"Do you have any other weapons?"

"If I did, I'd have used them already," Esme said.

"Mind if I check? Just to be sure?"

"Yes. I do."

"I'm going to have to do it anyway. You could make it easier by not struggling."

"You could make it easier by letting me go."

"That would defeat the purpose of me and King spending the last three days hanging around Long Pine Key Campground searching for you."

"Is that Cujo's name? King?" She'd stopped struggling. She'd either tired herself out or thought of another plan of attack.

"Yeah. Why?" Ian patted her down one-handed, refusing to release his hold. No matter how small she seemed, no matter how harmless, she was part of the crime family that had killed his parents.

New York Times Bestselling Authors

Shirlee McCoy
and
Lenora Worth

Survival Mission

Previously published as *Bodyguard* and *Tracker*

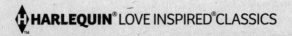
HARLEQUIN® LOVE INSPIRED®CLASSICS

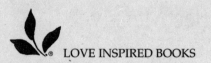 LOVE INSPIRED BOOKS

Recycling programs for this product may not exist in your area.

ISBN-13: 978-1-335-14304-4

Survival Mission

Copyright © 2019 by Harlequin Books S.A.

First published as Bodyguard by Harlequin Books in 2017 and Tracker by Harlequin Books in 2017.

The publisher acknowledges the copyright holders of the individual works as follows:

Bodyguard
Copyright © 2017 by Harlequin Books S.A.

Tracker
Copyright © 2017 by Harlequin Books S.A.

Special thanks and acknowledgment are given to Shirlee McCoy and Lenora Worth for their contributions to the Classified K-9 Unit miniseries.

www.Harlequin.com

Printed in U.S.A.

CONTENTS

Aside from her faith and her family, there's not much **Shirlee McCoy** enjoys more than a good book! When she's not teaching or chauffeuring her five kids, she can usually be found plotting her next Love Inspired Suspense story or wandering around the beautiful Inland Northwest in search of inspiration. Shirlee loves to hear from readers. If you have time, drop her a line at shirlee@shirleemccoy.com.

Books by Shirlee McCoy

Love Inspired Suspense

Military K-9 Unit

Valiant Defender

FBI: Special Crimes Unit

Night Stalker
Gone

Mission: Rescue

Protective Instincts
Her Christmas Guardian
Exit Strategy
Deadly Christmas Secrets
Mystery Child
The Christmas Target
Mistaken Identity
Christmas on the Run

Classified K-9 Unit

Bodyguard

Visit the Author Profile page
at Harlequin.com for more titles.

BODYGUARD

Shirlee McCoy

Have I not commanded you?
Be strong and courageous. Do not be afraid,
do not be discouraged. For the Lord your God
will be with you wherever you go.
—*Joshua* 1:9

To my beautiful and brave niece, Aaliyah Parker. The strongest young lady I know. I am so proud of you and so blessed to call you family! Keep smiling, sweetie. And I will keep praying! I love you dearly!

ONE

If the Everglades didn't kill her, her uncle would.

Either way, Esme Dupree was going to die.

The thought of that—of all the things she'd leave behind, all the dreams she'd never fulfill—had kept her moving through the Florida wetland for three days, but she was tiring. Even the most determined person in the world couldn't keep running forever. And she'd been running for what seemed like nearly that long. First, she'd fled witness protection, crisscrossing states to try to stay a step ahead of her uncle's henchmen. She'd finally found her way to Florida, to the thick vegetation and quiet waterways that her parents had loved.

Esme wasn't as keen. Her family had spent every summer of her childhood here, exploring the wetland, documenting flora and fauna as part of Esme's home-school experience. She preferred open fields and prairie grass, but her parents had loved the shallow green water of the Everglades. She'd never had the heart to tell them that she didn't. By that time, her older siblings were grown and gone, and it was just the three of them, exploring the world together.

Funny that she'd come back here when her life was

falling apart; when everything she'd worked for had been shot to smithereens by her brother's and uncle's crimes, Esme had returned to a place filled with fond memories.

It was also filled with lots of things that could kill a person. Alligators. Crocodiles. Snakes. Panthers. She wasn't as worried about those as she was about human predators.

Her uncle and the people he'd hired.

The FBI, too. If they tracked her down, they wouldn't kill her, but she'd put her hope in them before, trusted them for her safety. She'd almost died because of it.

She wiped sweat from her brow and sipped water from her canteen. Better to go it alone than to count on people who couldn't be depended on. She'd been learning that the hard way these past few months.

Bugs dive-bombed every inch of her exposed flesh, the insect repellant sweating off almost as quickly as she could spray it on. Things hadn't been so bad when she'd been renting a little trailer at the edge of the national park. She'd had shelter from the bugs and the critters. But Uncle Angus had tracked her down and nearly killed her. He would have killed her if she hadn't smashed his head with a snow globe and called the police. They'd come quickly.

Of course they had.

They were as eager to get their hands on her as Uncle Angus had been. It seemed like every law enforcement office in the United States was keeping its eyes out for her.

Thanks to the feds, the organization that had sworn to protect her. Witness protection was supposed to be her ticket out of the mess she'd found herself in. She'd hoped it would be. She'd probably even believed it would. She'd entered the program because she'd seen her brother murder a man in cold blood. She'd seen the look in his eyes, and she'd known that he was capable of anything. Even killing her to keep her quiet. What she'd learned since then was that there was no panacea to her trouble. No easy way out. No certain solution. Her best hope was in herself and her ability to keep a step ahead of her uncle until the trial.

"That might have been easier if you'd stayed with the police," she muttered, using a long wooden pole to move the canoe through shallow water.

There was no sense beating herself up over the decision to run again. Uncle Angus's hired guns had fire-bombed the tiny police station she'd been taken to after she'd been attacked. During the chaos that had followed, she'd seen the opportunity and she'd run.

It had seemed like the right decision at the time.

Now she wasn't so sure. The sun had nearly set, its golden glow still lingering on the horizon. Mosquitoes buzzed around her head. She didn't bother slapping at them. Her arms ached. Her head throbbed. Her body felt leaden. All she wanted was to get out of the Glades and back to civilization. She'd make different decisions this time. Head for a place she'd never been before. She'd buy colored contacts to change the bright green eyes she'd inherited from her mother. The reading glasses she'd bought and worn hadn't hidden them well enough, and Uncle Angus had told her that was how she'd been found.

"Those eyes, kid," he'd growled. "You can't hide them."

He was wrong. She could, and she would.

No more living in her delusions, telling herself that everything was going to be okay because she was a good person with a good heart who wanted only what was best for the people she loved.

A fool.

Because she really wanted to believe that good begat good and that the happily-ever-after she'd planned for so many clients would happen for her one day.

She might be a fool, but she wasn't stupid.

If she was found again, she *would* die.

But she wasn't going to be found. She'd sleep in the canoe again. Just like she had the past three nights, covered by mosquito netting, listening to things slither in and out of the water. By tomorrow afternoon, she should reach her destination—Long Pine Key Campground. She eyed the compass she'd bought before she'd left Wyoming, using a small Mag light to study the map she'd grabbed from the Everglades National Park information center.

She'd had a feeling she was going to need both.

As a matter of fact, she'd put together a survival pack, and she'd hidden it in the crumbling loft of one of the boat sheds that dotted the trailer park where she'd been staying.

She'd been able to grab it after she'd escaped the police.

Maybe she wasn't as much of a fool as her ex-fiancé, Brent, had said she was when she'd told him she was going to testify against her brother. She *was* tired, though. Tired people made mistakes. Like coming to the Everglades instead of heading for Texas or California or somewhere else where no one would think to look for her.

Death.

It had been stalking her for months, but now...

Now she could feel it breathing down her neck.

She shuddered, watching the edges of the murky water for a place to pull onto the shore. She needed a spot clear of vegetation. One that would allow her to drag the canoe far away from the edge of the water.

Tomorrow she'd be away from the slithering, slapping, plopping sounds of things moving through the water. She'd leave the canoe behind and make her way out of Florida. She still had money. Not much, but enough to get her to another state. She'd start fresh, build a new business. Nothing to do with weddings or brides. Nothing that anyone she knew would connect her with.

Not even Violetta.

Her eyes burned at the thought of never seeing her older sister again, her heart heavy with what that would mean—no family, no connections, no one who shared all her childhood memories.

If she could have, she'd have contacted her sister. But she didn't dare. Their brother, Reginald, would use Violetta's knowledge about Esme to his advantage. He'd probably been doing it all along. As much as she loved her sister, she also knew Violetta's weakness—greed. She liked the good things in life, and she was happy to let their brother, Reginald, give them to her. Even if his means to those ends was murder.

Esme winced at the thought, pushing aside the memory that was always at the back of her mind. She'd witnessed a murder. Her brother had been the murderer.

She'd watched the victim die, and she'd known that she couldn't keep quiet.

She'd turned on her family, betraying the deepest of all bonds.

That was what Uncle Angus had said when he'd broken into the trailer.

Turned on family, and that makes you the lowest of low. You have to die, Esme. Because family is everything.

It *was* a lot, but there was more to life. There was integrity, there was honor, there was faith. The last was what had enabled her to offer herself as a witness to her brother's crimes. She had what no one else in her family did—a certainty that God was in control, that He'd work everything out for His good.

She just hoped His good didn't involve her dying in the middle of the Florida wetland.

Esme flashed her light along the edges of the water, ready to stop for the night, to try to shut off her thoughts and get some sleep. Somewhere in the distance, a dog barked, the sound both alarming and comforting. She had to be on the right track, moving closer to civilization. The map and the compass hadn't steered her wrong, but civilization meant people, and that meant more danger.

Her light shone on marshy land. Eyes peered out from thick foliage, and she tried not to let herself think about what was watching her. She didn't mind the mammals. Mice, marsh rats, deer. Even thinking about panthers and bears didn't bother her. It was the reptiles that made her skin crawl—alligators, crocodiles, snakes.

"Cut it out!" she whispered, her voice filled with the fear she'd been working hard not to acknowledge.

Oh, what she wouldn't give to be back in her cute lit-tle Chicago apartment, making dinner after a long day planning weddings.

Esme sighed. She did not want to be in a place where predators were waiting to do what they did best.

The dog barked again—a quick sharp sound that made her wonder if she were even closer to civilization than she'd originally thought. She'd already planned her escape route and knew—in theory—how to get from the dock at the trailer park to the closest Everglade car-accessible campground. If cars could get in, she could walk out. And that was what she planned to do.

Her light glanced off what looked like a tiny boat-house, the old wood structure gray against the lush vegetation. She checked her map, circling the camping area she thought she'd arrived at. The glades were dot-ted with little places like this—areas where a couple of campers could bed down for the night. This time of year, though, the water was high and the risk was greater. There weren't as many campers. Just die-hard naturalists and explorers who wanted adventure.

Esme was neither of those things.

She liked home and books and routine.

She hated scary movies, danger, intrigue.

All she'd wanted was to plan weddings, marry her college sweetheart, have the nice life she'd been dream-ing of for years.

But here she was.

Ready to bed down for another night in a place that she'd rather not be.

She steered toward the wood structure, saw the clear-ing beyond it. There were lights in the distance—unexpected signs that she really was closer to civilization than she thought.

Esme dragged the canoe out of the water, her waders sucked in by the muddy ground. Behind her, something splashed, and she imagined a crocodile or giant snapping turtle moving toward her.

There were no other boats, no campers, nothing human that she could see. Whatever the light had been, it was gone now. Twilight turned the world deep purple, casting long shadows across the wet ground.

She climbed into the boat, traced the route she'd highlighted on the map, double-and triple-checking her coordinates. Two more camping spots before she reached her destination. Unless she'd missed a couple on the journey.

That was a possibility.

If she had, she might be at the last stop before the road-accessible campground. Something rustled in the brush, and she jumped, scanning the area, looking for whatever had made the noise. Not a mouse or rat. This had sounded large. A panther? A bear? Her heart thudded in her chest as she pulled the bowie knife from the sheath she'd strapped to her thigh. It glinted in the last rays of the setting sun, the blade new and wicked-looking. A great weapon for fighting something close-up, but she'd prefer to keep far from whatever was lurking in the shadows. In hindsight, a gun would have been a better idea. Purchasing a firearm would have been a problem, but she could have gotten her hands on one if she'd tried hard enough.

It wasn't like she didn't know how to use one. Her parents had taught her, and Reginald had reiterated the importance of knowing how to defend herself. Probably because he'd been afraid that his crimes would catch up to him, that the people he'd hurt would come back to hurt his family.

Family was everything, but he hadn't loved his enough to keep them out of harm's way. The irony of that wasn't lost on her.

The bushes rustled again—closer this time. Whatever it was, it was stalking her. She could feel it coming closer, see leaves shifting and plants shivering as something moved past.

"Please, God," she whispered, her fingers so tight around the knife hilt they ached. "Please."

And then it was on her, springing out from the brush in a flash of dark fur and dark eyes, her light following the movement as she scrambled back. Her knife hand moving as her brain screamed the truth—

A dog!

The *thing* was a dog, bounding across the open ground and stopping beside her. Sniffing at the air, at the boat, its nose so close she could have touched it.

"Hello," she said, her voice shaking, but the dog was already bounding away, barking wildly, the bright orange vest it was wearing glowing in the beam of Esme's light.

It took a second for that to register.

The vest.

The dog.

A search team. Either her uncle's henchmen or the police.

Looking for her.

She jumped out of the canoe, dragged it back toward

the water, her heart slamming against her ribs as she tried desperately to escape whoever was on her trail.

The lady was back in the water, tugging the canoe out of the shallows. She probably thought she could escape again, but Esme Dupree was about to be disappointed.

Ian Slade sprinted the last few yards that separated him from his quarry, his K-9 partner, King, barking ferociously beside him. Esme had to know they were coming, but she didn't glance back, didn't stop, she just kept dragging the canoe, splashing through the green water, alerting every predator in the area that prey was moving through.

He grabbed her arm, was surprised when she swung around, a bowie knife clutched in her free hand.

King growled low in his throat, a warning that Esme would be wise to heed. The Belgian Malinois was trained in protection. Smart, agile and strong, King had a bite as vicious as his bark.

"My partner," Ian warned, "doesn't like when people threaten me."

"Is that what I'm doing?" She tried to pull away, but after three days of tracking her, there was no way Ian planned to let her go.

"What would you call it?" he replied, dragging her back a few steps.

"Defending myself."

King growled again, and Esme's gaze shifted, her attention caught just long enough for Ian to make his move.

He disarmed her with ease, grabbing her knife arm

and twisting it until she dropped the weapon. Even then, he didn't release his hold.

Sure, her record was clean. She made a living planning weddings…pretty aboveboard, from the looks of it. But Esme was a member of the Dupree crime family, cut from the same cloth as her brother—a man who killed first and asked questions later.

Ian knew that more than most.

She yanked against his hold, forcing her arm into an angle that had to be painful. He might not trust her, but he didn't want to hurt her.

"Calm down," he said, shifting his grip. "I'm Agent Ian Slade. With the FBI.'"

"And that's supposed to be comforting?" Esme ground out as she continued to tug against his hold.

"More comforting than staying out in the middle of nowhere with your uncle still on the loose."

"He wouldn't be loose if your team would focus on apprehending him rather than me." She yanked hard, her boots slipping in the muck.

She'd have gone down if he weren't holding on to her.

She didn't seem to realize that there was no way she was going to escape. Ian was a well-trained federal officer, part of an elite group of agents. He was also a head taller than she was and seventy pounds heavier. Maybe more. Her bones were small, her wrist tiny, his hand circling it with ease.

As battles went, this wasn't a fair one, and he almost felt bad for restraining her.

Almost.

He knew what her family was capable of.

Until she proved differently, he had to assume she was capable of the same. Even if he'd been one-hundred-percent certain that she wasn't, he wouldn't have let her go. Protecting her was his assignment. Keeping her alive until the case against her brother went to trial was what he'd agreed to do.

Despite the fact that she was a Dupree.

"Do you have any other weapons on you?" he asked, his fingers curved around her wrist. She'd stopped tugging. Maybe she'd finally realized she couldn't get away.

"If I did, I'd have used them already," she spat.

"On a federal officer?" he asked.

"I didn't realize you were a federal officer at first. If I had, I wouldn't have pulled the knife."

"Good to know. Mind if I make sure you're telling the truth about weapons?"

"Yes. I do."

He could have forced the issue, but there wasn't any point. She might try to run, but he didn't think she'd attack him to do it. She had a clean record, no history of violence or trouble.

"All right," he said, releasing her.

"Thanks." She started walking to the canoe as if she thought he'd let her leave.

"I'm not checking for a weapon, but I'm not letting you leave, either."

"It would be easier on both of us if you did." She turned to face him, the darkening evening wrapping her in shadows. He couldn't see her expression through the gloom, but he could see the pale oval of her face, the tension in her shoulders.

"That would defeat the purpose of me and King spending the last three days hanging around Long Pine Key Campground waiting for you to show up."

"I didn't ask you to come looking for me. As a matter of fact, I would have preferred that you didn't, Agent Slade," she responded.

"Ian. We'll be spending a lot of time together. We might as well be on a first-name basis."

"I'm not going back into witness protection."

"That's fine. We'll work something else out."

"I guess I should have been more clear. I'm not going back into any kind of federal protection. I've been on my own for a few months now, and I've been doing just fine."

"Until your uncle tracked you down," he pointed out, and she stiffened.

"I was tracked down long before I came to Florida," she responded. "Or have you forgotten that poor woman who was murdered because she was in the same state you'd hidden me in?"

He hadn't forgotten.

None of the members of the team had.

Information about Esme's location had been leaked to the Dupree crime family, and a woman who'd looked a lot like her had been killed. "I'm sorry that happened. More than I can express, but I'm not part of the witness protection unit. I work for the FBI Tactical K-9 Unit."

"It doesn't matter who you work for. I'm not spending any more time with you."

"I wish that was how things worked, but it isn't. You agreed to testify against your brother."

"And I plan to."

"That will be really difficult to do if you're dead."

"If I'd stayed in Wyoming, I probably would be. Then we wouldn't be having this conversation."

She had a point. A good one. Esme was the sole witness to a murder her brother had committed. Her brother, Reginald, and Angus would do anything to keep her from testifying.

"We had a security breach," he explained, snagging her backpack from the bottom of the canoe. "It won't happen again."

"It won't happen again because I'm not going back into protective custody."

"I'm afraid you are."

She narrowed her eyes at him. "Have you ever been wrong before?"

"More than I'd like to be."

"Good," she retorted. "Then you won't be upset that you're wrong this time." She whirled around and would have walked away, but King blocked her path, pressing in close to her legs.

She shot a look in Ian's direction, her eyes still flashing with anger. "Call off your dog."

"Release," he said, and King pranced back to his side.

"Thanks." She probably would have walked away, but he held up her pack.

"Forgetting something?"

She reached for it and King growled.

"He doesn't like people taking things from me."

"I don't like people touching my things," she responded, her focus on King. She looked scared. He didn't blame her. At home, King was goofy and friendly, funny and entertaining. On the job, he was intimidating, his tan face and dark muzzle giving him a wolf-like appearance.

"Sorry. I've got to check the contents before we move out."

"I think I made it clear that—"

"You plan on going it alone. You've made it very clear. Unfortunately, my job is to get you to trial safely. I can't do that if we're not together."

"We're at cross purposes, then, and I don't see us finding common ground." She stepped back, and he thought she might be looking for an escape route. One that King wouldn't be able to follow.

"The common ground is this—we both want to keep you alive. How about you let me do what I'm trained to do?"

"Which is?"

"Protecting people like you."

King growled, the sound low and mean.

Esme froze, but Ian could have told her the growl wasn't directed at her. It was a warning. One that sent adrenaline shooting through Ian's bloodstream. He grabbed Esme's wrist, dragging her close.

"What—" she began, but Ian held up his hand, silencing her so that he could listen. The evening had gone eerily quiet, King's rumbling growl the only sound.

He pulled Esme to the thick brush that surrounded the campsite, motioning for her to drop down into the cover it offered. She slipped into the summer-soft leaves silently, folding herself down so that even he could barely see her.

King swiveled, tracking something that Ian could neither see nor hear. He wanted to think that it was a panther, a bear, an alligator, but King was trained to differentiate between human and animal threats. Besides, thanks to former team member Jake Morrow, the Dupree crime family seemed to always be just one step behind the K-9 team. There was every possibility that one or more of Angus's henchmen was wandering through the Everglades.

He thrust Esme's backpack into her arms, leaning close to whisper in her ear. "Stay down. Stay quiet. Don't move."

She nodded, clutching the backpack to her chest.

King's growl changed pitch. Whoever was coming was getting closer. It wasn't local law enforcement, and it wasn't a member of the K-9 team. They were back at headquarters waiting for word that Ian had finally found Esme's trail.

That left only one other option.

Angus Dupree or his hired guns.

Ian acted quickly, shoving the canoe into the water with just enough force to keep it moving. He gave King the signal to heel and went with him into the shelter of thick vegetation. Mosquitoes and flies buzzed around King's head, but the dog didn't move; his attention was fixed on a spot just beyond the clearing. Ian knew the area. He'd walked it several times the past few days, certain that Esme would arrive there eventually.

She was smart.

There was no doubt about that.

Ian had done his research. He knew as much as there was to know about her childhood, her schooling, her college years. He knew she'd built her business without the help of her older sister, that she'd never taken a dime from her brother. Everything she had, she'd earned on the right side of the law by using the brain God had given her.

The fact that she'd escaped witness protection and had stayed under the radar for months was even more proof of her keen intelligence. Smart people didn't go into situations without a plan. Ian had visited the trailer she'd been renting at the edge of the Everglades. He'd seen the old boathouse and the dock, and he'd known she'd had an escape route in mind when she'd chosen to rent the place.

All he'd needed was a map and a highlighter. He'd done some calculations, tried to think of how far someone like Esme would be willing to travel in a hostile environment. It hadn't taken any time at all to figure out that the quickest, most direct route out of the Everglades brought her here.

He'd staked out the area, walking a grid pattern every day, waiting for her to show.

Apparently, he wasn't the only one who'd been haunting this place looking for her. She was smart, but she'd have been better off leaving the area. She hadn't had the backpack with her while she was in protective custody with the local police, and she hadn't visited any of the local outdoor supply stores, either. He had to assume that she'd returned to the rental to retrieve the pack. Which meant there was something she needed in it. Money seemed more likely than anything.

King's growl had become a deep rumble of unease. Scruff standing on end, muscles taut, he waited for the signal to go in. Ian waited, too. He didn't know how many people were approaching or what kind of firepower they'd brought. Backup was already on the way. He'd called in to headquarters as soon as he'd seen Esme paddling toward the campsite.

A shadow appeared a hundred yards out, and King crouched, ready to bound toward it. Ian gave him the signal to hold, watching as two more people stepped into view. A posse of three hunting a lone woman. If

Esme had been bedded down for the night, they'd have been on her before she'd realized what was happening.

An unfair fight, but that was the way the Duprees did things.

One of the men turned on a flashlight, the beam bouncing across the camping area and flashing on the water. Twenty feet from the shore, the canoe floated languidly.

"There!" the man hollered, pulling a gun, the world exploding in a hail of gunfire.

TWO

If she'd been in the campground, she'd be dead.

Every bullet fired, every ping of metal against metal, reminded Esme that her family—the one she had loved and admired and been so proud of—wanted her dead.

Traitor. Benedict Arnold. Turn-tail. Judas.

Uncle Angus had whispered all those names as he tried to choke the life out of her four nights ago. The words were still ringing in her head and in her heart, mixing with the echoing sound of the automatic weapon Angus's hit men were using.

She wasn't sure what had happened to Ian and King. Either they'd run or they were biding their time, waiting for an opportunity to strike. One man against three didn't seem like good odds, and it was possible Ian was waiting for backup.

He could wait until the cows came home.

Esme was leaving.

She slithered through muddy grass and damp leaves, praying the sound of her retreat was covered by gunfire. Eventually, they'd stop shooting. When they did, her chance of escaping undetected would go from slim to none.

Who was she kidding?

It was already that. She might get out of the Everglades. She might get out of Florida. Eventually, though,
Uncle Angus would find her. He had money backing
him, and he had a lot riding on his ability to silence her.
If she testified against Reginald, everything the two
men had built—the entire crime family they'd grown—
would collapse. He'd been chasing her for months, and
he wouldn't give up now. Not with the trial date approaching. A few weeks, and she'd be in the courtroom,
looking at her brother as she told the jury and judge
what she'd seen him do.

She shuddered, sliding deeper into the foliage.

She wasn't going to give up on life, and she couldn't
give up on saving the one remaining bright spot in her
very dark family tree.

Violetta.

They hadn't seen or spoken to each other since Esme
had gone into witness protection, but they were sisters,
bound by blood and by genuine affection for each other.
As far as Esme knew, Violetta hadn't been involved
in any of Reginald's and Angus's crimes. Whether or
not she'd known about them, however, was a question
Esme needed to ask.

After she testified and shut her brother's operations
down for good.

The gunfire stopped, and she froze, her belly pressed
into damp earth, her heart thundering. They'd check the
canoe, find it empty, realize she'd escaped.

She had to get farther away before that happened.

Taking a deep breath, she slithered forward, her pack
slung over her shoulder, the soft rustle of leaves mak-

ing her heart beat harder. A man called out, and someone splashed into the water, cursing loudly as he went.

She used the commotion as cover, moving quickly, trying to put as much distance between herself and the campsite as possible.

"FBI, K-9 unit. Put your weapons down or I'll release my dog," a man called, his voice carrying above the chaos.

She froze again. Ian *was* still there. She hadn't intended on spending much time with him. The entire time they'd been talking, she'd been planning her escape, trying to work out a solution to the newest problem. Just like she did when she'd planned a wedding and there was a hiccup on the big day.

"I said, drop your weapons," he repeated sharply.

A single shot rang out, and someone shouted. A dog growled, and Esme could picture the dark-eyed, dark-faced K-9 racing into danger.

Two against three.

One weapon against many.

She couldn't leave.

No matter how much she wanted to.

She couldn't abandon a man to almost certain death.

Esme didn't have a gun, but she had surprise on her side. She scooted back the way she'd come, the dog growling and barking, men shouting, chaos filling the darkness. She was heading right toward it, because she didn't know when to quit. Another thing Brent had said to her.

He'd been right.

She never quit.

Not even when the odds were stacked against her. Hopefully, this time, it wouldn't get her killed.

She crawled closer to the edge of the campsite, dropping her pack and grabbing a fist-sized rock from the mud. Reginald had taught her to play ball when they were kids. He'd shown her how to throw a mean right hook, to take a man down with a well-placed kick. She'd loved him as much as she'd loved Violetta, and she'd soaked up everything he'd had to offer. Until she'd realized that the road he'd chosen was one she had no intention of traveling. Then she'd distanced herself from her brother and, to a lesser extent, Violetta. That had been eight years ago. Even after all that time and all the years away from Reginald's coaching, she still knew how to fight.

She stopped at the edge of the clearing, her heart pounding as she waited. The campsite had gone silent. No gunfire. No barking dog. Sirens were blaring in the distance, the sound muted by the thick foliage.

Somewhere nearby, a branch snapped, the sound breaking the eerie quiet. King barked again, and someone crashed through the brush just steps from where Esme lay.

She levered up, would have lobbed the rock at the fleeing man, but King was there, a shadowy blur, so close she could feel his fur as he raced past.

Surprised, she jerked back, her knees slipping in the layer of wet earth, her elbows sliding out from under her. She would have face-planted, but someone grabbed the back of her shirt, yanking her up.

"Hey!" She turned, the rock still in her hand.

"I told you to stay where you were," Ian growled.

"I was trying to help."

"Since when is getting in the way helping?" he retorted, King's wild barking nearly covering his words.

Esme didn't think he expected a response, and she didn't bother giving one. He was already moving again, sprinting toward his dog.

She followed, keeping a few steps behind him. Despite his sarcastic comment, she had no intention of getting in the way. The more gunmen he could take out, the safer they'd be. Once they were safe, she could go back to her plan. Get out of the Everglades and out of Florida.

Alone.

"Federal agent! Freeze!" Ian shouted, and she froze before she realized he hadn't shouted the command at her.

"Call off your dog!" a man replied, his voice tinged with a hint of panic.

"You want me to call off the dog, you freeze."

"This is all a mistake!" the man whined. "I was out here hunting gators and—"

"One command, and his teeth will go straight to the bone," Ian cut in.

The man must have stopped moving, because Ian stepped forward, gun trained toward something Esme couldn't see.

"Keep your hands where I can see them," he commanded, King still growling beside him.

"And you," he continued, and even though he hadn't turned to look at her, Esme was certain he was talking to her. "Stay where you are. The guy ditched his gun back at the campsite, but that doesn't mean he's not armed."

"I ditched my gun because your crazy dog was trying to kill me."

"You can explain it all to the judge."

"What judge? I was hunting gators. I can't help it if I got in the middle of your shoot-out."

"Like I said, you can explain it all to the judge. I'm sure he'll be really interested in your version. He'll also be interested in what your friend has to say. If he survives."

"I didn't come with a friend. Never seen either of those men before in my life."

Ian didn't respond.

Esme could hear the men walking toward her, their feet slapping against wet grass and soggy leaves. They reached her seconds later, Ian taller and broader than the man he'd apprehended. He looked fit and strong. The perfect bodyguard. If she were looking for one. She wasn't. What she was looking for was some peace. She wouldn't get that until her uncle was apprehended and he and her brother were convicted of their crimes.

"What now?" she asked, trying to think ahead, to figure out the best way to separate herself from the situation. Once she knew his plans, it would be easier to make hers.

"We're heading back to the camp. I've got one man down and cuffed there. The other ran off."

"He could return," she pointed out.

"Local law enforcement is close. Hopefully, one of them will pick him up."

"I stopped hoping for safety right around the time my uncle tried to murder me," she muttered.

He eyed her through the evening gloom, his expression unreadable. For a moment, she thought he wouldn't respond. When he did, his tone was gruff. "I hope you're not living in the delusion that your uncle is the one responsible for all of this."

"Who else would it be?"

"Your uncle might have tracked you to Florida, but your brother is calling the shots from prison."

"Maybe." Probably.

She didn't want to admit that.

Not even to herself.

She and her uncle had never been close. She could almost pretend they weren't family.

She and Reginald, though…

They were siblings. Sure, he was much older, but they'd been raised by the same parents with the same values.

Somehow they'd taken completely different paths, found value in completely different things.

She'd watched him kill a man.

She would never forget that. She *would* testify against him.

But this was by far the most difficult thing she'd ever done.

It was the right thing, but that didn't make her feel good about it. It sure didn't make her safe. Her family would do anything to keep her from testifying. She still couldn't wrap her mind around that.

The proof was here, though—the cuffed man walking beside a federal agent who had come to track her down. Both of them wanted Esme for different purposes. One wanted her dead. The other wanted her to stay alive. At least until her brother's trial.

The sirens had grown louder, and she could see flashing lights through the mangroves. Help had arrived. It didn't seem like Ian needed it. He motioned for his prisoner to sit on the raised sleeping platform.

"Guard," he commanded, and King snapped to attention, his eyes trained on the cuffed man.

"He's guarding you, too," Ian said, meeting Esme's eyes.

"It's not like I have anywhere to go," she responded. She could see the canoe, a dozen yards out, listing heavily to the right. Enough bullets had been fired to cause it to sink. If she'd been in it, she'd be dead. She shivered, suddenly chilled despite the warmth and humidity.

"There are plenty of places to go. You've proved that several times." He turned and walked away, moving across the clearing and crouching next to a man who lay near the water.

She thought he was checking the guy's pulse and rendering first aid, but it was hard to see through the deepening gloom. This would have been her third night out in the Glades. She should be used to how quickly darkness descended After so many months running from people who wanted her dead, she should also be used to skin-crawling, heart-stopping fear.

The cuffed gunman shifted position, and King growled, flashing teeth that looked as deadly as any gun or knife Esme had ever seen. He was focused on the prisoner. If she were going to try to escape, now would be the time to do it. She could see the emergency vehicles, hear people moving through the mangroves. She scanned the clearing and spotted her backpack abandoned near the edge of the campsite.

It would take seconds to grab it and just a little bit longer than that to disappear. She'd done it before. She could do it again.

But she was exhausted from endless running, tired from months of being on guard. She didn't trust the police or the FBI to keep her safe, but she wasn't sure she had the stamina to keep trying to do the job herself. Not that she had any choice.

The trial was just a month away. That seemed like forever, but it was nothing in comparison to the amount of time that had already passed. Once she testified, she'd disappear again. This time, she had no intention of being found. New name. New job. New beginning. Not the life she'd planned, but she knew she could make it a good one.

All she had to do was survive long enough to get there.

Just do it. Grab the bag and run! her mind shouted, and she was just tired enough and just scared enough to listen.

She darted forward, snagging the straps and lifting the bag in one quick motion. The rest was easy. Or should have been. The mangroves provided perfect cover, and she ducked behind one of the scrub-like trees, water lapping at her ankles as she moved.

She would have kept running, but something grabbed onto the bag, yanking her backward. She released the pack, but she was already falling, her ankle twisting as she tried to pivot and run.

She went down hard, splashing into a puddle of muck, the dog suddenly in her face, teeth bared, dark eyes staring straight into hers.

"I told you," Ian said calmly, his voice carrying through the mangroves, "he was guarding you."

She couldn't see him, and that made her almost as nervous as looking in the dog's snarling face did.

"He'd have been better off guarding the guy who tried to kill me," she responded, not even trying to get to her feet. Not with the beast of a dog staring her down, his teeth still bared. In any other circumstance, she'd have admired him for what he was—a handsome, fit working dog. Right now, she just wanted him gone.

"The perpetrator is in police custody. I guess you were too busy planning your escape to notice them moving in."

"I noticed."

"And did you think I wouldn't notice you leaving?" Branches rustled, and he stepped into view, his head and shoulders bowed as he walked through the trees.

"What I thought was that I wanted to live, and that being alone seemed like the safest way to make sure that happened."

"Esme, you really need to stop fighting me," he said, crouching a few feet away and looking straight into her eyes. There was something about his face—the angle of his jaw, the sharp cut of his cheekbones—that made her think of the old Westerns she used to watch with her dad, the hero cowboy riding to the rescue on his trusty steed. Only, this hero didn't have a horse; he had a dog.

"I'm not. I'm making your job easier. Go back to your office and tell anyone who cares that I refused federal help. I want to do this alone."

"What? Get yourself killed?"

"Call off your dog, okay? I want to get out of the mud." And the Everglades and the mess her family had created.

To her surprise, he complied.

"Release!" he said, and the dog backed off, sitting on his haunches, still watching her. Only this time, she was sure he was grinning.

King had had a great night. He'd found his mark twice and brought in an armed man. He was obviously pleased with himself, his tail splashing in a puddle of water, his dark eyes turned up to Ian.

"Good boy," Ian said, scratching behind King's ears and offering the praise he'd been waiting for.

"That's a matter of opinion," Esme muttered.

Ian flashed his light in her direction. She'd fallen hard but didn't seem to be much worse for the wear. "He did what I asked him to. That's always a win."

"That depends on what side of his teeth you're sitting on."

"He wasn't going to bite you."

"Right," she scoffed, tucking a strand of auburn hair behind her ear. She hadn't colored it. That had surprised him. It would have been the first thing he'd have done if he'd been in her position.

"He bites when he has to, but it's not in his nature to snap. Unless I give him the command."

"I'll keep that in mind," she said, a hint of weariness in her voice. She looked as exhausted as she sounded— her skin paper white in the twilight, dark circles beneath her eyes. He'd seen photos of her taken just a few months before she'd watched her brother execute a man. Her cheeks hadn't been as hollow, her shoulders as narrow.

He didn't want to feel sorry for her. She was, after all, part of the family that had taken his. Years ago, Reginald Dupree had called the hit on Ian's father. He'd been just starting out, sticking his toes in the water of his new family business. Ian's father had been a Chicago police officer, determined to undermine Dupree's efforts. He'd arrested two of Reginald's lower-level operatives. In retaliation, Reginald had paid a couple of street thugs to shoot him when he left the house for work. They'd opened fire as he'd stepped outside. The first bullet had killed him instantly. The second had killed Ian's mother, who'd been standing in the doorway saying goodbye.

Yeah. He didn't want to feel sorry for anyone in the family, but his father had raised him to be compassionate, to look out for those who couldn't look out for themselves. More than that, he'd raised him to do what was right. Even when it was difficult. The right thing to do was to protect Esme. Despite her last name and her family, she'd committed no crime.

"How about you keep something else in mind, too?" He offered a hand, and she allowed him to pull her to her feet.

"What?"

"Next time I tell you to stay somewhere, you should do it. It's a waste of King's energy to chase after you when he's supposed to be keeping you safe."

"You told him to guard me," she pointed out.

"Because the closer you are, the easier it is for me to make sure your brother doesn't get what he wants."

"Me dead, you mean?"

"I wasn't going to put it so bluntly, but yes."

"My uncle is the one who wants me dead, Ian. It's his hands that were around my throat the other night." Her tone was hard, her voice raspy, and the compassion he didn't want to feel welled up again.

"Does it make you feel better to keep telling yourself that?" he asked gently.

"It will make me feel better to be done with this. It will make me feel better to do what I promised and to get on with my life. So how about you leave me alone and let me go back to the business of staying safe until the trial?"

"Do you think this will all end if we have your uncle in custody?" he asked, calling King to heel and leading Esme back the way they'd come.

"I hope it will," she murmured, limping as she tried to keep pace with him. She must have hurt her leg or foot. He shouldn't have cared. She was a means to an end. Despite the clean criminal record, the supposedly upright business, she was who she was—a Dupree.

But he did care, because she was a person who'd found herself in an untenable position and had chosen to do the right thing. She'd witnessed a horrible crime, and despite the fact that her brother had committed it, she'd gone to the police and offered to testify.

"What'd you do to your leg?" he asked, and she shrugged.

"Twisted my ankle. It's fine."

"Then why are you limping?"

"Because I'm tired, okay? Because I want to get out of this stupid swamp and into clean clothes. I want to take a shower and wash three days' worth of bug repellent off my skin. Mostly, I just want to close my eyes, open them and find out that this has all been some horrible nightmare."

"I'm sorry," he said and meant it.

"For what? Being the one they chose for this assignment?"

"For the fact that all of this isn't just a bad dream. Your family has deep pockets, Esme. They can afford to pay people to do their dirty work. Which means you won't be safe until we shut down the crime ring your brother and uncle control."

"You're a wellspring of joyful tidings, Ian."

"I'm honest."

"And, like I said, I'm tired. So how about we discuss this another time?"

"You want to survive, right?" He stopped short and looked straight into her pale face.

"Would I have spent three days in the Everglades if I didn't?"

"Some people love it here."

"I'm not one of them," she huffed.

"And yet, this is where you ran when you left witness protection."

"My parents and I spent every summer here when I was a kid. They're—"

"Buried twenty miles from here. I know. I'm sure your uncle knew. Your brother. Your sister."

"I feel like you're trying to make a point, so how about you just get to it?" Her hands were on her hips, her chin raised. Of the three Dupree siblings, she was the one Ian understood the least. Reginald was all about power and money. He'd go to any length to get it. Violetta wanted the same, but she wasn't willing to break the law to get it. On the other hand, she wasn't willing to cooperate with law enforcement to make her brother pay for his crimes.

But Esme…

Ian couldn't wrap her in a tidy package and put a label on her. That bothered him. He'd spent most of his adult life studying people, figuring them out, deciding whether they were telling the truth, were dangerous or could be trusted. He'd missed the mark with Jake Morrow. A member of the Tactical K-9 team, Jake had put on a good show. He'd pretended to be everything the team believed in—a man of honesty, integrity, honor. That hadn't meant Ian had liked him. There'd always been something a little cocky about Jake, something a little off. Still, he'd trusted him.

That trust had been misplaced.

Jake had been on the Dupree payroll. He'd betrayed the team, and he was still on the loose, still causing trouble.

"Here's my point," he said, King panting quietly beside him. "You came to a place where anyone who knew anything about you would look for you. You would have been better off sticking with witness protection."

"One innocent person already lost her life because I was in the program. I'm not going to risk someone else dying for the same reason."

"We had a leak. We've sealed it. No one else is going to be hurt," he responded, keeping his tone neutral. He'd thought she was worried about her own safety, that she'd run from the program because she thought she'd be safer away from it. The fact that she'd been worried about others put a twist on things. A twist he didn't like. He wanted to lump her in with the rest of the family, but no matter how hard he tried, he couldn't seem to do it.

"You don't seem to understand." She swung around, her auburn ponytail flying in an arc as she moved. "One person being hurt is too many. I think about it every day. About how that woman died because someone mistook her for me."

"It wasn't because of you. It was because of your uncle and your brother. It was because they thought they were above the law, because they hadn't expected to ever be stopped. They like their money and their power, and neither of them want to give it up."

"Yeah. I know." She sighed, walking away, heading toward the distant emergency lights, her stride hitched but brisk, her shoulders straight.

"Esme," he said, not sure what he wanted to add, what he could possibly say to make things better or easier or right.

"I think we've both said everything we need to, Ian. How about you just let me do what I need to? I'm sure the police would like to talk to you, and I've got a long way to go before I reach civilization."

He could have stopped her.

He had the authority to do it. He had the strength. He had King.

But he let her go, because he thought she needed some space. It was five miles to the main road, and there were emergency vehicles everywhere. She'd be safe enough.

"All right," he said, and she met his eyes.

He thought he saw tears before she looked away again.

Then she was moving, putting distance between them, her backpack lying a yard away, abandoned on the muddy ground. He snagged it, figuring she'd want it later. He needed to check in with the local police, and then he'd get in his SUV and pick her up on the way out.

"King," he said, and the dog looked at him, eager for the next command. "Guard!"

The Malinois took off, racing across the clearing, his light brown fur visible in the darkness as he followed Esme through the trees and out into the main campground.

THREE

Long Pine Key Campground was not difficult to find. Esme simply followed the flashing emergency lights through a copse of mangroves and out into a field of vegetation. The vehicles were probably a quarter mile away, but the darkness made them easy enough to see. She picked her way across the field, the ground growing soggier with every step. If it got any wetter, she'd have to find another route. She didn't mind getting wet, but she didn't like the idea of being knee-deep in water that was filled with slimy, slithery, scaly creatures.

Esme was almost ready to turn back when she spotted a wooden walkway that stretched the remainder of the way across the area. She stepped onto it, the wood giving a little as she moved.

She was halfway over when she heard quiet panting and the soft pad of paws. Her heart in her throat, she spun around, her sore ankle nearly giving out. The dog was there. Of course. *King.* And he was so close she could have reached out and touched his nose, so close she could feel his panting breath on her hand, see his goofy smile through the darkness.

Because he was smiling again.

Why wouldn't he be?

She kept running. He kept finding her. A fun game for a dog. Not so much fun for Esme.

"Go home," she commanded.

The dog didn't even blink.

"Where's your partner?" She glanced back the way she'd come, saw nothing but the empty field and shadowy mangroves. "Did he tell you to follow me?"

The dog settled on his haunches, his dark eyes looking straight into hers.

"Release!" she commanded, pointing in the direction she wanted him to go.

Nothing.

"Go! Cease!"

Still nothing.

"Fine. Do what you want. I've got more important things to do than argue with a dog." She limped the rest of the way across the boardwalk, stepping onto wet grass, King close behind her.

The Long Pine Key parking area was straight ahead, the dark figures of emergency personnel visible in the flashing strobe lights of their vehicles. She'd seen way too many emergency vehicles the past few months. Beginning with the one that had been sent to the scene of her brother's crime.

She'd still been in shock—the memory of Reginald pointing the gun and firing it, of a man falling to the ground, blood spurting from his chest, taking up so much room in her mind, there hadn't been space to create memories of conversations she'd had, of people she'd spoken to. All she could remember were the emergency lights and the questions, barked one right after another—a series of words that had had no meaning.

Esme sighed.

She knew Ian meant well. She knew the FBI meant well. Law enforcement, witness protection, they meant well, too. But meaning well couldn't keep her alive.

Better to not take a chance of being waylaid by another well-meaning entity. She'd steer clear of law enforcement. She turned to the right, heading through a grove of cypress trees, aiming for the road that led into the parking lot. It should be straight ahead. She didn't have her map, but she'd memorized the topography and knew what landmarks to look for to ascertain how far she was from civilization. It would be a long walk to anyplace where she could make a phone call. Five miles on the back road, then out onto a main road that would eventually lead her to town. Once there, she'd borrow a phone and call...

Who?

Not Violetta. She loved her sister, but she couldn't count on her. Not the way she'd thought she could. Violetta's loyalties were torn. She wanted to support Reginald and see him freed from prison. Esme knew that, and she knew why. It wasn't all about love and family. At least not according to the FBI, it wasn't. Violetta had been happy to take whatever gifts Reginald offered—money for a new car, financial backing to support her business, new windows for her house. Esme had been shown a list of all the things her sister had accepted from Reginald.

At first, she'd argued that Violetta hadn't known where Reginald was getting the money. But, of course, the FBI had been prepared for that. They'd proved her wrong. Violetta *had* known...she just hadn't cared. She'd kept her hands clean, but she sure hadn't been willing to jeopardize Reginald's *career*. After all, she was benefiting too much from it.

The last time Esme had seen her sister had been six months ago. Violetta had looked just as cool and reserved as ever, her beautiful face not showing even a hint of stress or anxiety. Esme, on the other hand, had been a mess. But, then, she was the one who'd watched a man die. She was the one who'd had to make a choice between family and justice. She was the one who was swimming against the tide and doing exactly what her family didn't want her to.

And she was the one who'd pay with her life if her uncle got his hands on her again.

Esme shuddered, her skin clammy from the humid air, her body leaden from too many restless nights. She had to believe that she was going to get through this. She had to trust that God would keep her safe, that doing the right thing would always be best even when it felt so horribly wrong.

Betrayer. Traitor. Turncoat.

Her uncle's words were still in her head, the feel of his fingers around her throat enough to make her want to gag. She stumbled, tripping over a root and going down hard, her hands and knees sliding across damp earth, her shoulder bumping into a tree trunk.

She lay where she was for a few minutes too long, the muted sound of voices carrying on the still night air. Maybe she should go to the parking lot, turn herself in to the authorities and hope and pray that they could keep her safe. That seemed so much easier than going it alone.

It also seemed more dangerous.

A woman had died, and she'd almost been killed because of an information leak. Ian had told her the leak had been plugged, but she couldn't count on that. She couldn't really count on anything.

"Your pity party is getting you nowhere," she muttered, pushing up onto her hands and knees.

A cool wet nose pressed against her cheek, and King huffed quietly. She jerked back, looking into his dark face. He was a handsome dog when he wasn't snarling and showing teeth. Right now, he looked like he was smiling again, his tongue lolling out to the side.

"I think I told you to find your partner," she scolded, forcing herself up. Lying around feeling sorry for herself would accomplish absolutely nothing. Going back into the situation that had almost gotten her killed would do the same.

She had to stay the course—find a place to go to ground until trial, then contact the authorities and arrange to be escorted to court. Armed guards would be great. Six or seven dogs like King would be a nice bonus.

Right now, though...

Right now, she just had to find a safe place to hide.

She started walking again, trudging through saw grass and heading away from the emergency vehicles. There were no streetlights on the road, no beacons to lead her in the right direction. She went by instinct, the rising moon giving her at least some idea of what direction she was heading.

Northeast would bring her to the road.

The road would bring her to civilization.

She'd figure out everything else once she got there.

The grass opened up, the earth dried out and she could see the road winding snakelike through the Everglades. She stepped onto it, her ankle throbbing, her stomach churning. After three days and nights in the Everglades, it felt strange to be out in the open. No water surrounding her. No foliage to shelter in. She could see emergency lights to the left, so she turned right, trudging along the road as if she didn't have a care in the world.

Five miles wasn't much.

She loved hiking, biking and running. Before she'd entered witness protection, she'd been training for a half marathon. Walking a few miles should have been a piece of cake, but she felt like she was slogging through mud, her legs heavy with fatigue.

King pressed close to her leg, his shoulder brushing her thigh as they walked. He didn't look nervous, and she took that as a good sign. It wasn't good that he was sticking to her like glue, however, because eventually his handler would come looking for him. When he did, he'd find Esme, too.

Unless Esme could ditch the dog.

She patted the pockets of her cargo pants, found the package of peanut butter crackers she'd planned to eat for dinner. She opened it, the rustling paper not even garnering a glance from King.

She slipped a cracker from the sleeve, held it out to the dog. "Hungry?" she asked.

He ignored her and the cracker.

"King?" She nudged the cracker close to his mouth.

He didn't break his stride, didn't look at the food.

"It's peanut butter. Peanut butter is good. Fetch!" She waved it closer to his face, then threw it back in the direction they'd come.

It hit the pavement, and King just kept walking.

Esme blew out a frustrated breath. Great…just great.

Now she'd end up in town with a dog that didn't belong to her. Probably a very expensive dog. The FBI wouldn't be happy if she left the state with one of their dogs in tow.

For all she knew, she'd be charged with kidnapping.

Dognapping?

"King!" she said, trying to put an edge of command in her voice. "Sit!"

He didn't.

"Fetch!" She tried another cracker. "Retrieve!"

"Do you not speak English?" she asked, stopping short and eyeing the dog. He was still wearing his vest, a logo on the side announcing that he was a law enforcement dog. Esme wasn't sure about much lately, but she knew this—she did not look like a law enforcement officer. At least not one that was on duty. She didn't have a uniform, a gun or a holster. And no badge. If she made it to town, people would wonder what she was doing with a dog who was obviously supposed to be working.

"This is a problem," she said, crouching a few feet from the dog and watching him. He was watching her just as steadily.

"Listen, buddy, I'm sure your handler told you to follow me, but I'd prefer you go back to what you were doing before you got sent on this wild-goose chase."

He cocked his head to the side, then glanced back the way they'd come. He'd gone from alert to stiff with tension. She wasn't sure what that meant, but it couldn't be anything good.

"What is it?" she whispered, as if the dog could answer.

He barked once—a quick high-pitched sound that made her hair stand on end.

Someone or something was coming.

That was the only explanation.

She ran to the side of the road, plunging into the thick shrubs that lined it. She didn't know if King had followed. She was too focused on finding a place to hide. She crouched low, her heart throbbing hollowly in her ears. Lights splashed across the road and filtered through the leaves.

A car was coming. First the headlights, then the soft chug of an engine. She shrank deeper into the shadows, King's lean body suddenly beside her, pressing in so close his fur rubbed against her arm. Mosquitoes buzzed, dive-bombing the exposed areas of Esme's skin. She didn't dare swat them away. The car was closing in, the engine growing louder. She wanted to grab King's collar and make sure he didn't lunge out from their hiding place, but she couldn't get the image of him barking at the gunmen out of her head. No matter how hard she tried, she couldn't stop seeing his sharp teeth and snarling mouth. Sure, he currently looked like a sweet goofy pet, but she knew he could be vicious if he needed to be. She'd keep her hands to herself and hope for the best rather than risk losing one of her fingers to his sharp teeth.

"Don't move," she whispered, and the dog shifted closer, his shoulder leaning into hers.

The car slowed as it approached, the tires rolling over dry pavement.

Keep going, she silently commanded. *Please, keep going.*

The car stopped, the engine idling, the soft chug making her blood run cold. Could the driver see her? Did he know she was there?

A door opened, and she stiffened. She had no weapon. Her only option was to run. In a place as inhospitable as the Everglades, that could get a person killed.

Staying could get her killed, too.

She waited another minute, praying that whoever was on the road had stopped to look at a snake or save a turtle or do some completely normal thing that didn't involve hunting a woman through the swamp.

King barked, the sound so loud and startling, Esme jumped.

She didn't scream, but she came close.

And then she ran, darting away from the road as fast as her twisted ankle could carry her.

Two strides and Ian caught up, catching Esme's arm before she could run any farther.

She swung around, throwing a punch that nearly hit its mark.

"Hey! Cool it," he growled, dragging her arm down to her side the same way he had before. This time there was no knife, and she looked even more scared, her eyes wild with fear.

"Let me go!" she demanded, and he did, releasing his hold and stepping back.

"Calm down, Esme. It's just me."

She met his eyes, seemed to finally realize who he was and frowned. "You just scared six years off my life."

"Sorry about that."

"You don't sound sorry," she accused.

"Maybe because I'm tired of following you all over Florida," he replied, and she cracked a half smile.

"I'm not going to apologize, if that's what you're hoping for."

"I'm hoping we can get out of this area before we run into more trouble." He took her hand again, and this time, she didn't resist as he led her back to the road and his SUV.

He opened the back hatch and called for King, and she didn't say a word, didn't try to leave.

The Malinois jumped in, settling into his kennel and heaving a sigh that would have made Ian smile if he hadn't been standing next to Esme.

She was a problem.

Up until he'd tracked her down, he'd been resentful of the time and resources they were putting into finding her. The prosecutor had a good case against Reginald Dupree—even without his sister's testimony. She was the witness who would put him away for good, though. First-degree murder. Planned and executed with cunning and without remorse.

Esme was the only witness, and without her testimony, evidence was circumstantial at best. At worst, it was unconvincing. A good defense lawyer might get Reginald off. That wasn't something Ian was going to allow.

Yeah. He'd wanted to keep her safe for purely mercenary purposes. With her testimony, the Dupree crime family could be stopped. Without it, Reginald might go free.

Now...

He was beginning to feel sorry for her, beginning to see her as something other than the family she'd been born into. She'd given up her entire life to make sure her brother went to jail for his crime. She'd left her job, her friends, her fiancé. She'd done it all without complaining. Everyone who'd met her or worked with her had had only good things to say.

He'd told himself it was because she was a good actress and consummate manipulator. After hearing her talk about the woman who'd died, hearing the regret in her voice, seeing the tears in her eyes, he doubted that was the case.

Unless he was misreading her, she was who everyone else on the team seemed to think she was—a woman who'd been pulled into something she hadn't expected or wanted. A woman who'd been running from her family because she valued doing what was right more than she valued loyalty to her family.

A tough place to be standing.

A tough decision to make.

She'd made it. She'd continued to say that she would testify despite the obvious threats against her.

He admired that.

A lot.

He frowned, closing the back hatch and turning to face Esme. "Did you really think you were going to walk out of here?"

"I sure didn't think I wasn't going to," she replied, flipping her ponytail over her shoulder. A few strands of hair had escaped and were clinging to her throat and neck, the dark red strands gleaming in the SUV's parking lights.

"The nearest town is twenty miles away," he pointed out.

"I've walked farther."

"Did you do it when you had a price on your head?"

She pressed her lips together and didn't say a word.

"I'll take that as a no." He led her to the passenger side of the vehicle. "You keep walking on this road, and someone else is going to find you. If it happens to be one of your uncle's hired guns, you don't have a chance of surviving."

"I'm not sure my chances are any higher with you," she responded, but she didn't walk away.

Maybe she was too tired.

Maybe the injury to her ankle was worse than she'd been letting on.

Whatever the case, she stayed right where she was as he opened the door.

"How about we discuss it on the way to the local police department?"

"Ian..." She shook her head. "I believed your organization when I was told I'd be safe. They were wrong, and I can't see any reason to believe you again."

"And yet you're still standing here."

"Because I'm tired. I've been running for months, and I have at least another month to go before the trial. It's hard to sleep when you're worried someone is going to break in and kill you. Without sleep, it's really difficult to make good decisions."

Her honesty surprised him, and he touched her arm, urging her to the open door. "I've had plenty of sleep. How about you let me make the decisions for a while?"

She laughed without humor. "You're very convincing, but I think I'll pass."

"Then how about you sit in the SUV while I drive, and spend a little time thinking about what you want to do? It'll be easier doing it in a safe place than it will while you're out in the open."

"Like I said," she responded, finally stepping away. "You're convincing, but I'm going to have to pass."

"You're a long way from the state line, Esme."

"I was a long way from Florida a couple of months ago. Now I'm here, and eventually I'll be somewhere else."

"You agreed to testify," he said, trying a different tactic. She was coming with him. There could be no other outcome, but he'd like her to think she'd been the one to make the decision.

"I will testify."

"That's going to be difficult to do if you're off the grid and have no contact with us."

"Just because you can't find me, doesn't mean I won't be able to find you. I'll be at the trial." A note of weary resignation laced her tone. "I'll provide testimony that will put my brother in jail for the rest of his life."

"If you don't—"

"I know what will happen if I don't. I'll die. I may die anyway, but that's okay, right? A member of the Dupree crime family dies, and no one in a uniform is going to mourn." She started walking again, the limp more pronounced.

"You're not going to get very far with an injured leg."

"Ankle," she responded. "And I'll get wherever I want to go. Just let me, okay? Tell your boss and your team and the prosecuting attorney that I refused your help."

"I can't." That was the truth. He'd sworn to uphold the law. Just like his father and grandfather and great-grandfather, he'd always known he was going to be a cop. He'd worked the beat in Chicago, just like three generations of Slades had. And then he'd reached further, applying to the FBI, passing the physicals, the tests, the interviews.

His father would have been proud of him.

If he'd lived long enough to see it.

"Why? Because I signed some papers that said I agreed to witness protection?" Esme asked.

"Because you're more vulnerable than you want to think you are," he told her. "Because you're injured and you need to see a doctor. Because your backpack is in my vehicle, and without it, you've got nothing."

She hesitated, her gaze darting to the Suburban.

"It would be a lot easier for you to get where you're going with that pack, right?" he continued, certain he'd finally found the key to getting her to cooperate.

"Right," she agreed. "So how about you give it to me, and we can both be on our way?"

"How about I get you checked out at the hospital, and then I give it to you?"

"Are you bribing me to get me to cooperate?" she demanded.

"Yes," he responded, turning back to the SUV, and to his surprise, she followed. He helped her into the passenger seat and closed the door.

She was probably hoping to grab the pack and run, but he'd tucked it in next to King's crate. She'd have to reach over the backseat to do it.

That would take time, and he didn't plan to give her that.

He jogged around to the driver's side and climbed in. She was already on her knees, reaching into the back.

"Don't," he said, locking the doors and putting the vehicle into Drive.

"What?"

"Keep trying to run. It almost got you killed twice. The third time, you might not survive."

Pursing her lips, she settled into the seat, yanked her seat belt across her lap and didn't say another word. Her silence shouldn't have bothered him. As a matter of fact, he should have preferred it over conversation. She was an assignment, a job he'd been asked to take and that he'd accepted. No matter how much he hadn't wanted to.

He'd been after the Duprees since his parents' murders.

He and his team were this close to shutting them down.

Esme was a means to an end, but she was also a human being. One who'd been through a lot. One who deserved as much peace and security as he could offer her.

She shivered, pulling her hands up into the cuffs of her jacket. It had been hot the past few days, but she'd dressed to keep the bugs away—long pants, jacket, boots.

"Cold?" he asked, and she shook her head.

He turned on the heat anyway, blasting it into the already warm vehicle, wishing he could do more for her. Wanting to break the silence and tell her everything was going to be okay.

She wouldn't believe him if he did, so he stayed silent.

He wanted to think Esme had resigned herself to staying in protective custody. However, based on the fact that she'd spent the past few months on the run, he couldn't.

He dialed his boss, waiting impatiently for Max West to pick up. They'd spoken a few weeks ago, and Max had made it clear that he trusted Ian to do the job he'd been assigned.

Ian hadn't been pleased with the conversation. His past was his business, and he liked to keep it that way. The fact that Max knew about his parents' murders didn't surprise him. The fact that he'd brought it up had. The fact that he'd flat-out told Ian that he needed to focus on justice and forget about revenge?

That still stung.

Sure, Ian wanted to put an end to the crime family.

Sure, he wanted to avenge his parents' murders.

Justice always came first, though. That was the goal. The joy of seeing his parents' murderer sent to jail forever would simply be the bonus shot.

"West here." The team captain's voice cut through the silence. "You have her?"

"Word travels fast," Ian mused, his attention on the dark road that stretched out in front of him.

"It does when it involves one of the Duprees."

Esme tensed.

"You're on speakerphone, and she's in the vehicle," Ian cautioned.

"How are you doing, Ms. Dupree?" Max asked.

"I'd be better if your organization would leave me alone."

"I'm sure you know that's not possible until after the trial."

"You're assuming I'll make it to trial, but at the rate things are going, that doesn't seem likely."

"There's nothing to worry about. We've got things under control."

She laughed, the sound harsh and tight. "Like you did a few months ago when I agreed to enter the program?"

"Ms. Dupree—"

"How about we hash this out once I have her in a safe location?" Ian cut in.

"You're going to try to bring her to headquarters, right?" Max asked. "She'll be safer here than anywhere else."

"You think that's wise? Jake knows the setup there. He knows the security strengths and weaknesses." Jake Morrow had disappeared months ago. At first the team had assumed he'd been killed or abducted by the Duprees. The truth was a lot harder to swallow. He'd gone rogue and was feeding information to the crime family.

"You've got a point," Max said. "Tell you what. I'll see if we have a safe house available somewhere close to you. Once I locate one, I'll send a couple team members down to help with guard duty."

"I don't need to be guarded," Esme cut in.

"That sounds good," he said, ignoring her protest.

She'd agreed to enter the witness protection program, which meant she'd agreed to following the rules set up to protect her.

She was going to stick by those agreements whether she liked it or not.

And maybe, while she was at it, she could point the way to her uncle. Angus Dupree had been free for too long.

Ian wanted him behind bars.

Once that was accomplished, the Dupree crime family would be defunct. That was his personal goal, and it was the best revenge.

"Give me a half hour and I should have something set up," Max said. "Where are you headed now?"

"The regional hospital. Esme injured her ankle. We're getting it checked out."

"That's Big Cypress Regional Medical Center?" Max asked, probably staring at a map of the area, trying to figure out the easiest route there, as well as to the closest safe house.

"Right."

"I'll call for some local manpower. Angus is probably still in the area. He's smart. He's quick. He's not going to give up easily."

"He's not going to give up until I'm dead," Esme murmured.

"Or until he's behind bars," Ian added.

"That's the goal," Max said. "What's your ETA for the hospital?"

"Twenty-five minutes."

"We'll have someone there to meet you." Max disconnected, and the SUV fell silent.

Ian could have broken the silence.

He could have offered more reassurances, made a few more promises about keeping her safe. If she'd been anyone else, he probably would have. But Esme was a Dupree, and he was a man whose family had been brutally murdered by hers.

He needed to keep that in mind.

Because he couldn't afford to have too much compassion for her. He couldn't afford to let himself see her as more than just the sister of the man he wanted to destroy.

He scowled.

Destroy was a harsh word. It was the kind of word that, if spoken aloud, would make other people think he was out for revenge. Maybe he was. Maybe that really was what this was all about. Maybe Max had been right to call him on it.

In the end, though, he'd follow protocol. He'd use the law to get what he wanted.

And Esme?

She was part of that. An enemy by association.

Whether she knew it or not.

FOUR

The hospital was little more than a small clinic sitting at the edge of a tiny town. One story. Brick. Probably built in the early seventies. There was a main entrance in the front, and Esme assumed there were several other doors around the sides and back. She could see two police cruisers parked near the curb, lights flashing brightly in the darkness.

If that was the manpower Ian's boss had called in, she shouldn't have any difficulty escaping again. Once she had her backpack.

She waited impatiently as Ian opened the back hatch and attached King to a lead. Ian had been silent for most of the drive, and she hadn't bothered trying to make conversation.

She hadn't wanted to discuss her family and what they were capable of. She hadn't wanted to rehash the same tired conversation she'd had every time she'd spoken to a federal agent. They wanted to remind her of the crimes her brother and uncle had committed. They didn't want her to forget her obligations.

She'd been surprised that Ian hadn't done either of those things. His silence had been a welcome relief, the heat that he'd turned on for her chasing away the chill that she shouldn't have been feeling.

It was nearly ninety degrees outside, but she'd still been cold.

He'd noticed, and that shouldn't have mattered to her, but it had. It had been weeks since she'd had another human being around, months since she'd spoken to any of her friends. She'd never known loneliness before. Now it seemed it was all she had.

One day, one night, after another.

Just Esme and her thoughts, alone in whatever squalid little dive she could rent for cheap.

Her door opened, and Ian leaned down, met her eyes. "Do you want me to get a wheelchair?"

"I'm okay."

"No," he responded, his voice much kinder than she'd expected or wanted. "You're not. But you will be. Eventually."

And for some reason, that made her throat tighten and her eyes burn. It made her want to cry all the tears she hadn't cried in the weeks after she'd entered witness protection.

He offered a hand, and she took it, allowing herself to be pulled from the vehicle. He had her pack over his arm, and she reached for it. "I can take that."

"I've got it," he responded, shifting his hand to her elbow, his palm warm through her thin jacket.

"I'm not so badly hurt that I can't carry my own pack and walk unassisted," she muttered.

"I wouldn't want you to injure your ankle more."

Right. Sure. The way she saw things, he was probably trying to keep her from running.

It still felt good to have someone nearby, though.

She hated to admit that.

She hated that she was enjoying the warmth of his hand, the comfort of his company.

She'd been part of a couple for so long, it had felt strange to not be. To wake up in the morning knowing she wouldn't need to call Brent, text him, wish him good morning or ask him about his day.

He could have entered witness protection with her.

They could have gotten married and made a new life together. Maybe they would have, if Brent hadn't been so adamant about staying in Chicago. He'd made certain that she knew that he wasn't going to follow her into witness protection, that he wouldn't give up his life and his friends and his church group to be with her while she waited to testify. He'd also made certain she'd understood that he wouldn't be waiting for her. That if she went into witness protection, they were over. The wedding they'd been planning, the one that they'd sent out invitations for, that she'd bought a gown for, that she had a venue and flowers and cake for, wouldn't be happening.

If you leave, we're done, he'd said, and she'd almost thought he was joking. They'd been standing in a small conference room at FBI headquarters in Chicago, and she'd been given the offer of protection in exchange for her testimony. Six months wasn't that long. Not for two people who were in love. Well, apparently, she and Brent *hadn't* been in love, because he'd told her that six months apart was too much to ask.

For a split second, she'd considered suggesting that they move the wedding up, get married by a justice of the peace and go into the program together.

But then she'd thought better of it, because she hadn't

wanted to spend her life with a man who hadn't been willing to sacrifice a little time, a little convenience, a little of his own desires to help her do what she knew was right.

The FBI didn't know any of that.

They didn't care.

Faux concern about her ankle wouldn't make her think they did.

She reached the double doors that led into the clinic and opened them, limping into the air-conditioned lobby. After days of being out in the heat and humidity, it felt like she'd walked into an icebox. Her teeth were chattering, her arms covered in goose bumps as she approached the receptionist.

Her wallet was in the backpack. Along with her ID, her insurance card and her cash. Not just one ID. Several. The real her. The person she'd been in witness protection. The woman she'd become when she'd run.

"Sign in. We'll call you back shortly," the receptionist said, barely looking up from her computer.

She signed her real name—there didn't seem to be a whole lot of reason to do anything else. Angus knew she was in the area, but he didn't know she was injured, had no way of knowing she'd come to the hospital. Plus, he wasn't a fool. He wouldn't come after her when there were so many police around. He'd wait for a time when she was on her own again.

She rubbed the chill from her arms and settled into a chair. She thought Ian would follow, but he walked to the reception desk, leaning down and saying something that Esme couldn't hear. He took out his wallet, flashed what she assumed was his badge and jotted something on the sign-in sheet.

The receptionist eyed him as he turned away. She looked surprised and interested. Maybe because of the dog or whatever Ian had told her. Maybe because of him. He was a good-looking guy.

Better than good-looking. Dark hair. Light brown eyes. Tall and muscular. He looked like the kind of guy who could handle whatever came his way. The kind who could be depended on, who could fight his battles and everyone else's.

He must have sensed her gaze, because he met her eyes, offered a smile that made her heart flutter.

Fatigue was getting the best of her.

That much was obvious.

He crossed the room and sat beside her, his gun holster peeking out from beneath his jacket. "It shouldn't be long," he said.

"I'm not in a hurry."

"I am. This is a calculated risk. The likelihood that Angus will show up here is slim. We've got police watching all the entrances, but I'd rather be in and out quickly."

"We can skip it altogether, if you want," she said.

"I'd prefer you have the ankle looked at now rather than later. Once we get you to the safe house, you'll be sticking pretty close to it until the trial."

"So, basically, I'll be under house arrest?" she asked, not quite able to keep the sarcasm from her voice.

"Whatever keeps you safe, Esme," he responded.

"Whatever gets me to trial," she corrected.

"That, too."

She had nothing to say to that, and she found herself looking in his eyes again, studying his face. He had long lashes, and the beginning of a beard and mustache.

Clothes caked with mud and muck from the swamp, he was still one of the handsomest men she'd ever seen.

The fact that she was noticing didn't make her happy.

He looked about as annoyed as she felt. She couldn't blame him. He'd been assigned bodyguard duty. That meant hanging out and chilling, waiting for Uncle Angus's next move. It also meant giving up free time and hours that he could have been home with the people he loved.

"Just so you know, that's important to me, too," she said quietly, and he nodded, some of his annoyance seeming to melt away.

"I get that. I also understand that it's not fun having people come in and take over your life, but in this case, it's necessary."

"I'm sure it's not fun giving up your life to help protect a stranger. Your family—"

"Is gone," he bit the words out. "I have an aloe vera plant waiting for me at home, so I'm not all that concerned about my time away."

"You get lots of sunburns?"

He raised an eyebrow, and she blushed.

Blushed!

"It was a gift from a friend," he finally said, "who felt I needed something to take care of. That was in the years prior to King." He scratched the dog behind his ears.

"I see."

"Probably not, but we don't know each other well enough for a long explanation."

"Or for you to go back to the exam room with me," she pointed out, taking the opportunity that was presented to her.

"I'm going." The answer was simple, to the point and firm.

"That's not the way I do things," she responded, using her reasonable voice. The one she used with hysterical brides or overbearing mothers of the brides.

"It's the way my team does things, so it's the way it's going to be."

"Your team? Meaning the FBI?"

"Partly."

"Can you give me a plain answer, Ian, because I'm in no mood for riddles."

"No riddle. I work for a covert unit within the FBI. Our job is to take on cases like yours."

"Cases where witness protection nearly got someone killed?" she asked, and his lips curved into what she could only assume was a smile. Since there wasn't a bit of humor in his eyes, she couldn't be certain of that.

"Tough cases. Dangerous ones," he offered.

"Oh joy," she muttered.

This time, he really did smile. "Sarcasm?"

"How'd you guess?"

He chuckled. "You're an interesting lady, Esme."

"I plan people's weddings for a living. I go to church on Sunday and out to the movies every couple of months. There is nothing interesting about me."

"The federal government would beg to differ. To us, you are exceedingly interesting."

"Tell me how to change that, and I will. Hiding from my uncle would be a lot less complicated if I weren't also hiding from your people."

"Testify at the trial. Our interest in you will end at that point."

She rolled her eyes. "At least you're honest."

"About?"

"The fact that your organization will only care about me until then. Once I testify, I'll be on my own. If my uncle or my brother or anyone either of them is affiliated with comes after me, it won't be your concern."

He frowned but didn't deny it.

So, he *was* honest.

Which was nice, but didn't do much to make her feel better about the situation.

The door that led to the exam rooms opened and a dark-haired man stepped into the lobby. He glanced at a clipboard, scanned the room and finally called, "Esme Dupree?" as if she weren't the only woman there.

"Yes." She stood, Ian and King doing the same.

Ian had said he'd go into the exam room with her.

She wasn't going to argue. She wanted the pack, and it was currently hanging loosely from his left arm. Eventually, he'd relax enough to set it down.

"I'm Ryan. The PA on duty tonight. You said you injured your ankle?" The man glanced down as he spoke. "Left or right?"

"Right."

"Would you like me to get a wheelchair?"

"I'm fine." And the sooner they got this over with, the better.

"Come this way, then." He turned and strode through a narrow hall, pushing open a door and waiting as she moved across the threshold.

Just one door. A sink. A small supply cabinet with two drawers. A chair. An exam table.

And a window that looked out into a tiny paved lot and the thick forest beyond. If she could get out the window and into the woods, she might have a chance at escape.

"King has a very good nose," Ian murmured, as if he'd sensed the direction of her thoughts. Maybe he'd just seen the direction of her gaze.

It was a warning, and she knew it wasn't an exaggeration. King had tracked her through the Florida swamp and followed her so closely it would have been impossible to escape.

Nothing is impossible.

The words whispered through her mind, a gentle reminder that she wasn't alone, that she didn't have to do this herself.

God would never leave or forsake her.

He wouldn't abandon her. Not the way Brent had.

Not the way her family had.

The last part was so much more difficult to think about than the first. So she wouldn't think about it. She'd just keep doing what she'd been doing since the day she'd seen her brother shoot a man: running, hiding, keeping herself alive.

There'd be time to think things through, accept the facts, work through her sorrow and anger after the trial.

She limped across the room, ignoring Ian's dark gaze as she sat on the exam table, pulled off her boot, rolled up her pant cuff and eyed the swollen blue-black flesh of her ankle.

The ankle looked bad, but Ian didn't think it would keep Esme from trying to escape. If she had an opportunity, she'd take it. He had no doubt about that. She'd glanced at the window at least a dozen times while the PA poked and prodded her ankle. She'd answered questions in a brusque tense manner that was at odds with her soft green eyes and delicate features.

She looked fragile.

He'd thought that the first time he'd seen her photo.

He figured a lot of people made the mistake of believing what they saw. There was no other way to explain her escape from witness protection. From the time she'd shown up at local law enforcement offices in Chicago, she'd looked weak and soft and a little tired. He'd seen the videotaped testimony. She'd been crying, tears streaming down her cheeks as she'd described what she'd witnessed. She'd been shocked. Scared. Horrified.

She didn't break laws. *She* didn't get into public altercations. No drinking, smoking weed, playing the odds. She conducted her business in a way that had built a positive reputation in the community. She worked with high-end socialite clients who paid a hefty sum for her organized and creative approach to wedding planning.

He'd read all about it online.

He'd wanted to know everything he could about Esme Dupree before he started playing bodyguard to her. He'd been certain he'd dig up some dirt, discover something that would convince him of what he already knew—she was as rotten as her brother and uncle.

He'd come up empty.

She didn't even have a traffic ticket on record.

Everything about her screamed "law-abiding rule-follower."

It was no surprise that her handlers in witness protection had forgotten what cloth she was cut from. They'd forgotten that she was a Dupree, that the same blood that ran through her brother's and uncle's veins ran through hers.

She might look fragile, but she wasn't.

She might pretend to be a follower, but she wrote her own playbook, and she followed her own moral compass.

Whatever that happened to be.

He hadn't quite figured it out.

He didn't really care to.

His goal, his purpose, was to get her to trial.

Justice and revenge. All in one fell swoop.

Except for one thing.

He did care.

It was the way he'd been raised. He might want to deny it, might want to turn away from it, might want to tell himself all kinds of stories about how Esme was just a Dupree and her problems were hers to solve…

But he'd looked in her eyes. He'd seen her tears. Now he was in an exam room with her, watching as her ankle was prodded and poked. She didn't complain, barely winced, but she looked done.

"We could x-ray this," the PA finally said, "to make sure it isn't broken, but I feel pretty confident that it's just a bad sprain."

"No X-ray," Esme said with a strained smile. "It feels better already."

She hopped off the table. Probably to prove the point.

"Just hand me an Ace bandage, and I'll be on my way," she continued, grabbing hold of the backpack that hung over Ian's arm.

King growled.

Ian hadn't been lying. King didn't like people touching his things.

And the pack?

It was currently his possession.

"You're probably going to want to stop grabbing things that I'm holding," he suggested wryly.

The PA had already stepped back, his gaze on King. Esme didn't seem as worried about the dog.

She did release the pack, but she didn't back up. The ornery woman stood right where she was. Close enough that he could see dozens of freckles on her pale cheeks and the gold tips of her dark red eyelashes.

"I want to wash up and put on clean clothes before we leave." She tugged at the muddy fabric of her pants, her green eyes flashing with irritation.

"Okay." He handed her the pack, watching as her annoyance was replaced by surprise. She was easy to read. That would be helpful in the weeks to come.

"Just like that?"

"Sure."

"Why?" she asked, and he shrugged.

"Where are you going to go, Esme? Out the window?" He gestured toward it. "There are two marked police cars outside and probably five or six patrol officers surrounding the building."

She frowned but didn't respond.

"You wouldn't make it far before one of them spotted you. Even if you made it farther, you'd only be running from one danger into another. I think you're too smart to take that foolish of a risk." He glanced at the PA. "Can you bring that Ace bandage? My friend and I are anxious to get back on the road."

The PA scurried out of the room, nearly running down the hall. This was probably the most exciting thing that had happened in the clinic in years. He'd want to share every detail with as many colleagues as possible.

That was fine.

It didn't matter if Angus found out that his niece had been at the clinic. What he couldn't find out was where they'd be going next.

Ian glanced at his phone. No text from Max. Which meant he hadn't found a safe house yet. He was probably looking for one that wasn't in the FBI system. One that Jake wouldn't be familiar with.

"You know," Esme broke into his thoughts, "it would be a lot easier for me to get cleaned up and changed if you weren't standing in the room."

He met her eyes, trying to ignore the dark smudges beneath them, trying not to see the hollowness of her cheeks, the faded bruises on her neck that looked like fingerprints.

But he couldn't *not* see those things. She was a Dupree, but she was also a victim. His gut twisted at the thought. He'd gone into this kind of work to protect people like her, to prevent crimes, keep the bad guys off the streets and save other women from having to go through what Esme had. He couldn't look in her face and not realize how much she'd been through, how difficult it had been on her.

He turned away, closing the shades that covered the windows. "It would be a lot easier for me to do my job if I knew you were going to cooperate. I highly suggest that you do not attempt to leave this building, Esme."

He stepped into the hall before she could respond, closing the door with a soft snap that seemed to echo through the quiet building.

He stared at the closed door, trying to rid himself of the image of the bruises, the dark circles, the thin face and fragile body.

He didn't want to see Esme as anything other than what she was. He'd told himself that over and over again as he'd made the journey to Florida and begun his search. She was a Dupree. He wouldn't forget that. But she wasn't just a Dupree. She was a woman determined to do the right thing despite the danger. She was a person who'd given up her life to make sure her brother paid for his crimes.

She was a victim who needed someone in her corner.

Someone who would fight for her because she deserved it, not because of what he could get out of it.

Justice. Revenge. Closure.

They were what he wanted, what he'd been seeking for over a decade. He still wanted those things, but not at the expense of a woman who'd done nothing wrong, who—by all accounts—had done everything right.

King leaned against his leg, whining softly.

He didn't like the door separating him from the woman they were guarding.

But Ian needed the distance. Just for a few minutes. Because he didn't like the way he was feeling, didn't want the sense of responsibility that seemed to be settling on his shoulders.

Esme Dupree was an assignment.

She was the key witness in a federal trial, a fugitive on the run from a federal program. She was sister to the man who'd murdered Ian's parents.

But she had bruises on her neck and a price on her head, and that would change everything if he let it.

FIVE

She tried the window.

Because why wouldn't she?

It didn't open.

Ian had probably known it wouldn't.

Why else would he have left her alone with the pack?

Esme walked to the sink, turning on the water and splashing her face with ice-cold drops of it. She squirted soap into her hands and scrubbed her arms and her cheeks. Mud splattered the stainless steel and the counter, tiny brown blobs that slid along the smooth surfaces. She didn't bother wiping them away. Sure, she was tired, and her ankle hurt, but what she needed was a plan...and no matter how frantically her mind raced, she couldn't seem to formulate one.

She pulled black cargo pants and a light blue T-shirt from the pack. It was her only extra set of clothes, but it wasn't extra any longer. The set she'd been wearing was soaked through with mud and swamp muck. If Uncle Angus came hunting her, he'd smell the stench long before he spotted his prey.

Esme changed quickly, tossing the ruined clothes in the trash can, then she shoved her ID and money into one of her pant pockets. Her Bible was at the bottom of the pack—too big to fit in a pocket. She set it on the exam table. Beneath it was the photo of her family that she'd been carrying since she entered witness protection. Reginald, Violetta, Esme and their parents. Taken nearly twenty years ago, it was a reminder of what they'd once been—happy, connected, secure. A typical American family standing on a Florida beach that Esme couldn't remember. It was the only photo she had of the entire family, and she'd cherished it forever.

But now...

Now when she looked at it, all she could see was the sardonic gleam in her brother's eyes, the cocky way he held his head, the vast distance between Reginald and his parents. Esme and Violetta stood between them, arms wrapped around each other. Reginald stood a couple of feet away, slightly angled from the group.

She'd never noticed that. Not until after the murder.

She shuddered, dropping the photo onto the exam table and pulling her hair from the ponytail holder. The raw spot on the side of her head itched, and she ran a finger across the scabbed surface, telling herself she wasn't going to think about what had happened.

So, of course, she did.

She thought about the night Angus had found her, the swamp life teaming beyond the window. She thought about the quiet rustle of fabric and the horrible realization that she wasn't alone. She thought about trying to run. Thought about the way her uncle had grabbed her by the ponytail, yanking her back with so much force, a chunk of hair and skin had come out. She'd been blinded by the pain, terrified as he'd put his hands around her throat, looked straight into her eyes and tried to kill her.

If she hadn't been flailing, searching frantically for a weapon, if she hadn't felt the smooth domed surface of the heavy glass snow globe her mother had given her on the last birthday they'd spent together, she'd have died in the dingy rental near the swamp.

As it was, she'd smashed Angus in the nose with the snow globe. Blood had spurted out, and she'd run.

She was fast, but her uncle had almost been faster.

Because her hair—the long red hair that Brent loved so much, that Angus had used to stop her the first time—had caught in mangrove branches and nearly kept her from escaping.

Never cut it. Never dye it.

How many times had Brent said that?

"Not even if it's going to get me killed?" she muttered, walking to the supply cabinet and yanking open one of the drawers. Gauze. Bandages. Tape. She pulled open the other one and found suturing kits, alcohol wipes and scissors.

She didn't think through what she was doing.

One minute she had the scissors in her hand. The next, long strands of hair were falling to the floor. The scissors were dull, and she was tired, and the tears she'd been fighting for weeks kept trying to slide down her cheeks.

This wasn't the life she wanted.

This wasn't the way things were supposed to have worked out. She should be planning her wedding, not her escape from a federal officer, a crazy uncle, a corrupt brother.

"Everything okay in here?" Ian called.

"Fine," she responded, her voice catching on a sob.

"Fine," she repeated, and this time she sounded almost normal.

Good. Because there was no way she was going to let him know how broken she was.

"You're sure?" he asked.

She didn't answer.

She was still cutting her hair. No mirror. No way of seeing just how badly she was butchering it. Just the scissors slicing through thick strands, the hushed rasp of that the only sound in the now silent room.

She couldn't escape out the window, but she could do this.

She'd learned her lesson. Ponytails were weapons that could easily be used against women.

"Esme? I'm coming in," Ian said, his voice soft and soothing.

Had she made some sort of noise? A quiet sob she hadn't heard?

She touched her cheek, certain it would be wet from tears, but it was dry and hot, strands of hair sticking to it. She wiped them away as the door opened.

She heard his footsteps on the tile floor, but he didn't say anything. Not until he was beside her, his muddy boots surrounded by dark red hair.

"Need some help?" he asked, taking the scissors from her hand. For some reason, she didn't try to stop him. She didn't protest or speak or tell him to leave the room.

She wanted to sit for a minute. Catch her breath. Try to stop the images that were filling her head. Blood and death, men she loved who'd proved to be nothing like what she'd thought they were.

Her uncle.

His hands on her throat.

"Breathe," Ian said quietly, the scissors snapping off one thick hank of hair after another.

She sucked in a lungful of air.

"There you go." He ran his fingers carefully through her hair, cut off a few more strands. "Wish I were a hair stylist, Esme, but this is probably the best I can do."

She met his eyes, then saw the concern she hadn't been privy to before.

It surprised her.

She hadn't thought Ian had it in him to care. Not for someone with a name he seemed to despise from a family he obviously hated.

"He wouldn't have had the chance to strangle me if it hadn't been for the stupid ponytail," she explained. As if he'd asked. As if he really did care.

But, of course, she knew he didn't.

He was part of a well-oiled machine, all of it working toward one outcome, one result: shut down the Dupree crime family.

"Your uncle?" He set the scissors in the sink, his dark gaze never leaving her face. He was reading her. Easily.

"Yes."

"I'm sorry." He bit each word out. "Sorry we didn't do a better job of keeping you safe." His gaze dropped to her neck, probably to the bruises that still dotted it.

"I'm sorry my family's business is making money illegally. I'm sorry my brother has no moral values, no conscience and no regret. I'm sorry that my uncle is making your job more difficult. And I'm really, *really* sorry neither of them are who I wanted them to be."

"Or who you thought they were?" he asked.

"I wish I could say that. I wish I could say it and

know that I had absolutely no suspicions, but I'm not a fool, and neither are you. My brother had a boatload of money to spend on whatever he wanted. I *was* suspicious and worried about where it was coming from." She released a quavering breath. "I admitted that during my interview with your people. It's why I hadn't spoken to Reginald in a few months and why I only had contact with him once or twice a year."

"You accepted a client who was deeply affiliated with him."

"I accepted a lot of clients who knew Reginald," she clarified. "If I turned every one of them away, I wouldn't have a business."

Of course, when she'd agreed to plan the Wilson-Arnold wedding, she hadn't known that Maverick Arnold was deep in her brother's pocket. She hadn't known that he'd gone to the police and sold some information about the way Reginald ran his business. She hadn't known that Maverick was a snitch or that Reginald had found out or that she was going to walk into the house Maverick and his fiancée shared and see her brother pointing a gun at her client.

Esme rubbed her arms, willing some warmth into her body.

"I see," Ian said, lifting the photo from the exam table and studying it.

"No," she responded, snatching the photo from his hand and tossing it into the trash. "You *don't*. You're living in your cloistered world of law enforcement, and you've been assigned the task of protecting a woman you despise—"

"I don't despise you."

"From a family," she continued as if he hadn't spoken, "you hate."

He didn't deny that.

She hadn't expected him to.

"All you're doing is your job." She nearly spat the words. "I'm living my life, and right now, it's not a very good one." She kicked the pile of hair, whirling away on her bad ankle and nearly toppling from the pain.

She limped to the door.

He'd left it open, and she walked into the hall, ignoring the surprised PA who was walking toward her, a thick roll of gauze in his hand.

He didn't try to stop her.

Maybe her new haircut made her look unstable.

She *felt* unstable, emotions roiling through her so violently she could barely breathe.

Ian didn't try to stop her, either.

But he was following. She could hear the click of King's claws on the tile floor.

She didn't turn around.

She had nothing left to say. Not one word.

The light went off as she reached the lobby, plunging the clinic into darkness. She stood where she was, velvety darkness pressing in, surprised voices calling out.

She knew where the exit was.

She could have crossed the lobby and walked outside, but lights didn't go off for no reason. Not in a place like this. There was no storm. No wind.

She stepped back, bumping into a solid wall of muscle.

Ian.

She knew it before she tried to move away, before his arm wrapped around her waist, holding her still.

"Wait," he whispered, the words ruffling her newly shorn hair and tickling her cheek.

"For what?" she whispered back.

Somewhere outside, an engine roared, and Ian yanked her back as lights splashed across the lobby windows and the world exploded into chaos.

Bricks. Sparkling glass. Dust. Lights. People shouting.

She was moving, dragged backward away from the front end of the truck that had plowed into the building.

"Move, move, move!" Ian was shouting, dragging her into the still-dark hallway, the sound of gunshots following them.

And she finally understood. Finally got it. Finally realized that the driver of the truck hadn't just misjudged or made a mistake. He was there to finish what her uncle had started.

Suddenly, she didn't need to be prodded or pulled.

She ran, her ankle pain forgotten, her heartbreak gone. All the emotion she'd been feeling, everything that had been filling her up, replaced by cold hard terror and the driving need to survive and make sure her uncle and brother didn't have the opportunity to hurt anyone ever again.

Ian had been prepared for trouble, but he hadn't been expecting such a bold attempt on Esme's life.

He should have been, and he was angry with himself for the lack of foresight.

Reginald and Angus were desperate.

Desperate people did desperate things.

Including trying to kill someone in front of local law enforcement.

He scowled, his hand tight on Esme's wrist, his fingers digging into her smooth warm skin. He had to be hurting her, but she didn't complain. She was running through the hall beside him, her shoulder brushing against his arm.

Ian took a right turn at the end of the corridor, heading for the emergency exit that had been marked on a building map posted to the wall of the exam room. He'd noticed that, just like he'd noticed that the front of the clinic was comprised of large glass windows and a couple feet of bricks. Not a difficult facade to breach if someone really wanted to.

Yeah. He'd noticed. No extra points for that.

He and King worked protection more than anything else. They were good at it, but they generally worked with one or two other members of the team.

Right now, they were working alone, local law enforcement scrambling to contain the threat, but none of them specifically assigned to guard Esme.

He unhooked King's lead.

"Guard!" he ordered, and King growled, the sound deep and low. Not a warning. More of an acknowledgment that he was on duty and he knew it.

Good. The corridor was pitch-black. Even with his eyes adjusting to the darkness, Ian could barely see a foot in front of him. No generator cutting on to give some light to the situation. If there was a generator, the perp had taken that out, too.

They reached the emergency exit, nearly plowing into the door.

He felt Esme's arm move, knew she was reaching for the door handle.

"Wait," he cautioned.

"For what? The truck driver to come around the corner, guns blazing?"

"For me to open the door." He nudged her back until he knew she was against the wall. "Give me a minute to check things out."

"I'd rather—"

"Let's not waste time," he said, leaning in so close he could see her pale skin in the darkness, smell the fragrant soap on her skin. "The police probably already have the truck driver, but we don't know if he has friends."

She nodded. One quick, curt move of the head, and he turned back to the door, felt King pressing in close.

"Ready?" he asked, and the dog barked. "Let's go." He opened the door, and King sprinted out, racing across an empty lot that shimmered beneath a half-dozen streetlights.

Ian's cell phone buzzed. He ignored it.

His focus was on the dog.

He could see him running across the lot, heading toward a sparse stand of trees. He disappeared for a moment, the shadows swallowing him, then appeared again. Ian had trained other dogs, but none of them compared to King. The Belgian Mal was as smart and as driven as they came.

He waited for the dog to indicate. One quick sharp bark would be a warning that someone was nearby.

King was silent, loping from one area of the parking lot to the next until he was finally done and returning, tail waving jauntily in the artificial light.

"We're clear," Ian said, reaching for Esme's arm and pulling her closer.

"Are you sure?"

"He's my partner. We live by protecting each other's

better interest. I trust him to keep me safe. He trusts me. You could probably learn a little from that."

"I learned plenty about trust from my family. I don't plan to ever forget the lessons they've taught me." She followed him outside, her hand on the back of his jacket, her fingers clutching the fabric as if she were afraid that he might abandon her like so many other people had.

He could have told her that he wouldn't.

But King was moving ahead, scruff raised, tail stiff. He sensed something.

Whatever it was, he didn't like it.

"This way," Ian said, tugging Esme into the deep shadows near the corner of the building. Not wanting to alarm her more than she already was.

"What's wrong?" she whispered, and he knew she sensed it, too. The change in the air. The sudden charge of electricity.

King was off, running so fast he was just a blurry shadow in the streetlights as he headed back to the trees. To the darkness. To the shadows that could easily hide someone.

Ian pulled his gun, aiming in that direction. Not surprised to see the flash of light as a shot was fired. The bullet went wide, slamming into the back of the building a few feet from where Ian and Esme crouched.

A man shouted, then screamed.

No more shots. Just the vicious sound of King barking and growling.

A police cruiser raced around the side of the building, blocking Ian's view and his aim.

In any other circumstance, he would have run straight into the fray, gun drawn as he shouted for the perp to drop his weapon.

But these weren't other circumstances.

He had Esme to protect and no team members to guard her while he went after King.

The police officer jumped out of the cruiser, his gaze on the trees, his gun drawn.

"That your dog?" he said, his attention never wavering.

"Yes."

"FBI, right?"

"Right."

"You want to call him off or you want me to go in there?" the officer asked.

"The perp has a gun."

"I heard the shot."

"I'm not calling my dog off until I know he's disarmed."

"If I go in there and your dog attacks, I'm not going to have a choice as to how I react." The officer was issuing a warning, and Ian wasn't going to ignore it.

He shouted the command for King to return, praying the dog had managed to disarm the gunman. If not, there was a chance King would be shot as he ran away.

And Ian would have to live with that.

Live with the fact that he'd risked his partner's life for the sake of a woman whose family had destroyed his. The choice he'd just made only brought home the truth: he didn't want to protect any of the Duprees.

That was a fact.

It was also a fact that he'd walked into the exam room and seen Esme, scissors in hand, hair falling around her, and his heart had jerked with the kind of sympathy reserved for those who'd done absolutely nothing wrong but had still found themselves in untenable circumstances.

She deserved better than what she'd gotten.

That had been his first thought, his knee-jerk response.

She deserved better, and he could make sure she got it.

He *would* make sure she got it.

His first response, and maybe it was his second and third response, because he still felt it. Still wanted to turn back the clock and keep her from walking in on her brother's crime. Her only wrongdoing was having a name that made his blood boil. Her only mistake was in taking on clients that her brother sent her way. Those weren't things she should be punished for. They weren't things a rational man could hold against her, and he'd always considered himself rational.

Except when it came to the Duprees.

Maybe it was time for that to change.

He'd had more than one friend tell him he had to put aside his anger and move forward with his life. He'd told more than one of them to keep their opinions to themselves.

Not a very Christlike attitude.

His father would have told him that if he'd been around. He would have told him to let go of the need for revenge, to focus on justice and mercy and grace.

Ian didn't know if he could do that, but he could stop looking at Esme like she was the enemy. He could start viewing her as the victim she was. He could give her the protection she needed, offer her the support that was necessary when a person lost everyone they loved.

Could and would, because it was his job, because it

was the right thing to do and because his father wouldn't have expected anything less from him.

He called King again, was relieved when he barked in response. Seconds later, King emerged from the trees, tail high, ears alert.

"What a relief," Esme said, and he could hear the sincerity in her voice, see it in her face.

He turned away, focusing on King, on the darkness, the trees, the chaos still playing out. For now, they were safe.

He planned to make sure they stayed that way.

SIX

King raced back across the parking lot, silent, focused.

He stopped at Ian's feet, sitting at attention, looking straight into his handler's face.

"Good job," Ian said, scratching him behind the ears, his focus on the police officer who was jogging across the lot.

The dog didn't look like he believed the praise.

His happy smile was gone. In its place was tension that even Esme could feel.

"You did do good," she assured him and then felt foolish.

She'd never been much of a dog person.

It wasn't that she didn't like dogs.

It was more that she didn't have time for the training and the walks and the attention they needed. Plus, her sister had a small yappy poodle who despised Esme. The feeling was mutual.

Esme hadn't wanted to add another thing into her already hectic schedule. Planning weddings for demanding clientele took all of her energy and focus. If she couldn't have a dog that she could make part of the family, she didn't want to have one at all.

So she didn't have a dog.

She didn't want a dog.

She sure didn't spend her free time talking to dogs.

King didn't seem like a typical dog, though.

He seemed completely in tune with Ian and absolutely devoted to doing his job. This time, his job had been to take down the shooter.

Was he disappointed that he hadn't been able to finish what he'd started?

"If so," she muttered, "I know exactly how you feel."

"What's that?" Ian asked, his dark gaze suddenly on her.

"I thought the dog might be disappointed. I was just telling him that I know how he feels."

"You were talking to King?" He smiled, a slow easy grin that softened the hard angles of his face and made him look almost approachable.

Almost.

"Is there a problem with that?" she responded. "Do you have a rule about people talking to your dog?"

"He's my partner, and you're welcome to say anything you want to him. He probably is disappointed. He likes to be in on the arrest."

"Instead, he's here babysitting me." She eyed the canine. He was staring toward the trees, his body still tense, his hackles up.

"And instead of being home planning summer weddings for rich clients, you're here," he murmured. "Is that why you're disappointed?"

"I'm disappointed that the people I love don't love me. I'm disappointed that the people I trusted couldn't be counted on."

"You're talking about your brother and uncle?"

"No." She was talking about her sister. She was talking about Brent.

She was talking about two people she'd actually believed in and counted on. The sad truth was she'd stopped counting on Reginald years ago. And she'd never counted on her uncle. Angus was her father's younger half brother. A product of a second marriage, he'd made just a few appearances in Esme's life when she was a kid. He'd been thirty years older than her, but he'd acted like a child—bullying others into doing what he wanted, whining when he didn't get his way.

She'd never liked him.

His criminal activity was no surprise to her at all, and she liked to tell herself that he'd led Reginald into a life of crime.

The reality, according to the FBI, was that Reginald had been running his *business* for several years before he'd asked Angus to join him. Her uncle had been more than eager to comply, but he wasn't the boss.

He most likely wasn't the one who'd called the hit on Esme. That was probably the hardest pill to swallow, and it was the one thing she couldn't bring herself to admit.

Especially not to someone like Ian.

"Your sister, then?" he guessed. "Or your fiancé?"

Both, but she wasn't going to admit that, either.

"Do you think the police officer has found the guy who shot at us?" she asked.

"Changing the subject?"

"Just getting back to a more interesting one."

He smiled again. A gentle smile this time. The kind of smile that seemed to say he understood just how hard this was for her. "There was more than one person shooting, Esme. The guy in the building, and the one in the trees."

"I know."

"So which one do you want to find out about?" He took her arm, and she didn't resist as he drew her around the side of the building.

"Either. Both."

"We'll go around front. I want to get you out of the open, so we'll check in with the officer in charge and then get out of here."

"And go where?" she asked.

"Wherever my boss sends us."

"The safe house?"

"Yes."

"Will it be as safe as my witness protection location?" she asked and regretted the flip question immediately. Ian had been trying to be kind. She knew that, and she shouldn't have repaid him with attitude.

"Safer," he said without rancor. No excuses. No explanations. He'd already told her about a leak in the agency, and he'd already told her the leak had been plugged.

"I'm sorry. That didn't come out the way I wanted it to."

"What way would have been better?" he asked, King trotting along in front of him, heading toward the front of the building and the emergency lights that flashed across the pavement there.

"Silence?"

He chuckled, his hand still on her arm, his biceps brushing her shoulder. "Silence is the better part of valor. Or so my father always said."

"He doesn't say it any longer?" she asked, even

though she knew she shouldn't. The question was too personal, and she didn't expect him to answer.

For a moment, she thought he wouldn't.

The muscles in his arm were tense and taut, his jaw tight.

"I shouldn't have asked that," she began, and he shook his head.

"It's okay. I gave you the opening. My dad has been gone for ten years. He and my mother were killed in a drive-by shooting."

Her heart seemed to stop, then start again, beating the slow unsteady rhythm of grief.

She felt like an idiot. Worse, she felt like an ogre.

She'd stood in the hospital room and accused him of being in his cloistered law enforcement world making judgments about her life. She'd been sure he couldn't understand the grief and anger she felt over her family's betrayal, couldn't understand the sorrow of her losses.

She'd been wrong.

"Ian," she said, his name just a whisper in the warm night air, "I'm so sorry. I know that can't help, but I am."

"They've been gone a long time, but I still think about them a lot. I'm sure you understand that. Your parents were killed in a small plane crash, right?"

"You've done your research," she said, trying to lighten her tone, take some of the sorrow out of it. Time did ease the sting of loss. It never healed it, though. She understood that just as much as she understood his pain.

"It makes the job easier."

They'd reached the front of the building. The once nearly empty parking lot was filled with emergency vehicles and teaming with first responders.

No more hushed summer night. It was loud and chaotic, the shattered glass and crumbling bricks spilling into the lobby, spotlights shining onto the wrecked furniture and huge Ram truck that sat in the center of the mess.

"Were you folks inside?" an EMT asked, his skin ruddy from the sun, his eyes wide behind thick glasses. He looked young. Maybe early twenties, his uniform crisp and new.

"Yes," Ian responded, his fingers still curved around Esme's arm. She could have pulled away easily, but she didn't. There was something comforting about his touch, about the warmth of his palm through her sleeve.

She wouldn't think about that too deeply.

She wouldn't question it.

She had too much going on, too many details to work out. Sure, she'd have to run eventually, but she still didn't know which direction or how far she'd need to travel to reach a bus or train station. She'd have to take one or the other.

An airplane was out of the question.

And she didn't have enough money left to buy a used car.

She couldn't hitchhike, and she sure couldn't walk. She'd be too exposed, too easy to find.

"Are you okay?" the EMT asked, his gaze shifting from Ian to Esme.

"Fine," she responded. "Is everyone else?"

"Aside from the driver of the truck, there were no injuries."

"Where is the driver?" Ian asked.

"I'm sorry, sir. I'm not at liberty to give out information about clients."

"I'm a federal officer. Special Agent Ian Slade."

He pulled out his wallet and flashed his ID. The EMT seemed satisfied.

"He's being triaged in one of the clinic exam rooms. He was shot in the chest. I'm not sure he's going to survive."

"Do you know who the lead officer is?" Ian hooked King back to his lead.

He let go of Esme's arm to do it, and she stepped away, putting a little space between them.

She didn't want to like him. She sure didn't want to rely on him. She'd made it a habit to avoid getting close to any of the police officers, federal agents or prosecuting attorneys. They were using her to get what they wanted, and she understood that. She also understood that she'd been cut off from everyone she knew and loved.

She'd lost everything, and she was vulnerable.

Esme had her faith, but having a friend would be nice, too.

It would be easy to cling to any of the men and women who'd been shepherding her through what had become the most difficult time in her life.

Easy and foolish, because she'd already had her heart broken once in the past six months. She didn't want to repeat that. She didn't want to feel that sense of surprise and betrayal.

Love wasn't supposed to be limited by circumstances. It was supposed to grow during the hard times. Not just romantic love. All love—family, friendship. Instead, she'd found that it had abandoned her.

She needed to keep reminding herself of the way it had felt to know the people she'd loved didn't love her in return. She needed to remind herself that she was a means to an end. Nothing more, and that if she let herself forget that, if she let herself believe she was forging relationships with these people, she'd end up hurt.

Sighing, she took another step back, scanning the parking lot while the EMT pointed out the officer in charge.

Maybe Ian would get so excited about interviewing the gunman that he'd forget he was supposed to be guarding her. Maybe he'd be distracted for just enough time for her to slip away.

There had to be a store in town. She could ask for directions to the nearest bus stop or train station. She might even be able to call a taxi to bring her there. If there was a pay phone or someone willing to let her borrow a cell.

That was the problem with going off the grid. It wasn't easy to get help when she needed it. There was no one to call, no knight in shining armor ready to charge to the rescue. Worse, there was no one to consult with, no one to help make decisions. Her failures were her own. Which wasn't a bad thing. Unless failure meant death.

She eyed Ian and King, both deeply focused on the EMT who'd pulled out a business card and was scribbling something on it.

She could try to leave now, and they might not notice. She told herself to do it. The federal government had already failed to provide the safety it had promised. She had no reason to believe that things would be different this time, that somehow the organization that had failed her would suddenly find a way to succeed.

She took another step back, distancing herself from Ian and whatever security he offered. The intuition that had kept her alive, that had sent her running from witness protection, that had woken her from sleep when her uncle had broken into her trailer, kicked in. She could feel it in the pit of her stomach, a warning. Not to hurry. Not to disappear. To stay.

She scanned the crowd, suddenly terrified that she'd see her uncle hidden among the gawkers who'd begun to gather. She didn't find him, but she knew that meant almost nothing.

She felt dizzy with fear, sick with the thought of catching a glimpse of him. Her head ached where the hair had been torn out, and she touched the spot, remembered how short she'd cut it. How short Ian had cut it. He'd been kinder than she'd expected, more gentle, and she had the sudden feeling that if she were going to be saved from her family, he would be the man to do it.

That thought kept her in place, frozen two feet away from the man and dog she'd been telling herself to escape.

"Good choice," Ian said, turning in her direction as the EMT walked off.

She didn't respond, because she wasn't sure it was. She only knew it had been the only choice she could make.

Deputy Sheriff Kennedy Sinclair didn't much care to have the federal government messing around in one of her cases. She made that very clear to Ian more than once while he tried to get information on the truck driver.

In return, Ian had made it very clear that the case wasn't hers, that the federal government was already neck deep in it and that he wasn't going to back off. No matter how much she wanted him to.

Three hours after the truck had plowed into the medical center lobby, they were still at an impasse, Ian sitting on an uncomfortable chair in the corner of an interview room that smelled like vomit and mold, listening while Deputy Sheriff Sinclair asked Esme dozens of questions about her uncle, her family and her enemies.

"Her enemies," he stated, impatient with the process and wanting to move things along, "are her uncle and her brother. She's told you that a dozen times."

"Thanks for your input, Agent Slade, but I'm aware of what she said." The deputy sheriff tapped a pen against the old table that she and Esme were sitting at and frowned. "And I'm sure that you're aware of how common it is for witnesses to change their stories."

"Not this witness," he said, and she scowled.

"*Every* witness. Ms. Dupree might think that she only has two enemies in the world, but that doesn't mean there aren't more."

"I'm sitting right here. I can hear every word you say about me, so how about you stop discussing this case as if I weren't around," Esme muttered, her hands splayed flat, palms down on the tabletop. Probably to keep from fiddling with her hair. She'd been worrying at the short strands, smoothing them down and then fluffing them up again.

Nervous energy. Twice she'd gotten up and tried to pace the small room. The fact that King was lying smack-dab in the middle of the tiny bit of open floor had made that nearly impossible. Both times, she'd walked to him, looked down at him, frowned and taken her seat again.

King had seemed to think it was a game.

He'd followed her to her seat, nudged her hand to get the pet he thought he'd deserved and then retreated to the middle of the floor again. Currently, he was curled up, his nose tucked in neatly under his legs, his snout hidden, only his eyes visible. They were open. He was still on the job, after all.

"I'm sorry," the deputy sheriff said without a hint of remorse in her voice. "I'm just trying to get to the bottom of what happened tonight."

"I've explained everything I know. My uncle tried to kill me a few nights ago. He's probably responsible for what happened at the clinic, as well."

"Maybe." The deputy sheriff rested her elbows on the table and leaned toward Esme. Casual. Friendly. Ian had used the same interview technique more times than he cared to admit. "We found a jacket in the trees across from the clinic. Teeth marks in one sleeve. A little blood. I'm wondering if it could be your uncle's."

"I have no idea."

"You didn't see what he was wearing when he attacked you?"

"It was dark, I'd been woken from a sound sleep. Once I escaped him, I was too busy running for my life to pay much attention to what he wore," Esme said, a hint of irritation in her voice.

She'd planned to walk out of the hospital parking lot and run off again. He'd known it. He'd planned to give her the opportunity, and then he'd planned to stop her—a reminder to both of them that her agreement to testify against her family didn't mean they were on the same team. She'd stepped away. He'd been geared up to send King after her, and she'd stopped. Just…

stopped. No limping run toward the trees or the gathering crowd, no trying to dart away and hide somewhere until he gave up the hunt.

He thought her decision to put her life in his hands had surprised her as much as it had surprised him.

She'd spent the past few hours avoiding his eyes. She looked scared and shell-shocked, as if everything she'd been through the past few months had suddenly caught up to her.

"Yes. I guess that's true." The deputy sheriff paused, tapping the pen more rapidly. "Can I be honest with you, Esme?"

"It's better than feeding me lies."

"This is a small town. We don't get a lot of crime here. I've called in the state police to help collect and process evidence. As it stands, we know who the truck belongs to, but we have no idea who was driving it."

"Did you fingerprint the perp?" Ian asked, and the deputy sheriff frowned.

"We're a small town and not well funded, but we're not inept."

"It was a question. Not a statement of your abilities." He kept his tone neutral, and she seemed to relax.

"I know. I apologize for getting a bit defensive. But the fact is that I'm a woman in a position that has been held by men for nearly a hundred years. Sometimes, I've got to act tougher than I am." She released a breath and got back to the matter at hand. "We fingerprinted the guy at the hospital, and we're running him through the system. So far, we've come up empty. We did locate a handgun near the jacket. We found several prints on it, and we're running those, too."

"Any other evidence collected?"

"No, but I'm very familiar with the Dupree crime family." Her gaze shifted to Esme. "We've had run-ins with some of their drug transporters during the past few years. Cocaine. Heroin. There's a little airport ten miles outside of town. They fly the drugs in disguised as commercial shipments and transport it through the Everglades channels and out into the black market. I'm certain I've only caught one out of every ten drug shipments. We search the cargo, but they're good at what they do, and they know how to hide their product." She sighed in obvious frustration. "I've been begging the town council to fund a K-9 program. We need drug-detecting dogs to really shut the runners down. So far, I haven't convinced them to fund it."

"I'm sorry my family is doing this," Esme said, her voice raspy.

"You have nothing to be sorry for. You aren't responsible for your brother or your uncle. I'm only telling you this because I want you to know that this isn't a good place to try to hide. Someone around here is on the Duprees' payroll. Probably more than one person. I'm sure it wasn't difficult for your uncle to find someone willing to come after you."

"Kill me, you mean." Esme pushed away from the table, the chair scraping loudly on the old linoleum floor.

"Yes. That is exactly what I mean."

"I need some air." Esme didn't ask permission. She didn't seem to care if it was safe to leave. She walked out of the room, her limp obvious. She'd never gotten the Ace bandage, and she hadn't had time to ice her ankle. Ian would make sure she did both. It wasn't much to offer her, but it was more than he would have wanted to give her twenty-four hours ago.

A Dupree but not like the rest of the family.

He still wasn't sure how he felt about that.

All he knew was that he couldn't keep viewing her through the lens of his anger and vindictiveness.

He followed her into the hall, King off-lead beside him.

He kept his distance as she made her way down a narrow hall and into a dimly lit stairwell. She jogged down the steps ahead of him, and he forced himself to keep quiet about her ankle, to not tell her to be careful.

She knew he was there.

He had no doubt about that.

But she didn't acknowledge him. She slammed open the stairwell door with both hands, her narrow shoulders shaking.

Was she crying?

He hoped not.

Ian had never been great at dealing with the softer emotions. He could handle anger, frustration and disgust with ease. He dealt with them a lot in his line of work. And he knew how to assuage fear, how to calm nerves.

But tears?

They were a different thing altogether.

Tears were vulnerability incarnate. They were hints at the soul of another human being, and he was never quite sure how to respond when he was faced with that.

A pat on the shoulder? A verbal platitude? A gentle hug?

They all felt awkward and foreign and fake.

Esme reached the exit and would have opened the

door, but he touched her shoulder. Felt the fine trem-
ors, the tension.

"You can't go out there alone," he said softly, and
she whirled to face him, her short hair spiking out in a
hundred different directions, her face still deathly pale.

"I don't want to do this anymore," she responded,
her voice calm and quiet and reasonable. Completely
at odds with the wildness in her eyes.

"Talk to the deputy sheriff?" he asked, knowing it
was more than that. Knowing that she'd been pushed
too hard and been through too much.

"Be here. In this place. With an uncle who wants to
kill me. I don't want to keep running and hiding. I don't
like danger. I don't like intrigue. I hate scary movies
and books. I like weddings and happily-ever-afters and
cakes with sugar flowers."

"I can get you some cake. I'm not sure about the
sugar flowers," he offered, hoping for a smile, and felt
a spark of gratitude surge through him when he saw the
telltale curve of her lips, a subtle shifting of her energy.

She was calmer but not relaxed. "Thanks. Maybe I'll
take you up on that. If I survive until the trial."

"You will, but I thought maybe you could use some
cake now. When was the last time you ate?"

"I had a granola bar at noon."

"An empty stomach is hard on the psyche," he said,
and she offered a real smile.

"You're afraid I'm going to have a mental break-
down."

"I'm afraid you're going to cry. I'm as opposed to
tears as you are to scary movies."

She laughed a little at that, a hint of color returning

to her cheeks. "You're going to be very happy to hear that I almost never cry."

"And when you do, there's always a really good reason?"

"Usually. Sometimes, I cry at weddings. When the bride and groom are the perfect complement to each other, when I've worked with them for a year or more and seen just how deeply in love they are. I get a little teary-eyed then, because it reminds me of my parents. They were great people. You know what I keep wondering?"

"What?"

"Where they went wrong. How two great people could produce a son who has absolutely no moral compunction, no conscience, no remorse."

"Your brother made his choices, Esme. They had nothing to do with your parents."

"What about Violetta's choices? She could have stepped forward and helped, but she's refused to say anything."

It was true, and he wasn't going to argue the point. Two people from one family had decided they were above the law. Three, if he counted Angus. He did. "You can't blame your parents for that, either."

"I want to blame someone. It's easier than believing that the siblings I loved weren't worth it."

"Love is always worth it," he said, and she smiled again.

"Maybe you're the one who should be in the wedding business, because I'm kind of done with the whole believing-in-the-fairy-tale-of-love thing." Her voice broke on the last word, and he was sure there were tears in her eyes.

"Esme—"

"Relax," she said, sniffing once and then turning away. "I'm not crying. Just wondering how I ended up standing on the opposite side of the fence from the people who are supposed to love me."

She opened the door, and he motioned for King to move into place. The dog trotted outside beside Esme, ears alert, tail wagging. Warm, moist air blew in from the Everglades, bringing a hint of brine and rot. It was quiet here, the distant sound of highway traffic drifting on the still night air.

Esme didn't say another word. She seemed determined to leave, though, her limping stride carrying her across the parking lot to a cracked sidewalk that snaked through long grass.

"You know I can't let you go, right?" he said gently, and she shrugged, her hair glowing dark red in the streetlight.

"Esme," He tried again. "Don't make this more difficult for both of us."

"Sometimes, I get tired of following the rules, Ian. Especially when following them isn't doing me any good."

"It's doing you plenty of good."

"How so?" she countered. "I've nearly been killed more times than I care to remember. Maybe Violetta has a point. Maybe sitting on the fence and trying to stay neutral would be better than this."

Her words left him cold.

"You're not going to testify?" he asked, the question gruff and angry-sounding.

He needed to tone it down, rein in his own emotions. Esme clearly needed to talk this through. She didn't need him muddying the water with his less-than-positive opinion about her sister.

"Don't worry. I'll do what I said I would, and you'll get what you want from me." All the warmth had left her voice, and that bothered him more than it probably should have.

"What I want is for you to live. That's not going to happen if your brother goes free." That was the truth. Or part of it.

"You're twisting the truth to make yourself feel better, Ian. You want me to testify because you want my brother in jail. He's committed crime after crime with impunity, and his organization is only getting bigger. Look at this." She waved at the darkness that surrounded them. "Reginald started in Chicago. In the past ten years, he's expanded to Florida."

"And nearly every other state in the country," he offered.

"Exactly. I can't let him continue, but there is a part of me that wishes I could. There's a tiny little piece of me that would love to do what Violetta is doing. She's not committed any crimes, but she hasn't betrayed her family, either. She has support from the authorities and from my brother and uncle. All I've got is myself."

"You also have me and my team."

"For a while." She reached the end of the sidewalk and stopped, turning her face up to the night sky. A million stars dotted the blackness, and he wondered if she noticed, or if she was too caught up in her pain and regret to see anything beyond herself.

"It's beautiful," she said, answering the question he hadn't asked.

"Yes. It is."

"That's the weird thing about life."

"What is?"

"It goes on. Even during the most horrible pain a person can imagine, the earth continues to revolve around the sun, the seasons continue to change. Flowers bloom and crops are harvested and people are born and others marry. God is still on His throne, and life goes on." She sighed. "I guess we need to go back."

"If you're ready."

"What else do I have to do?" She skirted past, King close by her side.

"Call your sister?" he suggested and instantly regretted it. He shouldn't be encouraging her to speak with someone who had a different agenda than the FBI. Esme was already struggling. Speaking with her sister might pull her farther down the path of regret and farther from the job they needed her to do.

"That would be nice, but I don't have a phone. Even if I did, your people told me that if I tried to contact anyone from my former life, I'd probably be dead within forty-eight hours. Cell phone signals can be traced."

"Not mine," he said, continuing to give her the option. Despite his misgivings, it seemed like the right thing to do. Not for the FBI or, even, for Ian. For Esme. She deserved to have a little bit of peace, and if talking to her sister gave her that, who was he to deny her the opportunity?

"You're offering me your phone?" She met his eyes, and he could see the suspicion in her gaze, the wariness. He couldn't blame her. For six months, she'd been a pawn in a game she didn't want to play, shuffled around by people who either wanted to kill her or wanted to use her.

The fact that he'd been part of that made him feel guiltier than he should have. Or, maybe, as guilty as he should be. If he hadn't been so caught up in trying to bring her family down, he'd have thought more about what she was going through—the terror and anxiety and loneliness she must be feeling—rather than what her name meant to him.

"Your uncle already knows you're in this area, but I don't want you to mention our exact location," he said, and it felt right. It felt good. It felt like he'd stopped letting his emotions, his need for revenge, cloud his judgment and started seeing the situation for what it really was. Not a chance to destroy the Duprees. A chance to keep the one bright light on its dark family tree from being snuffed out.

"So, you *are* saying that." She grabbed his arm, and he let her pull him to a stop. Found himself looking down into her face, gazing into her eyes. They were dark in the dim light, her lashes thick and straight.

She was a Dupree, but she was smart, driven, decent.

Beautiful.

It was a winning combination, and if they'd been anywhere else, in any other situation, he'd have told her that.

"Don't tell her what happened tonight," he said instead, letting his gaze drop to King. He was relaxed and alert. No sign of danger, and Ian was glad. Not just for himself and King, but for Esme. She needed a break from the chaos and drama, a chance to breathe in a little peace. "No mention of anything that has transpired since you and I met, okay? I'll give you fifteen minutes, and then the conversation ends. You agree with those terms, or it doesn't happen."

"I agree!" she said with more enthusiasm than he'd have had if he were calling a sister who didn't care whether he lived or died. Violetta didn't seem to when it came to Esme. She knew more about the workings of the crime family than she'd admitted. Her silence had kept Angus from going to jail.

He shoved the thought away, taking Esme's arm and leading her back to the building. "We'll do it inside. It's safer there."

She nodded, but he didn't think she heard.

She was smiling, nearly skipping with happiness as they made their way across the parking lot and back inside.

Weddings.

Happily-ever-afters.

Cakes with sugar flowers.

Right then, she seemed filled with all those things. And suddenly, he understood why she was so good at her job; he knew how she'd built a wedding planning business from nothing into a million-dollar company. Her energy was difficult to resist. Her joy and enthusiasm were contagious.

But her uncle was still on the loose.

She still had a price on her head.

And until the Dupree crime family had been dismantled, all the joy and enthusiasm in the world couldn't keep her safe.

SEVEN

Ian managed to find a small room where Esme could make the phone call. He also managed to convince the deputy sheriff to leave her alone there.

Well…

Not alone exactly.

Ian was sitting in a chair a few feet away, King lying near his feet.

Esme would have preferred they both leave, but she hadn't been able to convince Ian to let her have privacy.

His way or the highway.

That was the impression he'd given.

But he was letting her make the call.

That was all that mattered to her.

Her fingers shook as she punched Violetta's number into the phone. She felt nervous and uneasy, no point in denying it. Six months ago, she and her sister hadn't parted on good terms. Violetta had been convinced that Esme was going to destroy the family.

She'd been right.

But the family had been destroyed long before Esme realized what her brother was. Families couldn't be built and sustained on lies. They couldn't be nurtured when

one or more of the members wasn't who he pretended
to be. Esme had explained all of that to Violetta. She'd
outlined her reasons for testifying against Reginald.
She'd tried to convince her sister to cooperate with the
police and FBI, to tell them anything she knew about
their brother's crimes. But it had backfired.

Big-time.

Violetta had been livid.

So, yeah. They hadn't parted on good terms, but
Esme still loved her sister. She longed to hear her voice,
to know that she was doing okay, that the police and
FBI hadn't come down too hard on her.

She punched in the last number and waited as the
phone rang. Once. Twice. The third time, voice mail
picked up, and all Esme's excitement and fear seeped
away. She leaned against the wall, every bit of her energy suddenly gone. She left a quick message telling
Violetta how much she loved her.

When she finished, she handed the phone back to
Ian.

"Thanks," she managed to say, her eyes hot with
tears she wasn't going to shed.

"I'm sorry she didn't pick up," he responded in a
gruff voice, tucking his phone into his jacket pocket.

She caught a glimpse of his holster and gun, and she
turned away from the reminder that he was there doing
his job, that he only cared about keeping her safe so that
she could testify.

Right at that very moment, Ian Slade was all she
had, and he'd given her way more than she'd expected.

"It's not your fault," she said, walking to the door.

"You're giving up a little easily, Esme," he responded, and she turned to face him again.

"What?"

"You escaped witness protection and kept ahead of your uncle for months. I'm surprised that you're willing to make one phone call and call it quits."

"That was the agreement."

"We agreed on the terms of your talk with her." He pulled out the cell phone and handed it to her. "Give it another try. Who knows? She might be screening her calls. Maybe she's gotten tired of hearing from my team and the prosecuting attorney."

She met his eyes, realized that he was doing this for her. Nothing else. No hidden agenda. No desire for information or control. He wanted her to have what she wanted, and that felt…different. It felt nice. It felt like what she'd hoped to have with Brent but had never achieved. She'd loved him, and she'd been willing to concede on almost every issue. They'd almost never fought, because she hadn't found much worth fighting about. It seemed easier and better to let him have his way.

Her friends had said they were the perfect couple. They'd all wanted to be in a relationship just like the one Esme and Brent were in.

She wondered what they were saying now.

She dialed her sister's number again, her heart thumping with memories and with anxiety. She really did want to hear her voice.

"Esme?!" Violetta's voice rang in her ear, sharp and a little frantic.

"Yes."

"I'm so glad. When I realized I hadn't picked up when you'd called…" She paused, and Esme could picture her pacing her posh home office. "I couldn't believe it when I heard your message. I should have picked up, but the number wasn't one I was familiar with. And the police and FBI and press won't stop hassling me."

"I... Someone let me use his phone. I wanted to make sure you were okay."

"Me? I'm not the one in trouble. Are you okay? The FBI said that you weren't in protective custody anymore. I've been worried sick." She seemed to have calmed, her voice taking on its normal clipped tone. Violetta had money. Lots of it. She liked to live large. Big house. Expensive cars. Gorgeous clothes. Her persona reflected an upper-crust background that she didn't have.

Esme wasn't sure when Violetta had adopted it. Maybe after her first marriage. Her ex had been rich and snobby, his money buying him friends that his personality couldn't.

"I'm okay. Just..." She glanced at Ian.

He was watching her, his eyes oddly light in his handsome, tanned face.

"Just what?" Violetta demanded.

"Wishing I could come home." To her surprise, her voice broke on the words, some of the emotion she'd been trying hard to contain slipping out.

"You can. Just tell the feds you won't testify," Violetta responded.

"You know I can't do that."

"You won't do it, sis. There's a difference."

"Reginald killed a man," she said, the words making her feel sick and light-headed.

She'd seen it all.

The gun.

The blood.

The red stain spreading across the cracked linoleum floor.

"Sit," Ian whispered in her ear, moving her to the chair and urging her into it.

"Is someone there with you?" Violetta demanded, her voice shrill.

"I…"

Ian shook his head.

"No," she lied and despised herself for it.

"Look, hon, I love you. You know that, but you've got to back out of your deal. You can't testify against blood."

"That's not what Mom and Dad would say. You know they wouldn't. They'd say I should do the right thing, and that the right thing isn't always the easy one."

"Maybe so, but they're dead. You're not. I'd like you to stay that way."

"Then maybe you could do what I have. Testify. If you tell the authorities what you know about the Dupree criminal enterprise, then Uncle Angus will be tossed into prison where he belongs."

"Here's what I know," Violetta said, her tone hard-edged and angry. "You could die for the sake of a man you barely knew, a guy who was probably as big a criminal as you think our brother is. That man you saw shot? He had a record. You know that, right? Just because you think Reginald shot him, doesn't mean he was an innocent bystander."

"Think? I saw him!"

"If you insist on testifying, you could die for the sake of some idealized belief about right and wrong," Violetta continued as if Esme hadn't spoken.

"I could die because my sister won't do the right

thing." The truth slipped out. Stark and real and harsh, and she despised herself for it as much as she had for the lie.

"I would do anything for you, Esme," Violetta said, all the affectation gone from her voice. She sounded like the person she'd been before she'd married into money and decided that having material possessions was more important than having relationships. "But both of us dying isn't a good solution to the problem. I love you, hon. I hope you know that."

She disconnected, the silence echoing hollowly in Esme's heart.

She wasn't sure how long she held the phone to her ear. Eventually, Ian took it, his fingers brushing against her cheek, warm and calloused and gentle.

She should have moved away, but she didn't. Not when he tucked the phone back in his pocket. Not when his hand cupped her chin. Not when he looked into her eyes.

"It's going to be okay," he said.

"You can't know that."

"Yeah, I can, because I'm going to make sure it is."

"Don't make promises you can't keep, Ian," she said, the words as hollow and empty as her heart felt.

"It's not a promise. It's a statement of fact."

"It's kind of sad that you're more determined to keep me safe than my sister is." Her voice broke, and to her horror, a single tear slipped down her cheek.

"Come here." He tugged her into his arms, and she went, because she needed his warmth so much more than she wanted to.

"All she has to do is tell the police what she knows

about Angus's involvement in the crimes my brother has been committing. If she did that, it would all be over."

"Some people have an easier time doing the right things than others do." He smoothed her hair, and she realized her head was resting against his chest, that she could hear the slow solid thump of his heart.

"Violetta is making a choice. Me or money. She's choosing money."

"Maybe, but your parents were right. Sometimes the right thing *is* the most difficult. Sometimes the easy path leads to the most dangerous places, and the most difficult road brings us home."

"I know."

"Obviously, Violetta doesn't. Not yet. So don't let her doubts shake your conviction." He said it kindly, his hand still smoothing her hair, the rhythmic thump of his heart soothing her soul.

It took a minute for the words to register, for her to realize what he was really saying: *Don't back out of your agreement. We need you to testify.*

The knowledge was like a bucket of ice water in the face. It woke her up, made her realize whose arms she was standing in. He wasn't any less biased than Violetta. He had just as much of an agenda, and she still wanted to stay in his arms, burrow closer, inhale the spicy scent of aftershave and soap.

She backed away. "You're afraid I won't testify," she accused. "Still. Even after I told you I wasn't going to change my mind."

"You're wrong," he said as she turned blindly and reached for the door handle. "I'm not afraid you won't do it. I'm afraid you'll spend the rest of your life regretting it."

"I won't," she bit out, her heart throbbing in her chest, her stomach churning.

"Are you saying you don't already feel like a traitor?"

"I'm saying that I know I'm doing the right thing. That's going to have to be enough."

"You didn't answer my question."

"Because I don't know what you want me to say," she responded, and she could hear the edge of sorrow and frustration and worry in her voice.

It surprised her.

She prided herself on her calm approach to life.

She'd won job after job because brides and grooms and their families had bragged about how easily she handled difficult situations.

She wasn't handling anything right now. She was just trying to get through this moment without completely breaking down.

Maybe Ian knew that.

He sighed, grabbing her hand and tugging her away from the door. "I wish you weren't in this situation, but you are, Esme. I wish I could give you some easy way out, but there isn't one. All I can do is offer whatever support you need and all the protection necessary to keep you safe."

"A personal bodyguard, huh?" she said, trying to smile but failing miserably.

"Call it whatever you want," Ian replied, brushing strands of hair from her temple and looking into her eyes, studying her face.

She wasn't sure what he was looking for, but he must have found it, because he smiled gently.

"It's going to be okay," he said, just like he had before, and then he stepped back, his hands dropping away.

"What now?" she asked, because she needed to say something, and because what she really wanted to do was step right back into his arms.

"We'd better get back to the interrogation room," he said. "The sooner we can convince the deputy sheriff to let us leave, the happier I'll be."

"Has your boss found a safe house yet?" She opened the door and walked straight into a tall muscular guy. She stepped back, nearly falling over in her haste.

He grabbed her arm to steady her, and she realized there was a dog beside him. Smaller than King, but watching her with the same kind of intelligence.

"I'm so sorry," she gasped.

"Don't be," the man said. "I never complain when a pretty woman bumps into me." He glanced past her, his smile broadening.

"I'm glad to see that they didn't toss you into jail, Ian," he said. "I was worried when Max said you were at the local police station."

"For once," Ian said, "I've stayed out of trouble. Esme, this is Zeke Morrow. He's a member of the Tactical K-9 Unit, and that's his K-9 partner, Cheetah."

"Nice to meet you." The words sounded stilted and awkward. Which was exactly how she felt. She'd been running from these men for months, hiding from the FBI and anyone affiliated with it, and now she was back in their custody.

She wasn't sure how she felt about that.

She only knew she was tired. No. Exhausted. There was an old vinyl chair sitting against the wall, and she dropped into it, her head swimming.

She closed her eyes for a second.

When she opened them, Ian was crouching in front

of her. "Are you okay?" he asked as King edged in between them and nudged her hand.

She scratched behind his ears and told herself she wasn't going to pass out from fatigue and hunger. "I'm fine."

"You're white as a sheet," he corrected, pressing his hand against her forehead.

"I'm a redhead," she muttered.

"I've never seen a redhead your particular shade of white," Zeke offered. "Maybe Ian was right. A little sugar might do you some good." He handed her a white paper bag.

"What is it?" she asked, her gaze shifting from him to Ian.

"Just something I thought you might enjoy after your hours-long interrogation. I asked Zeke to stop and pick it up before he drove here from the airport."

She peeked in the bag.

It contained a clear plastic container with what looked like cake inside.

She pulled it out.

Yes. *Cake.*

White with ivory icing and pretty yellow and pink flowers, and her heart hurt with the beauty of the gesture.

She met Ian's eyes again, and he was smiling, his face soft with what looked like affection, compassion and concern.

"It's cake," she murmured, as if it needed to be said.

"I told you I would get you some."

"Actually," Zeke interrupted, "I got it."

She heard him, but she was still looking in Ian's eyes, still seeing his smile.

She couldn't help herself, she smiled, too, some of her anxiety and fear seeping away. "Thank you."

"No problem. Like he mentioned, Zeke did all the work."

"Not just for the cake," she responded.

"No problem," he said again. "Now, how about you eat the cake while Zeke and I discuss how to get you out of here?"

He straightened, and she opened the container, found a plastic fork and a napkin in the bag. The first bite was sweet and light. Vanilla and sugar and flour and butter. If she'd had to put a name to the flavor, she'd say it tasted an awful lot like hope.

Things were looking up.

At least, as far as Ian was concerned they were.

Max had managed to find a safe house that was far enough away from town to throw Angus off their trail but close enough to be easily accessible. Zeke had arrived with Cheetah. Julianne Martinez was also on the way and planned to meet them at the safe house.

Three agents all devoted to getting Esme to the trial.

Yeah. Things were definitely looking up.

For him.

Esme didn't seem quite as happy, but she did have some color in her cheeks. The cake he'd asked Zeke to bring had done its job. The empty container was in her hand, empty but for a couple crumbs and a few smudges of frosting.

"Was it good?" he asked, and she patted her stomach, her hand shaking a little.

"It was the best cake I've had in months." She still sat in the old chair, her legs stretched out in front of her. Despite the food and the color in her cheeks, she looked exhausted.

"Good. Now, how about we get you out of here?"

"Deputy Sheriff Sinclair is okay with that?" she asked, glancing down the hall. Zeke was there, standing in front of a window, watching the parking lot as he and the deputy sheriff finished discussing plans for getting Esme outside safely.

Ian had left them to it, because he'd been worried about her. She'd been too quiet. For someone who'd been taking action and making decisions on her own for months, she didn't seem all that interested in the plans they'd been discussing while she ate cake.

That concerned him.

Months of fear and anxiety could wear a person down, make her feel hopeless and defeated. He didn't want that to happen to Esme.

"She said she has everything she needs from you. Come on. By the time we get to the safe house, there'll be a freshly made-up bed waiting for you." He took her hand, pulled her to her feet. She tossed the empty cake container and bag into a recycle bin and offered a shaky smile.

"That sounds great, because I think I'm crashing from my sugar high."

"Maybe you're just crashing from too many months of running," he replied, and her smile fell away.

"Don't, Ian."

"What?"

"Be so nice."

"I'm being me," he replied, leading her toward Zeke and the deputy sheriff.

"And making it really hard for me to not like you."

"Is there a reason why you don't want to?"

"Maybe I just don't want to be disappointed again."

"Again?"

"It's a long story. I don't have time to tell it."

"We're going to have plenty of time later," he replied, and she shrugged.

"You have something personal against my family, don't you?" she asked, the question so unexpected and sudden, it took a moment for it to register.

When it did, he stopped, turning so that they were face-to-face and he could look into her eyes. He wanted to see her expression while they talked, and he wanted her to see his.

Nothing hidden.

Nothing left out.

She deserved the truth, and he'd give it to her, if that was really what she was asking for. "Why do you ask?"

"I've been sitting there eating cake and thinking, and while I've been doing that, I've been remembering a couple of things you said about my family. Maybe not what you said, but how you said it. As if you despised everything we were."

"Not you," he corrected. "Them."

"See? Even with just those words, you sound angry."

"Do I?" he asked, but he knew he did. Just like he knew he was putting off the inevitable. They were about to spend a month in a safe house together. She deserved to know who he was, what he'd spent most of his adult life trying to do—take down her family.

"I'm too tired for games," she responded. "So how about you just tell me what happened?"

"I've known about your brother and his crimes for a long time. My father was a police officer in Chicago right around the time Reginald started making inroads into the crime world."

She frowned, and he could almost see her mind working, see her putting together bits of information and trying to connect them.

When she didn't speak, he continued. "My dad planned to shut Reginald down before he could gain more ground. He arrested quite a few low-level operatives, stopped several money-laundering schemes, intercepted a few drug shipments. Basically, he was making your brother's life very difficult."

He didn't continue.

He'd told the story to other people. He'd imagined telling it to one of the Duprees, standing in a courtroom somewhere and explaining the exact reason why he was going to make sure every crooked member of the family paid.

But he hadn't imagined this. Hadn't imagined looking in Esme's stricken face, seeing the knowledge in her eyes. She knew. He didn't have to tell her.

"Come on," he said, and he'd have walked away, but she grabbed his hand, her palm cold and dry.

"You said they were killed in a drive-by shooting," she murmured, her face so pale he thought she might fall over.

"They were."

"Are you sure it was him?" she asked, and he gave her credit for not denying it, for not insisting that her brother hadn't been responsible.

"Reginald showed up at the funeral. After everyone left, and I was standing by their caskets, praying that I'd wake up from the nightmare. I looked up, and he was there, standing a hundred feet away. He pointed his finger at me and pretended to shoot, and then he walked away."

"I'm so sorry, Ian," she whispered, tears slipping down her cheeks, the woman who'd said she rarely cried, swallowing back sobs as she stood in the stark white light of the police station. Her hair was deep red and spiked up around her head, her eyes deeply shadowed. He couldn't stop thinking about how she'd looked when he'd walked into the hospital room, seen her chopping off her hair because her uncle—her flesh and blood—had used her ponytail to keep her from running.

She must hate that, hate that she'd lost control in public, with Ian looking on.

She'd been through too much.

He'd made it worse.

If that was what wanting revenge led to, he didn't like it.

Didn't particularly like himself.

Let it go.

That was what his father would have said.

Let God deal with it.

He'd understood the truth behind that for a long time, but he'd never been able to make himself own it. He'd wanted revenge, and he'd wanted to be the one to dish it out. He'd wanted the Dupree family to suffer as much as he had. He'd wanted every last one of them to mourn and grieve and cry.

And then he'd met Esme.

She was as innocent as his parents had been.

He hadn't been able to protect them, but he could protect her. Maybe that was the key to peace. Maybe he'd come full circle, facing a choice about how he wanted to move forward in life. Maybe instead of taking two lives like Reginald had, he was supposed to save one. Save Esme.

Maybe.

"It's not your fault," he said, and for the first time since he'd been assigned this case, he knew that it was true.

"My family—"

"Isn't you." He wiped the tears from her cheeks.

"Ian—"

"You're tired. How about we discuss this when you're feeling more yourself?"

"Meaning not crying?" she asked wryly, swiping more tears from her cheeks. "You did say you were opposed to tears."

"On you," he responded, taking her hand and walking again, King trotting along beside them, "they look good."

She laughed, the sound husky and rough but still filled with warmth. "Better not say that, Ian. Next time, I might really let loose."

She was attempting to shove aside her grief and keep going with a good attitude. He'd never thought he could learn anything from a Dupree, but in the short time he'd known Esme, she'd taught him everything he needed to know about judging people on their own merit rather than on the merit of their family.

"You could let loose a floodgate of tears and you'd still look like the bravest woman I've ever met," he responded.

"I think that's the nicest thing anyone has ever said to me."

"Then I guess you haven't been around the right people," he responded.

She was silent for a moment, and then she smiled. Just a tiny little curve of the lips that made his pulse jump. "I guess running for my life has its perks."

"Like?"

"A bodyguard who knows how to say the right thing at exactly the right time."

"You two ready?" Zeke called, striding toward them, Cheetah at his side.

"I was ready an hour ago," Esme responded.

"Then let's head out."

She released Ian's hand and moved toward the door. He followed, more determined than ever to make sure she got to trial safely.

EIGHT

Esme didn't speak as she climbed into Zeke's over-size SUV. She didn't say a word as the two men got their dogs into the back. Zeke climbed in the front. Ian nudged Esme into the center of the bucket seat, grabbing her arm when she would have moved all the way to the other side of the vehicle.

"The middle is safest," he said.

She didn't respond.

She didn't have anything to say. She'd been fooling herself, believing in a fantasy, convinced that Reginald had committed only one murder.

One had been bad enough.

One had been horrible.

But he'd committed at least two more.

She had no reason to doubt Ian's story. She'd seen the truth in his eyes. She'd heard it in his voice. Apparently, Reginald had been killing people to get them out of his way for as long as he'd been running the *family business*.

How many lives had he taken?

And why was she telling herself that she was surprised, shocked, flabbergasted?

Reginald wanted his own sister dead.

He was working with Angus to make sure that happened.

Hadn't the FBI been telling her that for months? Hadn't they brought up his name every chance they got? It wasn't just Angus coming after her, it was Reginald. He was calling the shots and pulling the trigger.

"Are you all right?" Ian asked, his voice a soft rumble in the silent SUV.

"I will be."

"I shouldn't have told you about my parents."

"Of course you should have."

"It could have waited."

"Until when? Something like that festers the longer it sits." That was the truth. "Besides, I asked you. It's not like you just tossed the information out at me."

"It still could have waited. Seat belt," he said, and when she didn't reach to snap hers into place, he did it for her, his hand brushing against her abdomen, the warmth of his arm pressing against hers.

Comforting.

Just like his touch had been, his hug, his hands brushing tears from her cheeks.

Esme didn't want to think too much about that. About how much safer she felt when he was around, about how desperate she was to have someone she could count on.

She'd always been confident and had always known how to go after what she wanted. What she wanted right now was to be done with the trial and the testimony.

A month wasn't a long time.

She could do anything for a month.

Except maybe survive.

She shuddered, the warmth of the summer air drifting in the open driver's-side window doing nothing to chase away the chill that had settled deep in her bones.

"Here," Ian said, taking off his jacket and laying it over her, tucking the edges around her shoulders, his fingers brushing her collarbone and the side of her neck, lingering there. Soft and light and gentle.

That should have been all. Just a simple touch. His hand there and then gone. She met his eyes, felt something arc between them, the jolt of it making her pulse race.

"This is probably a bad idea," she said, and he smiled.

"What?"

"Whatever we're doing."

"Getting to know each other? We're going to be spending a lot of time together in the next month or so. Understanding a little about each other will make that easier."

"You're going to be staying at the safe house?" For some reason, that hadn't occurred to her. It probably should have. Ian had been talking about the safe house, about being her bodyguard and probably a bunch of other things that should have clued her in. Probably would have if she hadn't been so exhausted.

"What did you think was going to happen?"

"I guess I thought you were going to bring me there and leave."

"It would be difficult to be your bodyguard if I weren't close."

"Right."

"You don't sound happy about it."

"I don't really have an opinion." Except that he was the kind of temptation she didn't need in her life. That a few days with Ian could make her wonder what she'd ever seen in Brent.

Who was she kidding?

She'd spent a few hours with him and she was already wondering that.

"Sure you do," he said, and she frowned.

"Then my opinion is that my parents would roll over in their graves if they thought I was staying in a house with a guy like you."

"You think they'd take issue with me?"

"I think they'd have rather I stay in a house with a guy who looked like a toad, smelled like a troll and refused to shower regularly."

"No worries," he replied. "I won't be the only one there."

"And you couldn't have mentioned that before I went on my rant about trolls and toads?"

He chuckled, leaning back against the seat and giving her some breathing room.

She should have been happy about that.

Should have. Wasn't.

She liked having him close. He was a habit that could be easy to form and very, very difficult to break.

"You have the coordinates for the safe house?" Zeke asked as he pulled away from the police station and onto the road.

"Yeah. Hold on. I've also got another text from Max. He got a call from the local PD." Ian pulled out his phone and leaned over, speaking quietly to Zeke for several minutes. Esme heard a few words. Something about blood and DNA and a jacket. She could guess what they were discussing, and she could have joined in, but all she really wanted to do was close her eyes and sleep.

For the first time in weeks, she wasn't alone in the darkness listening to the sound of the Everglades, startling at every noise, pacing restlessly through the longest hours of the night. For the first time in weeks, she felt almost safe.

She closed her eyes, drifting into half sleep, the sound of a cell phone jerking her awake again. For a moment, she thought she was back in Chicago answering client phone calls and text messages. She opened her eyes, reaching for her purse and her phone.

No phone.

No purse.

Just Zeke driving the SUV, and Ian checking a text message, the blueish light from his phone deepening the hollows of his cheekbones, sharpening the angle of his chin.

Whatever he was reading, it wasn't making him happy.

"What's wrong?" she asked, and he tucked the phone away.

"Nothing you need to worry about."

"Which makes me worry more, so how about you just tell me?"

Rubbing the back of his neck, he let out a frustrated sigh. "Just a message from an anonymous friend."

"Another one?" Zeke asked. "Did Dylan forward it to you?"

"He forwarded it to the team. You should already have it."

"I really don't like being kept in the dark," Esme said.

"This has nothing to do with the trial," Ian reassured her.

"But it has something to do with my family, right?"

"In a roundabout way."

"Can you be any vaguer?" she asked.

"Probably. If I try hard enough."

"You might as well run the situation by her," Zeke interrupted. "Maybe she'll have some idea of who's sending the texts and why."

"What texts?" she asked.

Ian took out his phone, pulled up a text and handed it to her.

Word is that Mommy, Daddy and child have gone home.

She read it twice, trying to make sense of what she was seeing, attempting to put it in the context of the trouble she'd found herself in.

"Who are Mommy, Daddy and child?" she finally prompted.

"Daddy is the leak I mentioned. The one who gave away your location in witness protection. He's a rogue agent. He was working for your family." Ian frowned. "Your brother and uncle, I mean."

Esme narrowed her eyes, noticing the change in his rhetoric, the careful choice of words. She'd have thanked him for it, but she was reading the text again. This time out loud.

The words didn't make any more sense than they had before.

"Who are the child and the mother?"

"Penny and Kevin. His girlfriend and child. We think he's trying to get to his son. My suspicion is that he plans to take him and leave the country."

"What about the mother?"

"That's a good question," Zeke said, his voice tight and hard. "I wish I had an answer. The fact is, the agent is my brother, Jake Morrow. He's been on your brother's payroll for a while."

"I'm sorry, Zeke."

"Yeah. Me, too. If we could figure out who Anonymous is, we might be able to track Jake down, make sure he's stopped before he takes his son out of the country."

"We're sure it's someone who's familiar with your family and with Jake. Do you have any ideas, Esme?" Ian took the phone, tucked it back into his pocket.

"Me?" she sputtered. "I barely even know what you're talking about."

"We've been getting messages like this for months. Whoever is sending them seems to be trying to help us track down Jake. Unfortunately, the vague references aren't helping much."

"You think it's someone who works for my brother?" she asked, sifting through her memories, trying to find one that might be helpful.

There was nothing.

She hadn't spent much time with Reginald recently and the only vivid memory she had of him was his cold-eyed glare after he'd pulled the trigger.

"Probably," Zeke responded. "My brother was really good at making connections. He knows a lot of people. It's possible one of them is betraying him."

"I've never met your brother, so I have no idea if I've met someone who knows him."

"He went to a lot of your brother's functions. You might have seen him there."

"I didn't attend them." Not the extravagant Christmas parties, the over-the-top New Year's celebrations. Not even the birthday party he threw for himself every year.

She sent him a card.

She called him.

She made small talk about things that weren't important, but she never mingled with his crowd, because she'd never been comfortable in it. Violetta, on the other hand, had loved every bit of the lavish functions.

"But my sister…" She began, and then stopped herself.

"What about her?" Ian prodded.

"She might know something about Jake. She loved going to Reginald's parties. She enjoyed hanging out with his wealthy friends. I could ask her." Of course, that would mean calling again. It would mean having another dead-end conversation that would make her feel horrible. She'd do it, though, because she wanted to put an end to all of this. She wanted her uncle and Reginald in jail where they belonged, wanted peace for herself, justice for the man who died and for Ian's parents.

"Your sister has been less than cooperative," Ian said without a hint of judgment in his voice. He was trying hard to keep his opinion of her family under wraps, but his opinion was valid, his reasons justified. If she could help him, she would.

"She might be more willing to discuss things with me. We're family. That's important."

"It wouldn't hurt for her to try," Zeke said, glancing into the rearview mirror and frowning. "We may have a tail."

"Since when?" Ian shifted, angling his body so he could look out the back window.

Esme did the same. Not because she wanted to see danger coming for her, but because she wanted to be prepared for it.

Headlights.

Not close. Maybe six car lengths back.

"They pulled onto the road two miles ago," Zeke told him.

"And they've been hanging back all this time?"

"Yes. Pretty much the same distance."

"I'll call it in," Ian said. "See if we can get some local patrol cars out here. Turn off on the next road. I don't want whoever is in that car to have any idea of where we're going."

Where they were going seemed to be farther from civilization.

Esme hadn't been paying attention.

Now she was.

The town was behind them, pinpricks of light in the darkness. Ahead, there was nothing but an empty two-lane road. Thick marsh grass grew on either side of it. Farther away, a few trees jutted up toward the midnight sky.

No sign of any houses.

No business.

No golden arches spearing up from the landscape.

"If I can find a side road, I'll turn. Otherwise, we need to prepare for a rear attack. They seem to be picking up speed." Zeke accelerated, the SUV speeding around a curve, the headlights behind them disappearing briefly and reappearing again moments later.

"They're closing in," Ian said grimly as he pulled out his cell phone and dialed 911.

Esme didn't think calling the police was going to

do much good. The SUV was racing at a dangerous speed, and their pursuer was still closing the gap between them. She could see that as clearly as she could see the stars in the dark sky, the marsh grass sweeping sideways as the SUV passed.

"Hold on," Zeke said so calmly Esme wasn't prepared when he took a hard turn. She slammed into Ian, her shoulder pressing into his arm.

They bounced over a rut, and his arm slipped around her, holding her in place as the SUV hit another rut and another.

"Are they still behind us?" she asked, trying to free herself so that she could look.

He held her in place, his arm a steel band around her shoulders, his grip firm without being painful.

"Not yet," he responded, finally releasing her.

He had his gun in hand.

She hadn't realized that.

Hadn't realized how fast her heart was beating, how terrified she was. Not until she looked out the back window and saw the car. It was still on the main road but doing a U-turn, heading back the way it had come. Searching, she knew, for the turn.

"Looks like we're at a dead end." Zeke stopped the SUV and hopped out. No panic in his voice. No fear. He moved quickly and efficiently, grabbing a pack from the back, releasing the dogs.

Ian opened his door, letting the scent of briny water and decay fill the vehicle.

"Come on." He reached for her hand, tugging her out onto muddy earth. If they'd gone any farther, the SUV would be sinking. As it was, they were stuck. Going back would mean running straight into their pursuers. Going forward was impossible.

They'd have to walk out.

Run out.

Walking would do diddly-squat for any of them. She tracked the movement of the car as it crawled along. It wouldn't take long for the driver to find the road they'd taken. It would take even less time for him to find their SUV.

"We need to get out of here," she said, her voice too loud and tinged with a hint of desperation.

"We will." Ian snagged a pack from the back of the SUV, hooked a lead to King's collar and tossed his jacket into Esme's arms. "Put that on."

She didn't argue.

The faster she cooperated, the faster they could get moving.

That was how she saw things.

And she wanted to get moving, because she had a horrible feeling that Angus was in the car. Angus, the uncle who wanted her dead, who'd looked into her face and told her exactly why she had to die.

She shuddered, zipping up the jacket and following Ian as he headed through tall marsh grass, King on-heel beside him.

Zeke was a few feet ahead, his dog trotting nearly silently.

They weren't running, but they were moving fast, plowing through the grass and then on to drier land. She wasn't sure where they were heading. She didn't know if the men knew.

Wherever it was, it was away from that car and who-ever was driving it.

That was all she cared about.

That was all she needed to know.

She made the mistake of glancing back, of searching the darkness for the vehicle. And then she saw it, the headlights bobbing along as it sped toward the SUV.

She wanted to run. Wanted to sprint as far and as fast as she could. She probably would have, but Ian reached back and grabbed her hand, pulling her up next to him.

"Don't panic," he said in that same calm tone Zeke had used.

Did they go to school for that?

Did the FBI train them to keep their wits about them so that civilians didn't panic?

If so, it wasn't working on her.

"Why would I go and do something like that? Just because the car has almost reached the SUV and we're right out here in the open where any sniper can see us doesn't mean we should be worried," she retorted, the words spilling out in a rush of nervous energy.

"That's the spirit," he praised, not quickening his pace. Not glancing back. Not doing anything but moving forward.

Maybe that was a metaphor for life, but she wasn't in the mood to think about it.

Outwardly, she was staying calm, but inside?

Inside, she was a wild mass of hysteria.

Ian could hear sirens.

That was the good news.

The bad news was that their pursuers had already found the SUV. He didn't have to look to know it. He heard car doors slam. One. Then another.

At least two pursuers.

Probably armed.

Maybe with night vision goggles and long-range weapons.

That was more bad news, but it was also only speculation.

Angus had failed in his mission to kill Esme a couple of times. It was possible he wasn't nearly as well-versed in crime as his nephew.

He had found them, though. There was no doubt about that.

Ian wanted to know how.

He had a feeling it had something to do with Jake. The guy knew exactly how the Tactical K-9 Unit worked. He could have tapped into local databases and gotten a hit when Ian had checked Esme into the clinic. It would have been easy enough for him to pass that information on to Angus, and easier still for Angus to figure out that Esme would spend some time being interviewed by the local authorities.

After that, it was just a matter of waiting.

Anyone with enough money could hire people to do that.

Jake had the money.

That was what working both sides of the fence did for a person. It made him rich. It was possible it also made him foolish. If Jake were as smart as he liked to think he was, he'd have left the country when he'd disappeared months ago. At the time, the team had assumed he'd been abducted by Angus Dupree and that he would be used as a pawn to get Reginald out of jail.

It had taken months to uncover the truth. In that time, Jake could easily have found a way to disappear for good.

Instead, he'd stuck around, searching—it seemed—for his ex-girlfriend, Penny Potter, and their son.

As far as the team knew, Jake was still on the Dupree payroll. If that was the case, he could be hunting Esme. For all Ian knew, Jake was in the car that had been following them. If he were, he'd be a more challenging adversary than Angus. He knew exactly how the team worked, exactly how the dogs responded and reacted. He'd be able to anticipate and act accordingly. He'd know that they'd have abandoned the vehicle and would be hiking out with their dogs. He'd also know what weapons they had and how much firepower. What dogs they had with them and what each was trained for.

He'd probably assume that they'd be heading for the safe house. That was protocol. Get the civilian to safety as quickly as possible.

Jake would know all that because he'd done it. He'd lived it. But if Anonymous was correct, Ian's theory was wrong and Jake wasn't anywhere nearby. He was on his way home with his ex and their son.

That could mean Montana or something else, but it sure didn't seem to mean Florida.

He hoped.

Prayed.

They had enough on their plate. They didn't need to add Jake into the mix.

He glanced at his watch and adjusted their trajectory, making sure they were heading southeast. Toward the Everglades. The FBI had a house there. It hadn't been used in several years because it was too far from the nearest city. Most people didn't enjoy staying in such a remote location. Even if they were in hiding. At least that was what Max had said.

It was perfect for their purposes, though.

Ian wanted a place that was isolated. He wanted clear views and an easy escape route. Max had already arranged to have a small boat with an outboard motor delivered. If Jake or Angus managed to find them, they could escape into the Everglades.

First, though, they had to get to the house.

Up ahead, several trees jutted up from the soggy earth, their branches thick, their trunks broad. He moved between them, keeping Esme close. If there were snipers in the car, she was their target.

King growled, the sound filling the uneasy silence.

Danger. That was what the dog was trying to say.

Ian heard him loud and clear.

"Get down," he commanded, yanking Esme off her feet, covering her with his body. The first bullet hit the tree an inch from their heads.

She jerked, but he pressed her deeper into the earth as the second bullet struck, this time slamming into the ground, releasing bits of dirt and splatters of mud.

King was crouched beside them, and he growled again, his gaze on the area they'd just left.

"We're out of range for our handguns," Zeke whispered. "But I'm going to take a couple of shots and give you cover to move. There's a ravine straight ahead. They shouldn't be able to see you once you're in it. I'll circle around. Try to get a look at the perps. If the police show up, I'll deal with them."

He fired the first shot almost before he finished speaking, the loud report ringing through the night.

"Let's go," Ian said, rolling off Esme. "On your belly all the way. Keep the trees between you and the SUV. Don't stop until I tell you to."

"You mean between me and the gun?" she asked, sliding across the damp earth, her dark clothes blending in with the ground.

He followed, calling to King and smiling grimly as the dog pranced past. Zeke fired two more rounds, the sound masking what Ian thought was the sound of an engine firing up.

Were the perps on the run?

He didn't glance back to see.

He was focused instead on getting to the ravine and lowering himself into it, because Esme had disappeared somewhere up ahead, and he could only assume that was where she'd gone.

She might be out of sight of the gunmen, but she was also out of Ian's sight.

He didn't like that.

Not at all.

The ornery woman wanted to go it alone. She'd planned to hide until the trial. Without the protection of the team. She'd told him that. This had been the perfect opportunity for her to escape protective custody, and he'd handed it right to her.

He reached the edge of the ravine, lowering himself down and calling himself every kind of fool for letting Esme go ahead of him.

NINE

Esme's feet had hit the bottom of the marshy ravine, and she'd started running. Without thought. Without a plan. Just going as fast as she could toward some unknown destination, fleeing the gunshots, the car and, probably, Ian.

He'd been offering the protection she longed for, the security she craved. He'd given her comfort and smiles and, even, a laugh or two.

He'd been a port in the storm, a place to hunker down while the wind of Angus's wrath was raging around her.

But he wasn't a forever kind of thing.

He was a stopgap, a hero who'd run to the rescue when she'd needed him but who'd walk away when this was over and leave her exactly where she'd been when they'd met—alone.

Which was fine.

She liked solitude.

She enjoyed silence.

She didn't mind her own company.

And she certainly didn't want to be with someone just to fill a hole in her life.

Brent had taught her a lot about what she needed

and what she didn't. She hoped that she'd learned the lessons well.

Time would tell.

Time that wasn't filled with running for her life.

The marshy ground grew wetter, her feet splashing in a quarter inch of water. She needed to get out before she found herself in a creek or tributary up to her ankles or knees or shoulders. Wading through muck and dodging slithering, snapping, slimy reptiles.

She scrambled up the far side, feet digging into loose earth, hands grasping thick blades of grass. She was breathless when she reached the top, covered in dirt and mud. The sleeves of Ian's jacket hung past her fingertips, and she shoved them up, still moving fast. If she took off the jacket, she could leave it for King to find. That would let Ian know which direction she'd been headed, because she wasn't trying to outrun him or King or Zeke. She was trying to outrun the men who wanted her dead. If Ian and King found her, great. If not, maybe she'd find them.

For now, though, she was doing what she'd been told—running until Ian told her to stop. She shivered, her teeth chattering. Strange because the night was balmy and warm. She knew that. She could feel the sticky, humid air kissing her cheeks, could glimpse the clear sky and the moon resting just above the western horizon. The landscape was flat enough for her to see the distant flashing lights of emergency vehicles.

The police were on the way. It was possible they'd already reached the SUV and were rounding up whoever had been in the car. It was possible Uncle Angus was being arrested and that he'd be tossed in jail where he belonged.

Anything was possible, but she didn't think either of those things were likely. Angus had proved himself to be wily as a fox, moving mostly in the dead of the night, slipping in and then out without a sound.

Her uncle hired people to do the less subtle things— driving through clinic windows, shoot-outs in swamps. *He* liked darkness and enjoyed terrorizing people.

At least, that was the impression she'd gotten these past few months.

Her foot caught on a tangled web of marsh grass, and she went flying, landing hard on her hands and knees, her arms skidding in one direction, her legs in another.

She hit the ground with a thud, would have been up and running again, but a wet nose nudged her temple, warm dog breath fanning her cheek.

She looked into dark eyes, and then into King's grinning happy face.

His tongue lolled to the side, his eyes sparkling with what could only be joy. He'd found her, and he was very pleased with himself.

If she hadn't been lying flat on wet ground, the scent of decaying foliage in her nose, she might have smiled back.

"You don't have to look so pleased with yourself every single time. I'm not very difficult to find," she explained, but King had already darted away, heading back to his partner, tail high, carriage jaunty.

He was pleased with himself and ready to share the happy news of his discovery.

She could have gotten up and kept going, but she had as much hope of survival with Ian as she did on her own. More hope, because he had a gun. She had her mud-caked clothes and her will to live. Neither would stand much of a chance against a well-aimed bullet. Esme turned onto her back, staring up at the stars and the dark sky, her ankle throbbing dully. She didn't know what time it was…and she didn't care. In a few hours, the sun would rise, and she'd be facing another day of hide-and-seek. Winner took all. Loser lost everything. If Angus lost, he'd go to jail. If she lost, she'd die and her brother might go free. There'd be more crime, more drugs, more human trafficking and sorrow and terror and fear.

It was that simple and that awful. It was the reason she'd kept going for as long as she had. It was the reason she'd agreed to testify, and the reason why she wouldn't change her mind.

But right now, she really couldn't get up the gumption to care about any of it. She lay where she was, watching the night sky, thinking about how nice it would be if her life went back to normal, if she could simply close her eyes and open them and realize she'd been having some horrible dream.

The grass beside her rustled, and Ian was there, looming over her. She closed her eyes. Opened them again. Nothing had changed. Except that now he was crouched beside her. Not touching. Not talking. Just waiting, his eyes glittering in the darkness, King panting nearby.

"I wasn't trying to escape you," she explained. "I was just following orders. I guess running into the Everglades without any idea of where I was going wasn't the best idea I've ever had. I should have stopped at the bottom of the ravine and waited for you. I don't know why I didn't."

"Fear does funny things to people, Esme," he said,

offering a hand and pulling her to her feet. "How's your ankle holding up?"

"It's fine," she said, ignoring the throbbing pain as she walked beside him.

"*Fine* is the word most people use when they think the other person doesn't really care. For the record—" he stopped and turned to face her, tugging his jacket tighter around her and zipping it "—I care."

"It hurts," she corrected. "But I can walk on it."

"You never got the Ace bandage."

"We were distracted by the truck that drove through the window."

"Right. It's been a busy night." He started walking again, his hand on her elbow as he helped her through the thick grass. She didn't mind that. Not at all.

"Once we get to the safe house," he said, his voice a quiet rumble on the balmy air, "I'm going to let you call your sister. You can ask her about Jake or not. I'm not going to put pressure on you either way."

"I'll ask her," she said, because it couldn't hurt, and it might help.

"Is there anyone else you'd like to talk with?"

"No one important enough to risk my life for."

"Not even your fiancé?" he asked.

"Are you fishing for information?"

"Not fishing. I'm out-and-out asking. According to your file, you're engaged."

"My file is wrong."

"Let me guess, he wasn't ready to marry you, but he didn't want to wait for you to be out of the program?"

"Something like that," she responded. "It's old news, though. I've been over it for a while."

"He was an idiot," he said, and she smiled.

"According to him, I was. He didn't want me to testify. He thought I was asking for trouble. He told me Reginald and Angus were dangerous, and that he didn't want me to get hurt."

"Then he should have married you and entered witness protection with you to make certain you were safe."

"He's not much of a fighter."

"Not much of a man, if you ask me. As a matter of fact, if he was standing here, I'd call him a coward," he said bluntly.

"I guess he was, and he obviously didn't love me all that much. We had the whole wedding planned and paid for. I really thought he was going to be my forever. I was wrong."

"I'd like to say I'm sorry," he said softly. "But that would be a lie."

She could have asked him what he meant.

Should have, probably, but this thing between them? It seemed new and fragile and lovely, and she didn't want to ruin it by asking questions that would be answered in their own good time.

They'd reached a steeply sloping hill that led down to what looked like swamp—dark water snaking through thick foliage.

"Careful here. It's slippery," he said, his hand tightening fractionally as he helped her navigate the slick landscape. "You don't want to end up gator food. Fall into the swamp, and that could happen."

"Maybe we should head in another direction," she suggested nervously.

"If we do that, we'll never make it to the safe house."

"It's in the Glades?"

"Does that make you nervous?"

"I spent a few too many days alone there. I'm not all that excited about repeating the experience."

"You won't have to. I'll be there with two other team members and their dogs."

"Sounds cozy."

"It will be safe."

"That, too." Her foot slipped, and she'd have gone down if he hadn't dragged her back.

"Like I said," he murmured, "it's slippery."

"Any idea of how far we are from the safe house?"

"Too far to walk. One of my teammates is meeting us on the road about a mile from here. See that bridge?" He put his hands on her shoulders and turned her slightly, his forearm brushing her cheek as he pointed.

She'd probably have seen whatever he was pointing at if her heart hadn't been beating so fast, her pulse racing with something that had nothing to do with crocodiles or Uncle Angus or her near slide into the murky water and everything to do with Ian.

"She'll be right on the other side of it," he continued. "She'll pick us up there."

They'd reached the bottom of the hill, the pungent smell of the swamp filling her nose.

She could see lights in the distance, flashing rhythmically. Was it too much to hope that Angus had been in the car and that he'd been caught by the police?

"Maybe they caught Angus." She spoke the thought aloud, and he shook his head.

"Whoever was in the car drove away before the police arrived."

"You're well-informed."

He shrugged. "Zeke headed back to talk to Deputy

Sheriff Sinclair and to retrieve the SUV. He sent a text before I caught up to you."

"You guys work fast."

"We've been doing this a long time," he replied. "That means we've got a system, protocol, things that we prepare for."

"If you're trying to make a point, you can just go ahead and spell it out for me."

"Once we get in my coworker's vehicle and head for the safe house, your days of calling the shots are going to have to be over."

"I told you, I wasn't trying to escape," she started to explain.

"That's not why I'm saying this. You've been in witness protection. Being in a safe house is different. You'll be housebound for most of the next month. If the trial date is extended, it'll be longer."

"I understand that."

"Good, and I hope you'll understand when I tell you that my team expects your complete obedience to the rules."

"The term *obedience* seems a little…archaic."

"It can seem like anything, but we're still going to expect it. Following the rules will keep you alive. Breaking them could get you killed. Before we get in the car and make the trip to the safe house, before the team and I agree to play bodyguard for the next month, we need to know that we have your complete cooperation."

"You do," she said and meant it.

"Really?" He raised a dark eyebrow, and she shrugged.

"Yes."

"That was a lot easier than I thought it would be."

"Dying young is cliché. I'd rather live awhile."

He smiled. "Good to know. Come on. We need to get moving."

He took her hand, and she didn't pull away.

She wanted this moment of quiet, of walking beside a man who seemed willing to risk everything for her. She'd think about what it meant later. She'd mull over his words, wonder about his answers, ask herself if she were reading something into nothing.

Later.

Right now, she was content to let things be what they were—walking hand in hand through the moonlit swamp, King prancing along beside them.

The moon had sunk even lower on the horizon, the swamp creatures slithering just out of sight. Nothing had changed. Her uncle still wanted her dead. Her brother was still a murderer. Her sister was angry, and her friends probably thought she was dead. Her business was being run by employees, and she didn't know what would be left of it when she returned.

There'd be no wedding, no marriage, no children, because Brent was exactly what Ian had said—a coward.

Yeah. Nothing had changed.

But some of what had stayed was good: God was still on His throne. The sun would eventually rise. Life would go on for as long as it did.

And she wasn't alone.

She had a team of people working to keep her safe. She had a dog prancing along beside her.

And she had Ian.

Somehow that made her feel better than anything had in a very long time.

* * *

It took longer to reach the road than Ian had antici-
pated, the wet spring and summer creating boggy terrain that made walking difficult.

An hour into the walk and Esme was visibly slow-
ing, her limp more pronounced with each step. Julianne
had already texted twice, asking for updates on their
location and ETA.

She was clearly worried.

The safe house location couldn't be compromised,
and sitting on the side of the road waiting for Ian and
Esme to emerge was going to attract attention.

Or so she kept saying.

Ian knew she was right, but he couldn't push any
harder than he was.

"So," Esme panted as she pulled her foot out of thick
mud and managed another struggling step, "how much
farther?"

"Not much."

"You said that a half hour ago."

He gave her an apologetic look. "I didn't realize how
tough the terrain would be."

"It doesn't seem to be bothering King," she said.
"Or you."

"We're used to hiking through stuff like this."

"This happens a lot?"

"No, but we run training exercises with the team. We
don't make it easy. If you're going to be part of the tactical unit, you've got to be ready for just about anything."

"Sounds like wedding planning. But more dangerous," she joked, but her voice was flat and hollow, her
fatigue obvious.

"Want to take a break?" he suggested. "My colleague can walk in and meet us here."

"What good would that do? I'd still have to walk out."

"Julianne is good at improvising," he told her. "We might be able to create a gurney of some—"

"No." She said it emphatically.

"You didn't let me finish."

"Because you were going to suggest that the two of you carry me out, and it's not going to happen."

"It's okay to admit when we're done in, Esme."

She shot him a glare. "It's also okay to admit when you aren't making a situation better, Ian," she responded, and he laughed.

He couldn't help himself.

Esme was different. Refreshing. Totally and uniquely herself.

"Well," she huffed, "it's true."

"I apologize. I was trying to give you options. Not annoy you."

"Everything is annoying me. The bugs, the mud, the horrible smell."

"Yeah. The swamp does have a unique odor."

"I was talking about me," she said, and he laughed again.

"I'm serious," she muttered. "I smell like bug spray and swamp mud with a hint of cake batter."

"More like vanilla and whipped cream," he responded, and she smiled.

"You're a funny guy, Ian, but we both know I've rolled in the muck one too many times today. I want a hot shower and clean clothes and a comfortable bed. I want to lie down and not have to worry that I'll open my eyes and see Angus."

"You'll have all of that soon."

"If I don't collapse from exhaustion first," she replied, limping along beside him. Despite her joking complaints, she'd had a good attitude about the long walk. She'd asked questions about King and about the training program they used for their working dogs. She'd asked how he'd gotten into police work and what his father would have thought about his work with the FBI. He'd answered because she'd seemed sincerely interested.

It felt oddly good to be with Esme. Despite the circumstances, despite her family name, despite all the things that should keep him from being attracted to her, he was.

"We really can take a break," he said, and she shot him a scathing look, but there was humor in her eyes.

"I think I explained my need for a hot shower and a comfortable bed. Taking a break isn't going to get me any of those things."

"It's possible King needs a break," he offered, and she snorted.

"King could probably walk for days and not get tired."

Hearing his name, the Malinois trotted closer, bumping Esme's hand with his nose the way he did when he wanted attention.

She scratched behind his ears. "You're a good dog, King. If I ever get my first puppy, I hope he turns out like you."

"You've never had a dog?"

"We traveled too much when I was a kid, and now that I'm an adult, life is busy. Brent and I were planning to get one, though. I do a lot of my work from home. I just needed a home with a fence and a yard. We planned to get that, too."

"There are plenty of dogs that do well in apartments, Esme. If you really want one, I can help you choose one after this is over."

"A few hours ago, I'd have said no. Brent was really the one who wanted the dog. I was mostly on the fence about it. My sister has a little yappy dog that hates my guts. I'm not so keen on it, either, so I figured I wasn't a dog person. Now that I've met King, I can see the appeal. They're good companions. If I'm going to be a lonely old maid, I might as well have some pets to spend time with."

"Old maid?"

"Cat lady?"

"I doubt you'll be either of those things."

"I'm certainly not going to be married. I already spent my wedding savings on the wedding that wasn't." She patted King again, and Ian could see her hand shaking. She didn't want to stop, and he wasn't going to force her to, but maybe he could distract her from the arduous walk.

"When this is over, I can help you choose a puppy."

"You're assuming we'll be living somewhere close to each other."

"There are planes, trains, automobiles."

"There are also a million dreams that never come true, and if I let myself think about getting through this, of coming out on the other side of it with a house and a business and a friend and a dog…" She shrugged.

"What's the worst that could happen if you believed that?"

"I might be really disappointed if it didn't happen.

I've been through enough disappointment recently. I'm not up to facing another."

"I won't disappoint you, Esme," he said, the words pouring out before he could think them through. The promises right on the tip of his tongue.

Promises about being there for her, about helping her as she transitioned into whatever life she was going to create.

He might have said more.

He probably would have, but the soft hum of an engine broke the stillness.

Not a car or truck.

This sounded more like a bi-engine plane.

Which could mean nothing, or it could mean something.

Angus or his henchmen had driven away, but that didn't mean they'd given up.

He grabbed Esme's hand, pulling her with him as he sprinted toward the road.

TEN

She lost a boot and sock somewhere in the muck, but she made it to the road with one bare foot, a throbbing ankle and absolutely no breath in her lungs.

Esme would have stopped the minute her bare foot hit hard pavement. She would have stood for a couple of minutes, gasping and coughing and trying to catch her breath, but Ian was dragging her along as he sprinted up the road.

She knew what they were running from.

She could see the plane.

Worse, she could see its searchlight, aimed at the ground and highlighting the swamp and the marsh grass.

How far away was it?

A mile? Less?

They needed to reach shelter before it reached them. Otherwise…

She wasn't going to think about that.

Nope, instead she was just going to keep running, her hand in Ian's, King sticking so close to her side she knew that he sensed danger.

He barked. Once. High and quick, and then he shot forward, bounding over a small hill and disappearing.

Seconds later, he reappeared, another dog running beside him. A hound of some sort. She could hear it baying over the frantic slush of her pulse.

Her legs burned, her lungs ached, but she couldn't feel the pain in her ankle.

That was good.

What would be better was outrunning the plane.

It seemed to be heading toward them, swooping low over the marshy land they'd just left.

Were there footprints?

Was that what the spotlight was revealing?

"We're almost there," Ian said.

He wasn't even out of breath.

"Just so you know, when I get back home," she panted, "I'm going to train sprint runs. That way the next time a plane comes after me, I'll have a chance."

Her words were drowned out by the frantic baying and barking of the dogs, the drone of the airplane engines and the sound of a car motor.

Headlights flashed at the top of the hill.

There. Then gone.

Her imagination?

She wasn't sure, but Ian didn't seem concerned, he was heading straight for them, still running, still holding her hand.

The dogs met them halfway up the hill, the hound bounding excitedly, its vest glowing in the darkness.

A working dog.

A team member?

It had to be. Anything else would be too much of a coincidence.

Julianne's dog. That made sense, and so did the small SUV cresting the hill, idling there. No light, just gleaming paint in the fading moonlight.

It probably took only seconds to reach the car.

It felt like a lifetime, everything moving in slow motion. The plane. The dogs. Esme's legs.

The door opened as they approached, and a woman hopped out. Tall, muscular, quick.

Those were the impressions Esme had before the woman grabbed her arm, ushered her into the back of the vehicle.

The hound hopped in after her, scrambling for position as the door slammed shut.

And they were off. Pulling a quick U-turn and speeding down the other side of the hill.

Which would have been great.

Except that Ian wasn't with them. Neither was King.

"What's going on?" Esme demanded. Or tried to. Her voice rasped out, her lungs still heaving from the run.

"I'm taking you to the safe house," the woman responded.

"Where's Ian?"

"Throwing them off our tail."

"What does that mean?"

"It means that we don't want the airplane following us. Ian is going to make sure that if it's a search plane looking for you, whoever is flying it will think you're still running. At least—" she glanced in the rearview mirror and met Esme's eyes "—that's what I'm assuming the plan is. Ian and I didn't have much time to discuss it."

"More like you didn't have *any* time."

"True. He signaled me to take you and go. So I did.

I'm Julianne Martinez, by the way. Special agent, but I'm not big into titles. The dog is Thunder."

"He's cute."

"And loud?"

"That, too."

"I know! But it's useful when he's indicating. He's an evidence detection dog, and he likes to let us know when he's found something. He was very happy when he found you. He loves new friends."

Obviously, because he was nearly sitting in Esme's lap, looking at her expectantly.

"Usually, I crate him in the back," Julianne continued. "This is a rental, so I don't have that luxury. If he becomes a pest, just tell him no."

"Okay. Thanks," Esme responded by rote, but her mind wasn't on the conversation. It was on Ian, King and the plane. "They could have guns," she said, voicing the concern out loud. "They probably do."

"Ian can handle whatever they dish out. Don't worry about him."

"That's easier said than done," she muttered.

"Yeah. I know." She sounded like she did know. Like maybe there was a story hidden in the matter-of-fact reply.

She didn't give Esme a chance to ask for details.

"Do me a favor," she said. "Duck real low in the seat. We're going through a populated area. I don't want anyone to see you."

"Who'd be looking at this time of night?" she asked, but she did what she was told, pressing her chin to her knees, the scent of wet earth drifting up from her mud-coated feet.

One booted.

One bare.

She studied both, her back aching from the odd position.

She didn't straighten.

She'd told Ian that she'd cooperate, that she'd follow directions and do exactly what she was told. She'd meant it.

Esme desperately wanted to get through this alive, and she'd really like everyone else to get through it the same way.

"You doing okay back there?" Julianne called.

"Fine."

"Just a couple more minutes. This is kind of a shanty town, but there are definitely people around."

"And you think one of them is in my uncle's pocket?"

"I don't like to speculate, so how about I just tell you what I know? Your uncle and brother have been running drugs and people through the airport here for several years. They've made connections in the surrounding area, and they have several people on their payroll." She took a breath. "It wouldn't surprise me if Angus put out the word that you need to be found and stopped, and it wouldn't shock me if one of the people living in this little town was very happy and willing to make that happen."

"Nice."

"No. It's not. None of what my team deals with is nice, but that's why we do it. We want to stop people like your uncle from hurting and corrupting others."

"It's hard to be corrupted unless you want to be," Esme pointed out.

"Some people think that. I think that it's easy to fall into the wrong crowd when the wrong crowd is all you know. Angus and Reginald take advantage of that. They go after people who are already struggling, and they offer them a way out of poverty. Of course, the people who accept the offer don't realize they're selling themselves into modern slavery. They make money, but they're always beholden to the boss. If they try to break away, they die."

"It sounds like the Mafia," Esme said, sick at the thought of what her brother and uncle had created, disgusted by the image of an organization that fed off others, one that ate and ate but was never full.

"It *is* like the Mafia. I've heard a criminal profiler speculate that your brother was obsessed with the mob as a child, that he had a sense of helplessness brought on by your father's—"

"My father was a really great guy," she snapped and then was ashamed of herself for doing it.

None of this was Julianne's fault.

"I'm sorry," Julianne said. "I didn't mean to imply he wasn't. The profiler simply said that your father wasn't the kind of strong powerful man the Godfather represented and that your brother wanted to be what your dad was not."

"Or maybe," Esme said, the words tight and controlled, "Reginald was influenced by my uncle. Maybe he just wanted more than what he had. Maybe he didn't care who he hurt in his bid to get what he wanted."

"You're upset."

"This is my family we're talking about, Julianne. And I still can't believe they're such horrible people."

"The world isn't black-and-white. There are shades of gray. Your brother might be a murderer and a criminal, but he helped your sister a lot. That's something you can hold on to."

"He murdered a man in cold blood. He killed two people who'd done nothing wrong. He runs an organization that makes its money off criminal activities, and he doesn't care who he has to hurt to get what he wants." She blew out an angry breath. "That's pretty horrible, and it's pretty black-and-white. Should I not hold on to it?"

"What about your sister? She hasn't gotten involved in the business. She might not be cooperating with us, but she certainly isn't killing people for profit."

The words were supposed to be comforting.

Esme knew they were.

She knew Julianne was trying to offer encouragement, trying to make her feel better.

But there was nothing that could do that.

Saying Violetta wasn't horrible because she hadn't killed was like saying a boa constrictor wasn't deadly because it didn't inject venom into its victim. Snakes were snakes. And Violetta seemed to be one of them.

Esme shuddered, staring out the side window, Thunder lying on the seat beside her, his back pressed up against her thigh. She touched his warm fur, felt the soft rise and fall of his ribs as he breathed.

"You can sit up now," Julianne said quietly. Nothing else. She probably thought she'd crossed a line, but she'd only really spoken the truth.

Esme could have told her that. If she could have made the words form. Her brain knew what to say. It knew how to be gracious and kind. It knew how to put people at ease.

Right now, though, Esme could only sit mutely, staring out the window, watching as the darkness flew by.

Ian finally reached the safe house at dawn.

He'd hitched a ride with Zeke after he'd led the plane on a nice little joyride through marshy fields and swampland.

Eventually, the pilot had given up the chase. Either he'd realized that his quarry was really good at dodging the searchlight or he'd run out of fuel.

Either way, when he'd returned to the airport, the police had been waiting. They'd found an automatic rifle onboard. The pilot, a convicted felon who'd served ten years on drug charges, was arrested immediately. His passenger had an outstanding warrant, and he'd been taken into custody, as well.

Both were still being questioned.

Neither was talking.

That seemed to be the theme with the Dupree family's lackeys. They didn't talk. They were probably terrified of the consequences. A man who would murder family would murder anyone.

"This place looks interesting," Zeke said as he pulled the SUV under a double-wide carport. Julianne's rental was beside it.

The house did look interesting. Small. Purple. Standing on stilts that looked like a good hard wind would topple them.

"That's one word for it," Ian said, climbing out of the vehicle and stretching stiff muscles. He'd been going nonstop for days, and he was ready to crash. First, he needed to make sure that Esme was settled in and that the house was secure.

He opened the back hatch and released King, letting the dog explore the area as he did a circuit of the property.

Not much to see.

The front yard was mostly swamp scrub and mud. Beyond it, a small dock jutted into a deep green pool of everglade water. A canoe had been tied to a post, and he inspected it, checking for holes, life vests and supplies. Everything was where it needed to be, paddles sitting in the bow, life vests under the bench seats.

"How's it look?" a woman called, and he saw Julianne jog down stairs that led to the front door of the house.

"Good. Is this our emergency escape?"

"Yes. I'm hoping we don't need it, of course." She walked onto the deck, Thunder right behind her.

"Any trouble on the way here?"

"None. It was almost too easy."

"Meaning?"

"I don't know, Ian. I just don't feel comfortable here. The town we have to ride through to reach the property is probably owned by the Duprees. Someone there has probably noticed my bright shiny rental driving through. You think they aren't going to put two and two together?"

"Is there a reason why you think the Duprees own the town?"

"Crime. Drugs. Poverty. Do I need to say more?"

"I'll contact Max—"

"Already done. He's looking for another safe house while we speak. I want it somewhere less rural. We stick out like a sore thumb here."

Ian agreed. He didn't like the feel of the place any more than Julianne did.

"You guys having a party without me?" Zeke strode toward them, his dark eyes scanning the surroundings.

"No, but I'm thinking one of us better go inside and make sure Esme isn't planning another escape," Ian said, heading back across the dock.

"She's sleeping," Julianne informed him. "I made her shower, change and eat. She seemed upset when you didn't get in the SUV with us, and she was pacing around, asking me over and over again if I'd heard from you. I finally told her to take a nap. She did."

"You're sure?"

"As sure as I am about anything."

"You explained the rules to her when you arrived?"

"In detail. Shades closed. Windows locked. No walking outside without an escort. No phone calls, internet or contact with friends or family."

"Her response?"

"She didn't give me much of one. Just asked when I thought you'd be here."

There was a hint of something in the comment.

Curiosity maybe.

Ian made it a habit of keeping his private life private. He didn't enjoy sharing gossip about girlfriends or relationships, and he sure wasn't going to start sharing information now.

"I guess she'll be glad to know I've returned, but I'm not going to wake her. I'll shower, eat and get some shuteye, too." He walked up wooden steps that led to a deck that wrapped around the house. King must have heard him. He bounded up the stairs, ears up, tail wagging.

To him, this was a new adventure. New place. New scents. New people.

To Ian, it was a nightmare.

Too much cover too close to the house.

Too many places Angus and his goons could hide.

He reached the front door and was about to open it when his cell phone rang. He glanced at it, frowning as he saw that the number was unlisted.

"Is that Max?" Zeke asked, stepping onto the deck behind him. "The sooner he finds us new digs, the happier I'll be."

"Me, too, but it's not him. The number isn't listed." He accepted the call, put the phone to his ear. "Hello?"

"Having fun in the swamp?" the caller said, the voice so familiar, Ian's heart jumped.

"Not as much fun as I'd be having if you were around, Jake."

Zeke stiffened, moving closer and leaning in to try to hear the conversation.

"You never liked me. Don't try to tell me that you did."

"I'm sure the feeling was mutual. Which is why I'm surprised that you're calling me and not your brother."

"Zeke needs to stay out of this. I don't want him hurt," Jake growled. "You have the woman. Esme Dupree."

"And?"

"Angus wants her."

"Sometimes we don't get what we want." He glanced at Zeke, nodding when the other agent took out his cell phone and started texting headquarters. Jake was probably using a prepaid cell phone, but it still might be possible to back-trace the signal. If Ian could keep him on long enough…

"He'd better get what he wants. If he doesn't, the team is going to pay for it."

"You think he can get close enough to any of us to make that happen?" Ian said, cold with rage at the threat.

"He might not be able to, but I can. I know exactly how you work. I know where everyone is, and I know how to get close enough to take you down one by one until you give me what I want."

"I thought it was what Angus wanted."

"He wants her. I want my kid to survive. You produce the Dupree woman, because if you don't, he's sending someone after my son, and I'll be sending someone after you and the team."

"I doubt you have anything to worry about. Angus doesn't want to make you that unhappy. You've done a lot for his family over the years," Ian said, stalling for more time. Julianne had joined them, her brow furrowed as she read the texts that were going back and forth between team members.

"I've cut my ties with the organization. I think you know that. Angus doesn't like that I've gone rogue, and he plans to find my kid before I do. He's got more manpower and more money, and if he manages it, he'll make me pay. Unless I produce Esme Dupree. The team has her, I want her. Hand her over by tomorrow night, or someone is going to get hurt." His voice was stone cold, and Ian had no doubt he meant every word he said.

"You have a location for delivery?"

"There's an abandoned church near the rental where she was hiding. Bring her there by midnight."

"That's too soon."

"Too soon for you to come up with a plan to keep her safe, you mean? I'm not worried about that. I'm worried about my son. Midnight, Ian. I'm not playing around."

"You want to see your brother when we bring her? He's here. Part of the team protecting her."

Jake swore softly. Obviously, he hadn't realized his brother had been called in on protection detail.

"You come with the woman alone. If anyone else shows up, I'll kill her right in front of you. Understand?"

"You're saying you don't want to see Zeke?" Ian said, purposely prodding the bear.

"You don't seem to understand what's going on here," Jake said, every word clipped. "I don't want my brother hurt. I don't want you hurt. I don't want anyone on the team injured. I just want the woman."

"So she can be killed by her family?"

"So my son can live!" he roared.

That was it. He cut the connection, and Ian was left holding the silent phone to his ear.

"Did Dylan get it?" he asked, forcing a calmness into his voice that he didn't feel. The tech guru who worked with the team, Dylan O'Leary, was the go-to guy when it came to all things technical. If anyone could hack into a phone system and obtain GPS coordinates from a prepaid phone, he could.

As if in response, his phone buzzed, Dylan's number flashing across the screen.

He answered quickly. "Hello?"

"I got a quick trace for you. The cell signal on the prepaid you were communicating with was a hard capture, but I managed to find the signal tower that it was pinging from." As was his way, Dylan didn't waste time.

"Looks like he's somewhere in Montana. Unfortunately, I can't give you anything more specific."

"Thanks, Dylan. That helps."

"Anything else you need?"

"Just an all-points to the team. Jake Morrow is on the move, and he's threatening to kill team members if we don't hand over Esme Dupree."

Dylan whistled softly. "He's crossing a line here."

"He crossed it a long time ago. If you're able to do anything else to pinpoint his location, let me know."

"I'll give it a shot."

Ian disconnected and met Zeke's eyes. "I'm sorry about this."

"Sorry about what? We're half brothers, remember? Jake and I barely know each other."

"For someone who doesn't know you, he seems really concerned about your well-being." He'd seemed worried about the team, too. In his own bizarre sociopathic way. "He doesn't want you anywhere near the church when I bring Esme there."

"As if we'd do that," Julianne scoffed, her dark eyes flashing.

"We wouldn't, but why not make him think we're complying?"

"I like the way you think," Zeke said. "Setting a trap for the guy who is trying to trap us. Jake is nowhere nearby, so Angus will probably show up at the drop place. We can take him down and end this."

"Let's run it by Max," Ian suggested. "See what he has to say. If he likes it, we'll move forward and come up with a plan."

"Anything is better than sitting around in this house, twiddling our thumbs and waiting for the boogeyman to come crawling out of the swamp." Julianne eyed the blackish water that stretched out behind the dock.

"I think you mean the swamp monster," Zeke suggested, opening the front door and waiting while Julianne walked through.

Both their dogs followed, rushing into the house without invitations. When they weren't working, they were family, and they knew it.

The team was family.

All of them connected and committed.

The thought of any one of the members being hurt because of the Duprees left a hard knot in Ian's stomach and soul-deep fury in his heart.

He wouldn't allow Jake to follow through on his threat.

Of course, there was only one way to stop him: stop Angus Dupree and shut down the Dupree crime family forever.

ELEVEN

Julianne and Zeke left the safe house at 9:45 p.m.

Esme didn't know exactly what they were doing, but she was certain it had something to do with her. Julianne had compared their height, commented that she'd pass for Esme only if Angus was blind and stupid, then strapped on a gun, pulled on a jacket and strode out the door.

That had been three hours ago.

They still hadn't returned, and Ian was pacing the little house like a caged animal, moving back and forth across the living room, checking his cell phone, doing everything but walking outside and shouting for God to give him some answers.

"I'm sure they'll contact you as soon as they finish doing whatever it is they're doing," she finally said, and he turned to face her.

He'd showered and changed, shaved and napped.

She knew all those things because Julianne had seemed determined to keep Esme informed of everything except her plans for the night. She also knew that he was angry. She could see it in the tautness of his muscles, the tightness of his jaw.

"This is about my uncle, isn't it? He's causing more trouble."

"Your uncle wants us to turn you over to him tonight. If we don't, there's been threats made against team members."

"What kind of threats?"

"The normal, everyday someone-is-going-to-die threats," he gritted out, crossing the room and sitting down beside her.

She'd chosen the couch. It was the only piece of furniture in the room that wasn't covered in psychedelic fabric. The armchair was lime green and bright pink stripes. The love seat was robin egg blue with huge yellow and purple flowers.

The sofa was a muted ivory that was surprisingly clean and soft. She'd sat there because it had reminded her of her old life—of weddings and brides and dresses.

She wasn't sure why Ian chose it. There were plenty of other places to sit. She liked him there, though. She wasn't going to lie. It felt good to have his warm arm pressed against her shoulder. It felt good to not be alone.

He lifted her hand, frowning at the scratches that marred her palm. "I didn't realize you'd gotten hurt when you fell last night."

He traced a line from her palm to her wrist, his fingers warm on her cool skin. Heat shot through her, and she almost pulled away, but this was Ian, and being near him felt like being home—so right, so wonderful that she couldn't imagine ever wanting to be anywhere else.

"I got hurt when I realized what my family was. I didn't even feel the scratches," she admitted.

He studied her face. Not speaking for such a long time, she was tempted to fill the silence, to beg forgiveness for all the trouble her family had caused, all the people who had been hurt because of them.

"When I took this assignment," he finally said, "I wasn't expecting to like you."

"I got that impression," she admitted, and he smiled.

"Yeah, I know. I'm sorry about that. I'm also sorry that we didn't apprehend Angus before he got to you." He touched the side of her neck, sliding his finger along what she knew were the fading bruises her uncle had left. She resisted the urge to lean closer, to let her fingers slide into his hair.

"It's not anyone's fault. He's got a lot of money, and he likes to hire people to do his dirty work."

"I'm hoping he's planning to do his own work tonight."

"You think he'll show up?"

"I don't know. Julianne and Zeke are prepared for it. We went over all the variables."

"Are you upset because you had to stay here and guard me?" she asked softly.

"I'm upset that you have to go through this. I'm upset that Jake Morrow and Angus Dupree are wandering free while we hide in this house. I'm not upset about guarding you. I told you before, Esme, I'll keep doing it as long as it's necessary."

"Don't say that. It might be necessary forever," she cautioned with a laugh that sounded a little too loud and a little too phony.

"That's an interesting thought," he responded. "How about we revisit it after this is over?"

"You're kidding, right?"

"Why would I be?"

"Because I'm a Dupree and you're trying to bring

down my entire family?" she said, her mouth dry with something that felt a lot like nerves.

"I'm going after criminals, Esme. You're not one of them. I'm not going to lie. That wasn't my mind-set when we met. You were the last assignment I wanted to take. My boss had other plans." He shrugged. "Or, maybe, God did."

"Probably God did," she said, and he smiled.

"My father would agree."

"You don't?"

"If you'd asked me a week ago, I'd have said I didn't know. It's tough to see God in things that make us unhappy. Now..." He shook his head. "I can't deny that I see Him working. Getting to know you has mended something in me that I didn't know was broken. Revenge tastes sweet when you're first going after it, but it turns bitter in the end. I'm glad God didn't let me get that far down the path."

"My uncle and brother need to pay for what they did."

"They do. But there's a difference between revenge and justice. Spending time with you has clarified that for me." He brushed a few strands of hair from her forehead, cocking his head to the side, studying her again.

"You cleaned up your haircut, didn't you?" he finally asked.

"Julianne helped me."

"She did a good job. Next time, I'll drive you to the hairdressers instead of helping you with the scissors."

"You're planning a lot of things for a future we may not have."

"We're going to have a future, and I have a feeling

we're going to be spending a lot of it together." He ran his knuckles down her cheek, looked so deeply into her eyes, she thought he might be seeing her soul.

Her hand moved of its own accord, her palm sliding along the warm column of his neck, her fingers smoothing the silky strands of his hair.

He didn't pull back, didn't tell her to stop, didn't list a dozen reasons why it wasn't appropriate for them to be sitting the way they were. He just looked into her eyes and into her heart, and she looked into his, seeing things that she hadn't expected. Attraction. Interest. Compassion.

His cell phone buzzed, and she jerked back, the sound like a splash of ice water in her face.

He glanced down at his phone screen, frowning as he read the text.

"What's wrong?"

"Things didn't go down the way we'd hoped. Angus sent three men to the church. There was a shoot-out. All three are dead."

"What about Zeke and Julianne?"

"Zeke was hit. Doesn't sound like a serious injury, but Julianne is accompanying him to the hospital."

"And Angus is still on the loose." She said what they were both thinking, named the thing neither of them wanted.

"Right." He bit out the answer, his eyes flashing with banked fury.

She wanted to offer words of comfort. She wanted to tell him that Angus would be caught. She wanted to say that justice would be served, and that God would bring them all through this safely.

She wanted to say a dozen things that she hoped

would be true, but he was moving across the room, dialing a number, talking to someone, each word a hard staccato beat.

King walked next to him, whining softly in response to the wild energy that suddenly seemed to fill the room, and Esme was redundant—an extra in a drama she should have had no part in.

She stood, limping across the living room and down a narrow hall. Her room was at the end, a single door that opened into a plum-colored boxy space. The bed sat in the middle, a peacock blue comforter clashing with the walls. She turned off the light, let the darkness hide the garish decor.

She could still hear Ian, his voice drifting through the closed door. She thought she heard him talking about a new plan. One that involved Jake Morrow.

She didn't leave the room and ask him to clarify.

He was busy. Doing what he was paid to do. Protecting civilians from criminals like Angus.

She shuddered, pulling the pillow over her eyes, pressing it hard against lids that seemed to want to let tears seep out. She prayed for Zeke, that his injury really was minor and that he'd recover quickly. For Ian, Julianne and the rest of the team.

And then she prayed for her family. Prayed that Violetta would do the right thing, and that Angus and Reginald would pay for their crimes.

When she finished, she lay still, the house settling around her, Ian's voice silent, the only sound the soft lap of wind against the windows and the rhythmic click of King's claws as he walked from room to room, waiting for danger that Esme hoped would never come.

* * *

Zeke and Julianne arrived at the house an hour before dawn.

Neither of them looked happy.

Ian wasn't happy, either. The thick bandage that peeked out from under the short sleeve of Zeke's shirt was a stark reminder of just how bad the mission had gone.

Three gunmen dead. One federal officer injured.

And no sign of Angus.

He was out there, though.

Haunting the streets, waiting for news and for an opportunity to strike again.

"How's the shoulder?" Ian asked as Zeke dropped into the gaudy recliner.

"It would be better if I didn't have a bullet hole in it."

"Don't exaggerate," Julianne chided. "It barely grazed you."

"Tell that to my shoulder. Maybe it will stop throbbing."

"They offered you pain meds," she chided.

"I'm on duty."

"I can call Max and ask him to send someone else," Ian offered, and Zeke scowled.

"Don't even think about it. This—" he poked at the bandage "—has made things a lot more personal."

"Did we get an ID on any of the gunmen?" Ian asked.

"Locals," Julianne replied. "The deputy sheriff knew all three by sight."

"I guess you were right about the Duprees owning this town." Zeke stood and walked into the kitchen, opening the fridge and surveying its contents. "Eggs, anyone?"

"Are you cooking?" Ian asked.

"Only if I have to. The arm is a little sore."

"I'll take care of it." Ian needed to do something. Beating eggs seemed a whole lot less violent than beating Angus to a bloody pulp.

He frowned as he poured the eggs into a hot pan.

Justice. Not revenge.

But it was hard to keep that in mind when a guy like Angus was out there.

His cell buzzed, and he pulled it out, glancing at the text as he spooned cooked eggs onto plates. It was from Dylan, the message making Ian's pulse race.

Max has been injured. Shot while he was walking his dog. Should be fine. He'll call once he's been triaged.

Julianne and Zeke must have received the same text. They were moving toward him, phones in hand, looks of shock and outrage on their faces.

"Jake," Ian said. Just that. They knew. He knew.

No one else could have done this. No one else would have.

"I thought maybe he was yanking our chains, trying to get his way, but he really did mean he was going to pick us off one by one if we didn't hand Esme over." Zeke sounded as furious as Ian felt.

"He acted quickly. Didn't even wait a few hours. He must have gotten a call from Angus and gone after the closest team member," Ian said.

"Which means he's hanging out somewhere close to headquarters." Julianne frowned. "He's brazen."

"He's a fool," Ian corrected darkly. "He thinks he's too smart and too fast to be caught."

"So far, he's been right." Zeke smoothed down the edge of his bandage and grabbed a plate of eggs. He shoveled in a mouthful as he eyed the message.

"He's been right because he's been lying low. Now that he's showing himself more, we should be able to catch him," Ian responded.

"Catch him. Catch Angus. Go back to our regularly scheduled program," Julianne agreed.

Ian's phone rang. He glanced at the number.

Unlisted.

Again.

And he knew exactly who it was.

He answered, every bit of the rage he felt seeping into his voice. "What do you want, Jake?"

"Esme Dupree. I told you that. Apparently, you weren't listening."

"I listened. Now it's your turn. You're going down for this, Morrow. I'm going to make certain of it."

"You'll have to find me first, and that's proved really difficult for you and the team. So how about we call a truce? You promise me the woman, and I stop shooting at team members."

"How about you jump off the nearest—"

Julianne snatched the phone from his hand, putting it on speakerphone.

"Jake?" she said, her voice a lot calmer than Ian's had been. "It's Julianne. I think you know the team never makes deals with criminals. Back off and give us space to do our job. We'll protect your son, if you don't get in our way."

"Like you protected Max?" he said with a snide laugh that made Ian's blood run cold.

"I was shot tonight, bro," Zeke said angrily. "Going

after the goons your friend hired. How do you feel about that?"

"I told you to stay away. I warned you. Angus doesn't care who he kills."

"It doesn't seem like you do, either," Ian pointed out.

"You're wrong. I have to make tough choices. I got in deeper than I planned. Maybe I underestimated how much of a hold Reginald and Angus had on me, but that doesn't mean I want to do what I'm doing. This is for my son. If people have to die to keep him safe, so be it."

"Not just people, bro," Zeke snapped. "Family. That's what this team is. It's what we were supposed to be."

"I tried to protect you, Zeke. I warned you, and that shot at Max? I could have killed him if I'd wanted to. Consider his injury a warning. Next time, I won't miss. I'll be in touch soon, and I'll let you know where the next rendezvous will happen." He disconnected, the sudden silence heavy with tension.

"He needs to be stopped," Julianne muttered, pulling out her phone and punching in the number for headquarters.

She was calling Dylan.

Ian was certain of that.

Good. He didn't want to talk to anyone.

Not yet.

He needed to collect his thoughts and get himself focused. Two team members had been shot in one night. The situation with the Duprees was escalating. Angus was becoming more desperate. It wasn't just the team and Esme whose lives were at risk. Jake's son and ex-girlfriend might also be in trouble.

He'd let Julianne talk to Dylan, see how Max was and inform the team of the danger. Ian would stick to the plan and follow protocol. It was time to patrol the property.

He called King. The dog came immediately, ready to work or to play. Whichever Ian chose.

For now, they'd just walk, skirting the perimeter of the property, checking to be sure no one was lurking in the shadows.

Praying that maybe someone was.

Angus would be a good find. Bringing him in would be the culmination of months of hard work and years of planning.

A decade.

That was how long Ian had been waiting to bring the Duprees down.

He didn't want to have to wait any longer, but he would. He'd bide his time as long as it took, and when it was over, when Angus was in jail and the crime syndicate was defunct, he'd finally be able to move forward.

Out from the shadow of anger and hatred.

Into something bright and new.

An image of Esme filled his mind, her soft lips and vivid eyes, her silky hair falling straight to her nape.

Her smile.

A Dupree cut from different cloth. One who deserved all the good life could bring. He wanted to make sure she got it.

But first, he wanted to find her uncle, toss him in jail and throw away the key.

TWELVE

Seven days was a long time to be stuck inside a gaudily decorated swamp shanty. Seven nights was a long time to lie listening to the hushed voices of Ian and his team.

And now she was on night eight.

Doing exactly what she'd done for the past seven.

Counting the opening and closing of the front door, listening to the soft pad of paws on the floor outside her door, to the quiet bark of King as he patrolled the property.

Waiting for dawn to come and something to change.

She turned over in bed, eyeing the tiny cracks in the shades that covered the window. She wanted to pull the cord and open the bright yellow vinyl, to look out into the darkness and watch the moonlight reflected on the water.

She wanted a dozen things that she couldn't have, but mostly she just wanted this to be over.

Sighing, Esme climbed out of bed, padding across the floor on bare feet, wincing as the boards creaked. It was an old place. She'd learned that about it, the rough-hewn floors speaking of a bygone era, the window glass wavy from age.

Not that she was allowed near the windows.

Seven days without sunlight was beginning to get to her.

She could admit that.

If not for Ian, she'd have gone stark raving mad by now. He'd entertained her with stories of his childhood, taught her how to play chess, insisted she teach him how to bake her mother's award-winning pound cake. It was the recipe she used when she was meeting clients for the first time—pound cake and coffee or tea. Making the cake, laughing as she watched Ian measure flour and butter and try his hand at whipping cream had been cathartic.

It felt good to laugh.

It felt good to sit with someone who seemed to want to sit with her. It felt good to play chess and checkers, argue over who'd get the last piece of cake or the last slice of ham.

It wasn't just Ian, though.

She'd become friends with Julianne, offering suggestions on the wedding the FBI agent was planning with Brody Kenner, a man she'd broken up with years ago and had recently reconnected with. She'd run into him while she was searching for Jake Morrow. He'd been sheriff of the small town of Clover, Texas. Now he was training to join the K-9 team.

Julianne had told the story matter-of-factly, but Esme had seen the joy in her eyes and in her face. She'd promised to help her choose colors and decor, find vendors and, maybe, pick a dress.

Ian had heard them talking and gone on a mission, returning hours later with a bagful of wedding magazines.

Zeke had laughed, but he'd sat in the ugly easy chair and given his opinion about the dresses and flowers and food.

Funny. The seven days she'd spent in the ugly house at the edge of the swamp had taught Esme a lot about what friendship was and about what family meant. She could see that was what Zeke, Ian and Julianne were. They were a team, a pack with three leaders, all working together for the good of the group.

She liked that.

But she hated waiting. She hated wondering just how long their little group would stay together.

It wouldn't last forever.

She didn't want it to.

Esme paced back across the room, settling into the rocking chair that Ian had brought for her. She hadn't asked where he'd gotten it or how he'd known that she preferred simple wooden frames and plain blue cushions to anything ornate or fancy. Instead, she'd just thanked him and enjoyed it.

That was the thing about being in the safe house.

Things weren't complicated.

Not unless she thought too much about them.

Then she'd start to wonder and worry and ask herself questions she couldn't answer—like what she was going to do when Angus was finally apprehended and she could move on.

Ian had hinted that they'd move on together.

She liked that idea, but she was trying to enjoy the moment, to take what he was offering now and not question it too much.

Anything could happen while they were waiting for the trial, and this thing they were feeling—this fragile new relationship they were forging—could become old and blasé and boring.

She snorted.

If she were being totally honest with herself, she'd admit she didn't want that to happen. She'd admit that the more time she spent with Ian, the more things she learned about him, the more time she wanted to spend and the more she wanted to know.

She'd never felt that way about Brent.

He'd been a nice guy. She'd liked him. He'd seemed faithful, moral, hardworking—all the things she'd been looking for. He hadn't been the kind of person who'd told stories to make people laugh. He'd told stories to impress, and for a while, he'd impressed her. He'd done all the right things, gone through all the right motions. Flowers. Candy. Expensive dinners.

It had taken a lot of distance and a lot of perspective for her to understand the truth. Brent had been more concerned about what he could get out of the relationship than what he could put in it. Esme had spent the years they were together trying to please him, because she'd thought that was how love was supposed to work. Give and give and give, because that was what the other person expected.

But when she was with Ian, things flowed smoothly. Give and take. Back and forth. Exchanges of ideas and opinions without the need for either of them to be right.

Being with him was as natural as breathing, and she couldn't quite figure out why. Except that he made it easy to be herself. He didn't ask for anything other than the truth. He didn't expect anything more than her company.

The old glider moved beneath her as she pulled her feet up and wrapped her arms around her knees.

The house had gone quiet, the first and second patrol of the night over. If she listened carefully enough, she might hear one of the dogs moving restlessly. Other than that, things would stay quiet for a half hour and then grow busy again.

In a few days, they'd be leaving.

That was what Ian had told her.

He couldn't say where they were going. Just that it would be far away from the Everglades. Esme wasn't sorry about that. She wanted to leave Florida and all the bad memories she had of it. Fortunately, she had some good memories now, though. Memories that she knew would always make her smile.

Esme rested her head on her knees, closing her eyes for just a moment, drifting in the silence and the darkness, the hope of something new and wonderful nudging her into sleep.

She dreamed of Angus. His sharp eyes and hard features. His skinny body and sinewy limbs. She dreamed of his hand in her hair, yanking her backward, tearing at her scalp, his lips pressed close to her ear, screaming words she couldn't understand. In her dream she tried to run, her arms and legs refusing to cooperate. She could see a door. Knew that if she reached it, she would live, but she couldn't move. She was trapped by his grip on her hair and by her fear.

She tried to scream, but nothing but a whimper emerged.

He yanked her backward, slamming her into a wall and shouting into her face. She could see the pockmarks in his skin, the burst spider veins on either side of his nose.

She could see the hatred in his eyes, and, she thought, the evil. Panic-stricken, she clawed at his hand, trying to get him to release his hold, but that only angered him more.

He tossed her away, his hand still in her hair, his fist slamming into the side of her head.

She woke with a start, found herself on the floor, the gliding rocker bumping against her feet.

She'd fallen. That was all. Nothing sinister or scary about that. She sat up, gingerly got to her feet.

Nothing hurt. She was fine, but she felt uneasy, her skin crawling with the kind of fear she hadn't felt since she'd arrived at the safe house.

Somewhere outside, an owl hooted, the sound out of place and alarming.

She crept to the window, breaking the rule that had been drilled into her, pulling back the shades and peering out into the darkness. The owl hooted again, and she was certain she saw a shadow move at the corner of the yard.

Esme needed to get to Ian, let him know that someone was outside. They had to—

Her door opened, and she screamed, the sound shrill and high and filled with terror. She ran at the shadowy form that stood in the doorway, head down, ready to ram right through him if she needed to.

He caught her arm, and she knew the feel of the warm fingers against her skin, the gentleness of the touch.

"Ian," she gasped, and he pulled her up against his chest, whispered in her ear.

"There's someone outside. More than one person, I think. We've got to get out."

"Right." She started to move past, but he stopped her.

"We need to get out, but we need to be smart about it. There's an emergency pack in your closet. Grab that and put on the waders that are sitting beside it."

She'd seen the pack.

She'd even looked through it.

She really hadn't expected to have to use it, though.

Heart thudding in her chest, she ran to the closet, shoving her feet into knee-high waders and slipping into a jacket and then the pack.

Ian was still at the door when she returned, and he took her hand, leading her out into the living room. The lights were off, but she could see Julianne and Zeke standing near the kitchen, their dogs small shadows near their feet.

No one spoke. Esme could only assume they'd had an escape route planned out before they'd ever brought her to the house.

Ian urged her past his colleagues, down the hall that led to the back of the house and the rear deck. There was no way down from there. They'd have to walk around the front to escape.

She was sure Ian knew it, but she wanted to remind him, because she really really didn't want to be trapped on the deck, an easy target to whomever might be stalking them.

She opened her mouth, would have spoken, but one of the dogs growled, the sound sending fear racing up her spine. Esme had heard King growl before, but she'd never heard Thunder or Cheetah make anything but happy noises.

King…

She glanced back. Saw no sign of the dog.

"Where's King?" she whispered, the words barely breaking the silence.

"On the deck."

"He's not barking."

"We don't want our friends to know that we're aware of their presence. He'll only alert if they get closer."

"You said there's more than one?"

"I said I *think* there is," he corrected.

"Does that mean two? Three?"

He touched her cheek, his fingers brushing across her jaw and then her lips, stopping the frantic words.

"It doesn't matter," he said. "However many there are, we'll take care of them."

"Ian—"

"It's going to be okay," he reassured her, pulling her in for a quick hug before slowly opening the back door. Carefully easing outside, he gestured for Esme to follow.

She wanted to move with the same grace and confidence he'd had, but the waders seemed to catch on the old floor, and she nearly fell into the doorjamb.

He caught her, his hands skimming down her arms and resting on her waist.

"Careful," he said, the word more breath than noise.

She nodded but didn't speak again.

They were outside now, the full moon casting long shadows across the backyard. King stood a few feet away, his fur glowing gold in the moon's reflected light.

The canine didn't glance their way as they approached. He didn't move. She didn't think he even blinked. His focus was on the back edge of the property and the deep shadows there. His ears were up, his tail stiff, his posture tense.

Someone was there.

King knew it, and he was ready to act if he received the command.

Ian moved up beside the dog, offering a hand signal

that broke King's concentration. The dog trotted to the side of the house, scanned the area and headed back, nudging the back of his handler's calf.

"It's clear. Let's go," Ian whispered, taking her hand and leading her to the area King had just left. He stopped at the deck railing, and she wasn't sure what he thought they were going to do.

Jump?

She sure hoped not. It was twenty feet straight down, and she wasn't all that great at landing. Even if she were, she didn't think she'd manage to do it without breaking something.

Ian slid out of his pack, unzipping the front compartment and taking out a harness. He motioned for King, and the dog loped over, waiting patiently while Ian hooked him in.

"Ready?" he asked Esme, and she nodded even though she still had no idea what they were going to do.

The way she saw things, as long as his plan involved escaping with their lives, she was good with it.

He pulled something else from his pack.

Rope?

No. A ladder.

She watched as he hooked it to the deck railing and let it fall over the side. It made a quiet whoosh as it unfolded, and she had about two seconds to worry that sound had carried to the back of the yard. Then Ian was up, the dog strapped to his chest, as he climbed over the rail and started making his way down the rope ladder.

She was next.

That much was obvious.

She clambered over the railing, trying not to think about the twenty-foot drop as she started down the ladder.

* * *

Esme didn't hesitate; she climbed over the railing and scrambled down the ladder like she'd done it a million times before. He helped her down the last two rungs, his hands light against her narrow waist, her pack knocking against his hands.

He'd already released King from his harness and tucked it into the pack. They were ready to head around the front of the property. The dock was there. And the boat. If they were careful, they should be able to escape before their stalkers knew they'd left.

That was good.

What wasn't good was the fact that there were at least two people wandering through the swampy area that surrounded the house. Even if the dogs hadn't been growling and pacing, Ian would have known about the trespassers. He'd been awake and restless when he'd heard the first owl call. By the time he'd heard the second, he'd already gathered the team and put the escape plan into action.

Ian and Esme out the back.

Zeke and Julianne out the front.

They'd gone over the plan dozens of times while they'd waited for Angus to strike.

That was paying off.

He heard the front door open, listened for the quick hard tap of feet on wood.

There!

Julianne and Zeke were heading for the stairs. If things went well, they'd be down in seconds, climbing into the SUV and taking off. Hopefully, leading trouble away.

Ian and Esme would take the boat, rowing out far

enough to be out of sight of the house before starting the motor. There was a campsite twenty miles away. Not a long trip, but hazardous at night. Julianne had figured it would take two or three hours to safely navigate. She'd have the SUV there when they arrived.

From there, they'd head straight to headquarters in Montana, and then Esme would be flown out of the country.

She wouldn't like it.

He knew it.

He didn't like it, either. The truth was, he'd wanted to argue for a different location. Somewhere close to headquarters, a place he might be assigned to keep her safe. He'd understood the practicality of Max's decision. He knew that she'd be safer out of the country than in it. The Dupree crime family was a multi-limbed tree, its branches spreading through the United States. With the price on her head, Esme was too vulnerable. No matter where they hid her, there was a good chance she'd be found.

Ian and Max had discussed it. They'd agreed. The only way to keep her safe was to get her out of the country. He cared about her too much to want anything less than her total security. Eventually, she'd return, and when the trial was over, he was going to make certain they were never separated again.

First things first, though.

He tugged her to the edge of the yard, urging her down into thick grass that was tall enough to cover them both. They crouched there, his hand on her forearm, her head brushing against his shoulder. He wanted to tell her everything would be okay, wanted to remind her that he'd make sure of it. Instead, he pulled her closer, did what he would have done days ago if there hadn't always been someone around; he pressed a kiss to her forehead, her cheek, her lips. Soft. Easy. Tender, because that was how it felt to be around her.

The SUV's engine roared. Tires squealed.

He backed away, his heart thundering, his pulse racing. Not with fear. With longing for all the things he hadn't been looking for but had found in Esme. He could see her through the darkness, her face pale, her eyes wide.

"What was that?" she whispered, her fingers touching her lips.

"A promise."

"Of what?"

"Tomorrow and the next day and the next," he said, his lips brushing her ear as he spoke.

Somewhere in the distance, an owl called, the sound chilling Ian's blood.

That was the signal he'd been waiting for. The one that told him the enemy was on the move.

Beside him, King growled, a long low warning that Ian wasn't going to ignore.

The SUV pulled out of the carport, headlights flashing on the ground a few feet away. There. Gone. Julianne and Zeke were doing their part.

It was time to do his.

"Let's go," he whispered, pulling Esme through the thick grass and boggy water, the roaring engine masking the sound of their retreat.

They made it to the dock easily. He climbed onto it, pulling Esme up beside him, King growling and barking, trying to tell him something that took just a few seconds too long for Ian to figure out.

By the time he did, it was too late.

Angus was there, rising like a wraith from the boat, a gun in his hand.

Ian reached for his firearm.

"Stop," Angus said calmly. "I've got nothing against you, Ian. It's Esme I have a problem with."

"I've got a problem with you, too," Esme retorted. "So I guess the feeling is mutual."

"Shut up," Angus snapped. "Get in the boat."

"Or what? You'll kill me?" She was baiting him, trying to keep his attention. Maybe so that Ian could act. Or maybe so that she could.

He felt her shift, thought she might be planning to dive off the dock and into the swamp. She probably figured she'd have a better chance there than she would with her uncle.

Or, maybe, she thought she'd draw Angus's gunfire away from Ian, give him a chance to pull his gun and end the fight.

Ian wasn't going to let her do it.

He gave the command, and King took off, sailing through the air, knocking into Angus with so much force the other man went down, the gun going off as he landed.

One shot, but it was followed by another. This one coming from somewhere near the house. King was snarling, teeth around Angus's wrist, shaking it so hard the gun flew out of his hand and landed somewhere beside the dock.

Ian didn't have time to go after it.

A bullet whizzed by his ear, coming so close he thought he could feel the heat of it. He dived for cover, taking Esme with him, rolling off the dock as more bullets flew.

They landed in soft wet earth, and he covered her with his body, holding her in place when she tried to stand.

Suddenly, King was beside them. He'd disarmed Angus, and he was back, ready to do more.

Ian raised a hand, giving the command to apprehend, and King took off again, racing toward the house and whoever was firing the weapon.

Ian heard the growls and snarls of the fight, heard a man cry out in agony. There were no high-pitched yips from King. Which meant he wasn't being hurt, and that he'd taken the gunman by surprise.

Another human yowl, and the night went silent.

No noise but the soft lap of water against the shore.

"Is it over?" Esme mumbled against his chest. "Because you're suffocating me."

"Sorry." He backed off, caught the unmistakable coppery scent of blood, saw black rivulets of it running down Esme's arm.

"You've been hit," he growled, pulling off his jacket and pressing it against the wound.

She pushed his hand away.

"I'm fine. Go help King."

"King can take care of himself." He knew that for a fact, was certain the dog was already on his way back. He glanced around, searching the shadows for Angus. The guy had disappeared, but that didn't mean he was gone.

"Really." She stood and took a step away. "I'm okay. Call your dog back, and let's get in the boat and get out of here."

"I'm afraid that isn't going to happen." Angus moved out of the shadows of an old mangrove tree, a gun drawn and pointed, hand bloody from his fight with King. He'd obviously been carrying a second weapon. Something Ian would have checked for if he'd had the opportunity.

Ian reached for his Glock, freezing when Angus pointed the revolver at Esme's head.

"Don't," he said conversationally. "Not unless you'd like to see her die."

He let his hand fall away, let Angus think he had the upper hand.

"That's better," the older man said, grabbing the back of Esme's jacket and yanking her toward him. He slammed the barrel of the gun into her temple, and she winced, her reaction making Ian want to pull his Glock and take a chance that he could fire before Angus.

It was too big a risk, though. If he timed it wrong, she'd be dead.

"Now, take out the gun and toss it in the water. Slowly. Try anything funny, and Esme's brains will be splattered all over the swamp."

"Ian, don't do it. He's going to kill me anyway," Esme pleaded.

"It'll be okay," he said, looking into her eyes, willing her to calm down, to trust him. "I promise."

"Right. And promises mean so much," Angus sneered. "Toss the gun. Now."

Ian pulled it from the holster, looking straight into Esme's panicked eyes as he did exactly what he had been told.

THIRTEEN

They were going to die.

Esme wasn't certain of much, but she was sure of that.

Not only had Ian tossed his gun into the swamp, but he'd sent King off to chase down another gunman. Which would have been fine if Uncle Angus hadn't been armed with a second weapon.

The first one, the one King had shaken from his hand, had looked deadly enough. This one looked even worse.

Maybe because the barrel was pressed against her head.

"Happy?" Ian asked. The question was obviously meant for Angus, but he was still looking into her eyes.

He didn't look panicked.

He didn't look scared. She'd have found that comforting if she didn't know just how deadly the situation was.

"Very," Angus crowed. "This is what I like to see! Absolute obedience. Keep it up, *Fed*-boy, and you might just survive."

"I'm more concerned about Esme. How about we agree that she won't testify if you let her go?"

"Sorry. That's not going to happen. First, because

she's caused me a lot of trouble, and I'm ready to make her pay for that. Second, because I don't trust you, her or the United States government."

"We could offer something else in exchange for her life."

"Like what?" The gun dropped away, just a fraction of an inch, but it was enough to give Esme a little hope and a little wiggle room. If it dropped any farther, she'd elbow him in the stomach and make a run for it.

As if he sensed her thoughts, Ian met her eyes again, offering a subtle shake of his head.

A warning, she thought.

A week ago, she would have ignored it and gone ahead with her plan. Now she knew Ian. She knew how his mind worked, how he thought, the way he worked. He didn't believe in taking chances. He always had a plan A, a plan B and a plan C. He'd told her that one night while they were playing checkers.

Tonight's plan A hadn't worked out.

Maybe plan B would be better.

And maybe she'd be smart to wait a little longer, see what Ian had up his sleeve.

"Here's what I'm thinking," Ian said, shuffling forward a couple of steps.

"What *I'm* thinking," Angus barked, "is that you need to stay where you are."

"Sorry. I was thinking about other things. Like you. On a plane, heading for a tropical paradise."

"That sounds more like your friend Jake's cup of tea," Angus said, tugging Esme backward, dragging her into ankle-deep water.

"Jake's smart. He knows that the best way to stay out of jail is to get out of the country."

"He's smart, all right," Angus agreed. "I showed him a few pictures of this place, told him how many people were working protection, and he was able to tell me exactly how you'd react if you were under attack. He knew you'd send your friends off in the SUV. He knew you'd try to escape in the boat. He even knew that you'd only keep one dog back at the house."

"Like I said," Ian replied, no heat in his voice, no emotion. He was getting ready to move, Esme could sense it. She could feel the tension in him, the corded muscles and tamped-down energy. All of it was ready to explode. "Jake is smart. You'd be wise to take a page from his book."

"Meaning?"

"Agree to let us fly you out of the country. Stay away for good, and you won't have to worry about the police or the feds."

"I'm not much for tropical climates," Angus said, his beady eyes shifting from Ian to a point just beyond his shoulder. "That you, Eddie?" he called.

There was no reply, and he took another step back, dragging Esme with him.

She wasn't sure what he'd seen. She didn't care.

She just didn't want to have to take another step deeper into the water, because she had the horrible feeling she knew what he planned. One gunshot, and her body would fall, the loud splash attracting predators for miles around.

She'd probably be dead before they reached her.

The thought wasn't comforting.

"Who's Eddie?" Ian asked.

"One of the guys I hired to help out. Four people to

help me take you down and get my niece. That's what Jake said."

"Did he also say that I don't like to be fooled?" Ian asked. "And that I always make sure that I'm well armed?"

He moved so quickly, Esme almost didn't see it happen.

First he was still, then he was beside her, one arm sweeping in a downward arc, a glittering knife heading straight for Angus's hand.

Angus shrieked, jerking away, but maintaining his grip on the gun.

"Move!" Ian shouted, giving Esme a gentle shove toward shore.

She stumbled, landing on her knees, blood sleeping down her arm and dripping into the dark water.

Get up! her mind shrieked. *Run!*

She was finally up, stumbling through the water, screaming for King, hoping the dog would come running.

Praying he would.

Suddenly, he was there, flying across the yard, splashing into the water. He moved past, aiming for the struggling men, launching himself into the air and into the fray.

Angus cursed, stumbling from the pack, the gun still in his hand, his arms bloody and oozing.

He lifted the weapon, and King charged again.

"No!" Esme screamed, but it was too late.

The gun report was deafening, the sound drowning out everything else. She watched in horror, expecting King to fall away, but he was still moving, landing against Angus, pushing him over.

Or...

Maybe Angus was just falling, the gun splashing into the swamp as the sound of the gunshot faded away.

"I'd feel bad, but he deserved it," a woman said, her voice so close to Esme's ear, she screamed, whirling around and looking straight into her sister's gorgeous face.

Violetta Dupree had saved King's life.

No matter how hard he tried, Ian couldn't wrap his mind around that. He took another sip of the hot coffee Julianne had offered him, eyeing Esme's sister over the top of the paper cup.

She perched on the edge of a vinyl-covered chair in the waiting room of the ER.

She looked...

Tired.

Undone.

Her brown hair fell in messy waves around her pale face. Her mascara was smeared underneath her eyes. She'd been wearing red lipstick at some point, and lines of it feathered out from her lips. She was a beautiful woman. There was no doubt about that, but she looked like she'd aged ten years since he'd last seen her, and that had been only a couple of months ago.

"I don't understand what's taking so long," she complained, biting at a hangnail on the edge of her thumb. "You said the gunshot wound didn't look that bad."

"It didn't."

"Then why haven't they come to let us know how Esme is doing?"

"It takes time to clean a wound," Julianne offered, and Violetta huffed.

"It would be nice if it would take a little less time. I have things to do." She flicked a speck of mud off her dark jeans and frowned.

"What kind of things?" Ian asked, trying to see a little of Esme in her face.

"Nothing that concerns you or your people. A friend is having a birthday party this weekend, and I need to be home for it."

"So you just took a little jaunt from Chicago to Florida to kill your uncle, and now you're going back home to hobnob with your rich friends?" Zeke's assessment was harsh, and Violetta's eyes widened.

"I did not come out here to kill Angus. I came to save my sister."

"And you knew she was in trouble because…?" Julianne tapped her fingers on her thighs and eyed Violetta with a mixture of curiosity and suspicion.

It was the same look Ian was probably giving her.

Violetta didn't answer questions. At least, not any questions he'd ever asked. Now she seemed determined to tell them everything she knew.

As long as it was on her time frame.

"It was pretty obvious that our uncle wanted Esme dead, and that he wasn't going to stop going after her until he achieved his goal."

"You didn't seem all that concerned about her well-being when we tried to get you to tell us what you knew about your uncle," Ian pointed out, and she shrugged, flipping a strand of hair over her shoulder.

"Of course I was concerned. Esme means the world to me."

"Do I?" Esme's voice carried through the small waiting area, and Ian turned, saw her standing in the doorway. Her arm was in a sling, her hair was slicked to her scalp, her face was pale and streaked with mud.

And she was absolutely the most beautiful woman he'd ever seen. King must have thought the same. He barreled toward her, stopping at her feet and looking up at her adoringly.

"Hello, handsome," Esme said, swaying a little as she leaned down to pet the dog.

Ian cupped the elbow of her good arm, supporting her weight as she straightened.

"Thanks," she said, smiling into his eyes.

And, right then, he knew. Beyond a shadow of a doubt. Knew more than he knew almost anything else, that he'd be in Esme's life for as long as she wanted him there.

"It's not hard to give someone a hand when they need it," he said, helping her to the seat next to her sister.

"I meant for everything else," she replied, looking into his eyes and offering a soft sweet smile. "You've given up a lot to keep me safe, and I appreciate that more than I can say."

"You won't be safe until after you testify. You do know that, don't you?" Violetta lifted Esme's hand and squeezed it gently. "There are still plenty of people who would like Reginald to go free."

"I don't suppose you want to name any of them?" Julianne asked, and Violetta stiffened.

"Of course she doesn't," Zeke cut in. "She's willing to help her sister, but only if it doesn't interfere with her life."

"You have no idea what you're talking about." Violetta stood, her body nearly shaking with fury. "I have done nothing but help you people. I've kept my silence so that I could keep track of Jake Morrow. I knew he'd keep in touch with Angus, and I was right."

"You know where Jake is?" Zeke asked, and Violetta shook her head.

"I've heard he's going after his ex-girlfriend and his son. He won't leave the country without them."

"Who did you hear that from?" Esme prodded, leaning back in the seat and stifling a yawn. She was trying to cover up how bone-tired she was, but Ian noticed.

"Angus. I kept on his good side so that I could protect you. That was my only reason, my sole motivation. I hope you believe that, Esme."

"So you've been playing up to your uncle and getting information from him?" Julianne had taken a small notepad from her pocket and was jotting something in it. "Is that what you're saying?"

"That is exactly what I'm saying. I've made my mistakes. I'll admit that. I like nice things. Expensive things. I was happy to let my brother and uncle get them for me." Her gaze shifted to her sister, and she frowned. "But I love you more than any of that, Esme. I would have cooperated with the FBI immediately if I hadn't been afraid it would cost you your life."

"Sounds to me like you're trying to separate yourself from your brother's crimes," Zeke said, and Violetta scowled.

"You don't know a thing about me. None of you do. If I'd wanted to separate myself from my brother's crimes, I wouldn't be here. I'd have stopped Angus, and I'd have gone straight back to Chicago without letting any of you know I'd been here. It wasn't like you weren't distracted enough for me to escape. I stayed because I accomplished my goal. Everything I've done these past months has been to protect my sister."

"If that's the case, you shouldn't be hesitating to give us information about the way the organization runs," Ian accused.

"I'm afraid, okay?" Violetta nearly shouted. "Not all of us are like Esme—brave enough to risk our lives. I'm not. I never have been. Except when it comes to her. I'd do anything to keep her safe. Even play to my uncle's good side, pretend to be part of his team and convince him to confide in me." She hissed out a breath. "He told me all about Jake Morrow. He told me that he'd threatened Jake's son's and ex-girlfriend's lives. It made me physically ill. Who would hurt a child?"

"Your uncle," Ian said, gentling his voice, because he believed her, and he was starting to feel sympathy for the mess she'd found herself in.

"I know," she said just as gently, her gaze on her sister. "I'm so sorry this happened, Esme. If I could go back and change things, make different decisions, be a better person, I would. I promise you that."

"You can make different decisions," Julianne said, and there didn't seem to be a hint of sympathy in her voice. "As long as Jake Morrow is free, your sister may not be safe. Angus was a terrible person, but Reginald calls the shots. He may be trying to contact Jake, get him to follow through on the effort to silence Esme before the trial. We need to bring him in, and we need to do it quickly if you really want to keep your sister from harm."

Violetta frowned. "Some of the information I got was vague, but I'll tell you what I know. Angus told me Jake was going back home to find his ex-girlfriend and his baby. She despises what he's become and wants nothing to do with him, but he's not going to leave the country until he has his son."

The words jolted through Ian, and he fished his phone out of his pocket, scrolled through the texts until he found the one sent by Anonymous: Word is that Mommy, Daddy and child have gone home.

"You're Anonymous," he said, and she blushed.

"Yes. Like I said, I was trying to pass on as much information as I could without making things too easy to figure out."

"Easy would have been nice," Zeke grumbled.

"Easy would have gotten me killed," she responded through clenched teeth, dropping into the seat beside Esme. "I was the only one who knew about Jake Morrow. If I'd given you too much information and you'd passed it on to someone owned by Angus…" She shuddered.

"Tell us about Jake going home," Ian demanded, turning the subject back to the thing he was most interested in.

He didn't really care what Violetta's motivation had been. It didn't matter to him if it had been greed or fear that had caused her to get close to her uncle. What he cared about was the fact that she had information that could prove to be very useful to the team.

"He's in Montana. At least, that's where I think he is. Angus thought it was hilarious that he was going to be so close to your headquarters. He liked to say you were all farsighted, unable to see what was right in front of your faces."

"What else did he like to say?" Zeke asked, his irritation and anger obvious.

"That he was smarter than all of you put together. That he always came out on top, and the rest of us were flies buzzing around on the trash heap of his leftovers." She squeezed the bridge of her nose and shook her head. "He really was a horrible man."

"Maybe you should have gone to the police and told them that a long time ago." Zeke stalked out of the room, Cheetah bounding along beside him.

"I already said that I'd change things if I could. What more do you people want from me?" Violetta began, her frustration and irritation obvious.

Ian had the feeling that she was just gearing up, that she had a whole lot more she wanted to say about the way they were treating her.

Esme held up her hand, stopping her sister's diatribe.

"Do we have to do this right now?" she asked wearily.

"Of course we do," Violetta retorted. "I didn't come all this way to be treated like a criminal."

"Just stop, Violetta," Esme said. "It's been a long day. Actually, it's been a long six months. I'm tired, and I just want to go home. Except—" Her voice broke, and a tear rolled down her cheek. "I can't, because I have to keep drifting from place to place until the trial. You get to go back to the fancy penthouse Reginald helped you buy. Until his trial is over and he's been sentenced, there's no place that I'll ever feel safe. No place to throw anchor and wait until the storm blows over. I just have to keep riding it out until the bitter end."

"Oh. Honey! I'm sorry. I wasn't thinking about what you've been through." Violetta pulled tissue from her handbag and tried to give them to Esme.

Esme nudged them away.

"Esme," Violetta tried again. "Don't cry. None of these people are worth your tears."

"Yes. They are. And so are you. So, please, let's not do this right now." She swiped at the errant tear, her hand shaking.

Julianne met Ian's eyes. "You want me to handle the interrogation?"

"Yes. And update Max on the case. He'll be interested in hearing the information about Jake."

She nodded, touching Violetta's shoulder and somehow convincing her to walk out of the room.

Turning back to Esme, he saw that her eyes were closed. She had her head resting against the wall and her hands fisted in her lap, and when another tear slipped down her cheek, he couldn't hold back.

He lifted her good hand, unfurled her fingers and pressed a kiss to her palm.

"What's that for?" she murmured, not opening her eyes.

"Something to anchor you until you find your way home," he said, and she smiled, but the tears kept falling, and he finally tugged her into his lap, pressed her head to his chest and just let her cry.

FOURTEEN

She hated crying.

Hated it, but she couldn't seem to stop. The tears kept rolling down her face, soaking into Ian's shirt.

Ian!

She was cradled in his arms.

Crying all over him.

She pushed away, her left arm shrieking in protest.

Because she'd been shot.

By her uncle.

Her own flesh and blood, but he'd wanted her dead. In the end, he'd died because of that.

"Slow down," Ian said as she scrambled away from him.

"Your shirt is soaked," she pointed out.

"And?"

"I'd die of embarrassment. If that were actually a thing."

"What's to be embarrassed about?" He snagged her hand, holding her in place when she would have backed farther away.

"Look at me!" She gestured to her mud-encrusted pants, her hair, her tear-soaked face. "I'm a mess!"

"A beautiful mess," he responded gruffly, and her heart did a funny little dance. One that spoke of happiness and contentment and better things to come.

And suddenly the tears weren't sliding down her cheeks anymore. Suddenly, she was smiling. "Only you would say something like that," she said.

"And I'd only say it to you. How's the arm?"

"Sore, but I'll live."

"And the heart?"

"The same." Her voice broke, and the stupid tears started again.

"They'll both get better. Just give it a little time." He tugged her into his arms, his lips brushing hers. Once. Then again. Her hand slid up his arm, her fingers slid through his hair.

She could have stood there with him forever, tasting the sweetness of his lips, feeling the warmth of his hand resting on her back.

Someone cleared his throat, and she jerked back, nearly tripping over King.

"Sorry," she said to the dog, and his tail thumped.

"I'm probably the one who should be apologizing. I didn't mean to interrupt," a man said, and she turned, watching as he walked into the room. Tall and blond with a scar that slashed down the side of his cheek, he had the bluest eyes she'd ever seen.

"Max," Ian said. If he were embarrassed at having been caught kissing her, he didn't show it. "What are you doing here?"

"I decided to come help with the transport. The more people protecting Ms. Dupree, the better. I took the red-eye last night. If I'd known how much trouble you were going to be in, I'd have tried to get to Florida sooner."

He smiled, offering Esme his hand. "I'm Max West. Team captain and shameless romantic."

"Really?"

"No, but I thought it might make things less awkward."

"I really don't think anything can do that."

"Well, then how about we focus on the business at hand? Has Ian explained what our next step is?"

"There hasn't been a whole lot of time," Ian said, and Max nodded.

"Right. So here's how it's going to be, Esme. We're going to take you to our headquarters in Montana. You'll be there until our next safe house is ready."

"Is it going to be in a swamp?" she asked, too tired to argue with the plan.

"No." He laughed. "It's going to be really nice. Not in the States, though. We've arranged for you to have round-the-clock security in another country. We've already collected your passport. If there's anything else you think you'll need, let us know and we'll make sure you have it."

Yeah.

There was.

She'd need Ian, but she didn't think that was what Max was expecting to hear.

"Some air would be nice. If that's okay," she said, offering a poor facsimile of a smile.

She didn't think either of the men bought it, but neither tried to stop her. With Angus dead, she was safe. At least until Reginald could figure out a way to hire killers from prison.

Throat thick with emotion, she reached the exit and walked out into early-morning light. The sun was just peeking above the horizon, the ground dusted gold with it. King appeared at her side, his sturdy body pressing against her leg, warm and heavy and comforting.

"It's going to be okay," she murmured.

"Yes, it is," Ian said, and she wasn't surprised that he was there, wasn't shocked when he turned her so that they were facing each other.

"I don't want to leave the country," she said. Simple. Straightforward. To the point.

"I'm sorry," he responded, and she knew his hands were tied, that the decision wasn't his. "But your sister will be fine. She's very good at taking care of herself."

"That's not what I'm worried about."

"Then what?" he asked. "Your business? Your friends?" He touched her chin, offered a smile that should have made her heart sing. It just made her think of what she'd almost had, and what she was about to lose.

"You," she finally admitted, and he shook his head, tugged her into his arms, pressed her head to his chest.

"Why would you think I'd let you?"

"Because your work is here, and I'm going to be somewhere else."

"My work is with you. Keeping you safe is my assignment until after the trial. King and I have both been cleared to travel with you. I sent Max a text while you were getting your arm cleaned up. He was quick to agree to the plan."

"What if the trial takes years to happen?"

"I don't care if it takes a lifetime, Esme. As long as we're together."

"Are you sure?"

"Absolutely. Now, how about we go back inside and get started on our new adventure?" He took her hand, leading her back to the door. King loped beside him, his ears up, his nose to the air.

He stopped short, whining softly.

"What is it, King?" Ian asked, touching the dog's broad head.

"Is someone out here with us?"

"He'd be barking, but there's definitely something worrying him."

King whined again.

"Find it," Ian said, and the dog took off, racing around the side of the building, nose still to the air, ears alert.

They moved through an alley and then into a back lot.

That was when Esme heard it. Above the distant sound of morning traffic, above the pounding of her heart, the soft whimpering cry of an animal in distress.

"What in the world?" she asked, but Ian was striding across the back lot, following King to a Dumpster that butted against a brick wall.

"Whatever it is," he said, lifting the lid and peering inside, "it's in here."

"Maybe we should call animal control," she suggested as King stood on two legs and looked inside the bin.

She looked, too, because she had to.

The crying was pitiful, and whatever was making the sound needed help.

"I think we can handle this," Ian said, reaching for a box that was shoved up against the back of the metal container. Someone had taped it closed, and the thing inside bumped against the top.

"What if it's a rat?" She cringed as he pulled a utility tool from his pocket and carefully sliced through the tape.

"King wouldn't be going crazy over a rodent. I think it's a—"

He didn't get a chance to finish.

The lid popped open, and a dark-faced thing appeared.

No. Not a thing.

A puppy. Scrawny. All legs, boxy head and little potbelly, he tried to jump out of the box but ended up falling back in.

King nudged the puppy with his nose, offering a tentative lick.

"Good boy, King," Ian said. "Good find."

He lifted the puppy from what would have been its coffin, checked its gums, felt its ribs.

"He's skinny and dehydrated, but it's nothing a little food and water can't fix."

"Should we take him to the shelter?" she asked, touching the puppy's velvety nose and losing a little piece of her heart when he licked her hand.

"It would probably be the practical thing to do, but there's a lot more to life than practicality. I'm supposed to be looking for a puppy to bring back to our training facility. Kind of a reminder that we're part of a family of sorts, one that always sticks together."

There was a note of sadness in his voice, and she knew he must be thinking about Jake Morrow.

"You are a real family," she told him, because it was the only thing she could offer. "I felt that when we were in the safe house. Just because one member decided to go his own way, doesn't mean the remainder can't stay strong."

"I know, but thanks for the reminder. Some days I need it more than others," he confided, smiling in the way that always made her heart leap.

"So...what now?"

"Now we'll take this guy inside and introduce him to his new family," he said, holding the puppy in the crook of his arm. "We'll get him checked out by a vet, and we'll take him to puppy training school."

"He'll be an A student. Of course," she joked, feeling lighter than she had in weeks, happier than she'd been in months.

All the hard times, all the difficulties, had led her to this point, and for the first time since she'd witnessed her brother's crime, she was thankful for them.

"Of course," Ian agreed. "No kid of ours could ever be anything less."

"Kid of ours?" she asked.

"A figure of speech," he responded. "And maybe a conversation to revisit at another time."

"I think I'd like that."

"That's what I was hoping you'd say." He grinned, and she couldn't help returning his smile.

"I guess we'll have plenty of time to discuss it and everything else while we're waiting for Reginald's trial," she said.

"And plenty of time after the trial is over," he replied, tugging her close, offering a kiss that promised everything she'd ever hoped for and more.

When he backed away, they were both breathless, and they were both smiling. She noticed that. Just like she noticed the quiet hum of morning traffic, the soft trill of a songbird on a branch nearby. The sun glinting in Ian's dark hair, the puppy sleeping in the crook of his arm, King grinning at his feet.

It all looked fresh and bright and beautiful.

"What was that for?" she asked, and he took her hand.

"You," he said, "and our new beginning."

She laughed. "New beginnings are wonderful things. Especially when we get to start them with people we care about."

"You're right," he agreed. "So how about we get started on ours?"

"That," she replied, levering up on her toes and offering him one more sweet kiss, "sounds like a wonderful idea."

He called to King, and they walked back to the hospital. All of them together. And it was enough to fill all the empty spots in her heart. It was enough to sustain her through whatever the future might bring.

She hadn't wanted the trouble she'd found herself in, but she couldn't regret where it had led her. Where God had led her. Not just to a new beginning, but to the only place where she'd ever truly felt at home.

EPILOGUE

Ian didn't do nervous. He didn't know what it meant to be anxious. He'd spent years working in law enforcement and facing down thugs, druggies and murderers.

He didn't sweat.

He didn't panic.

He didn't lose his cool.

He was an FBI agent, trained to handle whatever crisis came his way.

So why was he sweating now? Beads of perspiration dotting his brow?

Why were his hands shaking as he tried to knot his tie. *For the tenth time.*

Why was his throat dry? His heart pounding? His pulse racing?

"Need some help with that, Ian?" Max said, a hint of amusement in his voice as he eyed Ian's unknotted tie.

He'd dressed up for the occasion—button-up shirt, dark slacks and a small rose that someone had tucked in his pocket. Probably Katarina. Ian wasn't the only one who'd found love while the team was looking for Jake. Max had found it, too. So had several other team members.

"I've got it," he said, smoothing the tie, and patting his jacket pocket. The ring was there. No box, because he hadn't wanted Esme to notice it. They'd come to headquarters to sign last-minute paperwork before they boarded the plane that would take them to a top secret location.

Even Ian wasn't sure exactly where they'd be.

As long as he was with Esme, he really didn't care.

"Is she here yet?" he asked. He'd spent most of the past few weeks at the safe house, but last night he'd had to pack his bags and get ready for the flight. He'd left Esme with three team members, but he'd still been worried.

Now he was just anxious to see her again.

Ten hours wasn't long, but it felt like a lifetime when you were away from the person you loved, the person you wanted to spend a lifetime with.

"Just arrived. I asked Julianne to keep her in the lobby for another minute." He glanced at his watch. "I've sent your bags ahead, and they're already being loaded onto the plane."

"Is that a hint that I should get this show on the road?"

"Not at all. Take your time. It's a private jet. It's not like it's going to leave without you."

"Then again," Dylan O'Leary said, glancing up from a computer he'd been working on, "things have been calm for a couple of weeks. That usually means trouble is brewing. You might want to get out of town before it arrives."

"Don't rush a man who's about to take one of the biggest steps of his life," Zeke responded, crossing the room and taking one of the cookies that team member Harper Prentiss had brought for the occasion.

"Hands off," she said, slapping his hand away. "Those are for after he pops the question."

She turned to Ian, gave him a quick once-over.

"You could have tried a little harder," she announced, straightening his tie.

"Meaning?"

"A tux? A bowtie? A huge bouquet of her favorite flowers?"

"I've been a little busy," he muttered. It was the truth. He'd spent the past three weeks working at the safe house and helping the team as they tried to locate Jake Morrow. So far, they'd come up empty. If Violetta had been right, if he was in Montana, they hadn't been able to find him.

Yet.

Zeke was still looking.

Or he would be once his doctor cleared him to go back to work. The little flesh wound he'd gotten in the shoot-out had been a bigger deal than he'd thought, and he wasn't happy about it.

As far as Ian could tell, he wasn't happy about a lot of things. Ian couldn't blame him. This had been a tough season for the entire team, but looking around the small conference room, he couldn't help thinking how blessed they all were.

They'd cut the Dupree crime family off at the roots.

With Angus dead and Reginald in prison, the organization was dying, crushed by its inability to run itself. He'd heard of at least a dozen arrests in cities all over the country.

And that was the kind of news he would never ever

get tired of listening to. For a long time, he'd thought that was all he wanted, that seeing the crime family destroyed was all he'd needed to make his life complete.

Every time he looked at Esme, every time their eyes met or their hands touched or he heard her soft laughter, he realized just how wrong he'd been.

That still didn't make this any less nerve-racking!

He ran his hand over his hair, tugged at his tie.

"Ian, really!" Harper brushed his hands away from the tie. "Stop fidgeting. You're making a mess of this."

She straightened the tie again.

"Leave the poor guy alone," Dylan said, glancing down at his phone and frowning.

"Trouble?" Max asked.

"About as big a trouble as a guy like me can get into," he responded.

"Meaning?" Ian prodded. He'd much rather focus on someone else's troubles than his out-of-control nerves.

"I'm going to have to go to a…" Dylan sighed. "To a dress shop to pick up Zara's wedding gown. She says they're in hiding and formulating a plan, but the dress is in, and she needs me to get it."

"That's it?"

"Yes."

"That doesn't sound so bad," Ian said.

"Have you ever been to one of those places?"

"No. Have you?"

"Of course not, and I wasn't planning to." He sighed, and Ian would have said something else, maybe offered a solution to the problem, but the door opened and Julianne walked in, Esme right behind her.

His breath caught, and he was sure his heart stopped. She was that beautiful, short red hair framing her face, her sundress skimming slim muscular legs. She'd put a sweater on over the dress, probably hoping to keep warm on the plane. The white knit seemed to highlight the vibrancy of her hair and her eyes.

"You're beautiful," he said.

"So are you," she replied, and he was pretty certain someone laughed. He didn't care. Didn't look to see who it was.

She was all that mattered.

King had walked over, was leaning against Esme's leg, offering a K-9 hug that made her smile.

Ian would normally smile, too, maybe comment on how much King loved her, how quickly he'd accepted her as part of the pack.

He didn't do either, he was too busy studying her face, memorizing the way she looked, so that he could tell their children exactly how gorgeous she'd been the day he'd proposed.

"What's wrong, Ian?" she said, probably sensing his nervous energy.

"I've been thinking," he said. "That I don't want to go into witness protection as your bodyguard. I wan—"

"I understand, Ian." She cut him off before he could finish, obviously assuming something that had never occurred to him.

"I don't think you do," he responded, taking her hand and pulling her closer, mentally kicking himself for making her think for even a moment that he'd walk away. "I don't want to go into witness protection as your bodyguard, because I'm hoping to change my job title before we get on the plane."

"To what?" She looked confused and relieved, her smile returning.

"Fiancé?" he suggested, pulling the ring from his pocket. He had purchased it at an antiques store, the teardrop-shaped emerald surrounded by small mine-cut diamonds, the gold band carved with dozens of infinity symbols.

Her eyes widened when she saw it, and she met his gaze.

"Ian," she breathed, and he didn't know what she meant to say. He only knew what he had to tell her.

The words spilled out. Not practiced or rehearsed. Not the canned little speech that a few of his buddies had suggested. Esme deserved so much more than that.

"I didn't realize what I was missing until I found you, Esme. You are everything I didn't know I was looking for, everything I didn't know I needed. When I'm with you, I'm home. When I'm not, all I can think about is finding my way back. I'd give all I have to spend the rest of my life with you. Will you marry me?"

"Yes," she said, the word choking out as she reached for him, pulled him in for a hug that spoke all the words she hadn't said.

He could hear them in the quiet hitch of her breath, the soft whisper of her hair against his jacket as she laid her head against his chest.

He could have stood with her forever, let that one perfect moment continue, but King nudged his hand, and he realized he was still holding the ring.

He looked down into Esme's face, smiling into her eyes as he slipped the ring on her finger.

"I love you," he said.

"I love you, too," she responded, a single tear sliding down her cheek.

"Then why are you crying?"

"Because this is the most beautiful moment I have ever lived, and I'm so glad I'm living it with you." She offered a watery smile, and he wiped the tear away, kissing her gently, letting the sound of his friends' warm congratulations fill his heart as he took her hand, signaled for King and walked out of the room and into their future together.

* * * * *

With over seventy books published and millions in print, **Lenora Worth** writes award-winning romance and romantic suspense. Three of her books finaled in the ACFW Carol Awards, and her Love Inspired Suspense novel *Body of Evidence* became a *New York Times* bestseller. Her novella in *Mistletoe Kisses* made her a *USA TODAY* bestselling author. Lenora goes on adventures with her retired husband, Don, and enjoys reading, baking and shopping...especially shoe shopping.

Books by Lenora Worth

Love Inspired Suspense

Undercover Memories

Military K-9 Unit

Rescue Operation

Classified K-9 Unit

Tracker
Classified K-9 Unit Christmas
"A Killer Christmas"

Rookie K-9 Unit

Truth and Consequences
Rookie K-9 Unit Christmas
"Holiday High Alert"

Capitol K-9 Unit

Proof of Innocence
Capitol K-9 Unit Christmas
"Guarding Abigail"

Visit the Author Profile page
at Harlequin.com for more titles.

TRACKER

Lenora Worth

Through the praise of children and infants you have
established a stronghold against your enemies,
to silence the foe and the avenger.
—*Psalms* 8:2

To the other authors in this series
who always help me, brainstorm with me
and laugh with me—Terri Reed, Valerie Hansen,
Lynette Eason, Laura Scott and Shirlee McCoy.
I love working with all of you! And to my editor,
Emily Rodmell, for putting up with me!

ONE

"I'm not leaving without my son."

He pressed the gun against her spine, the cold muzzle chilling against her thin shirt. Late-afternoon sunshine shot over the Elk Basin, giving the vast Montana sky a pastoral rendering. But right now, that sky looked ominous.

She didn't want to die here.

Penny Potter twisted around and tried to break free from the man who'd come crashing out of the woods and tackled her just seconds before. Heaving a shuddering breath, she screamed at her former boyfriend, "Jake, there is no way I'm letting you take Kevin out of the country! I told you last time, neither of us is going with you."

Jake Morrow's blue eyes matched the sky, but the bitter flash of anger seared Penny's heart. "Yeah, but you took my boy and ran away."

Apprehension and fear gnawed at her, but Penny tried to stay calm. She had to keep her head and get back to Kevin before her ex found him. "I can't leave the country with you. I'm not going to put Kevin through that. They're all looking for you, Jake. Just go and leave us alone."

"*You* might not be willing to come with me," Jake said, his actions filled with a wild recklessness that made her shiver in spite of the late summer heat. "But my son sure is not staying behind. You're going to take me to him. Now! Or you'll never see him again."

Special Agent Zeke Morrow moved silently through the underbrush, his K-9 partner, an Australian shepherd named Cheetah, taking the lead as they canvassed yet another grid of rocky hills and tall ponderosa pines. He'd checked in with several of the other members of the FBI Classified K-9 Unit who were scouring a ridge on the other side of the woods. Nothing yet. No sign of Jake Morrow.

"Where are you, Jake?" he asked in a low whisper, his gaze scanning every shift of leaves and every snap of twigs. He had to keep going in spite of the deep-boned fatigue that threatened to weigh him down.

Could his half brother, Jake, really be somewhere inside this vast wilderness? After picking up a tip that the former agent, now wanted by the FBI for turning corrupt and joining forces with the infamous Dupree crime syndicate, had been spotted buying supplies and ammunition at a truck stop a few miles from here, Zeke had talked to several of the residents who lived along the edge of the wilderness preserve. One of them, a young science teacher who'd been on a hike, had seen someone matching Jake's description going into the Elk Basin early this morning.

"And there was another man with him but he took off in a big black van," the nervous fellow had stated.

"Don't mention my name, okay? Those two looked loaded for bear."

The other guy had been described as short in stature with long, stringy hair and wearing glasses. Sounded a lot like Gunther Caprice, a wanted criminal who'd managed to fly under the radar since the Dupree family business had started to unravel. He'd probably dropped Jake off here and was hiding out somewhere. But what were they doing here of all places?

Unless this was another one of his brother's ruses to fool all of them. Or…perhaps this was the big break they'd all been waiting for.

Zeke's gut told him that his half brother was indeed somewhere in these woods. But that still didn't explain why Jake had decided to come back to Montana when he knew he was a wanted man. What possible motive could he have?

Jake, who'd once been a valuable member of the elite FBI Classified K-9 Unit, had gone off the deep end after joining up with the notorious Dupree crime family. Fellow agent Ian Slade had fallen in love with the only crime-free member of the Dupree clan. Esme Dupree was willing to testify against her brother, Reginald, but she'd left the witness protection program because she feared for her life. Ian grudgingly became her protector after a trek through the Florida Everglades, where eventually her older sister, Violetta, shot and killed Angus Dupree in order to save Esme's life. But now Ian and Esme had gone into hiding in another country until Jake was found and Reginald Dupree was brought to justice. Couldn't happen soon enough for Zeke. The whole team had been playing a game of cat and mouse with Jake all spring and summer.

Almost six months of searching for his armed and dangerous half brother had brought Zeke back to Montana a couple of days ago. Reports kept coming in—sightings of the rogue agent near the Elk Basin and in other areas close to Billings. Was he trying to get back to headquarters? Or was Jake just messing with the entire team?

I have to find him and try to reason with him, take him in alive.

Zeke stopped and gave Cheetah some water, patted him and checked the dog's protective FBI vest. "Good boy. You're doing great. Show me where to go next, okay?"

Cheetah would do his job. The medium-sized dog had a sweet temperament, but he was trained in search and rescue and could turn serious with one command. His K-9 partner never quit, so Zeke wouldn't, either.

Cheetah lifted his snout and sniffed the hot August air. Then the dog tugged at his leash and headed east, back toward the main trail out of the basin.

Zeke followed, the sound of distant voices causing his pulse to rise. Could he finally be on the right track?

"No!" Penny tried to break away, but Jake grabbed her by the collar of her shirt and jerked her back so hard pain shot through her neck. Praying her son was okay, she tried to stay calm so she could see a way out of this.

Shoving her ahead of him on the rocky path into the thicket, Jake kept one hand in a death grip on her arm. "Let's go. We're getting Kevin, and either you both go with me, or I'll take him and you won't even have time to regret it."

"You don't have to do this," she pleaded, wondering

how Jake had found her. She'd been all over the country, using fake names, constantly changing her appearance and hiding out in dives with her now two-year-old son. Penny hated dragging Kevin from pillar to post and hiding him in secrecy, but she had to protect him from his father. She'd thought since almost six months had passed and no one had found Jake, she'd be safe coming back to Montana. Especially here in the remote wilderness in the Elk Basin, an area she'd loved all of her life.

But then, she'd always underestimated the dangerous man holding her against her will now. Penny had wanted to believe Jake was one of the good guys, but she could tell even before he'd disappeared that he'd changed. She'd heard the rumors and a few cryptic news reports after he'd been presumed kidnapped by a member of the Dupree crime family. But as the months wore on, things had taken a sickening twist.

Now Jake was wanted by the very people who used to trust him and work with him—his own FBI team. Their work was classified, but she knew they'd searched her former house and probably taken some pictures she'd left there so they could easily identify her and Kevin. They were most likely searching for her, too. She'd taken off long before they showed up, and she'd had to leave several other temporary locations.

All because she'd been trying to get away from Jake.

Her ex was in deep trouble and from what she could glean, it had something to do with the criminal syndicate that his former unit had tried to infiltrate several months ago. Jake had gone missing once the dust had settled on that botched mission. She'd heard they'd captured Reginald Dupree that day, but his uncle Angus Dupree had escaped and taken Jake hostage. Angus was dead now, or so she'd heard. All she knew was Jake was a wanted man, according to the few news reports she'd heard.

The reports had also implicated Jake as a willing accomplice. He'd betrayed his unit for money and power. And yet here he stood, holding a gun on her in a desperate attempt to get out of the country. With their son. That would happen over her dead body.

"Jake, let me go. You can't take a toddler on the run. Let us be and…maybe one day I can send you pictures or…find a way for you two to reunite."

"No," he barked. "No, Penny. I lost my father. I won't let that happen to my son."

Her heart sank. Jake was in a mindset where he refused to listen to reason. "I understand," she said, not giving up but giving in for now.

It was too late for Jake to do anything but run. He would kill her and take their son. He wouldn't give up without a fight, but neither would she.

Zeke's phone buzzed. "What's the status, Agent Morrow?"

Max West, the Special Agent in Charge, checking on him again.

"Cheetah's picked up something, sir. I heard voices on the other side of one of the main trails heading east. Headed that way now."

"I'll send some backup. We got nothing here."

After ending the call, Zeke put his phone away and listened. There. Again. Shouts into the still, dry air. A woman's scream.

Cheetah growled low and alerted. Zeke's heart pumped new energy into his tired body. They hurried through the scrub brush and outcroppings, but he couldn't decide if he was relieved or if this dread burdening his soul would overtake him.

Help me make the right decisions, Lord.

Jake clamped a sweaty hand over her mouth. "That was a big mistake," he said, his tone full of rage. "But I doubt anyone heard you. You're so predictable, Penny, hanging around out in the woods with people trying to have a wilderness adventure. I've been watching you for days, getting a handle on your routine. No one will ever find you out here." He dropped his hand. "But if you scream again, you'll regret it."

He was right.

Penny blinked away tears of frustration and looked around frantically at the deserted trail. No one in sight. She'd finished guiding a wilderness tour over an hour ago and watched the busload of about twenty people head out in the other direction. Tired and hot and not as alert as she should have been, she'd started hiking the couple of miles toward home, her mind on seeing Kevin. Jake had waylaid her near the small town of Iris Rock, where her son was safe inside the Wild Iris Inn with the owner, Claire Crayton.

Claire knew what to do. Penny had explained when she first moved into the boardinghouse that her ex-boyfriend might show up and try to cause trouble. Under no circumstance was the older woman to allow Kevin to go with anyone except Penny. Claire had nodded toward the shotgun she kept behind the check-in counter and promised her she'd take care of Kevin, no matter what.

Now Penny wished she'd warned Claire that the father of her child might be armed and dangerous and wanted by the law. But she'd never dreamed Jake would hold a gun on her or threaten her life.

Please, God, keep Kevin safe.

Penny entreated that simple prayer over and over while she looked around for a way to escape. Since she'd been a trained guide for years, she knew this basin better than most. She knew the nooks and crannies, the hills, valleys and meadows and all the streams and waterfalls; knew the animals and the seasons. If she could make it across the trailhead to the open meadow, she'd be able to hide in the tall grass and inch her way toward the foothills.

"Don't even think about it, sweetheart," Jake said, his breath hissing like a snake against her neck. "You're smart and I have no doubt that you can survive out here. But it would be stupid to try and outrun me."

Penny glanced at the semiautomatic handgun he pressed into her ribs as a reminder, her heart pumping adrenaline while she thought of her sweet little boy. Kevin had his daddy's dark blond hair and deep blue eyes.

"What happened to you, Jake?" she asked, stalling but also wanting some answers. "Why would you risk everything and ruin your career? I've heard rumors—"

"Later," he snarled. "I'm not going to explain all of that right now. Besides, what do you care? You ran out on me."

Pushing her forward, his anger shimmering from every pore, he checked both ways along the path into the woods.

He wasn't going to talk, and he was too wired to tolerate her feeble attempts to save herself. Penny cast a desperate glance over the vast open country between the surrounding hills, the August heat burning her. Her only chance was to try to run as fast as she possibly could. She waited for Jake to loosen his grip on her arm before she broke free and plowed through the brush, only to stumble on a jutting rock and fall face-first into the dry bramble.

He caught up with her and jerked her back up. "Nice try." Stroking a gentle finger against her cheekbone, he said, "Now you're bleeding. Next time, things might get even worse."

Zeke followed the sound of voices, Cheetah taking him back into the woods. A woman. A scream. Even if this didn't involve Jake, someone could be in trouble. Not many people hung around here this late unless they were camping or had gotten lost on one of the many trails. The sun would be setting in about an hour. Needing to think this through, he halted Cheetah to get his bearings and hurriedly checked the map coordinates on his phone. They were about two miles from the small town of Iris Rock.

The town where Penny Potter used to rent a house.

Penny had been Jake's girlfriend and she was now the mother of his child. But she was so off the radar, no one had been able to find her. Could Jake have come back here looking for her and his son, one last time? While that didn't make much sense, Zeke's gut burned with the sure knowledge that someone was in trouble up ahead.

"Let's go," he said to Cheetah. The animal took off in an eager run, straight toward those echoing voices.

Then Zeke heard something else off in the distance. The hum of a vehicle hitting ruts in the dirt. Hopefully, his backup had arrived.

* * *

"We'll keep walking," Jake explained. "I have someone coming with a vehicle full of supplies to pick us up just over that north ridge. We'll have our son and we can leave tonight. I have plenty of money hidden away, baby. We can go somewhere warm and tropical, a place where they will never find us. I'll take care of both of you." His husky whispers sent a cold chill down her spine. "I've missed you so much."

Now he was trying to sweet-talk her? Penny closed her eyes and swallowed back the painful knot lodged inside her throat. Resolve and revulsion overtook any sympathy she might have once had for him. She was strong now, strong in her newfound faith and strong in her love for her child. "I'm not going anywhere with you, Jake, and neither is Kevin."

"He's *my* son."

The words held a threat.

She had to make a move.

Penny practiced self-defense on a regular basis since her job required her to be out in the middle of nowhere with strangers following her around and wild animals approaching unexpectedly. But could she take down a six-foot-three-inch muscular man? A deranged, desperate fugitive who didn't have anything to lose?

Except the one person he loved in the world. His son.

Her heart swelled when she thought about Kevin. So innocent and precious. He'd never know his father. But if she didn't make a move, he'd never have his mother, either.

"Quit stalling, Penny," Jake said, his voice as hard and dry as the surrounding countryside. She stared at the flat, brown land leading to the distant woods and hills and spotted a lone scarlet-colored fairy trumpet. The pretty flower beckoned her. It had survived the hot summer. She would, too.

Lord, help me in my time of need. Give me the strength to do what I need to do.

With a grunt and all the energy she could muster, she whirled and elbowed Jake in the ribs, one booted foot latching against his left calf so she could trip him. Still in motion, she jabbed at his eyes with two fingers, surprising him.

He put a hand to his face and went down with a groan, giving her just enough time to slip out of his grip and slam her heavy backpack against his head.

Clutching the bag against her as protection, she spun away from his crumbled body and took off toward the forest about fifty yards across the meadow. If she could make it to the tree line, she could hide up in the hills until nightfall. Or longer if necessary. But she couldn't hide. She had to call the boardinghouse and warn Claire before Jake got to Kevin.

But right now she had to outrun the man she once loved. Her heart hammering in her chest, she pushed with all her might and took off, her hiking boots kicking up dust.

Thinking she'd made it, Penny glanced back when she was about ten yards from the thick stand of ponderosa pines and aspens leading to another trail. Jake stumbled toward her, his gun raised.

He wasn't going to let her live.

TWO

A gunshot echoed through the meadow just beyond the woods.

Zeke started running.

"Search," he commanded, letting Cheetah's leash go. The dog took off toward the area where they'd heard the shots, Zeke jogging behind him. Cheetah must have picked up some kind of scent that he recognized. But had it come from the same vicinity as that gunshot?

The showdown that Zeke had been waiting for for close to six months could be about to happen. And none too soon. Roaming all over the country trying to track down leads, desperately trying to rescue his older half brother, only to discover that the man he'd always worshipped had turned traitor, had taken its toll on him and the entire team. He'd even taken a bullet recently and still had the sore spot on his upper left arm to prove it. Thanks to his brother, he'd have a nice scar as a permanent reminder.

But nothing was going to stop Zeke from trying to track down Jake. Maybe he could at least keep him alive and in prison instead of dead and gone. If Jake was willing to give them vital information that could finish off the last dregs of the Dupree syndicate, maybe they could work out a plea bargain at least.

"Find him, Cheetah," Zeke said, the urgency of their situation driving him on.

Cheetah had Jake's scent from an old T-shirt they'd found in his locker back at headquarters in Billings, but they'd also confirmed the blood on a shirt they'd found in a cabin in Texas belonged to his brother, too. That, along with a watch Zeke had given him when Jake had first become an FBI agent. Zeke asked to be on the case and he'd followed the tips all over the country, hoping to end this thing. Now it could all end right here in Montana.

Zeke had images of his brawny half brother serving as a dedicated FBI Classified K-9 agent, now turned outright criminal, to spur him on. Yet, despite everything, he didn't want to accept that Jake was all bad. He had called Zeke not long ago and told him he was in too deep now. Just another reminder of how confusing things had become.

Hot and exhausted, both he and Cheetah hurried out of the thicket. Cheetah's low growl and urgent trot told Zeke he'd probably find his brother.

But had Jake been shot?

When they made it out into the open, Zeke sucked in a sharp breath. He couldn't believe what he was witnessing.

Jake had a woman held at gunpoint.

A woman who looked familiar based on the pictures he'd seen. And scared. She was bleeding, her left cheekbone bruised and swollen. Her gaze slammed into Zeke's and he felt a jolt of adrenaline rushing over him.

Penny Potter? It had to be her.

Zeke didn't hesitate. He needed to end this now.

"Drop the weapon," he ordered, his assault rifle aimed at Jake and the woman. Penny was the mother of Jake's young son, Kevin. Her golden-brown hair and slim, athletic figure sure fit the description. Her hair was shorter and heavily streaked with lighter shades of blond, but he remembered her face from some old photos they'd found when they'd searched her last known address in Colorado. The K-9 team had been looking for her since late spring but she'd managed to elude them, too. Zeke never imagined he'd find her here again and with Jake holding her hostage.

"It's over, Jake," he called, his gaze trained on his brother. "Don't make it any harder."

Jake didn't even flinch. Shoving the gun closer to the woman's stomach, he shouted, "Hello there, bro. Long time, no see." Then he shook his head and chuckled. "They had to send you, right?" Jake's dark blue gaze slid over Zeke's tactical uniform with disdain. "All geared up and loaded down to come after me. Poetic justice and so much irony, don't you think?"

Zeke advanced a little closer. Cheetah was silent but waiting for his command with a controlled tremor. "Jake, Cheetah can take you down but I don't want to force that. Put the weapon down and let the woman go. We can find a way to help you. Maybe work out a plea bargain or something."

He almost added a *please*, but Jake used to tease him about being weak-kneed and impulsive. Zeke couldn't show any weakness now, and he wasn't about to make any impulsive decisions. A woman's life depended on it. And the life of her child, too, if he was guessing right on her identity.

Jake shook his head and jammed the gun against the woman's ribs so hard, she cried out. But she quickly recovered, a determined grit in her expression. "It's not over until I have my son safely out of this country," he informed them. "I need to get Kevin. I'll be out of everyone's hair soon."

"You can't do that," Zeke said. "You don't want to take your son away from his mother."

Jake's gaze scanned the woods and trails. "What's left for me to do except leave? The Dupree family is shattered and their lieutenants are scattered to the wind. I'm on my own and…there's really no other way. I just want my son, so I'm going to get him. *Now.*"

He gripped Penny's arm and pushed her forward.

"I can't let you go," Zeke said, wondering if he'd have the courage to shoot his own half brother. Jake's desperate statement only made things worse. Turning his attention to the frightened woman, he asked, "Penny, are you okay?"

She gasped and nodded, her eyes filling with both relief and dread. Zeke could see the resolve in her gaze, too.

"She's fine," Jake gritted out, anger echoing in each word. "Turn around, Zeke. Let me get to my boy. I won't hurt her, I promise." Then he added, "And I don't want to shoot you again."

"I don't trust your promises," Zeke said. "I'm going to ask you one more time to drop your weapon."

With an angry grunt, Jake pulled Penny closer. "You need to behave, sweetheart. Because if you try anything, I'll kill him and come for you. Nod if you understand."

* * *

Penny nodded, her gaze latching onto the other man while she prayed Jake wouldn't kill either of them.

Jake kissed her on her temple, the heat of his lips burning her damp skin with a desperate heat. "I told you, I'm not leaving without my son."

He backed up, using her as a shield, and then pushed her a foot away, behind a towering pine. "Don't move, Penny. I mean it."

Confused and frightened, she scraped her knuckles against the rough bark while Jake stalked around the tree, giving her a possible means of escape. She could run now. Just leave them to duke this out. She could get Kevin and go as far away from here as possible. She'd done it before.

But the man who'd come to her rescue caused her to stay. She couldn't leave him here with Jake. He'd called her by her real name so he obviously recognized her, which could only mean they'd been digging into her past, too. Then Jake had called the man Zeke and *bro*. What did that mean? He'd never wanted to talk about himself or his family because of the classified nature of his job. None of this made any sense.

But if this man was a friend or a true brother, he hadn't come here for a family reunion. He was dressed in a bulletproof vest and wore a black cap over his crisp, dark hair that clearly read FBI. His partner was a sleek, fierce warrior. She'd always had a heart for dogs. This one was also marked as FBI.

"Hey, Penny. If you run, I'll kill him and his loyal partner, okay?" Jake said again, glancing at her with a threatening look. "But since we're all here together, I guess it would be rude of me not to make the proper introductions." He held his gun toward where the man called Zeke stood with feet braced apart and his deadly-looking rifle raised.

Before Jake could tell her who he was, the agent said, "Jake, man, don't do this. We all want to hear your side of the story. Your unit is worried about you."

This man was from Jake's unit!

"Who is he?" she asked Jake.

Keeping his eyes on the other man, Jake said, "Well, you always badgered me about my family, and now you get to meet my little brother, Zeke. Not the best of circumstances, but that can't be helped."

"You have a brother?" Penny asked, watching the man at the other end of this standoff. Hoping he could figure something out that would save both of them. He certainly looked capable. Muscular and confident, he stood ready for Jake's next move. But he also held a hint of hope that Jake would give up.

That should reassure her but…she was afraid none of them would get out of this alive.

Jake shook his head, his eyes wild, his gaze darting between her and Zeke. But he kept his pistol trained on the man and the canine. "Actually, he's only my half brother. We shared the same father but that's about it. My old man left *my* mother and *me* for his new family."

He said that with such disgust, Zeke flinched but recovered before Jake even noticed. But Penny noticed. Her heart went out to the man standing there, his rifle aimed at Jake. What must he be going through right now?

Two brothers, one good and one bad.

She couldn't walk away from this. Jake would keep

coming. She had to do something now. But which one did she trust?

Jake's next words confirmed that decision and told her what she had to do. "Now you know Kevin has an uncle, but he'll never get to meet Uncle Zeke." Raising the handgun at the same time he grabbed Penny and pinned her in front of him, he said with regret in each word, "I'm going to have to kill you, bro. You know too much." His grip tightened on Penny. "You *both* know too much."

Zeke inched forward, the canine following. "Jake, think about this. Don't make things worse for yourself. Let her go and you and I can talk."

"No more talking," Jake said. Then he held the gun closer and moved it up to Penny's heart. "Back off or I'll kill her right now. I'm not playing. I have to get out of here. With Kevin."

Penny's gaze slammed into Zeke's shocked expression. She'd dropped her backpack when Jake had shoved her at the tree, and she couldn't reach it now. Panic-stricken, she looked around for a weapon. Anything would suffice. Glancing back at Zeke, she tried to send him a silent message. She made a big deal about looking past him as if she saw someone else. Straining forward, she shouted, "Jake, did you see that? I think someone's in the woods."

It was enough to cause her ex to lift his head and glance around. He shifted, his hard-edged gaze sweeping the area.

Penny slumped against him again, causing him to shift. She slipped down and grabbed a jagged piece of rock and managed to twist toward Jake, her arm raised as she lifted the stone toward him while his arms went up in the air. She'd been a softball pitcher in high school so she could pretty much aim for any sweet spot far away. But up close, it was too hard. Thinking quickly, she aimed for the weapon in his outstretched hand. The heavy rock made contact enough against the gun for Jake to lose his grip. His gun flipped out into the air and fell a few feet away.

"You shouldn't have done that, Penny," he snapped as he shoved her onto her back and slid toward the weapon.

Zeke shouted at her, "Run. Go. Get out of here!"

The canine started barking and snarling.

Then the FBI agent shouted again, "Run!"

Penny grabbed her backpack as she headed into the woods. Her cell phone was inside. She could call the inn and warn Claire.

Gunshots went off. The FBI agent commanded, "Attack!"

Glancing back, she saw Jake roll and then hop up, the gun now aimed at the dog as he ran ahead of the barking canine, shooting to keep him away. But the dog was quick. He nipped at Jake's booted foot, his teeth sinking deep.

Her ex grunted and let out a string of curses, all the while fighting to get free of Cheetah. But his efforts failed. His pants ripped and he managed to get up and stumble forward, the dog still on his heels.

Penny couldn't stop to watch.

The whiz of a bullet hit a tree near her. She heard the shots and realized Jake was making good on his word to try to kill her.

She heard more shots and pivoted around. Her crazy ex was now shooting toward the dog.

Zeke began returning fire. The medium-sized dog

was becoming more and more aggressive, barking angrily and dancing away from the continuous shots. The animal would gain on Jake again any second now. Penny turned and ducked behind a tree just as the dog leaped into the air and headed toward her assailant.

But Jake took one more shot and disappeared into the woods.

Zeke came hurrying by. "Stay there," he told her on a rushed breath.

Then Jake shouted from somewhere above her on some rocks, "Call off your partner, Zeke. I have Penny in my sights and I will take out her and the dog. You know I'm a good shot."

The words echoed out over the woods like an eerie wail. As if to prove he could do it, Jake shot above Penny's head. She ducked and held her breath.

Then she saw Jake running through the rough terrain in a zigzag pattern. Heard him shout, "I'm taking him, Penny. None of you can stop me."

He fired another round of shots, causing Zeke to rush toward Penny and push her down, his big body shielding hers.

"Halt," Zeke called to the canine barking loudly at the rock formation.

Cheetah whirled and stopped.

"Come," Zeke called again, the reluctance and frustration obvious in his tone.

The obedient dog returned and stood watch, his beautiful heavy fur quivering with awareness.

"Why did you let him go?" Penny shrieked at Zeke while she struggled to get up. But he was still blocking her, protecting her. Then she stared into his chocolate-brown eyes. The anguish she saw there only mirrored what she'd been feeling for the last few months.

Something swift and sizzling arced between them in a flash of emotion.

"I had to for now," Zeke replied softly as he placed his hands on either side of her shoulders and got up. Helping her to her feet, he added, "I know my brother. He'd shoot you and Cheetah, or he'd ambush us later. He wants you dead so he can take my nephew."

"*Your* nephew?"

"Yes," he replied, defiance in his eyes. "Kevin is my nephew. I have to get to him before Jake does."

She agreed with him there but wasn't so ready to accept him as Kevin's uncle. That sounded way too personal right now.

They'd discuss the rest of this later. "You're going after him even though you just let him slip through your fingers?" she asked, still in shock and worried about her son, still reeling from Zeke's touch and the way his dark eyes had probed her.

He placed a gentle hand on her elbow and steered her through the woods and underneath the shelter of a giant rock near a pine tree. "Right now, I'm going after Jake." Then he turned to the canine. "Cheetah, guard."

Penny looked from the dog now standing in front of her back at Zeke. "Oh, no. I'm not sitting here while my son is in danger." She tried to move past him.

Zeke held her back down. "Listen, I'm going up ahead to look for my brother, but we've got backup in the area. You need to stay here and wait for one of them to arrive, understand? Now, tell me where your son is right now so I can send someone to check on him."

Penny didn't hesitate on that. Holding her hand to

her sweat-dampened hair, she said, "The Wild Iris Inn on Elk Rock Road. Just inside the town limits. Claire is the owner and she babysits for me. He's with her. I need to—"

"Stay here," Zeke commanded. "Cheetah won't let anyone come near you."

"And if your partner here gets shot?"

He pulled a handgun out of his shoulder holster. "Do you know how to use a weapon?"

She nodded. "My grandfather taught me."

"Good. Then you know what to do with this one. You've got seventeen rounds. One already in the chamber, safety off. When the magazine is empty, run as fast as you can to the main road."

With that, he took off. "Hurry," she called, thinking she'd go where she wanted after he left. "Jake could be at the inn right now. He said he had a van stashed somewhere."

"Got it," Zeke responded, already running away.

Penny tried to move but the dog moved with her. Blocking her. Feeling helpless, she searched for one of the trails. The canine gave her a daring eye-to-eye stare. Too good at his job.

Frustration gnawed at her. What more could she do? Feeling lost and so very alone, she prayed, tears falling fast and hard down her face. *Please, Lord, help me now.*

"Please don't let it be too late for my son," she said out loud. The courageous animal standing in front of her looked at her with doleful eyes, as if he understood her prayers.

Penny reached out a hand, wanting to pull her protector close. But Cheetah was trained to do what Zeke told him. He stood straight and on the alert, his eyes never leaving her face.

Then she heard what sounded like a vehicle to the east. The sound echoed over the quiet woods. Crouching, she whispered to Cheetah, "What if Jake's coming back?"

The dog turned his head toward the sound but still didn't move. Penny held her breath and listened, her adrenaline spiking. Could she really do it? Could she use this weapon to kill the father of her child?

THREE

Penny stayed crouched behind the rock, her heartbeat pounding against her temples like a jackhammer. A black van pulled up on one of the trails, and a man wielding a gun got out and scanned the woods. Penny tried to make out his face, but he was too far away and the shifting light was too low. Barely breathing, she watched as Cheetah stayed with her and stood so still she thought the dog had turned to stone. The canine emitted a low growl, the dare in that whisper of aggression telling her she was safe with him.

But the man kept coming, slowly, deliberately, as if he knew exactly where she was hiding. Penny decided she wasn't going to wait around and find out. Lifting the weighty handgun, she checked the safety and put her sights on the man. She hadn't fired a gun since Jake had taken her to target practice so long ago. Could she shoot another human being?

Taking another long look at him, she tried to memorize details of his description. He wore dark glasses and had longish, stringy blond hair. He wasn't very tall but he was brawny and in good shape.

The henchman advanced but Cheetah's growls grew

louder, causing the assailant to glance up in shock and pivot back and forth. He started backing away, a definite fear in his eyes.

Penny used that fear to give her courage. Lifting up, she aimed and shot into the air near where the man stood, hoping Zeke would hear and come back. The man took off running. Cheetah's barks now turned brutal and loud.

The man hopped back in the van and started it up. Penny raised the gun again and shot toward the moving target. She missed but she thought she heard something else over the sound of the dog's barks.

The cries of a child.

Zeke followed the trail of broken bramble and loose rocks along the craggy ridge, stopping to take a photo each time he saw drops of blood on the rocks or dirt. Cheetah had at least injured his brother. Probably not a deep bite since Jake had been wearing heavy leather boots, but enough that a crime scene tech could get a sample to back up whatever Penny could tell them. The K-9 team could gather evidence and get it to Billings. They all wanted Jake.

Deciding he couldn't keep going along blindly, Zeke stopped at the top of the ridge and glanced down through the woods. It was hard to see with the growing dusk but he stilled and waited. Nothing. Jake had to be hiding down there somewhere but until help arrived, he had no choice but to turn around. He didn't want to leave Penny alone. Pivoting, he heard a crashing noise down below. Could be an animal or it could be his brother on the move again. He hurried to check it out.

The sound of gunshots in the area where he'd left

Penny had him running back in that direction instead. When he heard Cheetah's fierce bark, he knew she was in trouble. Had Jake set up yet another distraction so he could get to Penny?

After what seemed like hours but had only been a few minutes, Zeke returned, winded, fatigue coloring his eyes.

Rushing up to where she sat against the tree with the gun held tightly against her, tears streaming down her face, he sank onto the ground by her. "Cheetah, sit." Then he gently cupped Penny's arms in his hands. "Are you okay?"

She handed Zeke his gun, thankful that he'd come back so quickly. But she was so scared of what she might have done it took her a while to speak. "A black van, big with no windows. A man got out and searched the area. I decided to scare him away so I shot toward him." With each word, she began to sob in earnest.

Zeke nodded, concern deepening his frown. "Good, that's good. Did you get a look at him?"

She swallowed, trying desperately to tamp down the fear that assailed her. "Yes. Not too tall. Long, stringy blond hair and glasses. And a really big rifle." Then she grabbed his shirt. "Zeke, I can't be sure since it all happened so fast and Cheetah was barking, but I... I think I heard a cry. Inside the van." The terror took over and she started shaking. "I think I heard a child crying." Then she fell against him, the sick fear engulfing her, the reality of her fears paralyzing her. "Zeke, I shot at the man and I missed. But I heard a child's cry." Pulling away, she stared up at him. "What if my son's in that van?"

Zeke's eyes went wide. Lifting her up, he pulled her closer and looked down at her. "We're going to the inn. We'll find Kevin." Then, still holding her near, he took out his phone and reported everything she'd just told him. "Yes, sir. We'll be there as soon as we can get back to my vehicle."

He ended the call and turned to her. "Let's get you back to the inn."

She tugged at his arm and pointed toward the road. "We need to go after them. They went that way. I... I have to find Kevin."

She started to go around him and tried to reach for her backpack.

"I'll get it." He snatched up the flower-encased bundle, their gazes locking for a brief moment. "Let's go."

Zeke pulled her with him across the rocky terrain at a furious trot. "My SAC—special agent in charge— Max West, and another agent are already headed to the Wild Iris, and the whole team is here and scattered throughout the woods. We've put out a BOLO on the van and we've got Jake's face plastered all over the news and social media outlets. Max made sure the locals put out an APB."

"So you didn't see him anywhere?"

"No," Zeke said. "But I did find blood on some of the rocks. I gave Max the locations so the crime scene techs can do a sweep of the area."

We had him. Penny wished they could have stopped Jake but everything happened so fast. She prayed Kevin was safe, prayed she'd been imagining those wails. She had shot toward that van but thankfully, she'd missed.

Dear God, please, please. I couldn't bear it if my child were kidnapped. She wished this was just a horrible nightmare. Each step seemed like an eternity and each time she glanced back, she expected Jake to be trailing them.

Then she halted and gasped. "I remember something Jake said earlier."

"What?" Zeke queried, swiping at buzzing bugs.

"He said he had a van waiting. 'We'll have Kevin.' Then he went on talking about how we'd leave together."

Realization filled Zeke's eyes. "That does make it sound like Kevin would already be in the van."

She bobbed her head. "Yes, yes. I think I heard my baby crying." Putting her hands to her mouth, she tried to take another breath. "Zeke, what if Jake holding me here was all a distraction so that man could get to Kevin? And now…he could be hurt or—"

Zeke let out a frustrated sigh and took her into his arms. "Penny, think. Where did the shot land?"

She closed her eyes. "It hit a few feet in front of the van, thankfully."

"So if Kevin was in the van, he'd probably be in the back, maybe in a crib or a seat, or you could have heard something else." Softening his tone, he tucked a loose strand of hair behind her ear. "Don't think the worst until we can get to the inn, okay?"

She glanced up at him, wanting to believe him. "Okay. Hurry anyway. We need to find out."

Zeke started going over things, his voice calm while her heart screamed in agony. "We know someone else was with Jake. I have an eyewitness for that. And they were in a black van. Then you probably saw the same van. The locals and the FBI are searching for it right now."

"That person could have Kevin already and they

could be leaving *right now.* Can you check? Talk to your person?"

Zeke took out his phone again and made the call. "Yes, sir. Tell them to hurry." Then he turned to her. "We've got people at the inn. We'll hear soon."

Penny felt sick, her knees weak. "Hurry, Zeke. Please. We're wasting time. He went west on the main road."

He urged her forward. "We can't get anywhere without my vehicle."

When they reached a clearing, Zeke scanned the entire area and watched his canine for any signs of a scent. The dog sniffed the air and the ground and looked toward where they'd been before.

"I'll get you there," he promised her, his eyes as dark as the tree bark. "I can't let you out of my sight now."

She nodded, glad he'd moved quickly. "I need to call Claire."

He guided her to the SUV and came around to the driver's side.

Before she could dig for her cell phone, Zeke pulled the official-looking sleek black phone out of his pocket. "Make the call."

Penny dialed the number to the inn and waited. "She's not answering. Something's wrong."

Zeke took the phone back and pressed on the gas pedal. "We'll be there in five minutes. In the meantime, we've got people already going over the area where I found you with Jake. They're searching for the van and they might find something we missed."

Penny nodded and listened while he spoke to someone about the location. She was still shaking and the blast of cold air coming from the vehicle's air-conditioning made her shiver even more. Interrupting his conversation, she said, "I think we should have tried to find the van. I can identify it. Should we turn around?"

Zeke noticed her discomfort and hit the button to turn down the airflow. After discussing the situation with his superior again, he dropped his cell phone into a cup holder between them. "I have to protect you and Kevin. He'll keep coming for you. I'm to get you to the inn first. It's too dangerous to go chasing after that vehicle."

Frustration roared through Penny. "I was right there! I should have killed that man and looked inside myself."

Zeke reached over and gripped her arm. "Listen to me, Penny. In situations like this, it's always best if the parents stay out of the way and let us do our jobs. My team is one of the best. You need to take a breath and trust us."

"I know," she said, wondering how she'd ever find her next breath. "I know." She couldn't voice the terror ripping her apart. *What if it's too late? What then?*

Zeke zoomed the sleek SUV around curves and along dirt roads and watched the rearview mirror. Cheetah stayed in the back in a roomy kennel. She felt safe with these two, but Penny couldn't relax until she knew Kevin was safe.

When they got to the Wild Iris and saw a local police officer standing with two FBI agents holding canines on leashes, her heart sank. "I have to find my baby," she cried, hopping out of the vehicle before Zeke could turn off the motor.

She ran toward the big, two-story house, every cell in her body on overload. "Kevin? Kevin, Mommy's here."

An officer stopped her at the wide stained glass front door. "Ma'am, you can't go in there."

"She's with me," Zeke said, showing the officer his ID. "Her two-year-old son could be in danger."

"He's gone," Rex Harmon said when Penny rushed inside, shaking his head. Rex, an avid hiker, had a room across from hers. "That man—he had a gun and he took the little boy."

"No!" Penny put a hand to her mouth and moaned, a sick feeling pooling inside her stomach. "No…"

"What did he look like?" Zeke asked, pulling out a picture of his half brother. "Is this him?"

"Nah," the older man said. "This thug was short and muscular with long, greasy blond hair and funky eyeglasses. He got into a beat-up old black van."

Zeke's eyes flared with awareness, his gaze hitting on Penny. She grabbed onto a chair, her worst nightmares coming to the surface. The same man she'd seen in the woods. Kevin had been right there, inside that van. She could have saved him.

"Do you know that man?" she asked Zeke, each word a struggle, each beat of her pulse a condemnation.

He nodded. "Possibly. But we'll figure that out later."

"Was this man in the van?" Penny demanded, her finger jabbing at the picture of Jake.

"No," Rex said, sympathy in his eyes. "He was alone but he overpowered Miss Claire and hit her on the head. I heard her scream and I saw him with the boy. Miss Claire was hurt but she got to her shotgun. Only he had a gun, too, and he pointed it at the kid when we both ordered him to stop. Miss Claire dropped her gun and the man got in the van with your son and left." He glanced from the officers to Penny. "I tried to get a license plate but it was all rusted out." He gave Penny an apologetic look and waved a hand at all the officers swarming around. "I was about to call you when they showed up."

Penny's stomach twisted and recoiled. A cold sweat crept up and down her spine. She sank down on the stairs and pushed at her hair. "Is Miss Claire okay?"

"She's fine," Rex said. "She's in her room with a female officer. The EMTs looked her over but she won't go to the hospital."

Penny stood, dizziness overcoming her. Zeke reached out to her and guided her to a chair. "I'll find him. I promise. You stay here while I go and check on your babysitter."

He asked Rex to bring her some water. The front door swung open and another man wearing an FBI vest entered, along with another canine. She'd seen them outside and heard Zeke introduce him as Special Agent in Charge Max West. He had short, spiked blond hair and blue eyes that seemed to stare everyone down, but like Zeke, he seemed confident and born to be in charge. She also noticed a jagged scar on his left cheek.

That only reminded her of how dangerous this situation had become. Jake had sent someone to kidnap her son and now he was at their mercy. That man could have killed Claire and Rex, too.

She watched, impatient and numb, while FBI agents and K-9 dogs filled the inn, their presence a sharp contrast to the dainty furnishings and heirloom antiques placed all around the Victorian-style mansion turned boardinghouse.

Max West gathered all of them around and explained

what would transpire next. Roadblocks, an Amber Alert, all train and bus stations made aware, all flights out of nearby airports monitored. And all agents out on the hunt.

Penny put her head in her hands and prayed. Helplessness weighed her down, a sense of doom and despair causing her to catch her breath. Why, oh, why, had she come back to Montana?

Law enforcement set up electronic equipment on every available spot and stomped over the braided rugs and slammed the stained glass doors, moving, while she sat there, frozen in a nightmare. She had to do something, *anything*, to find her little boy.

Agent West came over to her and asked her several rapid-fire questions about Jake. Did he say where he was headed? What did he look like? What kind of weapons was he carrying? Did he mention an accomplice?

He explained to her that they were aware she'd been on the run and why. They knew she'd been in a chalet in Colorado earlier in the summer. Had Jake come after her there?

Penny nodded and answered all the questions, anger warring with fear and regret. "I came back here because… I wanted my son to be here, close to where I grew up. I thought I was safe."

"Did you come here hoping Jake would find you? Did he arrange to meet you out in the Basin area?"

"No."

Fury roiled through her. Did they actually think she'd wanted this? That she wanted to be sitting here, paralyzed with fear, wondering if her son was alive or dead?

Finally, Penny lifted her head and said, "He planned

to go live on a tropical island, and he said he has a lot of money stashed somewhere but I don't know where. He wants my son, not me. I didn't want him around Kevin, and I sure don't want him taking my son away from me. The man tried to kill me. Why are you questioning me when you should be out there searching for Kevin?"

Max West gave her a stern but sympathetic stare. "We're doing everything we can to help us find your son, Penny. We've taken prints on everyone who works here or is staying here, and we have officers going door-to-door around this area to see if we can find any leads or get any eyewitnesses. Don't go anywhere."

"I *know* who took my son," she said, her voice rising. "Why aren't you listening to me? I was an eyewitness. Up close. So close, I feared for my life. Go and find my son before it's too late."

Zeke pulled Max aside and said something into his ear. The other man shot a frown at her. Did he know what she was afraid of, what was tearing through her racing mind?

Zeke came over and bent down in front of her. "It's highly unlikely that they'd hurt Kevin, Penny. You have to keep telling yourself that. Jake wants him, so he would order them not to harm him."

Closing her eyes to the shattering nerves breaking apart piece by piece throughout her core, she said, "Sure. And while I'm at it, I'll keep telling myself that Jake doesn't have him in that van headed to another getaway car or to the airport."

Zeke stared at her for a brief moment but one of the other agents called him. "I'll be right back." Then he whirled around. "And, Penny, don't go anywhere, understand? That would only make this worse."

Penny didn't believe it could get much worse but if they didn't do something soon, she would sneak out to her Jeep and do whatever she had to do to find Kevin. And she'd take Claire's shotgun with her.

FOUR

Fifteen minutes passed and Penny didn't think she could take another moment of waiting. Here she sat, wringing her hands, the sound of people talking around her drowned out by the emptiness clamoring inside her heart. "Kevin," she whispered, closing her eyes. "Kevin."

"Oh, honey, I'm so sorry."

She opened her eyes to find Claire Crayton gingerly stepping down the stairs, a bright red bump shining on her forehead. Claire had been so kind to Penny when she'd pulled up in the parking lot a month ago, on her last ounce of gasoline, Kevin crying in his car seat. Claire had booked them a room immediately and offered to babysit anytime Penny needed her.

"I tried to stop him but he hit me hard with his gun and I went down like a rock. Grabbed my gun but…he held the child and…" The older woman's eyes watered and her voice wobbled to a halt. "He took our precious boy. It's my fault, too."

"It wasn't your fault," Penny said, standing to wrap her hands around Claire's plump, comforting shoulders, her own eyes wet with tears, her own bruises and scratches burning from the salt. "It's my fault. I knew his daddy was dangerous, but I never dreamed he'd send a henchman to kidnap my son."

Then she started sobbing against Claire's plaid shirt, the scent of rose water and cinnamon cookies overtaking her. "I want him back, Claire. I want my little boy back."

A strong hand touched her on the arm.

Zeke.

His dark eyes held the same despair that raged through her, raw and jagged and burning. He placed her back in the nearby chair and kneeled in front of her again, his eyes on her. "Listen, we've got people out looking already, and we've put out an Amber Alert. But I need you to take me to the room where Kevin sleeps, okay? Cheetah can pick up his scent. It hasn't been that long, so if I hurry I can locate him."

"Did the others search his room?"

"Yes, but they were looking for clues regarding the kidnapper. They're searching for him while others are searching for Kevin. Both of them, really. I want to focus more on Kevin since Cheetah is trained in search and rescue." Touching a hand to her arm, he leaned in. "I promise I'm going to do everything in my power to bring Kevin back to you."

"I'm going with you to search," she said, standing and hurrying up the stairs, her heart beating just as fast as her hiking boots.

Zeke took off after her. "No."

"Yes." She stopped on the second-floor landing and turned at the first door on the left. "This is our room. I have the bedroom and he sleeps here in the living room in this crib."

Pointing to a large mahogany baby bed full of blankets and sheets decked out in a cowboy design, she walked over and picked up a stuffed brown horse, tears streaming down her face. Holding it close before she handed it to Zeke, anguish cutting through her, she said, "I'm going with you. Do you understand?"

Zeke let out a sigh, compassion in his dark eyes, and leaned down so Cheetah could get a good sniff of the worn horse. The canine lifted his snout, his ears perking up. "Yes, I understand. And since I need to keep you alive, I will go along with it. But Penny, you have to stay out of the way, okay?"

"Okay." She wiped away tears and lifted her head, staring at him with a dangerous resolve in her heart. After grabbing some baby supplies and shoving them into a diaper bag, she turned to him. "Let's go."

Zeke's head pounded with fatigue and tension ten times worse than foot soldiers stomping on his brain, but he followed Cheetah through the house and out to the SUV. Penny had insisted on gathering up some things for Kevin, including the little stuffed horse she'd clung to while the techs went over her room. Cheetah had hopefully picked up the kidnapper's scent, too, since the man had been in the house.

Zeke had to make this right.

The situation here was under control so he needed to be out there looking. The Wild Iris had become ground zero to set up operations to find Kevin and Jake. Locals and FBI alike scoured the grounds and had laptops out on top of their vehicles, searching with maps and following leads on tips. They'd had calls about sightings of three different vans in three different areas, but none of them had panned out. This could take all night. Max had assigned Nina Atkins, the petite blonde rookie who'd recently joined the team, to stay at the inn along with a couple of other agents and two locals. Nina and her K-9 partner, Sam, a cadaver-detection-trained Rottweiler, were to watch over Claire and the staff and residents. Whoever took Kevin wouldn't like leaving behind witnesses.

Claire and her crew went to work on bringing them food and drinks and offered whatever else they needed in the way of comfort. Rex answered the phone and explained the situation to the few other boarders who'd drifted in from work or travels and directed traffic to the restrooms and the coffeepot.

Vehicles kept coming and going. But no sightings had brought any substantial information, and they'd had no word on any solid leads even though the local citizens were being vigilant about helping. No one liked to hear of a child being kidnapped. Zeke couldn't let Penny see his own anxiety, but the dread pooling inside his stomach made that last cup of coffee he'd downed turn sour.

Jake was a master at setting up distractions and false scenarios. It had been one of his best assets as an agent. He'd certainly proved that today but not in a good way. Worried, Zeke knew his brother could charm just about anyone into doing his bidding.

He'd obviously gone to a lot of trouble to set things up so that while he was holding Penny and shoving her through the woods, his accomplice, Gunther Caprice, had kidnapped Kevin.

Zeke wished with all his heart he could have hauled his brother in. But even then, Gunther could have been long gone with Kevin. That thought chilled Zeke to his bones.

To make matters worse, Max wasn't too happy with him right now. Zeke had Jake in his sights and had let him get away. The whole unit probably thought he'd allowed his half brother to escape. He'd get things straight with Max and the others later. Right now, he was worried about the woman trailing behind him. Trying to get a handle of things, he studied her closely. If he was going to protect her and Kevin, he needed to figure out who exactly he was dealing with.

She was pretty in an outdoorsy kind of way. All golden skinned and toned, not an ounce of wasted fat on her. Probably worked out on a daily basis. Her hair was cut in choppy shoulder-length layers that sprouted out like waves of wheat around her triangular face. Her eyes were almond shaped and a crystal clear blue. Not piercing like Max's, but more of a clear-sky blue that reflected her heart.

And that heart was breaking right now. To be so close to her little boy and realize she'd been so near the vehicle that might have been holding him, not to mention that Kevin was somewhere with a lowlife like Gunther Caprice. No wonder the woman was in shock.

She rushed ahead of him down the stairs with her ever-present backpack and a big diaper bag over one shoulder, a staunch determination in those Montana-blue eyes.

Zeke also let Cheetah smell the baby blanket Penny had given him. Cheetah sniffed the soft wool and lifted his head to sniff the air. Then he headed to the end of the drive and sniffed around before lifting his snout toward the west.

They made it through the maze of officers and staff roaming through the quaint old house and hit the porch steps as if they were in a race against each other.

Opening the SUV's back door with a remote key, Zeke commanded Cheetah to jump in and turned to find Max West coming his way.

"Going somewhere, Agent Morrow?"

Zeke wasn't in the mood for orders. He agreed with Penny that the sooner they got out there searching, the better. "Yes, I'm going to find my nephew."

"Not so sure that's a good idea," Max said. "You do know we have people out there already searching, right?"

Zeke didn't want to be argumentative but he would stand his ground. "Cheetah has the boy's scent, sir, and you know he's trained for this. I need to find Kevin while the trail is fresh." Then he leaned in. "As I told you in my report, I think we're looking for Gunther Caprice. He fits the description that science teacher gave me earlier and the description Rex gave us. The man saw him drive away from the basin in a black van. And later, Penny saw the same man, same vehicle, just like I told you."

Caprice used to be third in line with the Dupree clan and had once been chummy with Violetta Dupree—sister to the crime brothers—but he'd fallen on hard times and broke off with them when the FBI had captured Reginald Dupree in a raid close to six months ago. His uncle Angus had gotten away, taking Jake with him, but now Angus was dead. That left a lot of people scattered and scared. Had Gunther joined up with Jake for money or for revenge? Jake had edged him out, after all.

If Jake's accomplice was in fact Gunther Caprice,

they could get a wealth of information out of that man. He'd been missing and wanted for questioning for months and now, suddenly, he was back in the picture. Jake had obviously made him an offer he couldn't refuse. But Gunther couldn't be trusted to keep Kevin alive. That lowlife was only out to save his own sorry hide.

Max's phone buzzed and he held up a hand and took the call, indicating he wasn't through with this conversation. "Is that right?" He eyed Zeke. "I've got an agent about to leave now." He ended the call and turned to Zeke. "Your timing is perfect. A man and woman on a motorcycle heard the reports and spotted a black van about five miles from here, driving west on Old Fork Road out of town."

Penny gasped when she heard their conversation from her spot by the passenger door, her gaze slamming into Zeke's. "That has to be him."

"I'm on it," Zeke said. "Cheetah sniffed the spot where the van was parked here and he's already tracking in that direction."

"You'll take backup." Max motioned to another agent, who hurried over. After explaining the situation to team member Harper Prentiss, who held her German shepherd, Star, on a leash, Max nodded and pinned Penny with a solemn stare. "Miss Potter, you really should stay here and wait—"

"I'm going to find my son," she said, the resolve in her words and eyes telling Max they couldn't stop her. "I can't sit here and wait, and you can't make me."

Zeke glanced at Max. "I'd feel better if I can keep an eye on her, sir."

"Morrow, we have eyes on her now and it's safer if she stays here—"

"Stop arguing about me," Penny interjected. "We're running out of time. I'm going to find Kevin, with or without either of you."

Max West looked from Zeke to Penny, surprise and a grudging acceptance in his expression. "Well, I *won't* feel better but... I'm holding you responsible for her, Zeke." He lifted a hand. "Go. Do what you have to do and this time if you find Jake, don't let him get away."

Zeke nodded and opened the door for Penny, now fully aware that his superior did think he had *purposely* let his half brother slip through his fingers. And maybe he had. He could have let Cheetah corner Jake or continue to go after him. But his K-9 partner needed to stay with Penny while Jake tried to ascertain which direction Jake might have gone. When he'd found only footprints and bloodstains on those rocks, he knew Jake had been nearby.

Had he made the right call, giving up the chase to run back to Penny? He'd heard enough about Jake lately to understand his brother would kill anyone or anything to get what he wanted. He remembered that dark side of Jake, had seen it come out at the oddest times. Jake would have shot Penny without any remorse. A while back, he'd tied up Harper in a cave in Colorado, and after telling her he was corrupt and he liked having money and power, he'd left her there where she could have died if she hadn't ordered K-9 Star to chew apart the ropes holding her. Jake had no qualms about killing a canine or a human.

Zeke had to protect the woman Jake had threatened to kill. He'd made the only choice he could, but now he had a second chance to capture his traitorous brother and see justice done.

Penny got in the SUV, a look of relief mixed with the anxiety marring her expression. "Thank you."

"For what?" he asked gruffly.

"For standing up to your boss."

"I wasn't just standing up to him," Jake replied. "I meant it when I said I plan to protect you. No matter what."

She shot him a surprised but grateful look. "I appreciate that but right now you need to find my little boy."

"I'm going to."

Zeke checked with Max again, hoping for any reports that could help. "I've got Cheetah by an open window and we're heading west, sir. Old Fork Road. We're on the road now but nothing yet."

"Stay on it and be careful," Max replied. "I'll send backup if you and Harper need it." Then he added, "Zeke, I know he's your brother and you want to keep him alive but—"

"I understand," Zeke bit out. "I know my duty, Max."

He ended the call and slung his phone into a cup holder.

"I'm surprised they haven't yanked you off this case," Penny said. "It must be hard, tracking him down like this."

"My job," Zeke retorted, wondering if she wanted to pick a fight.

She didn't say anything else and he regretted being sharp with her. "It's not easy but…if I can get to him first I might be able to take him in instead of—"

"Killing him," she finished. Then she went silent again.

Zeke had to wonder how she felt about that. Did she still love Jake in spite of everything?

Anxious to get this over with, Zeke turned the truck toward the west and started searching for the road they needed. He prayed they'd also find the thug who'd taken Kevin before the man could meet up with Jake Morrow. Because if that happened, he feared they might not ever see Penny's son again.

FIVE

Zeke tried to keep her talking while he kept watch on Cheetah in the back, his snout searching the air and the woods rolling by. He told Penny he needed to hear her story and gather any details she might remember. But she knew he was just as curious about her as she was about him. He obviously didn't trust her since she'd been involved with Jake. She couldn't blame him for that. Look where it had gotten her.

"How did you meet Jake?"

She swallowed and held tight to the bottle of water in her hand, memories she'd tried to bury coming to the surface. "I'm a wilderness guide," she said, her voice raw and low. How could she talk about this when Kevin was out there, afraid and in the clutches of dangerous criminals? But she did talk. Anything to keep from crawling out of her skin. "We literally ran into each other a couple of years ago on a hiking trail."

"He hiked a lot," Zeke recalled. "All over the world."

Shooting Zeke a quick glance, she added, "He wasn't out on a leisurely hike that day. He told me he was a federal agent and explained how it could get dangerous for me to be in the area." She smiled but it hurt to do so since every muscle in her body was coiled like rappelling rope. "But he hurried back and asked for my phone number, in case I saw anyone suspicious. He called me the next night but it wasn't regarding the case."

Looking straight ahead, she said, "We were inseparable after that. He had some downtime once he finished the case and...we spent two weeks together, hiking, kayaking and fishing. He even made me practice my shooting skills. But after I had Kevin, I didn't want a gun in the house."

She stopped, gulping in the air she couldn't seem to find. "I don't want to go down memory lane, Zeke. It hurts too much. Can't you make this SUV go any faster?"

Zeke reached out and squeezed her hand. "Penny, don't think about that shot you made. You didn't know—"

"I should have been more careful," she choked out. "I can't get the sound of those cries out of my mind."

"The noise could have scared Kevin," he said. To reassure her, he added softly, "Besides, we haven't confirmed that Kevin is with the suspect."

She shook her head and wiped her eyes. "I should know. A mother would feel that and when I heard that baby cry out, I knew in my heart it was Kevin. Jake would at least get Kevin to a doctor if he's hurt, right?"

"I have to believe that, yes," Zeke said, the look in his eyes full of concern. "Jake wasn't always this bad. Obviously, you saw some of the good in him."

She shot Zeke an anguished look. "He sweet-talked me into seeing the good, yes. Which makes me pathetic."

"He always was a sweet-talker," Zeke said. "Jake has charisma and he can persuade people with a flash of his dimples. He usually had a pretty girl hanging on his arm."

Penny took in a breath at hearing that. "I certainly fell right into that pattern with him. I ignored that nagging feeling in my heart that made me question his long absences and all the secrecy. He was probably off having flings with other women the whole time he was with me."

Zeke shot her an apologetic stare. "I'm sorry, I shouldn't have said that. I don't know much about his escapades except what he deemed fit to tell me."

"It's okay," she replied, her head down. "I've turned my life around because of Kevin. My faith is strong now. I can overcome what Jake did to me but right now, I want to find my son."

Stopping between two roads, Zeke glanced back to where Cheetah sniffed the air again. When he seemed satisfied that they were still on the right path, Zeke turned southwest and said, "Jake fooled me, too. For a while there after he joined the FBI, he had me thinking we could be true brothers. Even encouraged me to follow in his footsteps to become a law officer."

"He never mentioned you," Penny said, wishing she'd known all of this from the beginning. She could have reached out to Zeke and maybe helped with the search for Jake. But instead, she'd run away like a coward.

You were trying to protect Kevin.

But she'd failed at that when she'd returned here.

If she'd reported Jake's demands to the authorities all those months ago, she might not be searching for her son right now.

That realization made her blurt out one of the things gnawing at her. "I have to wonder if Jake contacted me that last time only to get information on whether your team was searching for him. He asked a few pointed questions about anyone coming around to see me, but he promised he'd take care of us. I'm not used to depending on a man but I sure wanted to believe him. For a while I did believe him." Pushing her fingers through her hair, she said, "But everything changed."

"How so?" Zeke asked, his eyes on the road.

She took a sip of water. "He called one day out of the blue but sounded kind of off, you know? He kept referring to his days at Quantico and how this job meant so much to him, how people trusted him and depended on him. Then he said something else that struck me as odd. He said he'd lost trust in the FBI and his connections at Quantico and he wasn't sure about anything anymore. He wasn't sure of his next step. And that's not like Jake."

"No, it's not. But I can see him wanting to be able to take care of you, so maybe not being able to do that had him worried," Zeke said, his gaze sliding over her face. "You're pretty and capable. Jake likes strength in women. He must have admired that about you."

"I don't feel so strong," she whispered, another distant memory nagging at her. She'd doubted Jake's faithfulness to her many times and thinking of Quantico only reminded her of that. She was pretty sure he'd been close to someone he'd gone through training with since she'd found a picture in some of his stuff. One of him with a female recruit. But when she'd asked him about it, he refused to talk to her about anything related to work. She sighed, knowing she should mention this to Zeke, but she wasn't ready to share yet another shameful truth with him.

Pushing all that away, she said, "As I said before,

I'm tired of going down memory lane. I want my son back." The ache of not knowing if Kevin was okay cut like a knife slowly slashing at her insides.

"We'll find the man who took Kevin," Zeke promised. "Cheetah can pick up vapor scents in the air and any other kind of scent on the ground. He's a smart, highly trained K-9 officer. One of the best."

Penny looked back at Cheetah. The furry dog gave her a long stare to reassure her. She knew Zeke was trying hard to keep her sane, but right now her insides burned with a raw ache and every nerve in her body hummed with the need to find her child.

"Why don't you tell me what you think about Jake?" she asked, hoping to take her mind off the horror of not having her son with her. "Did he and his mother get along?"

"He used to say Velma Morrow was weak," Zeke said. "She died a few years ago and Jake barely made it to the funeral. He left right after the service and after that, things seemed to shift between us. We stayed close but his moods changed like quicksilver, so I never knew what to expect with him."

Penny could relate to that. "He was moody and he'd hold everything inside. I never knew what he'd been through. He talked about a few friends he'd made along the way, but nothing too revealing." She blew out a frustrated breath. "I wish he'd told me about his past. About you. You'd think he'd mention having a half brother and that you worked for the FBI, too."

"He's always been secretive," Zeke said. "But now he's in a bad way. Too late for him to turn this around."

He sounded almost sympathetic, but Penny refused to feel sorry for Jake right now.

"According to my mom, our dad was also moody and easy to anger," Zeke continued. "But he could be a real charmer when he wanted something. He was a successful lawyer and my mom worked in his law firm as a secretary. She fell hard for him but she didn't know he was married. It was a real mess. He left Jake's mother and after they divorced, he married mine but left when I was too young to understand. I found out I had a brother one night when they were arguing about it."

"And…is your mother still alive?"

"Yes. She lives in Salt Lake City. I don't see her much."

Penny didn't press him on that. Her heartbeat echoed with each bump in the rugged lane. They'd only been on the road for about fifteen minutes, but it seemed like hours to her. What if they didn't get to Kevin in time? "I… I need to find Kevin, Zeke. My son shouldn't have to pay for Jake's criminal activities."

"And neither should you." Zeke's expression became etched with slashes of remorse. "You fell in love with him when he still had some good in him. Kevin is part of that good."

Penny teared up again. "Kevin is so precious. He's my entire world. I changed my life and found my faith again because I wanted to be the best mother possible. I miss him. I don't know what I'll do if anything has happened to him."

"Even if Jake has him, he won't hurt Kevin," Zeke said, trying to reassure her. "You have to keep telling yourself that."

Penny stared ahead. "He wasn't happy about my pregnancy at first but once Kevin was born, he changed and tried to be a good father to him. I have to remember that. And…at first he seemed to love me, too."

Zeke shook his head. "That sounds like Jake. He always loved the ladies but I'm thinking he saw something special in you. You gave him a son."

"But he didn't love *me* enough to stay," she lamented, tears she refused to shed burning at her eyes. "He would come and go and he made me promise to never mention him to anyone because of his work. But now I think he didn't want anyone to know about us, either. I thought we had something solid between us but when I refused to leave with him, he turned ugly. Almost desperate."

"He *is* desperate." Zeke slowed the truck and let Cheetah do his thing. "That's why we have to be careful."

Looking out over the meadows and woods around the basin, she said, "He promised me a lot of things but none of those promises came to pass. He would come and visit Kevin, though, just pop in and out, usually late at night and gone by morning. He'd send toys and mail cash in envelopes with no return address. With just one note. 'For my son.'"

She lowered her head and raked her hands through her tumble of hair. "The money helped but his callous nature was a slap in the face. It showed me exactly what he thought of me."

Now she felt even more ashamed and disappointed, knowing the cash was dirty mafia money; knowing that the father of her child would stoop to kidnapping Kevin and possibly taking him away from her forever.

Zeke looked as if he wanted to comfort her but she knew he had to stay on task. "When did you talk to him last? Has he been in contact with you over the last few months?" he asked.

"Only once, no, twice," she said, turning to face him.

"A few months ago, he texted and said he wouldn't be by for a while since he was involved in a heavy case that required top secrecy and a lot of travel."

"The Dupree crime family," Zeke stated. "He went deep undercover and somehow, he never came out."

"I didn't hear from him for a while but about five months ago, I got a package in the mail. It was a little stuffed horse. The card attached said 'For my son.'"

Zeke's eyes widened. "The one you packed and brought with us? Jake sent it?"

She nodded. "He called me a month after that and told me to pack a bag and get Kevin ready. We were leaving the country." Shaking her head, she looked back at Cheetah, wishing the dog would signal something, anything. "I refused and hung up. I knew he was in trouble and I didn't want to risk getting involved or taking Kevin out of the country. So I left the Elk Basin and moved around from state to state, finding odd jobs where I could. After I saw a news report about all this, I thought he'd be long gone by now. I wanted to bring Kevin home but someone else was in the house I rented, so we found a new home at the Wild Iris. I'd only planned to stay there a few days but...we love it there." She stopped and put a hand to her lips. "We *did* love it there."

Zeke pinned her with a hard glare. "Why did you return *here* knowing Jake was still on the run? Were you hoping he'd come for you? Maybe take you with him after all?"

She glared back at him, heat washing over her. "Is that what you think? You all keep asking me that. Did I look like I wanted to go with him this afternoon when he had that gun on me? Do I seem happy about the fact that he might have my son on a plane right now?"

"I'm sorry." He shrugged and revved the truck. "I have to know the truth."

"The only truth you need right now is that I love my son and I'd never do anything to put him in jeopardy. That's why I left, to protect Kevin. As for Jake, I was hoping he was somewhere on the other side of the world." Leaning her head against the window, she sighed. "Now I wish *I'd* left the country. My son might be with me right now if I had."

SIX

Before Zeke could reassure her that it wasn't her fault, they arrived at Old Fork Road and Cheetah held his furry head out the back-side window and lifted his snout. Zeke skidded and turned onto the dirt lane and brought the SUV to an abrupt halt.

"Stay here," he told Penny while he checked his 9 mm handgun and grabbed his high-powered rifle. Harper pulled her SUV up behind him and came around with Star.

"Max is sending the locals, too," she said, probably to warn Zeke to be alert.

Zeke didn't argue with her. He wanted this over. "Cheetah's on fire, so let's go."

"Jake will get away if he hears sirens," Penny cautioned as she rounded the vehicle. "What are you doing?"

"I told you—"

But she wasn't listening. She headed into the woods, her hiking boots hitting against vines and bramble. She'd been antsy on the ride over here and now she was evidently in full warrior-mama mode.

Zeke did an eye roll toward Harper and took off, trailing Penny while he tried to follow Cheetah. Harper and Star had his back and they had a whole police department on the way.

He let Cheetah take the lead and followed him without hesitation. Search and rescue was Cheetah's specialty but the loyal dog had been at it all day. Zeke knew his K-9 partner wouldn't quit until he did, so he kept going. They finally caught up with Penny. She seemed to be wandering aimlessly, a desperate fear in her demeanor.

Whirling when she heard them approaching, she gazed over at Zeke, a tremor in her words. "What's wrong with me? I know these woods. I do. I should be able to see the signs of someone walking through here. A broken branch, a footprint in the dirt. But… I don't know where to start, where to go."

Zeke stilled Cheetah then reached out to lay a comforting hand on Penny's arm. "You have to trust me. I'll show you."

Her gaze moved over him as if she were searching for shards of his brother. "Okay." She calmed down and focused on getting her bearings, but Zeke heard the trembling in her voice. Scanning the surrounding area, she said, "I don't know this area as well as the one along the basin. This is more overgrown and less used. Not many trails but lots of places to hide out."

Then she took off toward some bramble. "Look." Pointing to where the heavy bushes and brush had been knocked down, she whirled. "I think they must have gone through here."

Zeke clasped her hand to keep her from crashing through the forest again. "I know you're scared and worried. I'm concerned, too. But the first twenty-four hours are the most crucial, and we've got the best people we could ask for out searching everywhere."

Penny nodded, her eyes misty. "I get that and I'm thankful for it, but I'm telling you, I think they went this way. This shows fresh tracks. It could have been from an animal but… I think we need to detour down into this incline."

Taking out a flashlight, Zeke studied the broken bramble and footprints in the dust and commanded Cheetah to sniff the dirt. The dog moved his snout over the path before turning back to Zeke.

"It seems you were right," he said, proud of Penny for keeping her head in spite of the agony he saw in her eyes. He wanted to hug her close, but that would go beyond duty and the urgency they both felt.

She turned back toward the path, her fingers dashing tears away. "Hurry."

Together they worked their way through the dense forest. Cheetah lifted his snout in the air, following the vapor scent and the foot trails that had brought them here. With the sun sliding closer to the horizon toward the west, the woods were becoming dusky and shadowed.

They made their way into an overgrown hollow where a rutted, jagged path led down a short incline. A perfect hiding spot. But why would the kidnapper bring Kevin into the woods?

Maybe the man had been trying to escape but had parked the van and come here to hide out and avoid the roadblocks?

When he heard stomping feet about twenty yards away, Zeke stopped and silently called Cheetah back. A man started shouting, obviously talking to someone on his phone. Penny lifted up, already scanning the woods ahead. Zeke grabbed Penny and held her against him, a finger to his lips. Then he leaned close and pointed toward the area below. "If you want your son back, let me do my job."

She nodded, tears forming in her eyes. But she stayed still and silent and followed a few steps behind him.

Zeke gave Cheetah a hand signal to keep quiet while they listened. The man went into a rant. "I got the kid but the heat's on, man. You need to get out here and get your brat. I left two live witnesses at that inn and I got shot at in the woods with some snarling animal nearby. I need to leave right now. It ain't safe. You'd better get in touch with your contact in Colorado. I hate Montana and I hate dogs."

He gave jittery directions to the location and turned toward the cluster of bushes where Zeke and Penny were hiding.

Penny's slight gasp caused Zeke to look over at her. She put a hand to her mouth and took a deep breath. The kidnapper didn't seem to hear. He whirled and started pacing again.

Zeke turned back to study the kidnapper's face and immediately recognized the man. Gunther Caprice. Motioning for Penny to get down, he rushed toward the man, Cheetah deadly silent beside him. Spotting Kevin sitting forlorn and confused in some leaves, Zeke breathed a sigh of relief but he didn't stop.

"FBI. Turn around now!" Then he gave Cheetah the attack command.

The surprised man pulled out a gun and whirled into the bushes, quickly firing off a round of shots. He barely missed Cheetah as the dog leaped toward the dense cluster of scrub oaks and rocks near where he had Kevin hidden.

"Halt," Zeke called, hoping to keep the suspect alive for questioning. But he was also concerned that Kevin could get caught up in a shoot-out.

The man fired again, the bullet hitting inside some bushes near Zeke.

Zeke brought Cheetah back and took cover but Penny took off at a run and skirted around trees and bushes before he could stop her. He kept shooting at the man to cover her and watched as she grabbed up her frightened, crying toddler and took off in a sprint into the shadowy woods.

A wave of panic and fury surged through him. What was she *thinking*? She could get lost out there or worse, run right into Jake's arms. Zeke couldn't go after her right now.

Zeke heard Harper behind him on her phone, calling in their location, and hoped Jake would be listening in on the radio and come anyway. He'd either rush out here, or he'd hear the scanner alert and sirens and go in the other direction.

But his brother wanted Kevin. That incentive might flush him out.

Zeke had to get to Penny and Kevin, but he couldn't let Gunther get away.

"Drop your weapon, Caprice!" Zeke called out again. "We have you surrounded."

The man kept shooting but took off toward where Penny had gone. Zeke could hear Kevin's fearful wails off in the distance. He called out to Harper. "Stay on him. I have to find Penny and Kevin."

Harper nodded and shouted at Star to search, but

when Zeke heard a vehicle cranking up in the distance beyond the tree line, he feared not only had the suspect gotten away but he might have taken Penny and Kevin, too.

Zeke ordered Cheetah to search. They took off in the direction of where he'd last heard the wails. Zeke hoped Cheetah would find his nephew quickly so they could whisk Kevin to safety. Zeke gave the eager canine a long leash. Cheetah sniffed here and there but the loyal dog was running out of steam, so Zeke gave him water and hand-fed him food to keep him going.

Thirty minutes in with constant communication with Max and the team, and still no sign of Caprice or Penny and Kevin.

Where had Penny taken the boy? And had the suspect taken both of them? As the sun sank behind the trees, a solid fear hammered against Zeke's heart. He radioed Harper again. "Anything?"

"Negative," she reported back. "The boss and the locals are searching the other side of the ridge where we heard a vehicle starting, but we think the kidnapper disappeared on foot or had another getaway vehicle pick him up. We spotted the old van but nothing there." She released a breath. "We've swiped it for fingerprints, but whoever this is knows how to work around that. Star alerted on a spot where we found what looked like four-wheeler or Rhino tracks. Probably how they got away but we can't be sure at this point. I'm sorry, Zeke."

"No sign of the woman and the boy here, either," Zeke reported, wondering if Jake could be listening in. He signed off and kept stalking through the heavy foliage. Soon it would be breeding season for elk in these woods, and even this early it could be dangerous. An elk could easily kill a woman or a child.

Zeke often prayed when he was out on a mission like this one. He'd grown used to the evil in the world, but this hit too close to home. At a young age, Zeke had found out he had a brother and so he'd tried to get to know Jake, but his mother had explained things pretty bluntly.

"Jake Morrow doesn't want to be your friend or your brother. Your father used women, son. He convinced me he loved me and I believed him. But he couldn't handle leaving his first wife for me and so…he just left all of us. He always wanted more. More money. More power. More women. No one could ever please the man."

At times such as this when he had to be on high alert and at his best, Zeke often thought about his dad. Was he still alive? Did he regret leaving his two sons or the women he'd hurt so badly? Zeke fought against becoming that kind of man. He wouldn't be that way, not after what they'd all been through.

Now he wondered why Jake had turned bad. But his mother had always warned him. "Jake has a mean streak and an appetite for the finer things in life, just like your father. He can be conniving when he wants something. You'd be wise to stay away from him."

Zeke had chalked that advice up to bitterness after he and Jake had become close, but now he had to wonder if his mother had been right.

"He left my mom for yours," Jake used to say with a dark frown. "What kind of man does that?"

Zeke could never answer that question. But he'd burned with the need to be a better man than his father. He'd joined the church at an early age and while he and Jake saw each other occasionally and he longed for his brother to join him at church functions, it had never happened. Jake had made fun of Zeke's strong faith and later had even teased Zeke about copying him and trying to outdo him by becoming first a K-9 cop and later joining the FBI. Zeke had taken it in stride since he looked up to Jake during those couple of years when they'd had a little bit of a bond. Now he could see that Jake had resented him from the beginning.

Now it had all come down to this.

Jake was on the run and Zeke was trying to save the mother of his child.

Why had she run?

Because she didn't trust any of them. And how could he blame her after what she'd been through?

Determined to find her, Zeke spurred Cheetah on and once they'd circled back and tried a different path, the dog became excited and took off to the east. Had she been moving in circles to throw them off?

Twenty minutes later, they'd made their way back to Zeke's vehicle but there was still no sign of Penny and Kevin.

Until Cheetah quietly alerted at the SUV, his ears and head up and his gaze bouncing back to Zeke in a sure sign that he'd located a possible friendly.

Or it could be Jake or the thug inside there, but Cheetah wasn't indicating danger.

Zeke praised the anxious canine, then carefully opened the driver's-side door, his gun drawn, to peek in the back where the tinted windows kept anyone from seeing inside. Penny lay curled up next to Cheetah's kennel, her son beside her while she shielded him with her body.

The sight of them hiding in such a tight space just about undid Zeke. But the dark windows and the padded kennel were a perfect camouflage. He commanded Cheetah to stay. "Penny, it's me. Zeke. You're both safe now."

She lifted her head, exhaustion shadowing her eyes in the setting sun. "Did you find Jake?"

Kevin's sleepy eyes opened and he sat up. "Doggy?"

Zeke smiled at that but shook his head in answer to Penny. "Not yet."

"Then we're not safe, no matter what you keep telling me."

She was right. Zeke had to protect his nephew. And her. "What do you want me to do?" he asked, knowing it really wasn't up to him or her right now.

She pushed at her hair and rubbed a gentle hand over her curious toddler. "My grandfather has a cabin deep in the woods on the other side of the basin. He left it to me but I never told Jake about it because I don't get over there very much. But I'm going to take Kevin there."

She was not asking for his permission.

Zeke understood but he wouldn't back down, either. "Then I'm going with you, but you have to come up front so Cheetah can get into his kennel."

She shifted and tried to lift Kevin.

"Hold on," Zeke said, rushing around to the back of the vehicle to pop open the automatic door. "Let me."

"Hey, Kevin," he said, offering the boy his outstretched arms. "I'm your Uncle Zeke."

Kevin looked confused but when he saw Cheetah, his eyes lit up. "Doggy." Glancing back at Penny, the little boy giggled.

"That's Cheetah," Zeke said.

He reached in and took Kevin into his arms, the feel of the little boy's sweaty, sweet skin hitting against all his protective gear and breaking the shell around his heart.

"Mama, Cheety," Kevin echoed, glancing back at Penny.

"I've got him," Zeke said, reaching out his free hand to Penny.

She took it, her eyes meeting his, an unspoken understanding threading between them. "You had the keys or I'd already be gone."

"Well, then I'm glad I had the keys. And I'm also glad I left it unlocked."

He was about to break every rule in the book but he wasn't going to take her back out there. Not when Jake was still on the run and after his son. So he called Max and gave him the report. "Kevin and Penny are safe and they're with me, sir. Gunther Caprice is the kidnapper. He's working with Jake. He mentioned a contact in Colorado."

"Where are you now?"

Zeke took a breath. "I'm on my way to a place where Penny already planned to go anyway, with or without me. I'm going into hiding with Penny and Kevin while I figure out what to do next. And you won't hear from me until I have a plan."

"Negative," Max said. "Morrow, you bring her in now."

Zeke ended the call, Max's warning command echoing in his head. He had to ignore the SAC, at least for tonight. Right now, he had to follow his heart instead of protocol.

He'd ask for forgiveness later. And deal with the fallout then, too.

SEVEN

"We're here," Penny said, pointing to the dark house looming up near a narrow ridge. "This is the Potter cabin."

Zeke drove at a snail's pace while he glanced over the dark woods. "Secluded and definitely off the beaten path."

"I'm not sure what we'll find," Penny admitted, apprehension bouncing off her. She took in the long front porch and the square, squatty home that had been in her family for generations. Her grandfather was her champion and he'd taught her how to survive in these woods and hills. He'd died a year before Kevin was born. Her son was named after him.

But this place that had once been a haven now looked sinister and intimidating. What if someone was lying in wait out here? They'd be ambushed and…her son could be taken again.

Earlier when she'd found Kevin, an overwhelming rush of relief had swept through her. But she knew they didn't have a second to spare. Desperate, she'd zigzagged through the woods and hurried back to Zeke's SUV, hoping to get in it and drive away. No keys, but it had been open. So she'd hidden her scared little boy in the best spot available. Now she still marveled that other than a few scratches and bug bites, Kevin seemed okay. She would not let him out of her sight again. But being in this isolated spot only reminded her of what she'd been through today.

Panic gripped her like a set of claws, choking off the air she needed to inhale. "Zeke, I don't know about this. I mean, it's overgrown and run-down. Maybe we should—"

He touched her arm, the strength in his hand warm and sure. "Hey, take another breath. Kevin is with us now. This will do until we can get to safety in the morning." He scanned the surrounding woods. "Cheetah and I will do a thorough check of both the house and the area."

Penny tamped down her trepidations. They didn't have much of a choice. "I came here for a while before I went on the run and cleaned it and thought about staying but…having a cabin in the woods isn't fun when you're alone and afraid for your child. Or when your ex-boyfriend isn't happy with you."

"It won't be fun when you're in hiding, either," Zeke replied, sympathy sounding in the words. "But it'll keep us safe. We'll make sure of that."

He parked the dark vehicle around back where a lean-to held rotting firewood and some rusty gardening tools. Penny surveyed the overgrowth around the cabin and tried not to think about rattlesnakes or salamanders. Or scorpions and spiders. She was so exhausted, every muscle in her body screamed for relief. But she was too keyed up to relax now. Kevin was asleep in her arms since they didn't have a proper car seat. And maybe because she didn't want to let go of him ever again.

"Stay here while Cheetah and I check things out," Zeke said, his tone firm. Then he handed her a flashlight. "Use this if you get concerned. Flash the light and check out the darkness. Or use it as a weapon."

Penny nodded. "The key is hidden over the right windowsill near the front door."

While Zeke and Cheetah walked through the shifting shadows, she sank back in the dark SUV with a heavy sigh. She could finally let out the breath she'd been holding and try to calm herself. She prayed, thanking God and asking Him to protect them. Surely Jake wouldn't find them here.

Zeke had been careful getting them out of danger. He'd taken back roads and crisscrossed around the many trails and old routes. She'd shown him some off-the-beaten-path roads that didn't qualify as safe in most people's minds. They'd hurried into an old general store about ten miles to the south and gathered a few supplies. No one was around, the place didn't have security cameras and the manager didn't even look up at them.

Surely her baby would be safe for a while.

She clung to Kevin, her heart pounding against his, her fears subsiding for a brief few minutes. When a dark figure came around the corner, she almost gasped. But it was Zeke.

"It's secure around the immediate perimeter. Let's get inside."

Zeke had become more and more brusque as day turned to night. He didn't want to be here taking care of her, obviously. He probably wanted to be out there on the hunt for his brother. The father of her son.

He wouldn't do a lot of talking tonight unless it was to grill her more about Jake. But she didn't know anything much more beyond what she'd already told him. Zeke was so different from his half brother. Dark and brooding and serious but so solicitous of her son. And her. He was risking a lot, going into hiding with them.

He wanted justice. He was the good side of Jake. She hoped.

When he took Kevin out of her arms and held his big hand to her sleeping son's head to steady the child against his shoulder, hot tears pricked at Penny's tired eyes. Kevin would be safe with Zeke.

Zeke cared about Kevin. It was that simple. And he'd been forced to bring her along while he tried to protect his nephew.

She thanked God for that and said a prayer for Zeke as she followed the man shielding her son into the darkness of the old cabin, the musky scents of aged furniture and stale tobacco smoke hitting her in a full-force rush of dry air. Granddaddy Potter had been a heavy smoker. That had certainly contributed to his early death. And she'd never been able to clear the air completely, no matter how many candles and air fresheners she'd tried.

"Electricity?" Zeke asked, his flashlight out and on. He handed it to her so he could hold on to Kevin.

"Nope. But we have kerosene lanterns and candles. I usually open the windows to bring in fresh air, but I guess that's out of the question for now."

"Yes. We'll just have to hope the air cools down for the night."

"Kevin is exhausted," she said. "I don't know if he'll even wake up to eat any dinner."

"I should lay him down," Zeke said, glancing around.

"Not before I check the bedding and the sofa."

She hurried and found a lantern and some matches. On the third try, she had the lantern burning bright into the corners and used the flashlight to check more thoroughly.

While Zeke stalked behind her, Kevin safe in his arms and Cheetah watching with fascination, she gingerly lifted the old mattress and pulled out sofa cushions. A few dead bugs and scrambling spiders, but nothing too much to worry about.

She whirled around after shaking cushions and fluffing pillows. "Let's lay him on his blanket on the couch for now. I'll find the sheets for the bed and get it covered."

"I'll take the couch later then," Zeke said. "Cheetah and I can watch out the window from that location."

She nodded, glad the cabin only had one big window in the living area and a small window over the sink. Tugging Kevin's favorite blanket and his cherished "Wittle Horsey" stuffed animal out of his diaper bag, Penny breathed deep, the smell of clean soap assaulting her. Her baby's smell—sweet and pure and innocent. To think how close she'd come to losing him.

"How did I let this happen?" she asked, not even realizing she'd said it out loud.

"You didn't let anything happen," Zeke replied. "Jake took advantage of you, same way he's been using people all his life. It's finally caught up with him."

She didn't want to analyze that observation right now so she swiped and dusted with one of the baby wipes she had in the diaper bag, expending what little energy she had left. Satisfied that the old leather couch was clean and safe, she motioned for Zeke to place Kevin on the superhero blanket, a threadbare sofa pillow at his head. After kissing Kevin and hearing him sigh when she snuggled the worn little stuffed animal next to him, she turned back to Zeke, her need to nest kicking in.

"Let's get this place cleaned up. I'll make us some soup."

"Okay." He ordered Cheetah to stay and the dog circled and sat down by the sofa. With his dark eyes on Kevin, Cheetah curled up as close to Kevin as he could possibly get.

That brought her a new measure of comfort. Her son had two fierce protectors. Penny felt a new sense of hope. Maybe they just might make it out of this alive.

Zeke found a broom and started sweeping away dust bunnies and spiderwebs. "Tell me about your grandfather."

Penny grabbed the matchbox and managed to get the old two-burner propane stove working. "Don't you already know everything about me?"

"We did some research and a background check," he admitted. "But I want to hear it from you."

She opened the large can of chicken noodle soup. "Why? What does it matter now?"

He kept sweeping, the gleaming low light of the old lantern casting shadows before him like scattering leaves. "It matters to me," he said, stopping to stare into her eyes. "We're here together. Might as well get to know each other."

She stirred the soup and found crackers and two chunky mugs. After rinsing the mugs with a little bottled water, she deemed them sterile enough. Was this his way of making sure she was a fit mother to his nephew?

That caused a new fear to spring into her mind. "Are you going to take Kevin away from me?"

Zeke whirled, both hands gripping the old broom, his eyes even darker in the glow from the kerosene lamp. "No. Why would you even think that?"

Penny turned down the burner and took their mugs to the old table. "I don't exactly qualify for mother of the year. I thought maybe—"

"You thought wrong," he said, a tremor of anger in his words. He finished sweeping dirt and grime into the dustpan and turned to toss it out beyond the screen door. "I wouldn't do that to you or to Kevin. I know what it's like to not have both parents raising a child."

"So do I," she blurted, wondering if he planned to step in as a male role model for Kevin. "I mean, my mother died when I was young and my dad kind of went off the deep end. Last I heard, he's somewhere in Alaska. He left me with my grandfather when I was nine."

Zeke's dark expression hardened and softened all in one breath. "Let me guess. He promised to come back for you."

She nodded. "Yes."

"I got that, too. Jake and I...didn't know each other until we were older. I always admired him, wanted to be like him. But...we have different personalities, different codes on how to do things."

"I kind of gathered that you two were complete opposites," she replied. "Soup's ready."

She didn't miss that sizzle of awareness that seemed to purr around them like some exotic wind. Was she projecting her tumultuous feelings for Jake onto his brother? Or were her feelings for this honorable man the real deal? She didn't want to think beyond that. Zeke was way out of her league and…she'd learned her lesson with FBI agents. Too secretive and too driven.

Now that the adrenaline of trying to stay alive and find her missing son was draining down, Penny only wanted to curl up in a tiny ball and cry for a long time. But she steeled herself against that and glanced at Zeke.

"What?" he asked, his hand on a high-backed chair.

"Nothing." She'd been staring. Couldn't stop doing it. "I guess I'm just comparing you to him."

Disappointment flashed through his eyes. "Many people have. I always used to fall short."

"Used to. But now, you're the brother who's doing his job."

"I'm the brother who *has* to do his job. I don't have any choice."

She sank down and opened a bottle of water. "Just like you don't have any choice being here with us."

"I'm here for two reasons," he said, his spoon dropping into his soup with a soft splash. "One, you're in danger. And two, you're family now."

His eyes, so different from Jake's, held her. Penny felt a chill even though she felt too warm. "I haven't had a real family in a long time," she said, touched and wary at the same time.

"Me, either." He shrugged. "Like I said, my mother is still alive but I don't get to see her much. She'll love Kevin."

She'll love. As in the future. Would he take her son to see his mother? This was all too much to comprehend at this point.

So she tried to dissuade him with a bitter question. "Even though he's Jake's son?"

"In spite of him being Jake's son."

She let that settle, deciding to focus on the hot meal instead of the good-looking FBI agent. So she chewed on a cracker and kept one eye on her sleeping son.

Zeke fed Cheetah and gave him a chew toy. The obedient dog took his reward and curled up beside Kevin. Then Zeke went back to his soup, eating in a quick, efficient way that showed her he was used to eating alone and in the dark. Cheetah guarded her son without any wasted movements, his every move at attention.

They were both well trained.

It scared her to think where she'd be right now if they hadn't found her. Shivering, she stood, the image of Jake's anger and threatening moves hitting her like a cold slap to the face. She had to get as far away from him as she could.

And she had no business having such strange, intimate thoughts about his half brother. The best thing she could do once this was over would be to leave Montana and start a new life somewhere else. Somewhere away from secrets and lies and covert operations.

"Are you all right?" Zeke asked her, sincere concern in the question and something more in his eyes.

"I'm so tired." She never divulged things such as that. She didn't like admitting defeat. "And I don't mean physically tired, although I am that. I just want to have that life I always dreamed of. A pretty house near a meadow and a stream, the work that I love, and a chance to raise my sweet little boy. The whole white-picket-fence thing, I guess. A real home. A real life."

Zeke walked over to her and took her hand. "C'mon, you're going to get some rest."

She tried to pull away. "I've got to clean up the dishes."

"I'll do that. Go ready yourself for the night and I'll stand watch while you and Kevin rest."

Penny couldn't speak past the lump in her throat, so she hurried into the tiny bathroom across from the back storage room. The cold well water dripped onto her hands and she washed her face and cleaned herself up the best she could. Then she came back into the living room and saw that Zeke had moved Kevin to the bed and placed him up against the protection of the wall. He stood at the kitchen sink, but he wasn't washing dishes. Instead, he was staring out the tiny back window. Staring into the night.

"I'll want to know more," he said, without turning around. "I just need to know more about why my brother went rogue. And I'll need to know more about your relationship with him, too."

"Okay." She took off her hiking boots and dusted off her feet and crawled into the small bed beside her son, the warmth of his little body giving her hope. "Good night, Zeke. You'll know all you need to know about me soon enough."

"Good night," he said, his back still to her, his gaze lifting out into the darkness beyond the cabin.

Penny lay there watching him, wondering what he must be thinking. Wondering how the anguish that wrapped around him like a dark mantle could ever be lifted.

He'd find Jake. She knew it. And when he did, he'd want answers from him, too.

Finally, she closed her eyes and prayed again. Over and over. But in the end, she wasn't sure what she should be praying for. Redemption, a reprieve or for all of them to simply survive this?

Or…for that little house by the meadow with the stream flowing nearby.

Alone, if need be. She could handle alone. She'd handled that feeling most of her life.

Or with a man who could love her son as his own.

Someone, but not the man standing watch over her tonight.

He didn't seem ready to be the loving kind.

EIGHT

Zeke hadn't slept much.

Every snap of a branch against the cabin jarred him awake and forced him to make rounds, Cheetah at his side. Every creak or groan from the old wood caused him to shift and reach for his Glock, his gaze always hitting the two people sleeping on the bed in the corner. He had to keep them safe. Somehow.

This was a strange twist in the already strange, twisted scope of this entire case. A little boy and a pretty woman. He'd somehow become their protector.

He'd come here to help find Jake, and for months now, that had been his goal. He'd never imagined he'd find Penny and her son again and certainly not like this, with Jake trying to kidnap them and take them out of the country. While he'd worked with the FBI Classified K-9 Unit to find Jake, he'd worried about Penny and her son. Jake's son. Now things had taken a more dangerous turn. Jake was back and determined. His brother wouldn't give up without a fight.

Now Zeke's goal had shifted. His first obligation was to protect them while he focused on finding his criminal half brother. So he stood there, watching the dawn lifting through the trees, and wondered what else he could do besides sit and watch. This work was so secretive, so classified, that he couldn't just blurt it all out to the world. He'd already told Penny more than she should know. But…the woman deserved some answers.

Over the last few months, he'd searched and re-searched to the point of exhaustion, but he couldn't find anything that would incriminate Penny. She couldn't be arrested for bad judgment and she seemed sincere in not knowing anything about what Jake had been doing. Be-sides…the man had tried to kill her. Because he wanted the boy? Or because she knew too much and he was afraid she'd spill it all? He hadn't seen anything in her words or manner to indicate that she wasn't telling the truth. But it was his job to question anyone connected to a suspect.

Zeke's gut told him she was innocent in all of this. He's seen the fear in her eyes when Jake had held her at gunpoint and when she'd realized her son had been taken. Even more than fear, he'd witnessed the complete agony of her realization that Kevin had been in that van.

"What are you doing?"

Zeke whirled to find Penny standing by the bath-room door, her hair disheveled and cascading around her face, her eyes sleep rimmed and full of questions.

"I'm thinking," he admitted. "We can't stay here for-ever. I need to get you to a safe house."

She moved toward him, the patter of her bare feet hitting the old wood with purpose. "I thought *this* was a safe house."

"Not really." He stalked past her to the old percola-tor-style coffeepot and poured some of the coffee he'd made earlier. "It's isolated but vulnerable. No security except Cheetah and me."

"You're the best. You showed me that yesterday." She took the coffee and stared into the steaming brew. "But you don't trust me, do you?"

"I don't trust many people."

Penny pushed at her hair and took a sip of the strong coffee. "But shouldn't you trust me? I've told you what I know but… I think you don't believe me. I understand why you wouldn't. I was close to Jake for a long time but… I can see him for what he is now. Any remaining loyalty I had for the man evaporated yesterday."

Zeke jumped on that one. "But before yesterday?"

She slammed her cup down so hard on the table, coffee splattered on the old wood. "Before yesterday, I was still too naive to see the truth. I ran from the truth and put my son at risk and now I'm paying for it. I wish I'd gone to the authorities when Jake contacted me and demanded that I leave with him. That would have been the smart thing to do. But…"

"But you held out hope, even when you were running?"

She sank down onto a rickety chair. "Yes. For my son's sake. I wanted him to know his father."

"No matter what?"

She looked confused, crushed, beaten. "In spite of it all, yes." Shrugging, she lowered her head. "I never had that as a child. I didn't want Kevin to suffer the way I had."

Zeke stopped grilling her and sat down to offer her an energy bar for breakfast. "I'm sorry he hurt you. But… I told you I wanted to know more. I'm trying to understand why he'd risk everything and give up a career he seemed to love. Why would he give up on a chance for a good life with you and Kevin?"

"That part should be obvious," she said, her head down but her eyes on Zeke. "He loves the thrill of the chase more than he loves his son and me. He's an adrenaline junkie. Aren't you all?"

Zeke took that in and shook his head. "So you don't trust me, either?"

"Why should I?"

"You sure are cranky in the morning."

She lifted her chin and gave him a haughty look. "I am, especially when an FBI agent is asking me too many questions before I've had enough coffee."

Zeke wanted to tell her she could trust him because he was trained to do his job, but mostly because he wasn't the type to allow a woman and her child to be in danger. But Kevin cried out and she immediately went to her son. Zeke would have to convince her that he was on her side or this could all go very bad.

And she'd have to show him she was on his side, too.

The day moved along at a slow pace that made Penny's skin crawl. She wasn't one to sit still for too long. She'd tried reading a book but Kevin was fussy so he demanded her attention. When she asked Zeke if they could go for a walk, he said no.

But he took Cheetah out. They scoured the woods and stayed close to the cabin, but she knew it was more than a bathroom break for the canine.

When they came back in, Zeke took Kevin in his arms and did the airplane thing, flying the little boy in the air while Cheetah watched in fascination but never uttered a bark. But late in the day, Kevin tired of play and began to fret again.

"He's confused and exhausted," she said, wishing she could ease her son's pain. "I have medicine in the diaper bag. I'll give him some of that. He's had some ear problems off and on, so he might be coming down with something."

"Maybe he's just tired, like you said," Zeke told her. "He had a traumatic day yesterday. Let me try rocking him."

After she gave Kevin the suggested amount of liquid pain medicine, Zeke took Kevin in his arms and sat down in the rickety old rocker where her grandfather had spent many hours.

Penny sat on the couch, watching. Her son took to Zeke without hesitation and listened aptly while Zeke told him all about Cheetah's heroic ways.

"Cheety," Kevin interrupted, clapping his hands. "Doggy. Woof."

Cheetah's ears lifted, his solemn eyes on Kevin. Kevin poked at Zeke's solid chest. "Talk! Cheety!"

Zeke laughed and started back up, the animation in his words making him sound young and carefree. And irresistible.

Did her son see something in the man that she kept denying? Zeke rocked back and forth, steady and sure, Cheetah curled up nearby. The scene took her breath away but Penny closed her eyes to that sweet image.

After Kevin had fallen asleep, Zeke carried him to the bed and turned to stretch. "This is hard work, isn't it?"

She smiled and nodded, too overcome to speak. Then she swallowed back her emotions. "Yes. But the best

work. I want so much for him. I don't know how to protect him and that scares me."

Zeke's gaze moved over her. "Well, for now, you
don't need to worry about that. I'll be with you until
we find Jake."

Kevin tossed and turned but he finally settled down
for a couple of hours but woke around two in the morning. Penny gave him some more liquid medicine and
Zeke walked the floor, holding him until he became
drowsy again.

Penny watched Zeke with her son, her heart bumping a warning that she was treading into dangerous
emotional territory.

After Kevin drifted off again, they shared another
power bar Zeke had fished out of his go-bag. "You're
right," she finally told Zeke after they moved from the
table to the couch. "It's hard for me to trust you even
though you seem to care about Kevin a lot. But Jake
brought us together, and now it's like walking through
hot coals. He's here with us, a constant reminder of
why we're together and in hiding. You know him as
well or better than I do. I should be asking you all the
questions."

"I told you, we weren't close until we were grown. I
didn't see then that he resents me because of what our
dad did to us. That's what drives him now, that need to
find power and control. He's not thinking straight, out
to kill all of us just to get even. He had a lot of pent-up
anger and bitterness inside him, a lot more than anyone
realized. I could have helped him, talked to him, if he'd
been willing to let me."

Penny decided Zeke needed to talk. So she listened to
him and responded back in reassuring tones. A tentative

honesty developed between them and they laughed and told each other childhood stories that held some good memories before they moved on to future hopes, well into the night. It was almost easy for her to forget that they were hiding out from a man who wanted to kill both of them. A man whom they'd both loved. After Zeke had painted an overall grim picture of his life and how for a brief time he and Jake had grown closer, he finally confided, "And now…everything's changed. I don't want to track my own half brother but… I have to do my job."

Penny understood that concept. "He's throwing away his life for greed and money."

"Yep. I think he's pretty much committed a few of the seven deadly sins."

"But you're different. You're solid."

"I'm not perfect," Zeke said, staring over at Kevin. "But I have faith that everything works toward the good."

"And yet, you fight the bad."

"I have to. I want justice."

"Is that because of your dad leaving you and your mom?" she asked.

Zeke's frown told her this turn made him uncomfortable. "No. His leaving only made me want revenge. I wasn't sure what kind of revenge, but I wanted someone to pay."

"But you chose justice instead."

He nodded. "My mom insisted I attend youth meetings at the local church where we lived in Utah. I didn't want to, but… I found my strength there. I had people willing to guide me and help me. Stand-ins for my dad, but good people. My faith is solid because of that."

It gave her comfort that he felt the same way she did. That he loved Christ and turned to the Lord in his times of need.

"You're a good person, Zeke."

He shrugged that compliment off. "I want to help people. I want the bad guys off the streets."

"It must be so hard, chasing after Jake." She'd seen his anguish, his pain, in that standoff yesterday.

"More than I can ever say."

They sat, silent, sleepy, and let this quiet bond form between them. Penny felt the wall around her heart tumbling away, little by little.

"It's almost dawn," he finally said, his voice low and husky. "You should try to rest."

Penny nodded, yawned and stood up.

A sound echoed out over the warm night. A shot rang out, shattering the window behind them.

Zeke threw her back onto the couch and shielded her with his body, his heart racing right alongside her own. Cheetah stood and woofed low.

"Are you all right?" he whispered, his breath warm on her earlobe.

She managed a nod and heard her son's soft cries. "Kevin."

Zeke sat up. Cheetah danced around, eager to get going. Zeke put a finger to his lips, gave Cheetah the quiet command, and went for his assault weapon.

"Stay with Kevin," he said. Then he pushed a hand through her hair and held her eye to eye and handed her his Glock. "I mean it, Penny. Do not leave this cabin."

Penny nodded, her heart trying to beat again. She might have thought about running on her own yesterday, but not now. She had to trust Zeke enough to keep Kevin safe at least.

He turned the kerosene lamp off and darkness surrounded them. A quiet hush settled around the cabin. Then another sound. Stomping through the woods. Footsteps coming closer.

Zeke motioned to Penny. "Get down."

She slid down on the couch but didn't stay there. Instead she did a quick crawl toward her sleeping son. Kevin whimpered, "Mommy." Carefully putting the gun down on the floor, she scrambled up on the bed. When she touched him, his skin was burning hot.

Fever.

Penny glanced toward where Zeke crouched by the front window, listening. Cheetah stood by his side. Someone was out there. Kevin stirred and coughed. Zeke glanced back, his finger to his lips again. Penny eased up onto the bed and stroked Kevin's forehead. His skin sizzled with a burning fire.

When footsteps sounded just outside the door, Zeke pressed against the wall. "Don't move, Penny," he whispered. "Understand?"

She nodded and waited. Zeke lifted up into a crouch and gave Cheetah a silent command. In one swift move, both man and animal opened the front door and pounced. One shooting and the other barking.

That commotion brought Kevin fully awake. "Mommy!"

He started sobbing and she took him in her arms and tried to soothe him. Hearing gunfire, Penny closed her eyes. Praying. Hoping. Holding her breath.

Silence followed. A deadly silence.

Dear God, protect us, please. Protect my son.

She prayed for Zeke and Cheetah and thanked the Lord for providing them to protect her and Kevin. She'd never doubt Zeke again. She only prayed he'd come back through the door at any minute now.

As dawn began to seep through the undergrowth and the sun's first rays shot off the jagged rocks like a golden laser, Zeke called the canine back. "Good job, Cheetah," he said, rubbing the eager animal's head. "We nipped at 'em good, didn't we, boy?"

He'd seen the dark figure lurking near a big pine about fifteen feet from the cottage. And he'd purposely shot into the air near the tree to scare whoever it was and maybe flush them out. A hiker or camper would have identified themselves and probably would have taken off. However, this person hid, quiet and waiting.

Until Cheetah began to growl and alert right near the tree, which meant the Australian shepherd had picked up a hostile scent. Gunther Caprice, who tried to take Kevin? Or was Jake crouching behind that tree?

"You can come out now," Zeke said in a low whisper. "Or I let my partner bring you down. He can bite through your leg and make you bleed out in about ten seconds."

When he heard heavy footsteps running away, he had his answer. Someone knew they were here. That meant more would show up. He could go after the runner but he couldn't risk leaving Penny and Kevin for too long. He'd kept one eye on the cabin the whole time.

He hurried back inside. "We have to go. Right now."

Penny got up to stare over at him, her eyes filled with dread. "Zeke, Kevin has a fever. And I don't have enough medicine left to contain it. We have to get him to a doctor."

Not the best news right now, but the boy had to come first.

"Okay. We need to leave and I promise I'll find him some help."

They loaded up their few things and hurried to where he'd hidden the SUV. Zeke looked around and spotted footprints. Heavy boots. Then what looked like tire marks from a possible off-road vehicle.

"They've found us," he said as they got into the vehicle. "They'll be back with reinforcements. But…their scout also knows I saw him."

"Did you try to kill him?" Penny asked, her words tight with dread.

"No. I shot at him once and tried to wait him out. I wanted to question him. But he ran away."

"Why didn't you call for help or go after him?"

"No reception and I didn't want to leave you and Kevin alone."

She slumped against the seat and stared at the woods. "You could do your job if you didn't have to worry about us. You had to let Jake go for our sake and now this. Your boss is going to get tired of that excuse."

"It's not an excuse, Penny. I am doing what I think is right for you. I told Max that I was staying close to you two and right now, he'll have to deal with that. He's out there working the scenes and searching for Jake and anyone else who's been wreaking havoc. We all want to bring in Jake and his hit man."

"I shouldn't be complaining," Penny said with a pensive sigh. "Not after yesterday. I want this over. It's hard not to want that."

"We're on the same page there," Zeke retorted.

He maneuvered the massive vehicle along the rutted dirt lane. "Once we're out on the main highway, I'm calling Max to tell him we need to move you to a secure location."

"How does Jake keep finding us?" she asked, a tremor in the question.

"I don't know," he admitted. "GPS? Or maybe... someone on the inside giving him clues."

"Is that possible?"

He shot her a grim glance. "With my brother, anything is possible."

NINE

They were halfway to the road when Zeke spotted two ATVs motoring through the trees, two men dressed in camouflage and armed with guns and bows and arrows. He couldn't make out if the two were Jake and Gunther, but he figured they'd both be somewhere calling the shots by now. These two looked as if they knew these woods and were prepared for a hunt, but he doubted that even if it was the early bow season.

"They're still here," he said, pointing up ahead to where the men were steering into the woods around a bend. "Two of them now."

Zeke slowed and turned off behind some heavy brush and scattered boulders. "Let's wait them out."

He knew he could take down the men on the four-wheelers but his first concern had to be his two passengers. If he got shot, Penny would be exposed and taken. Or worse.

This dilemma only added to Zeke's woes. Bad enough that he was up against his own brother and Jake had managed to get away, even worse that right now, Zeke was the only one who could protect Jake's ex-girlfriend and his son.

Zeke didn't want to think about how Max West would react when he finally called in. *Not positively, that's for sure.* But…he had to go with his gut and Max would just have to do what he had to do.

He watched as the ATVs moved on up the path and took off on another trail. Breathing a sigh of relief, Zeke knew they had to get out of these woods.

They waited a few more minutes, but Kevin was fussing and pulling at his right ear.

"I think this is another bad ear infection," Penny said, worrying clear in her eyes. "We have to get him to a doctor right away."

"Once we're out of here," Zeke said.

They made it to within a few yards of a row of cabins located just off the main road. Zeke figured the people looking for them would stay away from the more congested areas to avoid anyone seeing them. He was about to turn and take a back way out when a man came running out of the woods and tried to flag him down.

"Careful," he said to Penny. "This could be a setup." He pulled his Glock out of his shoulder holster, just in case.

But when he spotted a frantic woman and young girl with the man, he let down the driver's-side window and waited. "Can we help you?"

"Yes," the woman said, pushing past the man. "We were hiking and when we turned around, our nine-year-old son was gone. We don't know what happened. Have you seen a little blond-headed boy anywhere?"

"No. Have you called the authorities?" Zeke asked.

"We've tried. The reception is horrible and we can't get through to the ranger's station. We need help now.

The other cabins are empty. You're the first people we've seen."

Zeke glanced over at Penny. He needed to get her and Kevin out of here, but he couldn't leave a family in need.

"I know," she said, wariness in her words. "You have to try and find him."

"I can search for your son," Zeke said. "But I need to get a physical description and a scent from some of his clothing so I can let my dog help me track him. He's good at that."

The frightened parents bobbed their heads and then the dad said, "Whatever you need. But hurry, please. He likes to sneak away and play hide-and-seek and we've warned him about not doing that. We're worried about him being attacked." The frantic man waved his hand in the air. "I mean, we know the dangers—bears, elk and antelope, mountain lions. We've called and called and he's not answering."

"Show us your cabin," Zeke said. "We have a sick little boy and we can't linger here too long."

"Whatever you can do," the man replied. "We'll keep trying the ranger's station, too."

The man's shocked expression and nervous pacing proved believable. But people could be convincing when they were desperate.

"Thank you. We're here." The woman pointed to a cabin sitting up on a hill. "Right over there. We thought maybe he'd come back here but he's not inside."

Zeke followed the hurrying parents and parked the SUV close to the small cabin before turning to Penny. Whispering low, he said, "We're married and we were at another cabin for two nights. Our son got sick so we had to leave. Our *family* dog is good at tracking. That's all they need to know."

"I could assist you in the search," she said, nodding. "But I can't leave Kevin."

"I'm not sure I should leave you two with them. We'll check out the cabin and decide."

They made it into the cabin and the parents, Brian and Marcy Wilder, gave him a picture of their son, Cody. His older sister, Jessica, looked as frightened as her mother.

"Okay," Zeke said after they'd brought him a T-shirt. "Here's the deal. My…wife and son need to stay here while I conduct the search. I need all of you to stay put. If you go out on your own and get lost, it could hamper me finding your son, understand?"

"We understand," Marcy said. "Just hurry, please. He has asthma. I'm so afraid he'll have an attack."

"He has his inhaler," Jessica said, trying to help.

Zeke took it all in, his gut burning with instincts he'd honed over the years. Hard to say who was telling the truth. But he had to find the boy before he stumbled upon a wild animal or those two men roaming around.

Then he turned to Cheetah. "Let me do a quick search here in the cabin first. That will help my dog to pick up Cody's scent, too." He gave Penny a warning glance, hoping she wouldn't blurt out anything about him and Cheetah.

After he finished a sweep of the cabin, he nodded to Penny. "Stay here and give Kevin the last of the drops, okay?"

"We have medicine," Marcy offered. "Over-the-counter liquid. Cody has a hard time taking pills."

"Thank you," Penny said, glancing toward Kevin. "He has a fever. I think his ears are bothering him."

"We have a thermometer, too." Marcy buzzed with nervous energy while she gathered what Penny needed.

"I'm going," Zeke said to Penny. On a low note, he added, "Don't let anyone into this cabin. Do what you have to do. Use any weapon you can find. If I don't come back soon or if someone threatens you, take the SUV and leave."

"I won't leave you," she replied, that determination he'd seen the first day they'd met shining through.

"You will, to keep Kevin safe," he whispered. "I can take care of myself."

Realization overshadowed her stubbornness. "Okay."

"Good. Now, I need to get a plan going."

"Zeke, I have an idea," she said. She turned to the couple. "I'm a nature guide so I know most of this area. Did you pack walkie-talkies or two-way radios?"

"Yes." Brian hurried to a battered desk and grabbed a duffel bag. "We didn't use them this morning because we were only going on one last short hike before we headed back to Salt Lake City."

"Okay." She took one and handed the other one to Zeke. "I can guide you," she said. "We can stay in touch."

"Good idea," Zeke replied, admiration in his words. "And you can use it if you need me."

Penny glanced around the small room. "We need a map."

Brian found one. "Here's ours. It's one of those easy maps." He was right. The map was colorful and animated and included trailheads and mile markers. He showed Zeke and Penny the spot on the trail where Cody had disappeared not far from the cabin.

Zeke gave a curt nod. "I'll start there and see where Cheetah takes us."

"Are you trained for this or something?" Brian asked Zeke.

"We're just careful when we're out here camping or hiking," Zeke replied. "Since my wife works out here and knows the dangers."

"Let the man go," Marcy said, the urgency in her words heartbreaking.

Zeke gave Penny one last glance then headed out with Cheetah. He only prayed that the boy hadn't been taken by the men lurking about on the ATVs. If Jake had to kidnap another child to get his own back, he'd do it in a heartbeat.

And that would turn into a worst-case scenario.

Once they were on the search, Cheetah took off toward the trail where they'd spotted the men on the four-wheelers. Could they have already taken Cody? Zeke hoped not. Giving Cheetah the quiet signal by dropping his hand down firmly, he allowed the dog to lead him along the path. They stopped several times so Zeke could check the tire marks in the rutted lane and search for footprints. When he didn't see two sets of footprints, one big and one small, he breathed a sigh of relief. But it was hard to find solid prints in the dry dirt.

Then Cheetah alerted and emitted a low growl as they were moving through a cluster of evergreens. Zeke stopped and heard voices up ahead.

"He said an old cabin, away from the others. I'm telling you, the one we found last night has to be it."

"But he wants the boy. That cabin looked deserted when we went back."

"Somebody shot at you last night, remember? Someone with a trained dog."

"Yeah, and now that somebody is gone. The cabin is empty."

Gunther? He'd run away yesterday when he heard Cheetah growling, according to what Penny had told Zeke.

"We shoulda gone in last night," his friend said on a jerky whine.

"Not me," Gunther retorted. "He's not paying me enough to get eaten alive by a trained police dog. I don't like dogs, man. I'm not taking any chances." Cheetah glanced up at Zeke, apparently taking in that information for future use. *Good for you, boy.*

The other man sounded off again. "Look, let's find the kid and get out of here. We heard a kid crying. They have to be hiding somewhere around here. Boss wants that kid, bad. And as for the rest, well, that's why we brought all these cool weapons, right?"

Zeke heard stomping, followed by two motors revving to life. He watched from the shelter of the trees as the two ATVs took off toward the main trail out of the woods.

What if they found the wrong boy?

"C'mon, Cheetah," he said, giving his dog the go order. "We gotta hurry, buddy."

Cheetah took him deeper into the woods but back toward the circle of cabins. When Cheetah alerted near a small ravine about a hundred yards from the cabins and turned back to face his handler, Zeke glanced down and saw a stream below. And something else.

A little boy, curled up in the fetal position.

* * *

Penny checked Kevin's forehead again.

"How's he doing?" Marcy asked, her expression filled with worry.

"I think his fever is going down but I'm afraid his ear problems aren't going to get better until I get him to a doctor."

Marcy nodded, her brown eyes misting over. "Cody's always had allergies and when we realized he had asthma, I didn't know what to do. But we've learned how to deal with it."

She held a hand to her mouth. "I should have been watching him more closely."

"Hey, you're doing the best you can," Penny said, understanding the woman's fears. "We can't always be there to protect them."

"I… I just want him back with me," Marcy said, tears falling. "I have to pray that your husband will find him. God sent you two at exactly the right moment."

Penny hugged Marcy close and prayed for her. But the woman made sense. God had certainly sent Zeke to her at just the right time and now this. Maybe there was a greater purpose in all of this. If she hadn't met Jake, she wouldn't have her beautiful little boy. But her bad judgment had brought consequences.

And maybe redemption.

Zeke was a good man. She felt that at this moment with all her heart. He'd do his best to find Cody and he'd protect Kevin. Zeke had turned toward the right path, rather than choosing a life of crime and destruction. Remembering how earlier he'd called her his wife and Kevin his son, Penny tried to ignore the punch of longing in her heart.

"You're right," she said to Marcy. "God's timing is always perfect, no matter the outcome."

"But sometimes the outcome is bad," Jessica said, bursting into tears. "Sometimes God doesn't help."

Both women looked up at the girl. "Oh, honey." Marcy rushed to her daughter's side. "It's all right. It'll be all right."

"I teased him, Mom. This morning. I dared him to go into the woods."

Marcy gasped and stared down at her daughter. "Why would you do that?"

"I was mad at him for messing up some of my sketches. I'm sorry. I didn't think he'd run away."

Brian came over to stare at his daughter. Penny held her breath, wishing she didn't have to witness this.

But he took his daughter into his arms and held her close. "It's okay, sweetheart. Your brother can be a handful but…this man Zeke seems to know what he's doing, right?"

He glanced at Penny, hope in his eyes and a certain understanding that showed he wasn't going to ask any more questions. He just wanted his son back.

Penny knew that horror. Had lived it since Jake had taken her along that path. She needed to stop questioning Zeke, too. Maybe if she gave up being problematic and unyielding, she might remember some detail that could help them.

She stood and brushed her hands down her jeans. "He does know what he's doing so we have to trust him."

Brian nodded and patted Jessica's back. "We'll talk about the rest later. After your brother is safe again."

The walkie-talkie on the table crackled with static.

Penny grabbed it and held it tight while the anxious family waited to hear.

"I've found him," Zeke said into the walkie-talkie. "Copy?"

"Ten-four," Penny replied, her throat constricting. "Is he okay?"

The family gasped and rushed toward her, Marcy and Jessica crying, Brian looking anxious. She held up a finger, warning them to wait.

Zeke's voice cracked through the static. "Yes, he's calling out to us. But I can't get to him. He's down in a ravine by a stream."

Her heart constricted with fear but Penny tried to stay focused. "Describe the area. What's your location?"

Zeke called off the coordinates. "We're about a half mile off the main trail leading out to the highway on the left by a heavy cluster of evergreens." He described some nearby trail signs and the surrounding rocky hills. "We're near the direction sign for the ten-mile hike."

"I'm looking at the map," Penny reported back, her mind going over what she remembered about this area. "I think there's another way down to the ravine." She told him about a little-known path that followed the water. "It should be a few yards south of where you're describing."

"Thank you," Zeke reported back. "Keep everyone there until I can report in. I might need some help."

"Copy," she said. "Over and out."

She turned to Marcy and Brian. "He's okay but we have to stay here unless he calls us. It's too dangerous."

"I want to see him," Marcy insisted, turning to her husband. "Brian, let's go."

"We have to listen to Zeke," Penny told her, thinking about the dangerous men who could be lurking in those woods. "Marcy, let him handle this. He'll report back in when he has Cody safely out of that ravine."

"What if he can't bring him out?" Brian asked.

"Then he'll call us to come and help."

"I'm going to find them," he said, heading for the door.

"Brian, stop." Penny rushed toward him. "Listen, we saw what looked like some hunters in the woods earlier. It's too risky since bow-hunting season is open for antelope right now. Remember, Zeke told us he can't help Cody if he has to stop and find one of us out there."

Brian frowned over at her. "So we just wait and worry?"

She had to word this very carefully. "For now. We can't get any outside help so Zeke is doing everything he can." She gave Cody's parents a sympathetic look. "Zeke knows what he's doing and it's best we don't distract him."

She only prayed that would be enough, and she *really* hoped Zeke didn't run into any of Jake's men while he was out there trying to save that little boy.

TEN

"Cody, can you hear me?"

Zeke called out again, listening as the boy's sobs became clearer. Remembering the boy had asthma, Zeke hurried down the slippery rocks near the splashing stream, Cheetah rushing ahead.

"Hey, buddy. Are you okay?"

The boy wouldn't speak. Then Zeke saw him curled up shivering and holding himself tightly, as if he were trying to melt into the rocks and brush.

"Cody, your parents sent me. I'm going to help you."

The boy's scared voice echoed out over the woods. "I'm not supposed to talk to strangers."

Zeke couldn't identify himself as a law officer since his work was classified, and he was already pushing the envelope by even attempting to help this family.

"That's right. You're doing fine. But I've spoken with your parents. My name's Zeke and I brought my dog, Cheetah, with me. He's really good at finding people who are lost."

Cody raised his head, his eyes red rimmed and wide. "Is he a good dog?"

"The best," Zeke said, stepping an inch or two closer.

"He really likes kids. He knows not to bite someone who needs help. And you look like you could use some help."

"I lost my inhaler," Cody whimpered. "And I don't feel so good."

Not great news, but Zeke could work around it. "All right, buddy, well, the sooner you let me help, the sooner we can get you back with your parents. Meantime, take deep, slow breaths."

Cody started unfolding his bruised, scratched legs and stretched them out. "Okay. So you're not one of those scary guys?"

Zeke's blood went cold but he hurried toward the boy. "Did you see some scary guys?"

Cody was sitting up now. He wiped at his eyes and bobbed his head, his breath coming in shallow gulps. "Yeah. I hid from my stupid sister but I got lost and… I heard them saying they had to find the boy and they sounded mad. I ran away and I fell, then I ran again and I heard water running and Daddy always says to follow the stream."

"Your dad sounds real smart," Zeke said, his gaze sweeping the woods. The wind whistled and moved through the lush pines and leafy aspen trees that towered over them, blocking out the late-summer sun. In spite of the warm day, he was concerned that Cody could go into shock. Or have a full-on asthma attack.

So those goons had been nearby when the kid darted away. They'd probably heard Cody calling for his parents. Zeke sent up a prayer of thanks that Cody had been smart enough to hide and that the two on the ATVs had left the area.

Cody stared at Cheetah. "I've never seen a dog like that. He's all different colors."

Keep him talking. Zeke hadn't dealt with children a lot since his work was mostly about capturing criminals, but he knew if he kept the kid engaged, things would go better. Thinking of the time he'd spent with Kevin, he had to admit he'd love to have a kid.

Zeke smiled and squatted by the boy. "Cheetah is an Australian shepherd. But his breed actually got started in the American West, during the gold rush. You've probably heard all about that in school, huh?"

"Nope. But my dad talks to me a lot about stuff like that. He's a professor. He sure didn't know about this dog, though. I'll have to tell him."

The kid's breathing was leveling off.

"Okay, well, Cheetah is a special kind of dog. Most people don't know much about him, but his breed is also a good family dog. He's part of my family because I've helped train him to be a working dog. He's going to help me get you back to your parents. First, I need to check you over. Do you hurt anywhere?"

Cody nodded. "I fell and skinned my knees. And my arm hurts."

Zeke looked at his left arm. His wrist was purple and swollen.

"Mind if I touch that spot?"

Cody shook his head.

Zeke pressed the swollen wrist and the boy winced. "That hurts real bad."

"You might have a twisted wrist or…it could be broken."

Which meant he needed to get the child out of here, and soon. Shock could definitely set in and if the bone was broken, it would need to be set as soon as possible.

Cheetah stood guard but Zeke noticed the dog's ears lifting. Then he heard a grinding motor nearby.

Not good. The last thing he needed right now was a run-in with two criminals. Looking around, he figured they could hide here but the boy needed medical attention. He'd have to take his chances on getting Cody out of here.

"Okay, Cody, we're gonna take you to your folks. I'm going to lift you up, okay?"

The kid looked afraid. "Are you really going to take me to Mom and Dad? Am I in trouble?"

"I'm going to get you back to them and, no, you're not in trouble."

Slowly, he lifted the shaking boy. "You've been very smart and brave. Cheetah is impressed."

The boy stared down at the dog. Cheetah's curious stare seemed to satisfy him.

Zeke heard motors purring up on the trail. Trouble on the way.

"Is that someone else coming?" the boy asked, his eyes wide. "What if it's those mean men?"

"You let me worry about that," Zeke said. He didn't want to get in a shoot-out in front of the kid.

"Guard," he commanded to Cheetah. The dog would give his life to save them but Zeke hoped it wouldn't come to that.

He took the rock trail that followed the stream, but going uphill was tougher with the boy in his arms.

"I can walk, you know," Cody said.

"I have no doubt about that, but I got you, buddy."

Zeke would shield the kid if things got serious.

When the roaring motors grew louder, Zeke knew their time was running out. He couldn't let those men see him with this boy.

* * *

Penny held the two-way radio with an iron grip, wishing she knew what was going on. Already, she'd heard the hum of some off-road vehicles moving through the forest.

Marcy and Brian paced and whispered, holding each other's hands anxiously.

Kevin was asleep in one of the bedrooms, within sight.

And Jessica was sitting by the window, waiting and watching.

Penny went to her but took a seat where she could still keep a watchful eye on Kevin. "It's not your fault, you know. Brothers and sisters torment each other all the time."

Jessica wiped at her eyes. "He's such a pain but… I love him."

"Yes, he'll always be a pain. Brothers are made that way." She thought about the two very different brothers who were both now entrenched in her life. "But as long as you love him, you can forgive him."

Could Zeke do that with Jake? Would Jake bother to forgive Zeke for doing his job? And how was she supposed to forgive and forget after these last few traumatic days?

"Will he forgive me?" Jessica asked, a fragile hope in her pretty blue eyes. "And Mom and Dad? Will they forgive me?"

"Of course." Penny smiled at her. "When he gets back, he'll be so happy to see you he'll probably forget why he hid in the first place. And I'm pretty sure your parents have already forgiven you."

She only prayed that whoever was driving around out there wouldn't stand in the way of Zeke getting Cody back to his family.

Dear Lord, please help this family. Keep Zeke and Cody safe. Protect all of us.

Then they heard a crackle over the walkie-talkie.

"Come in," she said while the room went still. "Zeke, can you hear me?"

"We're on our way back," he replied. "Pack up and be ready to go. And tell the Wilders to be ready to move, too. Cody might have a broken arm."

She knew what that meant. Those guys were either chasing him or they were too close for comfort.

"Over and out," she said, turning to face Cody's parents. "Your son is safe and on his way here but he has an injured arm. You need to be ready to leave immediately."

They held each other and cried tears of relief then went into a frenzy of finishing up what little packing and cleaning they had left to do.

Jessica stood by Penny, hesitating.

When her mom turned and held her arms open, the girl rushed into her embrace.

Penny couldn't help but get all misty-eyed. She was tired and frightened and worried. Tattered and torn. She had to hold out hope that Zeke would get her and Kevin to a doctor and then to a safe house where they could all rest.

If he could only make it back here first.

Zeke held Cody against him, careful not to crush the boy's injured arm. "Keep that wrist up and close to your chest," he instructed. "You're doing great."

Cheetah scouted ahead, stopping now and then with his snout in the air. The slightest hint of a familiar scent and he'd alert them. Zeke came around a copse of aspens cluttered together in a thick symmetry. The ATVs had moved on for now, but those men could show up again at any minute.

When he heard a rustling in the woods behind him, Zeke ducked into some tall grasses and signaled for Cheetah to come. Then he put a finger to Cody's mouth. "Shhh."

The little boy clung to him and stayed silent. Someone was moving through the dirt and jutting rocks just below them.

Zeke held his breath and settled Cody against a tree, careful to shield the boy. "I'm right here," he said in a low whisper. "I'm not leaving you."

Cody bobbed his head.

Zeke took out his handgun from underneath the waistband of his pants. The boy's eyes went big but he didn't say a word.

The noise grew closer. Right below them now.

Zeke crouched in front of the child while Cheetah stood, protecting Cody on the left. They all waited, not moving, with insects buzzing around them like hungry wolves.

Then Zeke saw it. A magnificent male elk that looked to weigh about seven hundred pounds. The bull elk lifted his head, his antlers shooting out like a regal crown. He was establishing his domain. Which meant he'd picked up their scent.

"Wow," Cody said in an exhaled breath of a whisper.

"*Wow* is right," Zeke replied in the same awestruck whisper. "We'll let him pass."

"Can he hurt us?"

"Only if we provoke him."

Cheetah's ears stood straight up but the dog did his job and stayed still. They stayed quiet, watching the massive animal until he finally lowered his head and strolled away.

When that bit of excitement was over, Zeke waited several minutes before they started moving again. They were within sight of the cabin when he heard motors roaring to life behind them on the trail.

"Cody, hold on tight and protect your wrist," Zeke said. "We're gonna make a run for it."

With that, he signaled Cheetah to trot ahead. Zeke took off through the woods, the sound of gunshots firing all around them.

Penny heard the gunshots and rushed to a window.

"What's going on?" Marcy asked in alarm. "You said you saw some hunters earlier. Bow hunters."

"They had guns, too," Penny explained.

"But they shouldn't be shooting," Brian pointed out. "Not at this time of year."

"I know." She turned to them and said, "Once you get Cody back, I suggest you load up and get out of here. It's not safe."

Brian stared at her. "So…you're not talking about normal hunters, are you?"

"No," she admitted. "I don't know who they are, but they scared us enough that we're leaving. You should, too."

Before Brian could question her further, the door burst open and Zeke came barreling in with Cody in his arms and Cheetah on his heels.

"He has a possible sprained or broken wrist," Zeke said, handing Cody off to his dad. "A few scrapes and bruises but other than that, he seems fine."

Marcy and Brian fussed over Cody while Zeke turned to Penny. "Let's go."

She didn't argue. Turning to Marcy, she said, "There's a clinic up on the main highway into Iris Rock. On the left. Take him there."

"But…"

"We have to go," she said, wishing she could say more. She hurried into the bedroom and scooped Kevin into her arms.

When she came back, Zeke was already headed to the door. But he turned to face the Wilders. "You have a very brave son. He should be fine."

Zeke gave Cody a thumbs-up sign and the boy grinned. "Thanks, Mr. Zeke. We got to see an elk."

"We sure did, buddy. And you were a real trouper."

"We can't thank you enough," Brian said. "Is there any way we can help you two?"

Something passed between the two men. Brian had figured out Zeke was more than just a nature lover with a good guard dog.

"Yes," Zeke said. "Get out of here and…pretend you never saw us."

With that, he urged Penny out and into the waiting SUV.

"Thank you," Jessica called. "For saving my brother."

Zeke nodded and Penny gave the girl an encouraging smile. Then Zeke got in and started the vehicle.

The Wilders followed, carrying luggage and storage bags. They hurried into their own vehicle, Marcy holding Cody in her arms.

And not a minute too soon.

The men on the four-wheelers whirled around the curve and spotted the two vehicles leaving. They gave chase but Zeke made sure the Wilders were well on their way before he fired a couple of shots out the driver's-side window, blowing out a tire on one of the ATVs and hitting the fuel tank of the other one.

Those two weren't going anywhere for a while.

When they were on the main road, he turned to Penny. "First, I'll call Max and report in. Then we wait to hear where I move you next. And I'll get someone we can trust to come and check on Kevin's ear infection, I promise."

She bobbed her head. "Okay. How bad did things get back there?"

"Bad enough," he admitted. "An elk stalking through the woods and those two searching all around us. I'm so thankful I got Cody out of there. He could have died in that ravine or…they could have found him and used him for leverage."

"I'm glad, too," she said. "I hope they make it home safely."

"They will," he reassured her, his official phone in his hand. "Max will make sure of that when I give him the Wilders' license plate and ETA at the clinic."

"You think of everything," she said.

Zeke shrugged. "I've been trained to think of everything."

"Zeke?"

He glanced over at her, weariness cloaking him now that the adrenaline was dying down.

"Thank you."

Zeke smiled at the gratitude in her pretty eyes. "Yes, ma'am."

Then he hit the number for Max West and waited for the fallout.

ELEVEN

"Are you all settled in?"

Penny whirled from her spot at the kitchen counter, still shell-shocked. "Yes, thank you," she said in response to Zeke's question. "This place is definitely an improvement over my grandfather's cabin."

The handsome agent stood across the room near the empty fireplace. The new safe house was about thirty miles north of Billings in a spot on a hill with open valleys and rocks below. She should feel safe here and she did feel much better after a shower, a good night's sleep and a solid breakfast this morning. But she couldn't help but worry.

Zeke tried to reassure her. "Yes. Secluded, gated and posted with no-trespassing signs. Nothing out of the ordinary last night, thankfully."

She wondered when this man ever slept. He and Cheetah had prowled around last night like two crouching lions, always on the hunt.

Penny poured two cups of coffee. "Well, we are surrounded by officers with dogs."

Zeke took the coffee she offered, his dark gaze washing over her with all kinds of mixed emotions. "I can't be with you 24/7, so the team is stepping in."

Max West had stepped in all right. She knew from listening and watching Zeke's stoic expression that he'd received a royal dressing down for taking matters into his own hands. "You took a risk, hiding me like that. I'm sorry your boss isn't happy."

"Technically he's not *my* boss, but for now he's the man in charge. I insisted on joining the hunt when I realized the Dupree family had taken my brother."

"Or so you thought at the time."

He nodded and glanced over his shoulder. "I was also concerned about you."

That was a new revelation. Giving him a shocked look, she said, "I thought you only became worried about me when you found Jake holding a gun on me, what, two days ago?"

"I worried long before that." He told her about asking special permission to help with the search. "At the time, I was apprehensive about all three of you, but I told Max and the team about you and Kevin. I had a hunch Jake would try to contact you."

"Why?" she asked. "Did you think I would help him? Hide him?"

"I wasn't sure," he admitted on a gruff tone. "Mostly, I wanted to make sure you were both safe. I went with my gut and I was right."

Penny didn't press him. They'd talked a lot back at the cabin but he hadn't mentioned this at all. He couldn't tell her very much due to the classified aspects of his job, but she'd pieced things together enough to know he came here to help track down his brother but discovered the horrible truth. The same truth she'd had to accept.

Jake had willingly gone with Angus Dupree that day all those months ago. How long had he been playing all of them?

Penny dropped that topic since it made her broken heart throb painfully. "I wish I could just walk out of here and keep going."

"But you know that's not safe, so don't do anything that could cause you or Kevin more harm."

She'd already done too many stupid things, so his warning was unnecessary. Right now, however, she felt safe and sound and secure. As secure as she could feel under the circumstances.

The house was lovely. Rustic and solid, it sat up on a hill, which held a stunning view of the mountains and valleys all around. It wasn't too big. Just two bedrooms and a huge kitchen and living room area with a massive stone fireplace and glass windows lining one wall.

She'd been told to stay away from those windows.

"How bad are things with you and the boss?"

"Not so bad," he replied, shrugging. "I've been in worse trouble."

"But I heard him telling you that you couldn't go dark on him again. Does that mean what I think it means?"

"It means next time I take you away, I have to stay in touch." He took a long swig of coffee. "They knew we were together but they didn't know our location. Meantime, they've checked all along the basin. Jake might be long gone but he's still got people out there. The two thugs who came after us stayed well hidden until they thought they had us. Now apparently they're the ones who've gone dark. Right along with my brother."

Penny's insides went cold thinking about how close

they'd come to getting into a battle with those two henchmen.

"Well, we're here now, and we have guards," she said, trying to find the good in this. "I don't see us going anywhere soon. In fact, I think your team is watching us as much as they're watching for Jake and his goons."

"They're friendlies," he replied. "You've got Nina Atkins coming next with her Rottweiler, Sam. She'll help me with the next twelve-hour shift."

"Is her dog safe? I mean, around Kevin?"

"He's trained to do as he's told. He won't harm your son. Most Rottweilers can be safe if handled and trained correctly. Trust me, Sam is a pro." Zeke drained his coffee. "How's Kevin doing?"

"He's much better. Thank you for finding a doctor."

"We have our ways," he replied with a heart-stopping grin. "So the antibiotics are helping?"

"Yes, but the doctor said he might have to get tubes in his ears to finally clear things up for good."

"There is so much that goes into caring for a child." He settled into a deep, cushy leather chair by the fireplace. "I never realized how much. I admire how you always put him first."

"I love him. He's my life," Penny admitted, wondering if he was thinking of his own single mother. "I'll do what I need to do to protect him."

"When this is over," Zeke said on a measured note, his gaze capturing hers, "I'd like to be a part of his life."

"When this is over, you'll head back to Utah, won't you?"

His dark eyes flooded with indecision. "I might not. I don't know yet."

Penny sank down on an ottoman across from him.

Kevin was asleep in a pop-up crib in the guest bedroom right next to this room, the door open so she could see him and Cheetah. The dog seemed to know his duty was to protect her son.

She didn't know how to respond to Zeke's surprising uncertainty. What would *she* do after this was over? If this was ever over?

Here they were, forced together again, in a nice house with a breathtaking view. She could almost pretend that her life could be like this. Except that each time she glanced outside from her corner of this luxury prison, she saw armed people with canines walking the perimeter.

"What if this is never over?" she asked, fear in the one question and an image of always looking over her shoulder cluttering her mind. Jake could stay hidden for years. He had the means and the motivation to do whatever he wanted.

Zeke did a sweep of the room. They were alone. He got up and came to sit next to her on the cushy ottoman, the masculine warmth radiating from him giving her strength. And causing her to wish for things she couldn't have.

When he took her hand in his, Penny almost pulled away. He'd never touched her like this before. It thrilled her and frightened her. She didn't dare fall for Jake's half brother. It wouldn't be right. It couldn't work. But her hammering heart was having trouble accepting that fact.

"It will be over," he said, his fingers covering hers. "The outcome isn't going to be good, either way. But it will end. The team combed the basin and woods and those men are gone but they left a lot of evidence behind. They're searching for the make and model of the ATVs, hoping it will lead them to a tip. They managed to preserve some tire tracks and they found some casings but those could both be from other people."

"They might not ever find those men," she said, desperation coloring her tone. "Jake always did know how to cover his tracks."

Zeke held tight to her hand. "I gave a detailed report on what transpired, including us helping the Wilders. And I told the team that the men sounded aggravated and on edge. They keep getting thwarted and to a criminal, nothing is more frustrating. Sooner or later, they will mess up big-time or they'll grow tired and turn tail and run, leaving Jake and his bribes behind."

She'd given up but his words reassured her. Maybe those men would figure things out and decide it wasn't worth it. "So until then, I stay here?"

"You stay where I stay," he said, the look in his eyes going from professional to intensely personal.

The air between them hummed with an awareness that had little to do with an FBI agent keeping her safe. Penny tried to shake it off but her attraction to Zeke was overwhelming and hard to explain. He made her feel things she'd never felt before—security, respect and a newfound hope. So she tried to ignore the way he leaned in as if he wanted to kiss her.

When they heard a door opening, Zeke stood abruptly and turned to see Max West moving into the room from the main hallway, his all-seeing gaze hitting on their guilty expressions.

Putting down a box marked Petrov's Bakery, he motioned to Zeke. "A word with you, Agent Morrow."

* * *

Zeke winked at Penny and moved over to the kitchen with Max. "Sir?"

"What's going on here?"

"Um… I'm guarding a woman in danger?"

"Yeah, we've all figured that one out," Max said, his icy stare burning a hole in Zeke's brain. "Fraternizing?"

"Sir, I…"

Max actually cracked what might have been a grin. "I'm messing with you, but with a warning. Be sure of what you're feeling. Things have been crazy over the last few days and you're all mixed up in this because someone you care about is in a heap of trouble. Don't mistake fatigue and adrenaline for something else."

"You've been through this," Zeke pointed out, chafing underneath Max's burning assumption. "A lot of the team has. How did you handle it?"

"Not very well at first," Max admitted, referring to how he fell in love with and married Katerina Garwood, a woman who'd once been engaged to a drug trafficker involved with the Dupree family. "And I don't have any right to fuss at you since there seems to be a wedding in the works with every month that passes. It's just… you're close to everyone involved in this case."

"You mean my half brother and his ex-girlfriend and my nephew, Kevin?"

"Isn't that enough? You can't protect all of them. You're going to have to make some tough choices from here on out."

"No, sir, no choice," Zeke replied. "I'm doing my job." He shrugged. "And while I'd like to bring Jake in alive, I'll do whatever it takes to end this once and for all."

Max let out a grunt. "I'm going to believe you haven't been deliberately letting your brother and his cronies get away. Instead, your first priority is protecting the boy and his mother, right?"

"You can take that to the bank, sir," Zeke replied. "I couldn't very well leave them in the woods to fend for themselves. So, yes, I made the decision to stay close to them instead of pursuing any and all threats. I counted on my team to cover me on that."

Max gave him a hard-edged glare but he didn't dispute Zeke. "Okay, Zeke, I get it. So far, nothing from the basin area and most of the tips we've received haven't panned out. I think even though you had two people stalking you in the basin, Jake has pulled back or maybe left Montana. But make no mistake. He's hired underlings to finish the job and he'll still come after the boy even if he's not physically around to do it himself."

Zeke nodded brusquely. "He'll keep coming. He's just trying to figure out where we are."

"I don't know how he's finding you. We couldn't even locate you out there."

Zeke ignored Max's pointed comment. He didn't know how Jake managed, either. But he had the techs on it. "Dylan is checking for anything suspicious. Jake could have someone on the inside watching our every move."

Tech guru Dylan O'Leary worked tirelessly behind the scenes to uncover anything on the Duprees or Jake Morrow. He was good at digging up data where no data was supposed to be found.

"Are you accusing someone on my team, Agent Morrow?"

"No, but I'm saying Jake is smart and he had a lot

of people fooled. He knows people on both sides of the law and he can be very persuasive."

Max looked skeptical but finally nodded. "He does seem to slip through our fingers at every turn."

"Maybe someone should talk to Violetta again. Did she go back to Chicago?"

"Yes, but she should be back for Reginald's trial, whenever that might be." Max rubbed his scar. "Soon, I hope. Ian and Esme will be able to come back to the States once this is over."

Agent Ian Slade and Esme Dupree had gotten married and immediately went into the witness protection program until this was all over. Esme's brother, Reginald, might be in jail, but he could still put out a hit on both of them.

"I can't wait that long," Zeke said, hoping he'd be able to attend that trial. Max's frustration over both only mirrored his own.

With Reginald in jail and Angus dead, the whole organization had become fractured. The FBI had been rounding up underlings all over the country. But Jake still remained at large and now they had a bead on Gunther Caprice, too. He'd been a thorn in their sides since he'd slipped away before all the fireworks started. He probably knew where all the bodies were buried so why had he come back to help Jake? Did Zeke's brother have something on him?

"I want this over," he said, glancing toward where Penny sat reading a magazine. "Violetta showed up in Florida and shot Angus. She had a way of keeping tabs on her brothers and it makes sense she's doing the same with Jake."

"Why don't you ask Penny some more questions?"

Max suggested, his expression blank. "She's only one of a long line of women who've been involved with Jake. We've questioned several of them and they all describe Jake's habits and MO the same as she has, but she might remember something none of the others can." Max pivoted his head toward Penny. "Because of the boy."

"She doesn't know anything," Zeke replied, anger fueling each word. "We've all questioned her. I think she just got caught up with the wrong man."

Max put his hands on his hips. "I'll get in touch with Violetta and see if she has any inkling about Jake's current movements or past deeds. Meantime, you do what you're here to do. Protect Penny and her son. And bring down your half brother."

"Yep, there is that." Zeke gave Max a long stare, wondering if the man still doubted his loyalty. "Something else has been niggling at my brain."

Max's eyebrows shot up. "And…?"

"Dylan keeps me up-to-date on a lot of things and one of them is how concerned he is about Zara. They can't even communicate now. She's not responding to his texts or emails."

Zara was Dylan's fiancée but she was in training at Quantico and should be home in time for their fall wedding. If everything went according to plan. But something was up at Quantico. And that bothered Zeke. Zara had gone into training around the time Jake had disappeared with Angus. That, and Dylan's concerns, caused a nagging worry in Zeke's mind. If Dylan couldn't find out what was going on, no one could.

Max pulled out his sunglasses. "Yes, we're all concerned but Quantico is in charge of Quantico and Zara

Fielding knows what to do. She's there to learn. That's what recruits do. We have our own case to worry about."

"What if the two are connected?" Zeke said. "What if Jake is involved somehow?"

Max looked confused, his piercing blue gaze filled with resolve. "Do you think he's got someone on the inside at Quantico?"

"Anything is possible with my brother," Zeke said. "Penny did make one remark about him going on and on about Quantico once when he called her. About all the people depending on him, all the people he trusted. But he told her he couldn't trust them anymore."

"We all have friends who've been through Quantico, Zeke, and not all of them stay friends. What's your point?"

Zeke shrugged again. "She said he sounded off, scattered and unsure. Jake could have someone there watching and listening and maybe that person is willing to help him. And he has to know Zara is training there. He could be trying to distract Dylan so he can't dig too deep into Jake's case or...he could have someone watching Zara and hacking into her personal messages."

He took a breath and rushed ahead. "Zara wouldn't talk about *our* case. But another agent could give her the wrong intel just to throw her off, thinking to mess up our whole operation. We're a highly classified unit, Max. Jake's known for creating distractions to cover his tracks. He did that this week when he held Penny and let Gunther kidnap Kevin."

Max studied Penny then pinned Zeke with a stare. "Did Dylan put this weird theory in your head?"

Zeke shook his head. Dylan planned to investigate as much as he could, but Max didn't need to know that right now. "No, but I've been taking notes and trying to figure things out. The timeline fits. Dylan's been concerned since Zara left right about the time Jake went rogue on us. He could be trying to get just enough information to stalk out our whole case."

Max shook his head. "It's a long shot because we didn't even know Jake had turned until months later. All Dylan knows is that Zara's class has had some trouble. You need to leave it at that."

"Jake had already turned when we thought he'd been kidnapped. He probably started covering his tracks the minute he took off with Angus in that chopper." He tapped his fingers on the kitchen counter. "I'm hoping Dylan will prove me wrong but I'm not letting this go until I know what's behind it. Besides, we owe it to Dylan and Zara to stick our noses into this, don't you think?"

Max didn't argue with that. "This is far-fetched, Zeke. But I guess it's worth looking into since we don't have much to go on in the first place. Jake knows a lot of people at Quantico and if he convinced someone he's been wronged, they could be trying to dig up information on our every move to report back to him. That would explain how he's always one step ahead of us."

"And Gunther Caprice is helping him. Gunther could still have connections, inside and out. Another thing to consider."

They talked a few more minutes before Max left. The day passed slowly but Zeke did insist that Penny should get some rest, so he took over with Kevin for a while. He enjoyed feeding the little boy and playing games with him. Kevin loved it when Zeke grabbed his stuffed horse and made whinnying noises.

They were playing that game when Zeke looked up to find Penny standing at the bedroom door wearing clean jeans and a black sweater, her damp hair like dark liquid gold, her eyes full of both hope and trepidation. He saw the gentle longing in her eyes. It tugged at the emptiness inside him.

Kevin giggled and pointed at Zeke, bringing him back to the present. He kept trying to say Zeke's name but it came out as "'Eke."

"'Eke? Horsey?"

Both Zeke and the boy giggled. Even Cheetah seemed to be in on the joke. But Penny's smile froze on her face. The longing in her eyes turned to a wariness that left Zeke cold.

She still wasn't sure she wanted him in their lives. So he watched her take Kevin for his bath and bedtime then waited for her to come back to have dinner with him.

While he waited, he wished for so many things and told himself with each wish that he couldn't have those things. His father had been a womanizer and now his brother was a criminal.

What did that make him?

Penny came back into the living room and gave him a weak smile. "You wore him out. That's a first." Then she motioned to the kitchen, her smile gone. "Let's eat."

A man could get used to this, he thought later as the sun began to set over the mountains. They had a quick dinner of sandwiches and soup but didn't talk much, mostly because Kevin woke up again, full of energy, which didn't allow for any personal talk. Which was maybe for the best.

Penny had become distant and wary again, so she must have had the same doubts as he did. Had he gone too far in playing with Kevin and helping to take care of him?

He was about to delve into that question when Nina Atkins arrived with her K-9 partner, Sam, and went over the routine with Zeke. She'd done a good job guarding the Wild Iris so Max had rotated her around to helping Zeke. He'd put Timothy Ramsey on the inn. Another good rookie. His dog, Frodo, specialized in arson detection but they could both handle any situation.

"We have locals down by the gate and you and me up here inside the house," Zeke said, updating Nina. "I just need to grab a few winks. We can take turns."

"Grab a lot of winks," Nina replied, her short blond hair falling in spikey waves around her temples and chin. "Sam and I don't mind staying up. We're night owls."

"So is our subject," Zeke said, glancing at Penny. She'd rooted herself into a cozy chair pushed up inside the only corner without windows, probably because it was right next to the bedroom where Kevin was sleeping. Or maybe because she'd tried to avoid Zeke for the last few hours, too.

Something had almost happened earlier there on the ottoman. He'd wanted to pull Penny into his arms and kiss her. Which would only make matters worse. He was here to do a job, to find his brother and maybe spare Jake's life at least. It wouldn't be a good life. He'd be behind bars for a long time. But if there was a chance…

Then what? You take over as Daddy to his son? Bring his son to see him in prison?

Zeke turned back to Nina. "I think I do need to get some rest so I can get my head straight."

Nina nodded in understanding. "I'll go and introduce

myself to Penny and let Sam and her get acclimated to each other. Where's the boy?"

"Asleep in a crib in the second bedroom. We hope. He keeps waking up." Zeke pointed to the room with the curtains drawn and a single lamp burning. "He's been through a lot."

"I'll take care of them, Zeke," Nina said. "Sam won't let you down."

"I'm not concerned about you and Sam. You're a good agent," Zeke said. "I just hope *I* don't let Penny and Kevin down."

Then he turned and headed for the other bedroom so he could get a shower and catch some shut-eye. But he had a feeling he wouldn't be able to sleep. If Max, and now Nina, had noticed the closeness he and Penny were feeling, then everyone else would soon see it, too. He couldn't let his personal feelings cloud his judgment, though.

Zeke couldn't deny that his feelings for Penny had changed over the last forty-eight hours but it was way too soon—and too dangerous—to decide what those feelings could mean.

TWELVE

Penny heard the gunshots at the same time Cheetah started barking. Then the night turned chaotic. Zeke hurried into her room, barefooted. He carried his weapon and wore a black T-shirt and jeans. Kevin sat up and started sobbing.

"Get down on the floor," Zeke said, not waiting for her to reach her child. Instead, he lifted Kevin out of the crib and, crouching, passed the child to Penny. "Stay here and stay down."

He turned to Cheetah and ordered, "Stay. Guard."

Cheetah went silent and stood alert in front of Penny and Kevin, his body pointed toward the door.

"I'll be back as soon as I can," Zeke said before he hurried through the house. "Nina and Sam are right here."

Penny held her son and soothed his tears while she tried to stay strong. Cheetah became the consummate professional. The dog seemed to be frozen in stone in front of where she'd pulled Kevin to a dark corner by a chunky nightstand. Cheetah kept his snout in the air and his head toward the open door. Having been protected by the amazing canine before, Penny tried to stay calm.

Glancing around, Penny searched for anything she could use as a weapon. When she saw a set of black bookends enclosing three classic novels, she grabbed one and held it close. The heavy metal shaped like a ladder gave her a sense of confidence but her rapidly beating heart and the cold sweat trickling down her body reinforced her fears for her child.

She'd fight anyone to the death to save Kevin.

Even his own father.

Zeke rushed through the house and out the door, shouting to Nina, "Don't leave them alone."

The rookie agent, who'd been sitting with a view of the front yard, had already jumped into action. She had her weapon out and Sam was leashed and roaming around the big den. "I saw at least two out there, Zeke. They split apart. Be careful."

"Roger," he called.

Zeke made it out the front door in a low crouch, his bare feet hitting the rocky walkway in a silent thump, cold wind rushing over him. He heard more gunfire, barking dogs and voices echoing out over the yard. When a dark figure whirled toward him and fired, just missing his head, Zeke fired back and the man slumped to the ground.

Then silence.

It was all over in a matter of minutes.

Zeke held his gun on the figure sprawled out on the walkway. Then he leaned down and felt the man's thick neck for a pulse. He was dead.

Leo Gallagher and his Labrador retriever, True, who'd been patrolling outside, trotted up. "They were trying to get to Kevin. I heard them talking. 'Kill any-one but the kid,' one of them said. 'Keep the kid alive.'"

Zeke stared down at the man on the ground. "This one isn't going to talk. What about the others? Was one of them Gunther?"

"Hard to say. The one I saw was dressed all in black, including a mask, and he ran down the hill. I've got someone searching for him and the other one."

"Everyone accounted for?"

"Yes, we're all good," Leo replied. "I'll take care of things out here."

Zeke nodded and turned toward the house, relief rushing over him in great waves. "I'm going to check on our subjects."

When he got inside, he found Nina standing guard with Sam inside the den. The dog roamed around, sniff-ing and listening. While Sam specialized in cadaver detection, the animal could also take down a criminal in about zero seconds flat.

"We're all safe," Nina said, glancing toward the bed-room.

He nodded. "All clear outside, too." Then he went to the open bedroom door and called out. "Penny, it's Zeke. Everything is under control."

She didn't move from the corner.

He called Cheetah. "Come."

Cheetah hurried toward him but Penny stayed in the corner, holding her son with her left arm around Kevin and a metal object in her right hand. When he kneeled down in front of her, she lifted her head to stare into his eyes, a stricken expression on her lovely face. "Noth-ing in my life is ever going to be under control again."

* * *

Zeke couldn't get through to her. She was done. Penny was slowly giving up, that spunk he'd so admired in her turning into a sputtering spark that was about to fizzle out. He had to try and keep her going. They had to move again.

So he went back into the corner where she sat in the big chair, holding Kevin asleep in her arms.

Outside, dawn shimmered through the tall conifers, the sun's rays shooting against the rocky hills in a brilliant announcement of the new day.

"Penny, I know you're tired. We all are. But we have to keep moving." They should have left hours ago but she'd held on to Kevin and refused to move. "We've been compromised. We have to go."

"No," she said. "I'm not moving my son again. Unless it's to a place far away from Montana. I can't do it, Zeke. I'm tired of hiding in dark corners. And I can't be around you anymore. Every time I look at you, I think of Jake."

That angry comment floored Zeke. She'd never want anything to do with him even if he did catch the bad guy. Because she was probably still in love with Jake, and she was right. Being around Zeke only reminded her of all that she'd been through with his brother. Zeke didn't know how to deal with that kind of pain. He sure didn't know how to make her see that he could never do the things Jake had done, that he'd never intentionally hurt her. But he could hurt her in so many other ways if he didn't play this right.

He stood and scratched at his five-o'clock shadow. Giving Nina a blank stare, he headed to the kitchen for some coffee. They'd ID'd the dead man as Claude Baxter, formerly from Chicago. He had a record and he'd first been hired as a bouncer at a well-known bar owned by the Dupree family and moved on to join the ranks of the Dupree crime syndicate. Since that family was officially busted up now, Jake had to have taken over paying the man's salary. Apparently, he was bribing or blackmailing people to do his dirty work.

The other intruders had managed to escape in spite of canines searching all night long. The trail had gone cold down on the road. They must have hopped into a getaway vehicle and taken off for parts unknown. The team was searching for reports on stolen or carjacked vehicles in the area. So far, nothing.

Nina came to stand beside him, her dark brown eyes full of sympathy. "I can talk to her."

"Have at it. I'm at about the end of my rope."

Nina poured a cup of the fresh coffee and headed to the corner. Penny hadn't eaten any breakfast yet, but then neither had he. Someone had opened the muffins and pastries Max had left, but the thought of eating turned Zeke's stomach sour.

This had to end. Jake had some kind of hold on them and if he knew his brother, he also had spies everywhere. How else was he constantly finding them?

He hurt for Penny and Kevin. He mourned his brother's lost logic and lack of decency. What could he do?

He could pray, and he had prayed, over and over. Zeke thought about calling his mother, but he tried to leave her out of his work problems and since he couldn't explain what was going on, he refrained from doing that. But he wondered if Jake would try to contact her as a last resort. She'd call him if that happened. His mother had been a newshound since she knew a little about his work. She would have heard about Jake by now.

The world knew about him but he seemed to be hiding from all of them. Now Zeke had to wonder if he could ever get Penny to a truly safe place.

Then something hit him square in the gut. Whirling so fast he surprised Cheetah, Zeke headed for the corner where Nina sat talking to Penny. "I need to go through that bag you carry around," he said to Penny.

"You mean Kevin's diaper bag?" she asked, clearly shocked at the strange request.

"Yes. That and your backpack, too. Where are they?"

Nina gave him a questioning glance. "In the bedroom. I'll get them for you, Penny."

When Nina hurried away, Penny stared up at him. "I told you and I just told Nina, I want to go back to the Wild Iris Inn. I'll get the rest of my stuff. Maybe I'll buy a plane ticket to Florida. Or maybe California. Or... Canada."

"Just hold that thought," Zeke said, grabbing the colorful bags Nina brought to him.

When he dumped the contents of the diaper bag out on the big ottoman by the chair, Penny glared at him. "What are you doing, Zeke?"

"Looking for a GPS tracker," he said. "I think I've figured out how Jake keeps finding us."

Penny couldn't believe she hadn't known about the tiny metal tracking device that Jake had embedded inside the plush lining of Kevin's favorite stuffed animal. He'd had it sewn in so deeply, they would have never discovered it. A small slit in the horse's underbelly had been resewn with tight brown threads but Zeke had pressed his fingers all along the seam and after finding a pair of scissors, had opened the stitches.

After digging his fingers around, he had pulled out a small cylinder that wasn't much bigger than a dime. "It looks like a key fob," he said. "He'd have to be nearby to locate you, but it's doable. This is made to track pets within a certain radius but Jake's smart enough to have something state-of-the-art inside this thing."

"He sent that to Kevin right before he disappeared," she said, gasping. "He must have figured this would happen."

"He wanted to get back here and take his son," Zeke replied. "So he planned ahead. He must have driven all around the basin area before the inn showed up on his tracking device, probably his cell phone."

Then he held up the other one he'd found in her backpack. "He could have easily dropped this one inside your backpack when he took you the other day."

"He's been tracking me all this time," Penny said in a weak whisper after she'd put Kevin in his crib. "First the stuffed animal and now the backpack."

"Yes. If he wanted to keep tabs on you, this was a good way to do it without anyone knowing." He pointed to the diaper bag. "He put one in the toy to mainly keep tabs on Kevin, but he wanted to keep track of you, too. So he could distract you long enough for Caprice to take the boy."

She put a hand to her mouth and held up her backpack. "He's been watching us since the beginning! He was coming for me in Colorado but I got away."

Zeke let out a grunt. "He's had a bead on you for months now. That works much like a GPS. No cameras or recordings, just a little dot on the map he can follow on any electronic device. He lost you for a while there, so staying on the move was smart on your part, but he must have asked around and found out you were back working as a wilderness guide." A muscle ticked in his jaw. "He distracted you so the man could get to Kevin. The stuffed horse has been with us since then along with your backpack, and that's how he found you at the cabin and here."

"That and his ability to dig up enough info to hunt us," he added. "Jake can charm anyone into giving him information."

"And now?" she asked, getting up to pace the room. "Now you've disabled both of those things?"

"We have," he said, his tone grim. "But we have to save the trackers and the stuffed horse for evidence."

"Now Kevin loses his favorite toy, too?"

"I'm sorry," Zeke said. "I'll find him another one."

Penny rubbed her hands up and down her arms to get rid of the invasiveness that covered her. "And that will make up for everything, right?"

She hated the hurt she saw in his eyes. Wishing she could take back her careless comment, she lowered her head. "I'm sorry, but I can't believe this. Jake's been spying on me. I can't hide from that."

"Just another sign of how far he's willing to go to get his way," Zeke said, his voice husky with regret.

A shiver moved down Penny's body. She felt violated and exposed. And hurt. How could Jake do something like that?

Because he'd lost his soul through greed and bitterness and a need to…to what? Prove himself, brag about his dirty money? To give his son all the things he'd never had?

She whirled, dizziness overtaking her. "I can't—"

Zeke was there, holding her up, getting her to the sofa and into the beautiful midmorning light that she'd tried to stay away from. "Sit here," he said gently, his eyes holding hers.

Penny sank down. "Kevin?"

"Cheetah is guarding Kevin."

Zeke looked down at her, his dark gaze washing her in that same brilliant light. "I know this isn't easy."

"No," she said, "it isn't, and I shouldn't take it all out on you. I'm sorry for what I said earlier."

His expression changed. She could see the war within his soul. Then he sank down beside her and pulled her into his arms. "I can make you forget him, Penny."

She gasped, tears misting her eyes. Deep down she wanted that. Wished for it with every fiber of her being. "But Kevin is his son."

Zeke glanced around. They were alone, and that attraction pulling at them proved impossible to resist. He lowered his head and kissed her, a gentle brush of their lips that deepened for only a couple of seconds.

And burned through her soul.

Then he pulled away and stared down at her, the light in his eyes softening. "Kevin needs me in his life. And… I'm beginning to think I need both of you in my life."

She stood, running a hand through her tousled hair. "I can't do this now, Zeke. It's too much, too soon. You don't know me and I don't really know you. I can't risk it."

Zeke stood, too, and took her hand. "I know. We'll wait and see how this goes. We can't do anything until we find Jake. And after that…"

After that, they might not want to be anywhere near each other. Ever again. No matter what happened, the shadow of Jake's horrible downfall would haunt them.

"He's going to die, isn't he?" she asked. "They're going to kill him. You'll do it if you have to, right?"

Zeke's eyes turned dark and grim. "I'll do my job, yes. And right now, that means I'll get to anyone who tries to hurt you and Kevin."

"Is that it? Your sense of protectiveness has kicked in? Or is it more of a sense of taking down the older brother who betrayed you?"

"Penny…"

She saw the frustration in his eyes, saw that torment that had carried such weight with both of them. "Jake will always be there between us, Zeke. Whether he's dead or alive. And we'll both always wonder, won't we? We'll wonder about him and…we'll never quite trust each other."

She turned, wishing she hadn't hurt him, wishing for so many things that could never be. But the wall around her heart ached with a heaviness that would never go away. She'd believed Jake loved her. Finally. After her mother's death and her father's abandonment, finally, someone besides her precious grandfather loved her.

But she'd been fooled and abandoned yet again. And so had her child. So she couldn't trust herself to fall for Zeke. Not now. Not so soon after Jake's lies and deceptions. Her ex-boyfriend had stood between Zeke and her from the start, and he'd always be right here with them.

"This could never work," she whispered. "I need to remember why I'm here. My son has to come first."

"He does come first," Zeke said. "From the moment I knew you had a son, I wanted to put Kevin first."

There was that about him, too. That need to do the right thing when everything was going wrong. Penny had to trust Zeke for now. She didn't have anywhere else to turn. And…hadn't she thanked God over and over for sending him to her? Why fight it when the urgency of the situation demanded that *she* needed to do the right thing, too?

"Get me out of here," she finally said. "The sooner we move on, the sooner this can be over."

When she looked back, she saw the stark resolve in Zeke's eyes. "You're right. I want this over as much as you do. And the sooner the better. Just prepare yourself. This is not going to end well no matter what we'd each like to believe."

Penny kept walking toward the bedroom, the whisper of his gentle kiss still warming her lips. Did he believe that she still wanted Jake, after all of this?

That was a question that clamored silently between them.

And one she'd have to answer truthfully sooner or later.

THIRTEEN

Another remote cabin. Another stunning view.

Penny stood away from the reinforced windows but the mountains and valleys still stretched before her in the last throes of summer. Soon the leaves on the aspen and cottonwood trees would change and the tamarack conifers would turn golden and drop their fronds. These woods would change from burning orange, brown and gold to stark grays and whites, covered in snow. She'd been told these windows allowed those inside to see out, but no one could see inside. A special tinted and reinforced glass that allowed for privacy and yet showed off this amazing view.

A prison nonetheless.

She missed being free. Being out there in the fresh air and the wind. She missed so many things that she promised herself she'd never take for granted again once she was allowed to be on her own. If she ever got to go outside again. But she wasn't sure she'd ever feel safe in the woods after this experience.

"My whole life has been put on hold," she said, turning to where Zeke sat scrolling on his phone. "I hope Claire and Rex are okay. I've had them on my mind, too."

"We've got people watching out for them," Zeke replied. "Nina told me they're doing great. Rex said he wasn't going back to Florida until he knew you and Kevin were safe."

Penny smiled at that. "He's a widower who decided to travel the country after his wife died three years ago. He helps out around the inn. I miss Claire and Rex so much."

"Well, you'll get to see both of them again soon."

Penny hoped she'd see her friends again. But she knew Jake wouldn't want to leave any witnesses to testify against him. She'd brought this danger to the quaint inn she loved so much.

And yet here, she was surrounded by the best possible security team. Today, she and Zeke were alone in the cabin with Kevin while the rest of the team worked to follow leads and do whatever else they had to do to track down a wanted man.

But they weren't really alone. There were guards outside, waiting and watching, stalking around with loaded weapons.

This house was sixty miles west of Billings and centered high up on a rocky hillside. While it was clean and held all the modern amenities, it still reminded her of her grandfather's cabin. It wasn't very big but it was solid, more of a good hunting cabin than a vacation retreat. Someone from the FBI owned it, so it had been custom built for protection if needed.

The home consisted of one large room with a massive stone fireplace along one wall, a huge kitchen and dining area and a den, all with floor-to-ceiling windows, and doors leading out to a sprawling deck. One big bedroom with an arched open doorway along with a bath finished out the other side and offered another stunning view of a small lake below.

Lovely. She could imagine being here on a retreat, resting and having a romantic time. A fire in the fireplace, soft music in the background, holding hands with someone she loved while the snow surrounded the whole place.

But Zeke had gone over an escape route with her, just in case things went wrong. That sobering discussion came back to her full force now. The small mudroom hidden behind the pantry off the kitchen, with an enclosed set of stairs leading out to a path down the hillside, was her way out.

She was beginning to hate cabins.

"How long is this going to go on, Zeke?" she asked.

"I'm trying to get any information I can," Zeke finally replied. "But all the tips we've received on Jake's recent whereabouts keep running cold. Sightings here and there followed by nothing. The man is trained to blend in and he knows how and where to hide. We've taken down one of his hired assassins but the others have managed to get away. No one has managed to get a bead on Jake since the day he tried to take you and Kevin."

"He knows how to disappear," she pointed out. But then, that was obvious. "He could have finally given up and left the country without us."

She hoped Jake had taken off so she could get back to some sort of normalcy. But that shoot-out last night proved it was probably just wishful thinking.

Kevin walked up to her and smiled, his chubby finger pointing to the window. "Be-ars."

"Yes, bears," Penny replied softly. She didn't want

him to be afraid of the many animals that roamed the state, but bears had been the only logical reason she could give him for not going outside. "They play here sometimes."

"Play, Mommy. Outside?" Kevin ran to Zeke, his big dark eyes hopeful. "'Eke? Outside? Cheety?"

Zeke's gaze collided with hers and caused a sizzling awareness to burn like a wildfire between them. She saw the rawness edging his eyes. "I wish we could, buddy, but—"

"Let's play with the blocks," she suggested, taking Kevin's hand to lead him to a toy chest they'd found in a corner. Sitting on the floor, she adjusted the jeans and big sweatshirt Nina had brought her earlier and took the wooden logs out and faked a grin for her son's sake. "Build Mommy a cabin."

Kevin went to work, his efforts a bit wobbly but his smile as bright as the sunshine. At least he was feeling better now.

Penny loved him with such intensity, it took her breath away. How could she protect him? Thankful for Zeke and his team, she turned toward the man.

Zeke glanced up, his gaze holding her, the look in his eyes telling her what she couldn't deny. He was taking this protection duty very seriously, but he'd shown her signs of tenderness and understanding. The kind of signs a woman could interpret as attraction. She couldn't put much store into what could never be.

Or did she dare to dream?

She'd given up trying to deny her attraction to Zeke, but at least now she knew she truly did like him and that she wasn't projecting what she'd felt for Jake onto his younger half brother.

This was different. Secure and strong. Faith filled and warm with hope.

Did he feel the same way? As if his whole world had shifted and changed, the terrain rocky and unsure but beautiful, as if his heart had begun to mend itself piece by piece with each tumbling step. Or did he feel the fear and doubt that plagued her each time she looked at him? That kind of emotional tug of a warning mixed with an anticipation that shouted "He's different but don't make the same mistake again."

She managed a weak smile. He nodded and looked as if he wanted to say more.

Then his phone dinged and he stopped to read something. "Dylan got a match for the ATVs' tire tracks. A dealer in Billings sold two ATVs that match the ones we saw to a big muscled man with a distinctive accent."

Penny grinned at Kevin while her pulse increased. "That looks great, honey. Build Mommy a pretty house, okay?"

Kevin grinned and held up a connecting log. "'Kay."

Penny kissed her son's chubby cheek then hurried to Zeke. "Could that be the man you shot the other night?"

"Sounds like one and the same," Zeke replied grimly. "I never got a good look at his face when we were in the woods the other day, but I saw him up close the other night and I'm pretty sure he was one of the two driving around on one of the off-road vehicles. Dylan's going to send out his picture to see if the ATV store manager can identify him as Claude Baxter."

"How will this help?"

"Well, if we can trace that man's movements, we might find Jake. Or at least start a trail and keep it going. We need to somehow connect Jake to this man.

We have Jake's blood as evidence, too, from where Cheetah took a bite out of him."

"It's at least something to go on," she said, a little tickle of hope moving up her spine when she remembered that horrible day. He'd shared information he wasn't supposed to share and she appreciated knowing. But that hope was overshadowed by what might come next.

Zeke put his phone down and stood up, relief softening his rugged features. "This is major, a good lead at last. We're gonna celebrate this small step forward tonight since Dylan is doing all the footwork and reporting to Max, too. I have two new guards hidden on the property—local hires who are trained for this type of work. And the whole team scattered from the road to the woods all around us." He released a breath. "Jake is smart. He'll send someone else if he finds us but if we can snare one of his henchmen and get that one to talk, we'll turn a corner on this."

Penny glanced at Kevin still playing with his logs. Cheetah lay nearby, his alert gaze on her son. "I do feel safer here. The one big room with the adjoining open bedroom and the reinforced tinted windows all help."

"That and the new security measures. Plus, this place isn't even on the map. No GPS can find it."

"Right. And we've checked for those kinds of devices." She shook her head, remembering how they'd taken her phone and gone through the diaper bag and her backpack, even their clothes and the SUV, doing what Zeke called a full sweep. "Okay, I'll try to relax."

At least she had a big, good-looking man sitting at the table in front of her. "I'll cook something."

"No. I'm cooking. I make a mean chili."

"You cook?"

Zeke's grin wiped away the strain he'd been under and made him look younger. Her breath seemed to leave her body. She couldn't even think about this—them together in a secluded cabin, enjoying a meal. Kevin safe and playing with the family dog. Life in such a sweet shade of gold, a too-bright gold that sparkled like the potted mums sitting on the front porch.

"Yes, I cook," Zeke replied. "My mom worked a lot of long hours as a hotel desk clerk and she still works part-time. I've had to fend for myself a lot."

She sank down beside him. "Tell me more about your mom."

"Deidre Morrow," he said while he went about pulling out frozen hamburger meat and all the ingredients he needed for the chili. "She's petite but powerful. She's tough but… I know she's also lonely, but she's happy for the most part. She taught me to keep going no matter what, and that's what she does. She has a good network of friends in Utah. A little town with a nice church, so she's always busy. But I miss her. I can't tell her what I do but she knows I'm in law enforcement."

"I can see those traits you mentioned in you," Penny replied as she went about chopping onions and peppers. Keeping busy and being normal did calm her shattered nerves.

"I'm tenacious," he admitted. He stirred the onions and peppers, the smell of spices filling the air. Then he looked at her with those mysterious dark eyes. "I don't do things halfway. I became a cop as soon as I could get through training then worked my way up to the K-9 Unit in Salt Lake City. Transferred to the FBI and trained at Quantico. Worked for Homeland Security until I came here and…took Jake's place." He paused, his eyes searching her face. "I thought temporarily but now… I don't know how long I'll be here."

Penny felt the heat of his questioning appraisal all the way to her toes. Did his decision to stay or go depend on her? To hide her confusion, she hurriedly microwaved the meat to thaw it then helped him toss it into the big pot. He took a wooden spoon and broke it down, his precise actions belying the quizzical expression on his face.

She decided to stay on a safe topic. "Wow. You do work fast. Did you follow in Jake's footsteps or did you always want to be in law enforcement?"

"A little of both, I think," he answered, a trace of disappointment shadowing his face. "Jake decided early on he wanted to be a cop, even after he got into some trouble for petty crimes, since he had a relative who worked the beat and helped him out of some jams. But he went all FBI after the Bureau took over a local case and solved the murder of one of his best friends. Some kind of drive-by shooting." Shrugging, he added, "Maybe he never got over that murder. It hit him pretty hard."

Zeke stared at the steaming stew in front of him. "As for me, I watched a lot of cop shows when my mom was at work and, like Jake, I wanted to be a cop. I guess I did try to follow in our dad's footsteps since I admired him and looked up to him." He cleared his throat. "Our father was a businessman and a lawyer but… I never knew what kind of business or what kind of law. I think he might have been an ambulance chaser or maybe he worked for the mob. I went for this type of work because my brother made it sound so heroic and noble and… I think because I did need answers. But I never got those answers from my mother or Jake and I have no idea where my father is."

Penny realized something standing there in the rustic kitchen with Zeke. "It must be so hard on you, tracking your brother and praying you won't be the one to have to bring him down."

Zeke gave her a sideways glance and nodded, his dark eyes misty with emotion. "Yes, I guess I'd like to keep him alive and I've never tried to hide that fact. But... I don't know. Jake wouldn't like prison."

He turned down the burner but went back to mixing and stirring. "I bulldozed my way into this case. But I wanted to be here to help find Jake. We were all concerned about him, of course, and when I told Max about you and Kevin, well, we worried about you two."

Penny leaned against the counter and watched him mixing up the chili. "I need to thank you again...for saving my life the other day and for protecting Kevin and me yet again." She shrugged and a shiver ran through her. "It's only been a few days but it seems as if—"

"As if we've known each other for a long time?"

Their gazes met and held. "Yes. You saved me and you saved my son. I won't ever forget that, Zeke."

He went back to stirring, his expression brooding now. "You mean, after this is over and you go back to your own life? You won't forget me? Or you won't forget what I have to do? I might not be able to save Jake."

Penny took a chance and touched her hand to his arm, the feel of his strong muscles only reminding her of his true character. "I'll never forget *you*, Zeke. Never."

He dropped the spoon onto the spoon holder and turned to her, taking her into his arms. "I sure hope not. Because like I said, I'm tenacious when I want something."

Then he kissed her, his lips on hers, making Penny forget everything but this moment. But the sound of tiny logs crashing to the floor brought them apart and served as a reminder of all that could keep *them* apart.

Zeke's expression held hope and aching tenderness. He kept her close, waiting for her to react, to say something, his gaze washing her in a need that broke her heart.

"Jake was that way, too," she said, her hand cupping Zeke's face. "And that should be enough to remind me of why we can't be together."

Then she turned and hurried to check on her giggling son.

Zeke couldn't sleep. That kiss. He'd felt *her* in that kiss. Had realized she felt the same way he did. She was attracted to him but she didn't want to admit it. So she'd pulled away again, using Jake as her excuse. Maybe out of misguided loyalty or maybe out of pure guilt. No matter. Zeke would bide his time and hope they could find their way through this together.

He couldn't blame her, though, if she didn't want him in her life. Falling for each other would be a big mistake. First, his career took him away too much—like all the time. How could they have a relationship if he was never around? And…they'd both feel guilty over Jake. Always Jake. Whether his brother lived or died, he'd always have control of both of them.

Unless they could find a way to get past the hurt and betrayal and heartache. None of this was fair or right, but it had to be dealt with before they could have a chance at getting to know each other.

Zeke suddenly gave into his own bitterness and resentment and got up off the couch to stomp around in the dark. Living in Jake's shadow hadn't been easy but he'd pushed through, the way his mother had taught him to do. Unfortunately, he'd hit a wall.

Because now he wanted more than to simply do his job and be a good FBI agent. He wanted more than to impress his tragic, tormented brother who seemed on a path to self-destruction. Now he wanted a life with a wife and son.

Penny and Kevin.

But that was crazy. He'd only met her a few days ago and under the worst possible circumstances. He had to take this slow and get past this current crisis before he could even consider anything more with Penny and Kevin. Right now, he was edgy and exhausted and not thinking very clearly.

He glanced into the open room where mother and child both slept, cuddled together underneath the puffy comforter, Cheetah on the floor at the end of the bed.

What a beautiful sight.

A picture-perfect illusion.

Zeke yanked at the heavy curtains caught up on hooks on each side of the big archway and closed them to give Penny and Kevin some privacy.

She had made it clear she couldn't take things to the next level with him. So why was he pushing this when he had to finish the job and accept the worst-case scenario?

Zeke shifted his thoughts back to the case. He'd gone over and over it with a fine-tooth comb and still didn't have the answers he sought. Where was Jake? Stalking them or long gone?

Opening his phone, he studied the last picture he had of his brother in a candid moment. Jake, wearing a dark T-shirt and smiling. They'd gotten together to watch a football game. Zeke studied the photo, hoping to get a clue. His brother always wore a necklace when he wasn't in uniform. A chain with a silvery snake coiled and hanging from it.

He'd asked Jake about the necklace when he'd first started wearing it.

"A woman once called me Jake the Snake," his brother had said with a steely laugh. "She gave me this right before she walked out on me."

"What kind of man did you become?" he whispered to the grainy image. "Why didn't I take better care of you, see this coming? Try to bring you in before it was too late?"

Putting down the phone with a heavy sigh, Zeke got back to work.

They'd brought down one of Jake's henchmen but another one stood out in his mind.

Gunther Caprice.

Gunther had been a made man within the Dupree family until things started falling apart. He'd been flying under the radar this whole time. Missing and wanted for questioning by the FBI. But he was here in Montana now, right under their noses. Why would he risk his life for Jake?

His former employers had probably tried to track him and kill him, so it made no sense why he was now helping Jake orchestrate this whole thing. Unless… Jake had gotten to him and promised him a ticket out of the country, the same way he'd promised Penny when she'd turned him down.

That nagging gut instinct told him that Jake had to have had some help somewhere. Some high-up intervention, since he kept finding the team and they kept losing him.

Could there be an informant within the unit? Or somewhere within the FBI? Zeke thought back over his conversations with Dylan. Zara had been dealing with something since she'd entered into training at Quantico. All the trouble there had started at about the same time that Jake had gone missing.

But why would Jake try to mess with the trainees at Quantico? Jake and Dylan had been friends. Dylan mentioned that once to Zeke but didn't speak about it since his focus was on helping with the case and keeping track of Zara.

Dylan's fiancée couldn't reveal anything about what was going on but maybe she'd been trying to give them all hints?

He thought back over what little he knew. Dylan had told Leo Gallagher that Zara was afraid she wouldn't graduate on time because something weird was going on with the NATs—new agent trainees. This had started early on and at about the same time Jake had gone missing. He had dates he could document on that, at least.

Zara had cautioned that they didn't need any help. The trainees wanted to handle this on their own. That shouted "Stay out of it."

Maybe this didn't involve all the trainees but only a few? Maybe Zara was in trouble but couldn't tell Dylan that?

Then her roommate had quit unexpectedly. Zeke

tapped a note on his phone to remind him to find out more. Maybe the friend would be willing to give him some information. It took a lot for an FBI trainee to quit. They were put through rigorous tests before they were even accepted into the academy. Had someone intimidated or threatened the roommate? Or had the roommate purposely failed as some were inclined to do when they'd had enough? Would she be willing to talk?

Harper reported the trainees had been moved to a safe house. Again, very suspicious. FBI trainees not safe at Quantico? The place was iron tight. What if they'd been moved because the threat seemed to be coming from within?

Last they'd heard, Zara would do her best to be home for her wedding to Dylan. What did that mean? Were the trainees working on a secret case or...were they being protected because they were vulnerable?

Who could get to them like that?

Zeke's gut burned with each unanswered question. His brother could get to just about anybody. Somehow, he had to connect Jake to Zara and the trainees. Penny and the two witnesses at the Wild Iris had identified Gunther Caprice but they needed him to spill the beans.

The rest of this was an out-there premise but Zeke was running out of options. They were like sitting ducks just waiting to be shot down. If something didn't give soon, he'd go to ground and take Penny and Kevin as far away from here as possible.

Meantime, he had to prove that Jake had been messing with Zara to distract the team and gain information from the inside out. He'd have to have solid proof of Jake paying off someone on the inside. Or, if he knew his brother, charming someone on the inside. The roommate? Or someone with a lot more clout and authority?

Exhaling roughly, he shoved a hand through his dark hair. But how could he ever find that proof and try to protect Penny and Kevin, too?

Remembering Max's suggestion, Zeke decided maybe he did need to question Penny about Jake again after all.

FOURTEEN

"You want to do *what*?"

Zeke didn't flinch at Max's growl of a question. Instead, he plunged ahead. "I want to interview Zara's former roommate at Quantico and see if she knows anything about Jake. And I want to find Gunther Caprice. He's on Team Jake now, but if we could get him to agree to a plea bargain, he might spill his guts."

"We're looking for Gunther, Zeke. You know that. I'm not sure about finding the roommate. She left the program. That's pretty clear."

Zeke didn't cave. "But why did she leave? I know there are myriad reasons for an NAT to quit but most don't want it to come to that. Zara implied the woman was running scared."

"You didn't hear that information firsthand," Max reminded him.

"Which is why we need to send someone to interview the woman," Zeke retorted. "Surely the FBI can track down a former trainee."

Max rubbed at his scar. "Look, I get that you want to talk to anyone who can possibly lead you to your brother. The Dupree syndicate has collapsed, but Jake's still out there with one goal left—to get to his son. Why don't you focus on that?"

"I am focusing on that, Max. It's all I think about. Caprice is missing. Zara is in trouble but can't tell us why. The roommate is gone without any explanation. Can you at least agree that someone from Quantico could be helping Jake and that these things could connect us to him?"

Max frowned. "Yes, I'll give you that, but it's still a long shot. We don't have proof but we're pretty sure some of his cronies are still along for the ride. They'd have to be desperate, but they're scattering like rats. Plus we have no idea where Gunther Caprice is right now."

"He's out there somewhere and he sounded extremely frustrated last time I heard him talking on the phone."

Zeke had stumbled on some interesting facts in the reports Dylan had pulled up for him. Caprice had a parting of ways with the Duprees after Reginald was hauled into custody. Maybe because Jake had taken his place within the organization?

But he had found his way back to Jake now that Angus was dead and Reginald was awaiting trial. Gunther could have tracked Jake down and for all Zeke knew, Gunther might have made demands on Jake.

"We need to find him," Zeke continued. "Now that the syndicate has been dismantled, the underlings are getting antsy. If we could just nab one of them and get him—or her—to turn, we might get to the truth. Gunther might have taken off to parts unknown by now. Or he could be hanging around trying to stay on Jake's good side. Or worse."

Zeke knew his theory was far-fetched but he couldn't

let go of it now. "We need to ask Violetta about Gunther, too."

Max's expression hardened. "To accomplish what? She was trying to save her sister, Esme, and she did that. She wants nothing else to do with the crimes her uncle and brother committed, and I'm sure she doesn't know a thing about Gunther."

"Remember when I asked you to talk to Violetta?" Zeke said.

Max let out a sigh. "Yes, I called the Dupree estate and requested to speak to Violetta. Apparently she's on a cruise somewhere in the Caribbean." He halted and took a breath. "And, yes, I've got eyes on her."

"That makes sense. She's out of the country, too," Zeke said. "Dylan found strong evidence that she and Gunther were once close but the affair ended badly."

Max didn't even blink. "Yeah, we'd kind of discovered that already but… I don't see how that plays into your theory."

"How can we be sure of anyone from that family?" Zeke asked, his voice rising. "She might be on that cruise ship, waiting for Gunther. Or, worse, my brother."

Max took a look around the cabin, careful to keep his voice low since Penny and Kevin were still asleep. "You're tired and frustrated and grasping at straws. Maybe you're too close to all of this, Zeke."

He lowered his head and put his hands on his hips. "I'm fine but… I have to make sense of this. Jake might be good at putting up distractions, but I'm good at looking at the big picture and putting together pieces of the puzzle that most don't see. I've got Dylan checking into some other things, too. If he doesn't find anything more concrete and if Violetta doesn't cooperate, I'll let this go."

And he'd take Penny and Kevin and leave. For good if he had to. Max looked skeptical but he nodded. "Fair enough." Then he walked to the windows and stared out at the distant foothills and mountains. "How's it going here?"

"We had a quiet night," Zeke said. "Any other leads?"

"No. We've canvassed homes all around the Elk Basin and throughout the wilderness areas around Billings, but every trail runs cold," Max replied, frustration underscoring his words. "I came by to see if you needed to get away for a while. I can keep watch while the crew is switching out. Julianne and Leo will take the next shift."

Zeke checked the closed curtain to the bedroom. Cheetah was working overtime, keeping watch over Penny and Kevin. "Good, sir. Leo and True are strong." Leo Gallagher had been with Jake the day his teammate disappeared and had blamed himself until they'd all realized the truth. "And Julianne has proved herself with Thunder over and over." He smiled. "That foxhound is one smart animal and Julianne Martinez is a great agent."

"I'm glad you approve," Max said on a dry note. "Still, you might want to get out of here for a while."

"No, sir," Zeke replied, deliberately not taking the hint. "I'll keep busy working on this angle while I wait to hear from Dylan regarding Quantico."

"All right," Max said. "But next time, that won't be a suggestion."

Zeke got that the SAC wanted him in control and not so on edge but…his instincts had never let him down before. When he thought back, he'd sensed something going on with Jake but chalked his moods up to him becoming a dad. Jake had never talked about wanting children but Kevin had changed his notion on that. But a good father wouldn't force his child away from his mother. Or try to kill the woman who'd given him a son.

Zeke wouldn't stop until he found his brother. Dead or alive. His phone buzzed. Dylan.

"I've just heard from Violetta Dupree," Dylan said on a winded voice. "She texted me a clue."

"What?"

Lights and siren syndrome. That's what Jake the Snake is all about.

Zeke's whole body went cold. His gut burned hot. That was a term sometimes used in FBI training. It referred to how some people never got over the adrenaline rush of becoming an agent. Jake had always been one of those people. The hint screamed Quantico.

And proved that Zeke was on the right track.

"What's going on?"

Penny stood at the bedroom door staring over at Zeke. He was turned, speaking low into his phone. She'd heard voices earlier and after checking on Kevin, she'd opened the privacy curtains to the den. That's when she'd overheard Zeke and Max talking about Quantico. She'd remembered that one memory she'd either blocked or maybe held back out of embarrassment and regret. But now, after hearing more rumblings she thought Zeke should know. If he'd level with her in return.

Zeke put away his phone and turned and faced her but she saw the tension in his expression. "Max was here. We're trying to establish some things that might help us to find Jake. I need to ask you—"

Penny's heart hammered against her ribs. "But we still don't know where Jake is, right?"

Zeke gave her a puzzled stare. "No. I've got people working on some new angles."

"I'm only asking because I heard you mention Quantico again," she said. "I remembered something else, something I should have told you about sooner."

Zeke's eyes went wide. "I was just about to ask if you knew about certain things. Talk to me, Penny."

Seeing the eagerness mixed with a tinge of disappointment in his eyes, she hoped she hadn't waited too late on this. "Once when Jake was at my house, I was washing clothes and I picked up a pair of his jeans. A photo of Jake and a woman fell out. I immediately expected the worst—that he was cheating on me. When I asked him about the picture, he got angry and told me to leave his clothes alone. Then later, he apologized and explained that he had fallen for another trainee years before. But things ended badly and they both went their separate ways. I accepted that and let it go but...he'd obviously kept that photo a long time."

Zeke's expression hardened and his eyes held a trace of dread. "Did he tell you her name or anything else?"

Penny shook her head. "No. He refused to talk about it." She tugged her hair behind her ear. "It happened right after Kevin was born and honestly, I didn't think much about it after that since Jake seemed so devoted to our son. But now I wonder about it. That day when he called and sounded so upset and off-kilter, he did mention Quantico and how he believed he still had friends there. Do you think he kept in touch with this woman?"

Zeke's features softened but he pressed her. "You said he'd lost trust in someone, too."

"Yes." Penny hated to admit it. "I wonder if he wasn't having an affair with this woman all along and when I got pregnant, he ended it. Or maybe she did." Her heart bumping a warning, she asked, "Do you think he could have reached out to his friend again? She'd be long gone by now, but he could have contacted her recently, given his situation."

Zeke pulled out his phone and started tapping away as if he didn't even know she was in the room. "I'll get Dylan on it but…you just might have helped us get to the bottom of this case, Penny."

"I should have told you sooner," she said, her voice tinged with regret. "But… I kind of blocked any thoughts of him with other women."

"It's okay," he said. "I planned to jar your memory anyway so we were on the same page. This is a major breakthrough."

"Zeke, tell me what's going on."

"I can't," he said, putting his phone away. "Too many details. But…we're so close."

"Close to finding Jake or close to building a solid case against him?"

"The case is solid enough but yes, we need to keep everything by the book."

Penny sensed a distinct difference in him even while his eyes filled with excitement. Maybe he couldn't talk about the details. He'd been careful with what he shared with her but…she heard things, suspected things. She'd opened up with this information, hoping he'd do the same with her.

Not sure what to say, she headed straight to the coffeepot.

He moved closer. "How'd you sleep?"

"Okay." But in actuality, she'd tossed and turned all night, aware of their kiss in the kitchen last night. Aware of her wants and needs and the myriad reasons why she couldn't fall for Zeke.

And he obviously wasn't in a talking mood this morning. Probably regretting that kiss.

They'd eaten the chili with very little conversation and Zeke hadn't kissed her again. Kevin had taken up much of their time and energy before he'd worn himself out. Penny had put him to bed and after a few quiet moments together where Zeke tapped on his phone, she'd gone into the bedroom to read a book.

Now she wished she could take back what she'd said after they'd kissed, but she'd spoken the truth. She could wish she'd never kissed Zeke, but…that wonderful, warm memory wouldn't leave her mind. That kiss had scared her way too much. And made her feel alive again even when her heart was so caught up in misery and regret.

Jake had been tenacious, too. She'd panicked and pulled away from Zeke because she was so afraid of going through that kind of pain again. But she shouldn't have said those spiteful words to Zeke.

Jake's impulses were quick and swift and he made decisions based on those impulses. But Zeke was determined and thorough and he made decisions based on facts and logic. One went after what he wanted out of life, regardless of who he hurt, and the other one went after those who committed crimes and ruined lives and tried to be kind and considerate in spite of the dangers. A bad trait in Jake. A good trait in Zeke. She heaved a frustrated sigh. Why did she have to always compare them anyway?

But what if Zeke up and changed one day, the way Jake had? Jake managed to hide his issues but the day she told him she was pregnant, Penny saw his true nature.

Now she had to consider what she'd pushed out of her mind so long ago. Had he resented her pregnancy because he was still in love with another woman?

"He never wanted a child," she blurted, hoping to see Zeke in a different light. She knew the truth but her heart was so broken and battered she didn't want to acknowledge the truth. She needed to test him a little more. "He got really upset when I told him I was pregnant."

Zeke turned to face her. "I know. He told me about it."

Humiliated, she recoiled, a hand to her mouth. So Zeke pitied her? "You've known that all along?"

"Yes, but—"

"But you didn't tell me." She didn't know why that hurt so much. She needed to remember that her feelings for Zeke couldn't see her through. This new revelation was just one more reason she had to find her own way in life. She shared a painful, uncertain memory with Zeke and now this. Embarrassed and tired, she turned away.

But a strong hand pulled her around. "Penny, how can I convince you that I'm not like him? When he told me, I worried about you and the baby and prayed that he'd do the right thing. But it wasn't my place back then to interfere. Jake said he had things under control." He shrugged. "I should have told you but… I didn't want to add to your agony over this."

"So all this time, you're helping me out of pity and duty?"

"Duty, yes. Pity, no," he said, a firm determination in his words. "You're so wrapped up in Jake and what he's done to you that you can't see me. The *real* me. I'd like to stay a part of your life when this is over. For Kevin's sake and…because I care about you, Penny."

When she didn't respond, he tugged her close. "I could have told you a lot right up front, but I was more focused on keeping you alive. I can't give you all the details." Then he brought it home. "And I could say the same for you. This intel about another woman is huge. Yet you kept it from me until you heard me discussing Quantico with Max."

"I'm sorry," she said, some of her anger dissipating. "It was painful and I… I tried to put it out of my mind. I played blind but now I can see it all so clearly. You're right. I can't seem to get past the man who betrayed me and is now trying to kill me. I'm not in a good place to make decisions right now."

Stepping back, Zeke nodded. "Okay, neither am I. But don't take anything I do or say as pity. I admire you."

She smiled at that. "Thank you."

"Jake tried," Zeke replied. "You said he gave you money to help take care of Kevin."

Bobbing her head, she quit smiling and pivoted to stare out at the mountains. "Yes, he did. Guilt money. Dirty money."

Zeke stood behind her. "Yes. But perhaps that was his way of showing you that he wasn't all bad."

"Now you're making excuses for him?"

"I'm trying to understand him. I'm not proud of what he's become but… I'd like to think he still has some trace of decency in him."

"Well, you're wrong. I think the good in him has been long dead."

She didn't want to break down but her emotions were bubbling like a running brook. She'd held it together, piece by piece, for months now. This kind of intimate talk could only lead to her falling into Zeke's arms.

"You were there in the chalet in Colorado, weren't you?"

Shocked, she came around so Zeke could see her face-to-face. He seemed to want to pick a fight with her but she wasn't going to fall for it.

"I was, but I took Kevin and left when I thought Jake had found us."

"Why did you think he was coming there?"

Feeling cornered, she glared at him. "Why do you care?"

"I need to know. I told you I'd want to know more."

"I got a call on my cell. But no one was there. The connection ended and I panicked."

"So you thought it was Jake?"

"Of course, I thought it was Jake. It wasn't as if I was waiting for him. More, like, expecting him to track me down. Which he has, time after time, or we wouldn't be standing here."

Zeke's expression changed, shifted, relaxed.

He must have been going over every detail of this

case and while he'd been doing that, he'd also tried to figure out a few things about her, obviously.

"How'd you get away?" he finally asked.

Penny wanted to end this conversation but she had to be truthful. "I'm a wilderness guide, remember? We found a path down the mountain into town." Getting closer so he'd fully understand how terrifying her ordeal had been that day, she added, "I carried my son in my arms for three miles, Zeke. Three miles of mountains and rough terrain, streams and jagged rocks and several near encounters with wild animals."

He almost said something but instead he asked, "And you paid the hotel clerk to lie about you booking a room?"

"Yes, to throw Jake off my trail. I'm not proud of lying but… I didn't know what else to do. Why are you asking me about all this now?"

"I told you I'd planned to interrogate you again."

"Yes, you did." She tried to turn away, but he put a hand on each of her arms, the strength in his touch warming her in spite of this roiling tension between them.

"I need you to understand something, Penny. We're closing in on Jake and before we do, I need to know how you really feel about him."

"For the case?" she asked, thinking he was as ruthless as Jake. "To prove that I've done something wrong…or to show that I'm telling the truth?"

"No." He leaned in, his face inches from hers, his dark eyes burning hot. Then he put his hand on her face and held her there, the brush of his fingers like a promise. "For *me*. I need to know for my own sanity. Because

I want to believe you don't still have feelings for him. I need to believe that. I need to know that…before *I* give into these feelings *I* have for you."

Penny didn't know what to say. She'd often asked herself that same question, regarding Jake and…regarding Zeke. What did she feel? She wanted to tell him she had strong feelings for him, too. Feelings that were different from the fast and furious attraction she'd thought she'd had for Jake. That crush of strong emotions was gone now, to be replaced by something slow and simmering and equally strong. Zeke had won her over the moment he'd called out her name in the wilderness. But she wasn't ready to admit that right now.

She didn't love Jake. Not anymore. Maybe she never had. She'd loved the idea of being in love and having a handsome, dynamic man take notice of her. But now that Zeke had spoken these things out loud, she had to swallow hard and bite down on her emotions. How could she be sure that this wasn't the same kind of infatuation and that she'd regret running right into Zeke's arms? She wanted to say the right thing, but fear gripped her, rendering her speechless.

But Zeke took her silence for something else.

"I see," he said. Then he turned around and stalked away.

Bitter and hurting, Penny couldn't let it go that easily. "And what about you, Zeke? You watched him get away the other day when you could have shot him. Why don't you analyze your own feelings instead of nitpicking mine?"

He didn't even turn around. "I've analyzed everything about my life since the day I found out I had a brother, and right now I'm trying to reconcile that I might have to be the one to bring him down."

Penny's heart skipped a beat. She almost ran to him to comfort him. But Kevin cried out, giving her a reprieve from having to watch Zeke walk away.

FIFTEEN

Zeke's cell buzzed later that day, a welcome distraction from Penny's stormy silence. She didn't want to care about him, and maybe she was right to keep pushing him away. He'd been telling himself the same thing, hadn't he? So he put the memory of their kiss and their last heated conversation out of his mind and answered his phone. He'd immediately consulted with Max about the cryptic hint Violetta had shared with Dylan. Finally, things were moving along.

"Dylan, do you have something?"

"Yes," he said. "I pulled in a lot of favors and kept Zara out of this so she wouldn't get any heat, but we've located her roommate. Her name is Brandy Ridgeway. She's been hiding out in Colorado."

Zeke did a sweep of the room. Penny was taking a shower and Julianne was entertaining Kevin, her K-9 partner, Thunder, guarding them. "Hiding out? Why?"

"The woman fears for her life," Dylan said. "We sent two local agents to talk to her and she tried to run. After they explained that they were there just to question her, she finally told them why she'd left Quantico."

Zeke held his breath, wondering if his brother had pulled some strings. "And?"

"It took some doing, but Brandy finally admitted that one of the instructors has been keeping in touch with Jake Morrow."

Zeke rubbed his forehead, his gut clenching. "That's not surprising. What else? Who is the instructor?"

"A woman named Rebecca Carwell who trained with Jake years ago. They were close. For a long, long time. So the information Penny gave you about the Quantico thing is correct." Dylan lowered his voice. "Here's the thing. Zara and Brandy stumbled on some information that suggested this instructor and Jake had been communicating in recent months. Maybe even meeting in out-of-the-way places."

Zeke closed his eyes. Had his brother been two-timing Penny the whole time? She'd suspected that but hearing it out loud infuriated Zeke. Not to mention an FBI instructor not alerting them about Jake. The woman had to know from the beginning that he'd gone missing. And later, that he was wanted and considered armed and dangerous. "Go on. Give me all of it."

"Special Agent Rebecca Carwell doesn't have any stains on her record. She worked in a California field office for a while and still has ties there. She's been back as an instructor for three years now. But she did graduate with Jake, and…others who knew them said they had been an item for a while."

So that matched what Jake had told Penny about not trusting anyone—no, *someone*—at Quantico anymore. Someone he'd depended on. Fraternizing amongst trainees was a big no-no, but it happened and sometimes those ties were hard to break.

This made perfect sense when he matched it to Violetta's clue. Jake still had someone on the inside at Quantico.

"Explain what happened," Zeke said, already getting the picture.

Dylan went on. "Apparently this all started when the word got out that Jake had been taken by Angus Dupree. Special Agent Carwell got all antsy and upset. Zara and Brandy heard her talking on her phone one night and… they started putting things together. It started as a joke. Rebecca tended to be very strict and by the book, so they wondered if she ever had any fun. Once the NATs were able to take leave on the weekends, those two followed her just for something to do. But when they saw who she was snuggling up with in a dark park, they panicked."

Zeke's anger flared but he stayed quiet, allowing the other man to go on.

"The man could have been Jake Morrow but they weren't sure," Dylan explained. "So they decided they'd watch and wait for verification since Jake was still considered missing. Zara couldn't say a word to us since she couldn't be sure the man was Jake." He took a long breath. "Plus, she found it hard to believe Jake would be anywhere near Quantico."

"Does this roommate think that was the case?" Zeke asked, wishing his hunch hadn't paid off. "That Jake and Rebecca were in cahoots even after the FBI realized he'd flipped?"

"Yes," Dylan replied. "But we have to gather more intel, Zeke. So don't do anything yet, okay? The recruits are still in a safe house."

"I won't," Zeke said, trying to remember the agent in

question. He'd never heard Jake mention her but then, why would he? "Is Max aware of this?"

"Yes. I went straight to him…since he'd ordered me to do that before I brought any of this to you. But before anyone does anything, Zara needs to graduate and get home. Somehow the NATs got involved in this secret sideline investigation and things went downhill from there. They'd have to report this, unless, of course, they don't trust anyone." Dylan stopped and took a breath. "I just want Zara back here and safe in time for our wedding."

Zeke understood the need to be discreet. Dylan had been waiting on Zara to return for months now. She could be in danger, especially if someone found out their unit had recently talked to her roommate. "So… what? We're watching and waiting?"

"Yes. Max has informed people, and he arranged to personally fly to Quantico last night and interrogate Agent Carwell in private. He should arrive back at headquarters here any time now. Meantime, we have Brandy Ridgeway's statement and Max has sent someone to protect her. She's willing to testify since her career is ruined."

"So this caused her to leave? Was she threatened while still at Quantico?"

Dylan let out a grunt. "Rebecca approached Brandy after Brandy and Zara started putting things together. She turned the tables, saying she'd heard rumors that *they* might know of Jake's whereabouts due to Zara's connection to our team. Rebecca hinted that Brandy should keep tabs on Zara in case we passed her any information. In case I slipped up and divulged anything classified, which of course I didn't."

He blew out a huff of frustration and cleared his throat. "But Agent Carwell didn't know that they'd already figured things out. Brandy took the fall since she wasn't sure she wanted to stay in the program anyway. She never squealed on Zara because Zara hadn't done anything wrong. She told Carwell she didn't come to the academy to turn on another agent. She agreed to forget the whole thing if Rebecca would let her leave, but Rebecca wouldn't agree to that. She began making things difficult for Zara and Brandy."

"Such as?" Zeke asked.

Dylan dived right in, explaining. "Their dorm room being searched. Both being used as an example during training runs, being harassed when a scenario case wasn't solved immediately. Accused of trying to give confidential information to someone on the outside. Which they didn't do. They proved they didn't do anything but she didn't let up."

"So Carwell wouldn't let Brandy leave? Did she try to blackmail her or something?"

"She made life hard and threatened both of them with exposure, yes," Dylan replied. "At least according to Brandy. I hope Zara can tell us everything once she gets to come home."

"But Brandy did drop out," Zeke said. "How did that come about?"

"The old-fashioned way," Zeke said. "Brandy failed some of the training courses and got herself kicked out. Carwell couldn't stop her without exposing what they knew about *her*, too. But after that, again according to Brandy, Zara worked hard to stay in the program. I don't know why they're in lockdown."

"What was Jake hoping to gain?" Zeke asked, his head throbbing.

"Who knows. A distraction. Information on where we were and if we were tracking him. He used Agent Carwell and he tried to trip up Zara and Brandy, too. But Zara stuck to the plan and didn't spill anything because she didn't know anything. She could only prove that she wasn't passing information." He exhaled heavily. "I can't believe she's been dealing with this all along, but that's what she's training for. So we have to keep quiet and solve the case."

Zeke didn't like it, but he agreed. They couldn't march in on the word of an ex-trainee and snatch a senior instructor who'd been a loyal agent for over a decade. They needed Zara's take on this, but he doubted even Max could have nabbed an interview with her. Too risky. If Max had gotten to Rebecca Carwell, it would be in a secretive meeting to hear her side, not accuse her. Even that could get Zara in hot water, but her former roommate *had* volunteered the information.

He thanked Dylan and told him he'd check with Max. "And, Dylan, send me a picture of Carwell and the roommate, any pictures the agents who interrogated Ridgeway might have taken for evidence, too."

"Sure. I guess Violetta did us another favor, grudgingly, of course."

Zeke shook his head. "Yes. It would have been nice to hear this earlier, but we can only assume that she's been in touch with Caprice and he let something slip. Probably how she kept tabs on all of them."

"Yep, but I guess she's not willing to forgive and forget. According to our sources in Chicago who've been watching her closely, Violetta refuses to even let

Caprice in the gate. She left on that cruise to get away from all of this. But…she obviously hasn't let it all go."

"Thanks again," Zeke said. "This information means we're getting somewhere at least."

When he turned back to the room, Julianne stood and walked over to him, her dark eyes full of questions. "Some news?"

"Yes. But not the good kind." Glancing toward the curtained bedroom, he added, "And I can't go into detail right now."

Julianne nodded and touched a hand to her dark, upswept hair. "Understood."

Zeke gave her a thankful nod and went to play with Kevin. Though Penny already suspected this, he planned to hold off on telling her that Jake had possibly been involved with another agent while with Penny. She obviously still cared about Jake from the way she'd gone silent on him earlier then turned the tables on his own feelings regarding his brother. A part of her still loved Jake and maybe she needed to hang on to that feeling a little bit longer. Until this was all over and she could see things clearly again.

Once that happened, he'd tell her the truth. That Jake had used all of them and he was no good for any of them. Especially no good for her and Kevin. It was a bitter truth, but just like Penny, Zeke had been in denial about his brother. This latest news ended all doubts on trying to save Jake. Prison or worse, Zeke had to do what needed to be done to bring down his brother.

But he also had to continue safeguarding Penny, even going so far as to protect her love for Jake. For her and Kevin's sake.

He couldn't add to her doubts and trauma by telling

her this and verifying her worst pain. She'd had enough heartbreak without hearing about this new wrinkle.

Besides, it was highly classified information. Period. He'd go with that rationale for now and ignore how his own emotions were beginning to take over his usual logic.

Penny spent most of the day getting to know Zeke's team member, Julianne Martinez, and enjoying Kevin while she tried to ignore the way Zeke was avoiding her. While Julianne was a delight and had caught her up on all the newly formed relationships developing within the team, including her own reunion with former love Brody Kenner, Penny wished Zeke would talk to her. They hadn't had any time alone so she wasn't able to explain her true feelings to him. But now wasn't the time to convince him she no longer loved Jake. And now sure wasn't the time to tell him she had strong feelings for him but she was afraid to act on those feelings.

So after Julianne went outside to do a sweep, she kept to herself and hugged on Kevin, showering her confused son with love. At least this forced isolation had given her some precious quality time with him. He was growing so fast, even the few clothes she'd brought with them were going to get snug soon. Would she ever be able to go back to the Wild Iris and get what few belongings they had left?

Dusk was settling over the mountains now and she had yet to talk to Zeke. He'd been scrolling on his laptop and verifying things on his phone all day, and now he'd disappeared into the bathroom. Penny wished she could go outside and take in the fresh mountain air, especially since this time of year the temperature would start going down with the changing seasons. August temperatures sometimes changed dramatically from day to day. Fall was wonderful in Montana. Unless you were in hiding from a desperate man.

"How you holding up?" Zeke asked, surprising her as he came out of the bathroom, all fresh and clean from his shower. They'd only shared clipped small talk for most of the day so his question threw her. But the way he looked threw her even more.

The man was gorgeous.

"I'm okay," she said, trying to keep her tone neutral.

Penny breathed in the crisp scent of spicy soap and decided that would have to do as far as getting some fresh air. His dark, close-cropped waves, still damp from the shower, caressed his ears and forehead in a way she wished she could. He wore a clean black T-shirt and faded jeans. But the gun in his shoulder holster only reminded her of why they were here.

He didn't remind her of Jake, however. In fact, she wasn't thinking of her ex at all in this moment with Zeke's mysterious eyes capturing hers with a hint of remorse and regret.

He held something back, something he wasn't ready to tell her.

Swallowing back the implications of that realization, she stood and smiled at him. She could be civil at least. "I'm good, all things considered. Kevin is safe and you've all been very considerate to me."

Zeke moved toward her, his gaze never leaving her face. "Considerate? Is that what you think this is between us? Just a consideration for a woman who's being threatened?"

"You know what I mean," she replied, hoping he

wasn't about to accuse her again and hoping she could apologize for her earlier remarks. "Your team has been watching out for me for almost a week now. *You've* gone beyond being considerate, Zeke."

But he had become distant since their last conversation. He'd been on edge all day, in a mood she couldn't quite read. That, and not knowing what he might have found, scared her but she'd done some heavy praying for the Lord to help her see him in a different light. In a light outside the shadow of his big brother.

Zeke was his own man. A good man. Why couldn't she just go with that and put her trust in him? And God.

Zeke hooked his thumbs into his jeans pockets and looked down at the floor. "Yeah, well, you've gone beyond letting me know that I'm looking at a lost cause. You're still in love with Jake. End of conversation. So I'm going to do my job and leave the rest to fate."

She shook her head and lowered her voice. "For someone who's so smart, you sure are being thick-headed about my feelings."

"You shouted your feelings loud and clear when I asked you directly, Penny," he said in a snarl of a whisper. "You couldn't even look me in the eye and tell me the truth."

She had to tell him the truth now, though. "Zeke—"

"I have to get back to work," he said, interrupting her. "Dylan just sent me some photos." He sat down at the big table and opened his laptop.

Angry, Penny came to stand behind him, her gaze hitting on the pictures. A close-up of a pretty woman and more photos of the same woman. Then she spotted something that caused her to take in a breath. "Zeke?"

He shook his head and tried to shut the laptop. "I don't have time to talk about this right now, Penny."

"Zeke," she said again, her hand on his so he couldn't close down the open file. "I recognize that necklace."

Penny pointed to the intricate necklace around the woman's neck. "The silver snake," she said in a shocked whisper. "Jake the Snake. That belonged to him."

"What?" Zeke leaned in and let out a held breath. "It does look like the one he wore. Are you sure?"

"Yes," she said, bobbing her head, her stomach clenching with the final gut-wrenching truth. "He always wore it. Who is she?"

Zeke's phone buzzed before he could respond.

"What?" he rasped into the phone, his gaze holding Penny's while his tone and expression showed a heavy frustration. He listened, silent and stern, his gaze moving over Penny, his frown turning dark with concern. "Yes, I understand." After a few more minutes of intense back and forth, he asked, "How much time do we have?"

Penny knew what was coming. She could tell from his actions that something significant had happened. He started stalking around the room while he barked replies to whoever was on the line. He finally ended the call and turned toward her. "We've got trouble."

Julianne hurried through the door, apprehension clear in her eyes. "I got a call on the radio. Six of them, Zeke, armed to the teeth. They're surrounding us."

An explosion down below rocked the air.

Penny's heart stopped. Were they going to bomb the cabin? She rushed to grab Kevin so fast that she startled him. "Mommy!" he cried out, fretting as his eyes widened.

Cheetah and Thunder both stood at alert. Penny pivoted to Zeke. "Zeke, I—"

He lifted a hand to her face then dropped it, his eyes full of regret.

Then she heard a round of shots being fired down below the deck. "He's found us again."

"Yes." Zeke grabbed her close, his jaw clenched tight. For a moment, she thought he'd tell her everything, whatever he'd just heard but instead, he stood there for a lifetime of precious seconds, his true feelings shining through the darkness in his eyes.

Then he said, "This is all going to be over soon."

Penny had tried to put this nightmare out of her mind, but in her heart she'd known it was coming. And this time, she had a feeling Jake wouldn't send others. This time, he'd be the one to storm her sanctuary and take her child right out of her arms.

SIXTEEN

Zeke took in the scene, his mind still reeling with what Max had rapidly reported. Rebecca Carwell wasn't in cahoots with Jake. She'd met Jake in the park that night and tried to get him to turn himself in. When he refused and held a gun on her, she let him go and wished too late that she'd brought backup. Max had interrogated her in a secret location and she'd told him the truth—that she had to keep this a secret or end her career. She begged Max to stop messing in something she needed to finish.

But Max couldn't stop what had been set into motion.

Zeke had to move, the fast-paced conversation he'd had with Max still looping through his head. He'd get the details later. Right now, he had to get Penny and Kevin out of this cabin.

If they were surrounded and the team members hiding in the woods couldn't get to them, they had no way out. The shots fired could mean the team had taken down some of the people coming for them.

Or it could mean the two extra guards they'd had stationed at the main door were gone.

He went with the worst-case scenario and called out to Julianne. "We have to go. Now!"

"I'll check the mudroom entrance," Julianne told him, already headed that way. "They must have cut the security system."

"Yeah," Zeke said. "Not good."

Zeke drew his gun and shoved Penny, who was holding a frightened Kevin, behind him. Then he commanded Cheetah forward to guard. "Stay with me," he ordered. "No matter what, Penny. Stay with me."

That plea echoed inside his head as he heard more shots, these near the front door of the cabin. Cheetah glanced back but the dog stayed silent and moved forward, following Julianne and Thunder.

Getting between Penny and whoever came through the door, Zeke pushed her to the side door. "Remember how we discussed this," he said. "We go down to the basement and exit out the back through the heavy vines hiding the door. The path is hidden there. If something happens, you take the path down. Keep going and don't look back."

She nodded and held her now-crying son close to her chest. "Got it. Zeke—"

"Shhh," he said as they rounded the corner to the small mudroom past the wide pantry.

"Hurry," Julianne whispered. "Both guards are down. We don't have much time."

The front door up on the other side of the house burst open just as they rushed through the hidden side door beyond the pantry. Zeke heard footsteps panning out. More than one set.

Off in the distance, more shots rang out and dogs barked. They made it through the door and onto a small landing. Julianne shut the door behind them and shoved an old wrought iron deck chair against it to give them precious seconds.

Zeke pushed Penny and Kevin ahead of him down the enclosed spiral stairs. They made it to the bottom and he shielded them against a wall while Julianne and Thunder hurried around him and opened the door leading into the woods. Julianne gripped her rifle and shifted left to right.

"Clear," she said in a harsh whisper. Thunder stood with her. She turned to Zeke after he pulled Penny and Kevin close behind him. Then she shut the door to the cabin. "I leave you here. I'll hide behind those rocks over there and fire a round or two to give you cover. Thunder and I can double back and find the rest of the team."

Zeke wanted to tell Julianne no, but this was her job and she'd only resent him if he did that. "Okay. As long as you have backup on the way."

"Roger that," she said, already heading for cover.

Zeke looked down at Penny, Kevin between them. "Hold on to your son and stay as close to me as possible."

Penny bobbed her head, her eyes holding his. "Zeke?"

He kissed her, hard and fast. "I'm going to get you out of here."

They worked their way down the rutted, rocky path leading to a small waterfall and stream. Zeke radioed for a vehicle to be waiting for them on a dirt road at the bottom of the ravine. He prayed they'd make it that far without being ambushed.

Cheetah led the way, his snout up and sniffing for any danger. Zeke kept Penny in front of him and she shielded Kevin in her arms. They'd left without any provisions except Kevin's blanket and the night air was chilly, but she moved through the moonlight without a word, her hand on her son's head in a protective measure that broke Zeke's heart.

I promise, Lord. If I get them out of here alive, I will spend the rest of my days trying to show them the love they deserve.

Kevin's sobs had turned into feeble whimpers and now, with the constant bump against rocks and jutted earth, the kid seemed to be drifting off to sleep against his mother's shoulder. Zeke longed to take the boy, to lift that sweet weight off her shoulders and put the precious burden on his own. But he needed to stay free in case he had to use his weapon.

He'd have to be the one to stay and fight while they got away.

They silently worked their way down the path, the moonlight both a blessing and a curse. They'd rounded a bend when gunfire erupted off in the woods.

Zeke grabbed Penny's arm. "Get down," he hissed. Then to Cheetah, "Stay. Guard."

Cheetah stood in front of Penny and Kevin while Zeke searched ahead, trying to watch for shadows or movement in the scrub brush and bramble along the way.

"Nothing up ahead," he said, relief washing over him. "We're almost to the cutoff road. Someone should be waiting there to get you to safety."

"What about you and your team members?" Penny asked. "Julianne and…the rest. Zeke, I can't bear it if one of them gets shot. I can't let you—"

"They're pros," he said, trying to keep his tone confident. "They know what to do. And you don't need to worry about me, either."

"But that explosion—and we keep hearing gunfire."

"Part of the process," he said, wondering if anyone would survive this. When his radio crackled to life, Zeke immediately reported in.

"Agent Morrow." It was Max West. "Are you safe?"

"Ten-four, sir. Package is secure." Then he asked, "Everyone accounted for?"

"Affirmative. Two guards down. Team secure," Max replied. He didn't linger. "Report in when extraction is complete."

"Yes, sir."

Zeke turned to Penny. "See, they're all okay. And we'll be on our way out of here soon."

"And where will we go next, Zeke?" she asked, her voice quiet and husky. "Where can I hide?"

"I don't know," he admitted. "But I will promise you this. I'm going to take you and Kevin as far away from here as possible."

The look in her eyes told him what he needed to know. She wanted that, too. But he also saw the despair in her gaze. Zeke leaned over to kiss her but froze in place. The breaking of a twig crunched a few yards off the path. Cheetah's ears went up and the dog emitted a low growl.

Penny heard it, too. She inhaled a breath and held tight to Kevin. Zeke crouched and turned only to see a dark figure rushing toward him. The butt of a rifle came down on Zeke's temple, hard and swift, causing him to fall forward, his weapon sliding out of his grip. Jake. Cheetah's barks turned aggressive. Zeke caught a glimpse of a dark figure behind Jake and heard a swish of sound. Cheetah fell to the ground before Zeke could order him to attack. Zeke blinked and tried to call out, but Cheetah lifted his head then fell back, a dark stain covering a white spot on his back.

Zeke looked up at his brother standing over him, seeing a dark rage in Jake's eyes, the sound of Penny's screams radiating through the searing pain in his brain. He tried to stand but couldn't find the strength to push himself up.

Jake kicked him back down and stalked toward Penny. Throwing his rifle strap over his shoulder, he lowered the gun and said, "It's time to get this over with, once and for all."

"No!" Penny started falling backward and tripped. Kevin slipped out of her arms to the ground.

The boy plopped on his bottom and cried out. "Mommy!" His sobs echoed down the hill and tore straight through Zeke's heart.

Zeke watched in horror, dizziness pushing at his consciousness, as he saw Jake reach down and grab Penny.

"Get my son," Jake called to the man with him. Then he turned back to Penny and grabbed her around her throat. "This will be the last time you try to hide my boy from me."

Zeke grunted and lifted up, blinking back the throbbing pain that surrounded his brain. Jake's hands circled Penny's neck, trying to strangle her. Zeke saw the terror in her eyes, saw her trying to claw her way to Kevin. Penny's hand caught on a rock and she tried to reach out and hit Jake with it, but he shoved her hand away and the rock fell to the earth.

Zeke called out. "Stop, Jake. Please, stop." He searched

for his weapon and noticed Cheetah trying to get up. "C'mon on, boy," Zeke said. "Come. Attack."

He had to do something. He'd failed all of them and now he'd be forced to watch Penny die right in front of his eyes. Jake would win after all.

"I said, 'Grab Kevin,'" Jake called to the man standing there with a gun in his hand. He wore a dark cap and dark heavy clothing.

Zeke lifted to his knees and spotted his weapon. Then he saw the man's face. Gunther Caprice! He'd shoot to kill.

"Stop," Zeke called. "Jake, don't do this."

Jake ignored Zeke, his hands still on Penny. "Caprice, get Kevin and take him down the mountain. You know the plan."

Gunther started toward Kevin. "I'll get him all right. But I'm taking him with *me* and none of you will see him again until I get the money you promised me months ago, Morrow. I'm tired of this."

Penny started thrashing against Jake, her eyes wide with terror, her hands over Jake's. But she'd never be able to fight him off.

"I mean it, Jake," Gunther Caprice called out. "You're holding out on me. I know it. I want my money now so I can get out of this place. I hate it here." He lifted his weapon to where Kevin now stood, crying and calling out for Penny. "Your mama's kind of caught up in something, little fellow."

He held the gun down toward Kevin.

Zeke grunted with all his might, stretching to reach his weapon. Jake turned to Gunther and watched as Gunther went for Kevin, his gun aimed at the boy.

"If you don't give me my money, I'll kill the kid," Gunther shouted while he stomped toward Kevin.

Zeke slid toward his weapon. Jake screamed a curse and let go of Penny, violently pushing her to the ground. Then he whipped his rifle back around and held it toward the other man.

"Don't you go near my son, Gunther," Jake shouted, his hands trembling. "He's the only good thing I have left and I won't let you hurt him."

"Too late," Gunther said. "I want you to suffer the same way I've had to suffer. You ruined everything, Morrow. Everything." Inching closer to Kevin, he said, "Drop your weapon, right now."

Jake lifted his gun away and dropped it to the ground, but Gunther kept his weapon trained on Kevin. The click of Gunther's silenced handgun echoed out over the night like a death knell.

Everything after that happened in a rapid-fire cadence that left Zeke dazed and in a state of shock. He called out to Cheetah and heard Cheetah's growls behind him. Jake watched Gunther, shadows coloring his haggard face, then dived toward Kevin just as Gunther pulled the trigger.

A gunshot rang out in the night.

Jake went down a couple of feet away from Kevin, his eyes on his crying son. He reached out a hand then let it fall. Then he went still.

Stunned, Gunther stared down at Jake and lifted his weapon toward Kevin again.

Penny screamed and crawled toward her son. Then she grabbed the powerful rifle Jake had dropped and turned it toward Gunther Caprice. She shot him once, twice, tears streaming down her face. Gunther fell down onto his knees. Penny dropped the gun and ran for Kevin.

But Gunther grunted and tried to get back up, his face twisted in pain and rage, his right shoulder gushing blood.

"Attack," Zeke managed to call out, praying Cheetah had the strength. The dog started barking and rushed the man and brought him down, his big teeth sinking into Gunther's flailing left arm.

Zeke checked on Penny and Kevin, his eyes meeting hers in relief, then he rushed to Jake.

She lifted up her crying son to hold him close. "It's okay. Mommy's here. You're safe now."

Zeke grabbed his phone, his hands trembling. Then he dropped it by his side and lifted Jake's head. He could hear sirens squealing down on the road. "Don't die on me now," he said, tears in his eyes. "Jake, you hear me?"

"I hear you, bro," Jake said in a weak whisper. "Kevin?"

"He's safe. You saved his life."

Jake grinned. "Got some good left in me, huh?"

"Yes." Zeke glanced up at Penny, his heart hurting for her and his brother. "Yeah, you did one last good deed. Your son will be proud of you."

Jake grabbed Zeke's shirt. "Need to tell you where the rest of them are. Record this."

Zeke turned on his phone recorder. "I'm listening."

In a weak whisper, Jake gave Zeke the locations of several warehouses scattered across the country, from the East Coast to the West and, his voice fading, named some of the missing and wanted henchmen still left.

Coughing, he smiled up at Zeke. "That ought to do it."

He closed his eyes, but Zeke shook him gently. "Jake, I've got help on the way. Don't go to sleep on me."

He looked down, trying to decide what to do to save his brother. Taking off his lightweight jacket, he held it tightly to Jake's stomach and tried to staunch the bleeding. Then he checked Jake's pulse.

Barely there. But he did open his eyes again.

Zeke held on to him, willing him to live. "Why'd you turn, Jake? You had it all. Why did you let this happen?"

Tears rolled down Jake's face. "Got caught up in the power and the money and…too late to get out. I had a price on my head, either way." He swallowed and held on to Zeke's shirt. "And so did my son."

Zeke nodded. "We'll get you help. Hang on. They're coming."

"Nah," Jake said, patting Zeke's arm. "I'm done for. Kevin?"

Penny heard him and stepped forward, her horrified gaze clashing with Zeke's. Holding Kevin close as she tried to shield him from noticing the blood flowing through Jake's dark shirt, she murmured, "Kevin is safe, Jake. He's right here."

Zeke wanted to jump up and hold her tight but… these last few minutes with Jake had to count for something. He silently offered his brother forgiveness and hoped Jake would ask the Lord the same thing. When he looked up at Penny, Zeke wondered if she'd ever forgive either of them.

Had he lost her, too?

Jake lifted his head, his gaze jumping here and there until he saw Penny and Kevin standing nearby. "Tell him, Penny. Tell him I loved him."

"He knows," she said, her distraught gaze moving from Zeke to Jake. "He'll always know that, I promise."

"Sorry I hurt you. Everything went wrong. Story of my life."

"You did the right thing tonight," she said, tears streaming down her face.

Zeke nodded. "Kevin is safe now, Jake."

Jake gave a thumbs-up sign, his eyes on his son. Then he died in Zeke's arms.

It was over at last.

Zeke held his brother, Cheetah by his side, even after the first responders showed up on the scene. He wished things could have ended differently. He thought of the good memories and he found it hard to let go.

The paramedics told him Penny and Kevin were both fine but all he could do was stare at them from a distance. Max came by and kneeled on the ground beside him, asking him questions in a firm but gentle tone. Zeke asked him about Cheetah—he'd been shot. Max had one of the paramedics examine the dog, and they deemed the courageous canine as fine. Just a flesh wound.

"Zeke, we need to check on you, man. And we need to remove Jake's body."

Zeke didn't move. The other agents all tried to talk to him but gave up and went about the work of documenting the scene and taking statements.

Finally, a hand touched his arm.

Penny. In the pale moonlight, she looked windblown and tragic, deep grief and fatigue washing her features in despair.

"Zeke, you need to let someone look at your head."

Zeke stared up at her and saw the tears in her eyes, but he was too numb and full of agony to care about himself right now. But he cared about her. He'd done everything he could to save her and his nephew. He only wished he could have saved Jake, too. He didn't know how he could ever face Kevin again, knowing how the toddler had witnessed all of this violence. Knowing he hadn't really protected any of them, after all.

"Zeke, please? You have to let him go now, okay?"

He heard the catch in Penny's words but he couldn't speak to her, couldn't tell her that he'd fallen in love with her. It was too much, too raw and messy after the tragedy of this night. He had to absorb all of this and try to find some peace and forgiveness before he could think about a future with her and Kevin.

"Go take care of your son," he said. "I'll find you later." Watching her walk away, her head down, her heart crushed, Zeke knew he loved her. But did he love her for all the right reasons?

Or did he now feel an obligation to make things right for all of them, including Jake?

An hour later—after he'd watched them take Jake's body, zipped in a dark bag, away on a stretcher—Zeke hurried to find Penny and Kevin. He only hoped to hold them both close one more time before he left the scene with Cheetah.

But Penny and her little boy weren't anywhere to be found. They were gone.

SEVENTEEN

A few weeks later, the whole team sat inside the conference room at headquarters in Billings, watching the highlights of the courtroom proceedings on the evening news. Several of them had been in the courtroom to give official reports and testimonies, Zeke included. But seeing it again now, it all seemed like a nightmare that still looped inside his head.

After the reporter signed off, Max got up and turned off the television.

"The Dupree crime family is no more," he said, a touch of grief mixed with obvious relief. Then he went on to give an updated report on the phone call he had with Zeke the night Jake died.

But Zeke knew it all. Had gone over and over it in his mind. The others knew most of it but today's debriefing would put an end to any speculation once and for all. Even though Zara had been cleared, Max wanted her reputation intact and all rumors squelched.

Jake had a previous fling with in-going trainee Brandy Ridgeway, who at the time had been a rookie police officer he'd met in Colorado, and he'd been in touch with her almost the whole time he'd been undercover. He knew she was interested in becoming an FBI agent so he convinced her she should do it, and he'd even given her some pointers on how to prepare. But he'd cautioned her not to mention his name since he was so deep undercover. He'd also told her he'd keep in touch, just in case. Then he'd taken off with Dupree.

Brandy had passed the initial exams for training and was accepted. She didn't see Jake for months but she was in love with him, so when he contacted her for help and convinced her that he'd been set up, she told him she'd do anything he needed. He told her to get close to Zara and he got a message to her that she should watch instructor Rebecca Carwell closely.

He fooled Brandy into thinking *Rebecca* was the one stirring up trouble. So Brandy, jealous that Rebecca and Jake had once been close, goaded Zara into going to the park with her that night. Jake had hoped to talk Rebecca into helping him but she refused and didn't turn him in, thus causing an investigation to focus on her. Angry at Rebecca, he'd coerced Brandy to get the goods on her. So they launched an all-out attack on Rebecca's NATs, targeting Zara since she was so close to the K-9 team.

Nina Atkins let out a sigh. "So Agent Carwell got to the bottom of all of this without reporting it to anyone."

"Yes, but Zara knew. She had to pretend to go along with it. A kind of trial by fire," Max replied. "Rebecca followed the evidence and at first thought Zara and Brandy were both out to get her fired. So she started pushing them, hoping to make one of them crack. Apparently Rebecca figured things out pretty quickly, but she made the decision to stay quiet until she had more proof. She enlisted, or rather forced, Zara to be her eyes and ears. She was afraid Zara would report they'd seen her with a man who looked like Jake."

Dylan, who'd been listening quietly, added, "Once she realized Brandy was lying to everyone, she really needed Zara's help anyway." He looked grateful but he was still worried about Zara getting home in time for their wedding.

Max shot Dylan a grim stare. "Why don't you explain that part?"

Dylan stood. "The truth is—Brandy Ridgeway was the one who tried to sabotage the trainees, hoping to make Zara look bad. When things got too heated, Brandy panicked and deliberately failed out. Since then she'd been waiting in Colorado for Jake to come and take her out of the country. Which, by the way, he never intended to do since she failed him."

Dylan pushed at his glasses. "Meantime, Rebecca was afraid Jake would send someone to possibly harm Zara, so she gave the NATs what they thought was a false situation to solve and put *all* of them in a safe house—off-site. Only Zara knew the truth."

"Rebecca should have reported this." Nina said, anger in her words. "She should step down."

"She will step down," Max replied. "She was caught between hiding her relationship with Jake and knowing he'd betrayed her yet again and this time with one of her own trainees. She knows she used bad judgment but she did everything she could to protect Zara."

Zeke stared down at the table, a heated rage burning inside him. Jake hadn't even cared about Brandy or any of the women he'd used, nor had he cared much about Penny and Kevin, either. The battle to forgive his brother still raged in Zeke's soul. He thought he'd done so, but sitting here now, Zeke felt the same old conflicted rage.

Max continued. "Rebecca couldn't find enough on Brandy to confront her, so she kept tabs on Brandy after she left the program. When I showed up to speak to Rebecca, she knew it was all over. Rebecca sent agents to Brandy's location, hoping to get to her before we did. But we beat her there. Of course, Brandy lied to our agents and reported back to Jake immediately."

When he heard grumbles, he held up his hand. "Yes, Rebecca should have alerted us the night she met Jake in that park. Her actions after that proved she was in a panic. She made the wrong call, but in the end, she cooperated with us."

Zeke wondered if Penny knew any of this. He'd wanted to tell her but she wasn't talking to anyone these days, especially him.

The FBI had taken Brandy into custody. She'd confessed everything and told them Jake was on his way to a cabin to get Kevin. Jake had remembered hiding a witness in the safe cabin years ago. He checked it out and discovered they were there. He'd told Brandy about the cabin and how he was going to get his son, finally. But she didn't know where the cabin was located.

"Why did he do all of this with Quantico?" Leo asked now, shaking his head. He glanced at Zeke, but Zeke didn't respond.

Max's unreadable gaze hit on Zeke, but he went on. "Jake's motivation surely stemmed from a strong need to make the FBI Classified K-9 Unit look incompetent. And it worked at times. He tracked Penny and Kevin right under our noses, kept a young recruit in his pocket and ruined her chance at becoming an FBI agent. He also tried to sabotage Zara's time in training and managed to get a senior instructor to put her career on the line for him."

Zeke couldn't take it anymore. He slammed a hand on the table. "He's dead now, and the Duprees are done. Case closed."

Max stared at Zeke for a long moment. "I'm sorry for your loss, Zeke. But…your brother took a wrong turn and we *all* lost him. Long ago, we lost him. It happens to the best of agents. And you need to remember he was one of the best before all of this took place. We know in the end, Jake proved to be a hero. He saved his little boy's life and he gave us the information we needed to finally finish off the Duprees."

The other team members gave Zeke encouraging, sympathetic glances. He remembered when he'd first walked into this place. They hadn't trusted him but they'd accepted him. Now Leo Gallagher, Julianne Martinez, Harper Prentiss, Timothy Ramsey and Nina Atkins all considered him as one of them. And the other team members had consoled him, telling him he'd done the best he could.

Max West had stood by him when he'd taken Jake's body back to Utah for burial, just Zeke, the SAC and Zeke's mother there to watch them put Jake in the ground. And a lone figure Zeke had noticed standing near a tree by the drive into the cemetery.

His father? He'd never know and he didn't care.

Earlier today, Max had offered Zeke a permanent position with the K-9 Unit. "We need people like you. You care not only about our work here, but you have good instincts and a strong sense of justice. You have a heart, Zeke. Don't forget that and don't go all cold and numb on me. I'd like you to stay and help us heal from this. We need to get back on track and get back out there doing our jobs."

"I'll think about it, Max," Zeke had responded numbly. "I just need a few days."

"Take as long as you need. I'm not going anywhere soon," Max had replied. Referring to the woman he'd met and married after investigating several bombings in California, he added, "Katerina and I have plans of our own. I think it involves horses and…maybe a house full of children."

Zeke wanted plans, too. Plans for a future with Penny and Kevin. He could see that now that he'd had time to step back. But had he waited too long?

Penny might make good on her need to get away from Montana forever. He might have already lost her.

Penny served Rex and the one other boarder, a businessman just passing through, their noon meals, her smile as fake as the burgundy silk mums Claire had arranged in the center of the antique dining table.

"Why don't you have lunch with us?" Rex asked, ever the gentleman. "You worked hard all morning making this chicken potpie. Should eat some of it, too. Claire's joining us."

Rex had come here to go hiking and fishing for a week. But he'd apparently stayed here with Claire the whole time Penny and Kevin had been on the run and he was still here, two weeks later. Penny couldn't help but notice that those two seemed mighty chummy.

More power to them, she thought. Smiling at Rex, she said, "I nibbled while I was cooking. I'm not hungry."

Claire came ambling by, a sweet scent wafting

around her. "You look like skin and bones to me, honey. We'd love to have you share a meal with us."

Claire had dressed in a pretty floral blouse and black pants. Not her usual sweatpants and baggy sweaters. Love was definitely in the air around here.

"I'm fine, Claire," Penny said. "I'm going to take some of this up to Kevin once it's cooled down a bit. I'll finish what he doesn't eat."

"I love that little boy," Rex said, winking at Claire.

Love. She felt that love and she loved both of them for watching after her and pampering her and Kevin.

But just thinking the word hurt Penny's heart so much she had to hurry back into the kitchen before she burst into tears. She cried a lot these days. For Kevin, for Jake. For Zeke...

She'd lost him the minute Jake had died. She'd seen it there in his eyes. She and Kevin would always remind Zeke of his brother. The brother he'd tried so hard to save instead of kill.

But... Jake had dived in front of Kevin to save him from Gunther's bullets. Not Zeke's. Zeke never got in a shot.

She still remembered that awful night. Woke up in cold sweats after having shadowy nightmares. She'd killed a man and in front of her little boy, at that. But how could she ever explain the terror that had captured her heart that night?

If Jake hadn't let her go and thrown himself in front of Kevin—

Her son's voice on the monitor caused Penny to race out of the kitchen and up the stairs. No matter that Claire had installed an alarm system and bought a more powerful shotgun. No matter that even now, Penny knew the FBI had people watching out for her until the trial was over and done. She'd seen them cruising by at least four times a day. No matter that Zeke had left messages and had come by to try and talk to her several times in the last few days.

None of it mattered. She couldn't face Zeke yet. She just wanted her son safe.

The minister had told her she'd be okay. That grief took many forms and came at the most unexpected times.

"I don't know why I'm grieving," she'd blurted. "Jake betrayed all of us."

"You grieve for what could have been," the kind older pastor had told her. "You grieve for what you've lost." Then he'd motioned to where Kevin sat playing with some of the new toys people had brought him after the news reports started coming in. "But Penny, you still have one thing to bring you joy and not grief. You have your son."

"I have my son," she'd echoed, smiling for the first time since this nightmare had ended.

Penny tried very hard to focus on that. So now, she swooped up her toddler and snuggled him close. "Hey, baby. Did you have a good nap?"

Kevin grinned and nodded. "Horsey?"

Penny offered him one of the other stuffed animals people had given him. "How about Giraffe?"

Kevin took it and threw it across the room. "Horsey?"

"Horsey isn't here, baby." She wouldn't cry. She couldn't. It might upset Kevin too much.

So she distracted him with the promise of outside.

They both loved outside, after all. If she could ever actually leave this yard again. She'd have to get over that phobia if she wanted to go back to work.

EIGHTEEN

After Max's reminder that they'd all lost Jake, Zeke swallowed the lump that seemed to be permanently lodged in his throat. "Thank you, sir."

It had been weeks since Jake had died in his arms. Esme Dupree had testified against Reginald Dupree, telling the jury that she'd witnessed her brother committing a murder. Her sister, Violetta, her brown-gold hair and dark cat eyes giving her an exotic flare, had been there with her, her own grief obvious in the way she held her head high and refused to wipe at the tears everyone saw in her eyes. Her brother was going to jail for life. She'd shot and killed her uncle to save Esme and now Gunther Caprice, the man she'd once loved, was dead. Violetta had verified a lot of things for them, yet again proving she had a love/hate relationship with her powerful family. But after the trial, she'd hugged Esme close and stood by her when the press had asked questions.

"My sister and I just want some peace and quiet," she'd proclaimed. "We are free now and we want to live in privacy. We can both make our own way without the help of blood money."

Esme's husband, team member Ian Slade, had also been by her side. Now that the trial was over and they'd been able to come out of the witness protection program, they planned to hold a wedding reception to celebrate.

Reginald's life sentence would ensure that he'd die behind bars and the knowledge of that at least brought the sense of justice Zeke craved. The Dupree organization had been entrenched in every type of crime from drug running to human trafficking, prostitution and gun smuggling, bribery, racketeering and murder. Sickening. But Jake's final tips had panned out in a big way. They'd raided warehouses and homes and found laptops and flash drives that told the tales of excess and greed and exposed the Dupree criminal activities across the globe.

The carnage had brought down his brother. Jake had been a good FBI agent because he needed an outlet for his rage and pain, but that same rage and pain had also caused him to covet money and power, two things he'd never had growing up.

A tragedy all the way around.

After glancing around the room, Zeke closed his eyes to *his* pain. Jake was dead, and Penny was still grieving. He'd tried to see her and console her once she was back at the Wild Iris, but she only wanted some time with her son.

"She stays up there with him mostly all day," Claire had said, shaking her head after Penny had refused to come downstairs the last time he'd come by. "They walk out in the back garden and she pushes Kevin on the tree swing but honestly, I don't think she's ready to venture past the yard yet."

Zeke understood that feeling. "Kevin will need some therapy. I know people at church who can help both of them."

"She's already had someone come by to see Kevin and she's visited with our minister, too," Claire assured Zeke. "You know how kids are. They bounce back."

But not all kids. Jake hadn't bounced back.

Now Zeke wondered if he ever would, either.

After they'd been dismissed but were still milling around inside the big briefing room, Dylan came up to him. "Hey, man, thanks for forcing us to take a closer look at Zara's situation. We haven't been able to talk much but she did get one message to me. She needs me to pick up her wedding dress but I can't peek at it. She promised me she'd be here for our wedding this weekend."

"That's good," Zeke replied as they walked toward the lobby. "I wish you both the best."

Dylan stopped him with a hand on his arm. "We want you there, Zeke. At our wedding. I'm counting on you. Don't let all of this with Jake ruin things for you, man."

Then Dylan motioned for Max. He and the entire team gathered around Zeke. Getting antsy, he glared at them. "Is this some kind of intervention?"

Max held out a stuffed animal. "Yeah, I guess you could call it that. We… The team…uh…had this made for Kevin. We tried to get it as close to Cheetah as we could. You know, because the boy loves Cheetah."

Zeke took the fluffy black-and-white-spotted dog, his hand gripping the soft fur, his eyes getting misty. "This does look like Cheetah."

Dylan pushed at his glasses. "We thought this might

kind of help you when you go and talk to Penny. You know?"

Leo folded his arms over his chest. "We're trying to give you an in, man. Don't blow it."

Zeke hadn't shed any tears since the night Jake died, but now he gritted his teeth against the gut-wrenching need to bawl like a baby. He could only manage a rapid nod and held tight to the stuffed animal.

Everyone dispersed just as rapidly as he stood nodding and swallowing around the lump in his throat. None of them were very good at emotions.

"So…you will show up at the church, right?" Dylan asked.

Zeke slapped a hand on Dylan's back and regained his senses. "I wouldn't miss the wedding, buddy. It'll be good to celebrate with you."

He'd be there. But first, he had to go and convince the woman he loved that they needed to be together.

Kevin ate a good bit of the chicken potpie. Penny cleaned him up and took him down the backstairs off the wraparound second-story porch. He took off running for the play area where swings and climbing equipment worked perfectly for toddler-sized adventures.

Penny sat down on a bench and laughed and clapped at his antics. He really did seem unfazed by all that had happened to him. She owed part of that to Zeke. He'd tried hard to keep Kevin occupied and distracted while they were hiding out.

She missed him so much. Too much. True, he had tried to reach out to her, but she figured it was only to tell her goodbye before he headed back to Utah.

Deep in thought about what might have been between them, she realized her minister was right. She was grieving so many things. And losing Zeke was the main one.

"'Eke!"

Penny's head shot up at her son's joyful exclamation.

"Mommy, 'Eke!" Kevin pointed behind her, his smile melting her heart. He'd probably seen a black SUV go by on the road and thought Zeke was coming to see them.

"Hi."

Pivoting up and off the bench, she saw the man himself standing there, his heart showing in his dark eyes.

"Hi." Her pulse leaped so hard, she had to take a deep breath. In spite of the cool day, Penny's hands turned clammy.

Kevin ran up to him. "'Eke! Cheety?"

"Cheetah is resting back at headquarters," Zeke said before he scooped up the little boy into his arms. "But, hey, buddy, I brought you something."

Penny watched as he showed Kevin the medium-sized stuffed animal he'd been holding with one hand behind his back. "It's a K-9 dog that looks like Cheetah. The gang at headquarters had it specially made just for you."

Kevin giggled and grabbed for the toy. "Cheety!"

"Cheety," Zeke said, his gaze moving from Kevin to Penny. Dropping Kevin to his feet, he smiled while Kevin ran around with the new stuffed animal, barking the way he'd heard Cheetah bark.

Tears pricked at Penny's eyes. "That's…so nice, so kind."

Zeke stood a few feet away, but the scent of spicy soap wafted in the air. He wore a black T-shirt and worn jeans and a black leather jacket. Why did he have to look so wonderful?

"You look good," he said, his eyes sliding over her face.

"I look awful and you know it," she replied, wishing she'd bothered to comb her hair and put on some makeup. Had she even put on clean jeans this morning? Yes, thankfully. And a lightweight blue sweater, too.

"Okay, so you've lost some weight. How about you and Kevin come with me? I have something I need to do and I can't do it alone."

Penny wanted to run straight into his arms but…she had to be sure. "Just like that? You come and want me to take off with you?"

Zeke moved closer. "Yes, Penny, just like that. After too many sleepless nights and worrying myself sick with regret and guilt and grief. Just like that, I want you in my life and I want Kevin in my life. But… I can't have Jake there with us."

She gasped and put a hand to her mouth. "You still don't believe me when I say I don't love him anymore. I didn't love him when I met you, Zeke. And everything I've heard on the news in bits and pieces about him and how he used those other women made me see that I was right to run from him."

He was now only inches away. "Are you sure? Because you've refused to see me for over two weeks now."

"I've been sure for a long time. I didn't want to see you because I was afraid I'd lost you. The night he died—"

"I was a wreck," Zeke replied. "I needed some time, too. But…today after Max summed it all up, I realized I need you more than I need anything else."

Penny checked on Kevin and let out a sigh she'd been holding for weeks now. "I thought you didn't want us, Zeke. It was awful, watching you there with Jake. You went cold and dark on me. I couldn't reach you."

He pulled her into his arms and rubbed his nose against her hair. "I've wasted too much time, Penny. I can't deny how I feel about you. I just want to give it a chance. You and me and Kevin. I need both of you in my life. I want that. No more wasted time, no more regrets. We'll make our way, together."

Penny held him there, savoring his strength. She'd never felt so safe in her life. "I want that, too. Just the three of us. We can heal together."

"I like that idea," Zeke said, his hands sifting through her hair. "I need you." Then he kissed her, showing her in a tender moment that he was the real deal. Solid. Warm. Loving. True. All the things she'd been searching for.

Penny pulled away and touched her fingers to his dark bangs. Then she looked up at him and smiled. "Where are we going?"

Zeke couldn't believe she wanted to go with him. "I'm supposed to find a shelter puppy that we can train to be a future K-9 officer dog. It became a tradition... when Jake went missing. After we discovered he'd turned, the team decided to keep doing it anyway, to strengthen the unit and to honor those who've died in the line of duty, both human and canine."

He stopped once they reached the back steps of the house. "But now I'm not so sure. I said I didn't want Jake between us. Maybe we should go to a park or something.

I just want to be with you and Kevin. Let's focus on that instead. I don't need to get a puppy."

"Wait," Penny said. "Zeke, I love you. Kevin loves you. There is no one here between us. We'll never forget Jake but if we're going to make this work, we have to face the tough times together. Getting a puppy will make Kevin happy and I love animals, too. We can do this one special thing, our first time together without having to look over our shoulders. Jake is gone now. We're here with you."

"Cheety," Kevin said, grinning at the stuffed dog he refused to let go of. "Woof, woof! I like puppies."

Zeke looked from the boy to Penny, his heart tripping over itself. "You do realize you just told me you love me, right?"

"Wuv," Kevin mimicked with a giggle.

"Yes," Penny said, a tentative question in her eyes. "But…how do you feel about that?"

"I love you," Zeke said before he lost his courage. "Both of you. So much."

Penny cradled his jaw in her hand. "Then let's go find a puppy. And when that dog is trained and ready to do his job, you can be proud and remember that the day we found it was also the day we found each other, okay?"

Zeke nodded, unable to speak. They headed inside and told Claire and Rex where they were going.

Claire beamed and clapped her hands together. "And?"

"And what?" Penny said with a smile.

"And if you two are getting hitched, I want to have the wedding here, out in the garden. I'll cater it and you don't have to worry about a thing. My gift to you."

Penny blushed, her skin as fresh as peaches. "Uh… I'm not so sure…"

"We'll accept that offer," Zeke said, giving Penny a grin. "That is, if Penny *is* willing to be my wife."

The big dining room became silent. Only the ticking of the old grandfather clock sounded off the seconds.

"Wuv," Kevin said, showing Claire his miniature Cheety.

"Love," Penny echoed, tears in her eyes. "I'm willing. So willing."

Claire squealed and caught Kevin up in her arms, causing the toddler to giggle even more. Rex wiped at his eyes. And Zeke grabbed Penny close and kissed her.

"Now, go find a puppy," Claire said, her smile beaming.

They hopped into Penny's Jeep, Kevin safe in his car seat, and headed toward the local shelter. But they only made it about a mile down the road when Kevin kicked at the seat and shouted, "Puppies."

Zeke saw them, too. A little boy who looked to be about ten or so was standing by a big oak tree next to the road. A handwritten sign printed on cardboard said Puppies—One Dollar Each.

Penny gave Zeke an imploring glance. "Let's stop here."

They got out and Penny held Kevin's hand to keep him from running toward the box of yelping dogs. "Hold on. We'll see what we have."

Zeke looked at the dark-haired boy selling the puppies. He reminded Zeke of Jake, but this boy had tears in his eyes.

"I gotta sell 'em," he explained. "We're moving into Billings for my dad's new job and I can only take Muffin cause we're renting a smaller house. Muffin is their mom." He hurried on, smelling a deal. "They're part Chocolate Lab and part…we don't know. But they're good little puppies. Want one?"

Zeke picked up the runt of the litter, his heart pounding with the sure knowledge that God was always in the details. The brown-colored puppy licked at his hands and face. "I'll take all four," he said. "I hope they can be trained to possibly become K-9 dogs."

"Those are good dogs," the boy said, smiling for the first time. "They save lives and catch bad guys."

"Yes, they do," Penny said, her gaze holding Zeke's.

"Listen," Zeke said, kneeling with Kevin by the box. "I'm gonna give you one hundred dollars, but only if you promise to come and visit these puppies at the training center in Billings." He handed the boy five twenties and gave him a business card with all the information. "And I also need to speak to your parents."

The boy bobbed his head and took the money and the card up to where two people sat on the porch steps, watching.

"Why do you need to speak to them?" Penny asked, glancing up toward the house.

"Look around," Zeke replied, awe in the words.

Penny glanced at the house and the yard. "Zeke…"

"A house with a picket fence and a nice yard, Penny," he said. "And I'm guessing there might be a stream in the back. If not, we'll make do with the house and this amazing view."

The boy's parents came down and thanked Zeke for his generosity. "You've done us a big favor," the dad said. "He's been fretting about these puppies since they were born."

Zeke smiled and explained the training program. "I hope you'll come and visit, take a tour." Then he gave Penny a hopeful smile. "And I was wondering… I don't see a for-sale sign. Do you rent this place?"

The man shook his head. "No. We just talked to a Realtor last week about putting it on the market. I have to be in Billings in about a month or so. Are you interested?"

Zeke gave Penny another expectant glance. "Are you ready?" he asked her.

"We could look," she replied, tears in her eyes.

"It's a nice piece of property," the woman said. "There's a quiet little stream out back."

Zeke smiled at Penny. She smiled back. "We'd appreciate a tour, if not today then whenever we can arrange it."

"C'mon in," the boy's mother said. "I just cleaned it up for the Realtor anyway."

Leaving the boy to guard the puppies, Zeke lifted Kevin into his arms and they all went up to the white farmhouse-style home with the big, deep front porch.

He held Kevin close and took Penny by the hand. "Are you sure about this?" he asked, still in awe.

"Very sure," she said, her beautiful eyes filled with hope and love. "You're going to make a great daddy, Zeke."

Kevin bobbed his head, not really understanding but picking up on the words anyway. "'Eke." He pointed to the man holding him. "Daddy."

EPILOGUE

"Is she here yet?"

Penny turned to the worried groom standing in the church hallway behind her. "No. I promised the brides-maids I'd let them know the minute Zara gets here, but… Zeke got word that she's on her way from the air-port. ETA is any minute now." Then she pushed Dylan back. "And you can't see her before the wedding, so go get ready to take your place at the altar."

Dylan's blue eyes were bright with hope. "Is my tie straight?"

Penny glanced over his dark suit and crisp white shirt. He wore a blue tie that matched his eyes. "Your tie is perfect. Stop being so nervous."

Dylan nodded and took off to the front of the church. Penny had been given the task of scouting for Zara. After hearing what had happened at Quantico, she couldn't wait to meet the newly minted FBI agent. Zara's experience had been harrowing, so Penny felt a bond with her already. And wished for the hundredth time that they could have all saved Jake.

"Hey."

She whirled around to find Zeke standing there,

smiling at her. "You make the cutest lookout." His eyes moved over her flowing burgundy dress. "I don't think I've ever seen you in a dress before. I like it."

"You told me that already," she said through a grin. "Several times." She patted her upswept hair. "And Claire did me up nice."

"She sure did," Zeke said, giving her a gentle kiss.

The last week had been amazing. Claire had offered her a job as manager of the Wild Iris. "So Rex and I can take that trip across the country I've always dreamed about."

Those two were getting married at Christmas.

And Zeke and Penny had agreed on a Valentine's Day wedding, after Claire and Rex returned from their honeymoon.

"One good thing came out of this," Zeke said as he stood there with her, his dark suit fitting his broad shoulders to perfection. "We all found someone to spend the rest of our lives with."

Penny laughed. "So Max is married to Katerina and they have two dogs and two training puppies and lots of horses."

He nudged her hair with his nose. "Yes. And Leo and Alicia are married. They got married a few months ago."

"Okay, then we have Riley and Harper. Harper and I talked about her wedding plans."

"Yes, they're engaged. Riley's mother moved in with him to help with his nephew, Asher, but Asher is much better now." Zeke had told her about Asher's mother being murdered and Asher being severely injured. Riley and Harper took down the killer.

"Then Julianne and Brody are planning to get married here in Montana, before he heads off to Quantico this spring."

"You're getting good at this," Zeke said, his lips touching on her neck. "They're training two pups, Cooper and Hawk."

Penny enjoyed being near him but slapped at his shoulder. "And Ian and Esme will renew their vows next week."

Zeke tugged her close. "Yep. You're all caught up, except for one couple." He grinned and touched his forehead to hers.

"Us," she said. "We're buying a house, I have a new job and we're getting married on Valentine's Day." She laughed. "And we're training two very active Chocolate Lab–mix puppies."

"You *are* good at this." He kissed her again. Penny closed her eyes and almost pinched herself.

But when she opened her eyes, she spotted a taxi and pulled away with a squeal. "Get lost. The bride is here!"

Zeke watched as Zara rushed up the aisle to her waiting groom, her full white skirt swishing. Dylan left the altar and met her halfway up the aisle and lifted her into his arms while the organist tried to keep up.

"You made it," Dylan said, tears in his eyes.

"I'm here." Zara's dark hair was caught up in a careless ponytail and she had one bright white flower tucked into the band holding her curls. But her smile said it all. "I'm ready to get married."

Everyone in the church clapped with happiness. Zeke turned to Penny and took her hand in his. Together, they watched their friends say their wedding vows.

An hour later, the whole team and all the people who worked behind the scenes with Dylan, various friends

and family, and Claire and Rex, who'd brought Kevin
to see everyone, gathered out behind the church where
tents and tables had been set up in a beautiful fall motif
and a huge cake from Petrov's Bakery stood in three
tiers decorated with burgundy and green edible flowers. Zeke's heart, once so cold and numb, now held hope
and the beautiful promise of having a true family at last.

"I love you," he whispered to Penny as they danced
to a soft waltz.

"I love you back," she said, her eyes glimmering with
that same hope and promise.

Dylan and Zara took off toward the parking lot, holding hands and laughing.

"Are you leaving?" Zeke called.

"No. We have a surprise for everyone," Dylan called out.

In the next few minutes, several handlers unleashed
a pack of trained K-9 dogs and several still-in-training
puppies that soon overtook the dance floor.

Every K-9 partner was there, including Cheetah. The
curious canine hurried when Zeke called him and was
soon dancing with them while the puppies flipped and
flopped over each other and everyone else. A lot of
laughing and yelping ensued.

"Chaos," Max said as he whirled by with Katerina.
"And I wouldn't have it any other way."

"Me, either," Zeke replied. "For once, we're all here
and accounted for."

"And we're happy," Penny said, laughing.

He looked into the big-sky sunset and then he looked
back at the woman he loved. "Happy…and blessed."

* * * * *

SPECIAL EXCERPT FROM

*When a guide dog trainer becomes a target
of a dangerous crime ring, a K-9 cop and his loyal
partner will work together to keep her safe.*

Read on for a sneak preview of Trail of Danger
*by Valerie Hansen, the next exciting installment
to the* True Blue K-9 Unit *miniseries,
available September 2019 from Love Inspired Suspense.*

Abigail Jones stared at the blackening eastern sky and
shivered. She was more afraid of the strangers lingering
in the shadows along the Coney Island boardwalk than
she was of the summer storm brewing over the Atlantic.

Early September humidity made the salty oceanic
atmosphere feel sticky while the wind whipped loose
tendrils of Abigail's long red hair. If sixteen-year-old
Kiera Underhill hadn't insisted where and when their
secret meeting must take place, Abigail would have
stopped to speak with some of the other teens she was
passing. Instead, she made a beeline for the spot where
their favorite little hot dog wagon spent its days.

Besides the groups of partying youth, she skirted
dog walkers, couples strolling hand in hand and an old
woman leaning on a cane. Then there was a tall man and

enormous dog ambling toward her. As they passed beneath an overhead vapor light, she recognized his police uniform and breathed a sigh of relief. Most K-9 patrols in her nearby neighborhood used German shepherds, so seeing the long floppy ears and droopy jowls of a bloodhound brought a smile despite her uneasiness.

Pausing, Abigail rested her back against the fence surrounding a currently closed amusement park, faced into the wind and waited for the K-9 cop to go by. His unexpected presence could be what was delaying Kiera.

"Come on, Kiera. I came alone, just like you wanted," Abigail muttered.

Kiera had sounded panicky when she'd phoned.

"Here. Over here" drifted on the wind. Abigail strained to listen.

The summons seemed to be coming from inside the Luna Park perimeter fence. That was not good since the amusement facility was currently closed. Nevertheless, she cupped her hands around her eyes and peered through the chain-link fence. It was several seconds before she realized the gate was ajar. *Uh-oh. Bad sign.* "Kiera? Is that you?"

A disembodied voice answered faintly. "Help me! Hurry."

Don't miss
Trail of Danger *by Valerie Hansen,*
available September 2019 wherever
Love Inspired® *Suspense books and ebooks are sold.*

www.LoveInspired.com

WE HOPE YOU ENJOYED THIS BOOK!

Love Inspired® SUSPENSE

Uncover the truth in these thrilling
stories of faith in the face of crime
from Love Inspired Suspense.
Discover six new books available
every month, wherever books
are sold!

LoveInspired.com

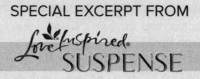
Rookie K-9 officer Lani Branson took in a deep breath as
she pedaled her bike along the trail in the Jamaica Bay
Wildlife Refuge. Water rushed and receded from the shore
just over the dunes. The high-rises of New York City,
made hazy from the dusky twilight, were visible across
the expanse of water.

She sped up even more.

Tonight was important. This training exercise was an
opportunity to prove herself to the other K-9 officers who
waited back at the visitors' center with the tracking dogs
for her to give the go-ahead. Playing the part of a child lost
in the refuge so the dogs could practice tracking her was
probably a less-than-desirable duty for the senior officers.

Reaching up to her shoulder, Lani got off her bike and
pressed the button on the radio. "I'm in place."

LISEXP0919

The smooth tenor voice of her supervisor, Chief Noah Jameson, came over the line. "Good—you made it out there in record time."

Up ahead she spotted an object shining in the setting sun. She jogged toward it. A bicycle, not hers, was propped against a tree.

A knot of tension formed at the back of her neck as she turned in a half circle, taking in the area around her. It was possible someone had left the bike behind. Vagrants could have wandered into the area.

She studied the bike a little closer. State-of-the-art and in good condition. Not the kind of bike someone just dumped.

A branch cracked. Her breath caught in her throat. Fear caused her heartbeat to drum in her ears.

"NYPD." She hadn't worn her gun for this exercise. Her eyes scanned all around her, searching for movement and color. "You need to show yourself."

Seconds ticked by. Her heart pounded.

Someone else was out here.

Don't miss
Courage Under Fire *by Sharon Dunn,*
available October 2019 wherever
Love Inspired® *Suspense books and ebooks are sold.*

www.LoveInspired.com